VALLEY COTTAGE LIBRARY
110 Route 303
Valley Cottage, NY
10989

www.vclib.org

Yours Truly,
JACK THE RIPPER

Yours Truly,
JACK THE RIPPER

Robert Bloch

Subterranean Press ✣ 2011

First Edition

ISBN
978-1-59606-424-9

Subterranean Press
PO Box 190106
Burton, MI 48519

www.subterraneanpress.com

TABLE OF CONTENTS

THE WRITER AND THE RIPPER

by Norman Partridge

Some writers only have one story in them. They tell it over and over. Some even make a career of it—turning out one cloned novel after another, running a playbook that makes their publisher happy, churning out the literary equivalent of McDonald's Happy Meals for the reading public at large.

Robert Bloch wasn't one of those writers. While prolific, Bloch's work was varied. His fiction ranged from horror to crime to gothic and even the occasional foray into science fiction, from Lovecraftian pastiches to classic shudder pulp to excursions into the *conte cruel*.

Of course, that doesn't mean Bloch didn't mine familiar territory on occasion. He did, and he wasn't averse to returning to a promising vein if the opportunity arose. Perhaps the first place he sunk his shovel was a series of tales featuring fantasy-minded con-man Lefty Feep, though by some reports the Feep sequels stemmed more from editorial demands than Bloch's own love of the character. His proto serial-killer novel *Psycho* inspired not only the Alfred Hitchcock film but several sequels manufactured by the Hollywood machine. Of course, these later movies had nothing to do with Bloch's own novelistic follow-ups to his most famous work.

End result? Hollywood and actor Anthony Perkins took Norman Bates in one direction on the screen, while Bloch took the character's legend in quite another direction on the page.

Legend. Now there's a word that'll provide a proper *segue.* After Bloch's *Psycho* turned the traditional crime story on its ear and Hitchcock's film made its inevitable mark, *legend* wasn't too strong a word to apply to Norman Bates. And it's definitely not too strong a descriptor to use when it comes to another murderer who made repeat appearances in Robert Bloch's fiction.

Namely, a fellow named Jack the Ripper.

• • •

"Yours Truly, Jack the Ripper," may be Bloch's best-known tale. In its way, the story is just as much of a career cornerstone for the author as *Psycho* was, combining a fantastic sensibility with the ultimate unsolved mystery from the annals of true crime. Bloch favors the unadorned style of pulp fiction in the tale, for the most part slapping the handcuffs on his signature black wit. Sure, some neo-Bohemians are served up for skewering, including a party-goer whose eyes are "as red as the maraschino cherries in his Manhattan." But in many ways "Yours Truly…" is an echo of a story from another time, right down to the hero who favors a traditional tufted moustache, tweeds, and a monocle. In other words, he's exactly the sort of gent who'd comment on the Ripper thusly: "Like a vampire, he battens on blood. Like a ghoul, he is nourished by death. Like a fiend, he stalks the world to kill. He is cunning, devilishly cunning. But I'll never rest until I find him, never!"

I first encountered "Yours Truly…" in junior high, thanks to a buddy who had a paperback collection of Bloch's work. I was spending the night at his house, and he practically shoved the book into my hands. "You've got to read this Jack the Ripper story," he said. "It's kind of like *The Night Strangler!*"

And it was, though neither of us knew that Bloch's tale predated Dan Curtis' second Kolchak movie by a thick hunk of calendar pages. All we knew was that "Yours Truly, Jack the Ripper" captured our imaginations. It was one of those stories that came off the page, slithered into your brainpan and coiled up around the cerebellum, determined to stay a while.

Once comfortable, it sank in its fangs and didn't let us go. We talked about the story long into the night. Bloch's tale stirred a couple of dangerous words into our conversation: *what if?* As in: *What if Robert Bloch's solution to the Ripper murders might be true?*

Really, it wasn't such a strange question for two kids to ask as the clock ticked past midnight. As young teens, my buddy and I lived for those kinds of questions. Our brains were already dark nests. We were the kind of kids who knew the Dewey decimal number for the nonfiction ghost story section at the library by heart.[1] We'd been trading horror comics and Alfred Hitchcock anthologies for years, along with Ray Bradbury paperbacks and anthologies by Rod Serling and Peter Haining. We'd grown up watching *Alfred Hitchcock Presents*, *The Twilight Zone*, and *The Night Gallery*. In short, we knew how to kill a vampire, slaughter a werewolf, and banish a ghost...in theory, anyway.

But we weren't thinking about any of those monsters that night. Thanks to Robert Bloch, we were thinking about Jack the Ripper, and another serial killer who stalked the streets of our very own town.

His name was the Zodiac.

At least, that's what we called him up until that night.

But after reading Bloch's masterful tale, we began to wonder if the killer's real name might really be *Jack*.

• • •

Unless you're a kid bent on terrifying himself into sleeplessness, you can file that solution to the Zodiac's identity in a folder marked *Not Bloody Likely*...though it wouldn't surprise me if an amateur sleuth with a book to sell has given it some play somewhere along the line. Personally, I'm fairly confident that sorcery wasn't part of the Zodiac's *modus operandi*, because I do not possess a fantastical turn of mind unless I'm operating on paper within fictional parameters. Still, if your name's Horatio (and even if it's not), I'll simply remind you that there are more things in heaven and earth than are dreamed of in your philosophies, and leave it at that.

And I'll do that for one simple reason: Like Jack the Ripper, the Zodiac was never caught. That leaves the door open (or at least, slightly ajar) to possibilities, even long-shots of the supernatural variety. Odds are we'll never know anything more about the killer who stalked my hometown than we know right now. And perhaps

---

1   133.1. See, I still remember.

that's why he endures in popular memory, just as the notorious Whitechapel slayer does.

It's my guess that Bloch understood that about the Ripper. He knew that the key to Red Jack's mystery was its lack of resolution. And though Bloch was obviously a student of the case (as you'll see in a pair of essays included in this book), I'm sure he understood that the Ripper wouldn't have cut quite the same figure[2] as a known quantity than he did as an unknown shadow in the fog, a killer who might have been an everyman…or anyman…or anywoman… or perhaps even an any*thing*.

And that's one reason Bloch returned to the Ripper in his fiction. The Whitechapel crimes provided an enduring mystery, and knowing the facts of the case made the insertion of a fantastical wild card into his Ripper tales that much more engaging. Bloch knew how to play that logic in his fiction, and as a result the construct worked. And perhaps that's why Bloch crafted tales featuring other historical characters—the Marquis de Sade, Lizzie Borden, and Edgar Allan Poe (to name a few).

But the Ripper was the one Bloch returned to time and time again. "Yours Truly…" was adapted several times for radio, and it made the jump to television on Boris Karloff's *Thriller* series (though truth be told, it's not one of the stronger episodes). On the page the Ripper showed up in other tales, including "A Toy for Juliette" in Harlan Ellison's landmark *Dangerous Visions* anthology. And thanks to Bloch, Red Jack appeared on the decks of the Starship *Enterprise*, deviling Kirk, Spock, and (mainly) Scotty…the one member of the *Enterprise* crew who had just a little bit of working-class Aberdeen fog in his blood.

Before all was said and done, it was inevitable that Bloch would write his own novel about Saucy Jack, *The Night of the Ripper*. I only wish he'd gotten around to that project a few years earlier, because it might have made a great Amicus production in the days when Bloch was working for the studio on projects such as *The House That Dripped Blood* and *Asylum*. Or perhaps he might have switched up and pitched a Ripper movie to Hammer, the home studio of his friend Christopher Lee. Either way, Bloch's novel is perhaps the most straight-up piece in this volume, and definitely the meatiest

_____

2   Or: carved himself a similar reputation? Or: sliced himself quite as big a helping of kidney pie? Hey, you've got to expect at least one bad pun in an essay about Robert Bloch. And I just gave you three.

when it comes to possible solutions to the Ripper's mystery. That alone makes it a treat for those who've never read it.

• • •

Me? I'd taken all of the aforementioned fog-shrouded walks with Mr. Bloch long before publisher Bill Schafer sent me the manuscript for this book. After reading "Yours Truly, Jack the Ripper" at my friend's house lo those many years ago, I became a Robert Bloch fan. I especially enjoyed Bloch's short stories, and collections like *Nightmares* and *More Nightmares* were prizes when I managed to find them while haunting used bookstores and library sales as a teenager. So was the *Psycho* paperback I snagged with a screaming Janet Leigh on the cover. Along with Bradbury (who I discovered thanks to my older brother) and Matheson (who I discovered thanks to Rod Serling and *The Twilight Zone*), Bloch was a favorite writer from the night I first encountered his work.

And I'm sure I don't need to tell you that those gentlemen are three aces, right there. Four if you count Serling. They're also four good reasons why I decided to become a writer myself.

Which I was by the time I met the author of "Yours Truly, Jack the Ripper." Bloch was (literally) the grand old man of the horror genre by that point. Well into his seventies, he was on the road to promote his "unauthorized autobiography," *Once Around the Bloch*. I went to a signing up in Sacramento along with a couple of buddies who published a horror 'zine called *The Scream Factory*. Both John Scoleri and Pete Enfantino were well-versed in the history of horror and Bloch's own work…plus by an odd turn of coincidence Pete just happened to be Bloch's daughter's mailman. He'd talked to her a few times about her dad, and she had passed on word to Bloch that Pete was coming to the event. Go figure. It really is a small world.

Anyway, we all figured Pete's *mailman connection* was a good enough excuse to approach Bloch before the signing. Luckily for us, the dapper guy in the burgundy sports coat who was busy flipping through a stack of old paperbacks didn't mind being interrupted. Neither did he need much encouragement to get rolling. A convention veteran and natural *raconteur*, Bloch soon had us all laughing as he shared stories about his career, pulps and paperbacks, writers and publishers and actors he'd met along the way. I'm sure I don't have to mention that Bloch's stories were heavy on the puns, wry, and told with the natural timing of a born comedian.

Of course, look at it one way and that was all part of the gig. I'm sure Bloch had told those stories a hundred times before, entertaining fans at conventions or signings. But standing there listening to him, it occurred to me he didn't have to do any of this. Hey, he could have been in the back room taking a nap. But it was obvious that he was enjoying the conversation as much as we were.

Like I said, by that time I'd made my first dent in the writing business. I'd published my first short story collection, won a Bram Stoker award, had stories in the *Year's Best* anthologies for horror and crime. In fact, Bloch was one of the writers who had the kind of career I aspired to. He'd been jumping effortlessly from genre to genre for years. There were a dozen questions I might have asked him that day. Hell, there were probably a hundred.

But standing there with a gentleman I'd known for years from the other side of the page, a man I'd learned from and admired, a writer's writer who'd piled up an Everest of fiction and was still at it with his seventy-fifth birthday already in the rearview mirror, I just couldn't imagine myself saying: "Gee, Mr. Bloch, I'm a writer, too."

Nope. That wasn't going to happen.

What did happen was that I got Bloch to sign my well-worn paperback copy of *Psycho*. Handing him the book, I said, "You know, Norman was a perfectly good name until you came along. You won't believe how much misery Norman Bates has caused me over the years."

It wasn't the best joke in the world, but Bloch laughed anyway. He shook his head, and there was a twinkle in his eye. Maybe it belonged to a guy who really did write with the heart of a young boy, or perhaps a cackling little creature who lived somewhere deep down inside him who kept that heart in a jar on its desk so it would have something to jab with a pitchfork when it was bored. Either way, Norman Bates' creator enjoyed the joke.

A few strokes of his pen, and Bloch handed back my copy of *Psycho*. I didn't read his inscription until I was home, later that night.

Best to Norman's namesake!
Robert Bloch

That one's a keeper.
And so is Robert Bloch.

FOREWORD

(from the anthology, *Ripper!*)

Who was Jack the Ripper?

For almost a century this question has challenged crimi-
nologists, plagued psychologists, intrigued investigative reporters,
authors, playwrights, and the general public throughout the world.
Millions of words have been expended in speculation, a thousand
theories propounded, scores of theories and solutions offered in
books, articles, essays, stories, drama on stage or screen. But the
identity of Jack the Ripper remains a mystery.

And an even greater mystery is this: Why, after a hundred years
of hypotheses, do we still seek an answer?

Consider the facts.

On the face of it, the victims of the elusive murderer were
scarcely such as to inspire interest. In London's slum of Whitechapel,
during the fall of 1888, the Ripper killed five prostitutes. Four were
women in their forties who, from descriptions, medical reports,
and photographs, were hardly glamorous sex objects. Destitution
and dissipation had aged them beyond their years to a point where
they resembled the bag ladies of today. The fifth victim was twenty-
four, but no beauty; big and burly, she was over three months
pregnant at the time of her untimely death. So continuing interest
in these crimes cannot be connected with the physical charms of
the females who met their fate at the hands—and knife—of their
mysterious assailant.

True, his methods inspired morbid imaginations. The blade that cut throats also slashed bodies, and each successive slaying involved increasing mutilation, even the removal of internal organs. The third and fourth murders occurred within the space of an hour on the same night. The fifth—the only one which took place indoors—culminated in carving up the corpse so hideously as to defy description.

But the history of homicide abounds with accounts of atrocities accompanying murder: prolonged torture, dismemberment, cannibalism, necrophilia, and other embellishments.

It can be argued that mass murder was a shock to Victorian sensibilities; aside from historical horrors perpetrated by Gilles de Retz, Countess Báthory, and a few others plus the perhaps apocryphal atrocities of a Sawney Bean or Sweeney Todd, there seemed little precedent for serial slayings.

Still, since that time multiple homicides have become commonplace. Only three years later, an exploration of the so-called Murder Castle in Chicago yielded ghastly hints of perhaps as many as two hundred killings over a period of eighteen months. Their perpetrator, a man who called himself H. H. Holmes, was also believed to have done away with many other victims prior to that time. Holmes was apprehended following his callous and calculated murder of a partner and his three young children.

In their heyday Henri Landru, Peter Kurten, Fritz Haarmann, Neville Heath, Reginald Christie, Albert Fish, and a dozen others horrified newspaper readers, but their fame or infamy faded in the mists of passing time. In our own era came a multiplicity of multiple murderers—a sniper atop a tower shooting down dozens of innocent victims at random, the savage slayer of eight nurses in a single night of nightmare, the serial slaughters committed by the Hillside Strangler, the Son of Sam, the Skid Row Slasher, and scores of others whose murders and methods exceed the Ripper's both in number and in nature.

But it's the Ripper we remember.

He came silently out of the midnight shadows on August 31, 1888, emerged again on September 8, reappeared on September 30, then made his final fearsome bow on the night of November 9. He vanished afterward, but the shadows remain; the shadows cloaking his deeds, his motives, his identity.

Perhaps this is why we continue to remember him. We can identify the other mass murderers, for they were caught and punished.

But though he was hunted by hundreds of police, sought by thousands of self-appointed avengers, and dreaded by millions of potential victims, the monster with the knife escaped without a trace. His trail of blood led nowhere, and to this day we do not know his name.

Thus the Ripper remains as a symbol of all our secret fears—the fear of the stranger on a darkened street, fear of the neighbor whose commonplace exterior may conceal the beast within, even the fear of a friend we *think* we know; a friend who may become a fiend once the mask comes off and the knife comes out.

The mystery of the Ripper's identity was constantly challenged, both during his reign of terror and ever since. An entire literature of explanations has been created by those whom my learned colleague Colin Wilson calls "Ripperologists." In a fascinating treatise, the pseudonymous Alexander Kelly lists over fifty types of suspects who have been proposed as the killer in both fact and fiction, including a Druid, a black magician, an invisible man, a time-traveler, an orangutan, and even a gorilla.

And not all seeming solutions have been so fanciful. More reasonable choices involve members of the medical profession—doctors, students, veterinarians, abortionists, mid-wives—persons whose comings and goings in the nighted slums would attract scant notice, but all of whom would be skillful in wielding a knife. Other candidates include police, military men, sailors, lunatics, syphilitics, and a catalog of citizenry ranging from nonentities to the nobility.

There, perhaps, lies a clue within a clue. Can it be we continue to seek the Ripper not just as a symbol of our secret fears but also as a symbol of our innermost hatreds?

Does the Ripper serve as a scapegoat?

If we are prejudiced against any profession, any class of society, any race or religion, we can probably find a candidate for our convictions among the suspects. If we dislike Russians, Poles, Jews, Americans, Spaniards, Latin Americans, Frenchmen, Norwegians, Asiatics, or even Texans, we may take comfort in knowing that each in turn has been suggested as the mass murderer. Jack is all things to all men.

Of course many of the allegations are fanciful and farfetched, but over the years various students of Ripperology have advanced more detailed and serious theories of identification.

One of the best known concerns a "Dr. Stanley," whose son was infected with syphilis by a prostitute and died of the disease. Bent on vengeance, the good doctor tracked down the guilty party, Mary Jane Kelly, killing the other whores to prevent them from warning her. Kelly was his last victim, and after butchering her he disappeared. Before his death in Buenos Aires he supposedly confessed his crimes in a Spanish newspaper story. But the news item has never been found and none of the "factual" details hold water. It normally takes ten to twenty years for syphilis to cause death, and since Mary Jane Kelly was only twenty-four when she was murdered, it seems unlikely that she cohabited with the doctor's son when she was between the ages of four and fourteen. More to the point, medical reports show that Mary Jane Kelly didn't have syphilis.

Another and more startling accusation is leveled against none other than Edward, the Duke of Clarence, a grandson of Queen Victoria. It is claimed that hints of his guilt were found in the private papers of the Queen's physician, Sir William Gull. According to the story, Clarence was syphilitic and died in a madhouse rather than during the 1892 flu epidemic. But Clarence was reputedly homosexual. And even if he chose to murder whores out of hatred, his excursions into Whitechapel would involve many difficulties, for he was an easily recognized public figure. Yet none of the self-proclaimed witnesses who insisted they'd seen the Ripper near the scene of his crimes ever mentioned a resemblance to Clarence. And on the dates of several of the slayings his whereabouts are listed and accounted for in the official Court Calendar.

His former tutor and supposed lover, James Stephen, also is proposed as the killer, but semi-invalidism after a head injury tends to cast doubt on his ability to perform the killings. And the motives attributed to him, including a weird conspiracy involving high-ranking members of the Masonic Order, are a bit hard to accept. Moreover, he, too, would have encountered great problems visiting the slums and committing multiple slayings without detection.

A Polish Jew named Kosminski—not to be confused with Severin Klosowski, a Russian who committed other types of murders in the 1890s under the name of George Chapman and lived with a woman named Chapman who was no relative of the Annie Chapman killed earlier by the Ripper—is sometimes named as a suspect, along with another Russian, Michael Ostrog. Klosowski, in turn, may or may not have been the alias of another Russian, Alexander or Alexei Pedachenko, whose real name was Vasili Konovalov, but who also called himself Andrei Luiskovo. If this is a trifle difficult to follow, so is the convoluted "evidence" regarding the reputed barber-surgeon or medical doctor who may or may not have been planted in London as a secret agent to stir up anarchist elements in Whitechapel. Explanations also involve the existence of a "double," allegations of homicidal mania, and even statements made years later by Rasputin—purportedly written in French, a language he didn't know—which were found in the basement of Rasputin's house after his death. But Rasputin's house didn't have a basement, and the theories themselves lack a solid foundation.

One of the most popular suspects is Montague J. Druitt, a barrister who failed at law, became a tutor at a private school in Blackheath, and voiced fears that he was going insane. Shortly after the last of the five slayings credited to the Ripper, Mr. Druitt weighted his pockets with stones and drowned himself in the Thames, from which his body was recovered a month or so later. Since the killings stopped at the time of his suicide, it is most convenient to propose him as the guilty party. But nomination isn't election, and the trouble with Druitt's candidacy—aside from the fact that there's no evidence linking him to the crimes—is his ability as a cricketer. On the mornings following two of the Whitechapel murders, Druitt was playing his heart out on cricket fields many miles away from London. That he could kill and mutilate two women in the city slums shortly before dawn, then board a train and go directly to join his team in contest matches in the country is hardly plausible. To do so just isn't cricket.

None of these or other suspects seem likely sources for the flood of mail which inundated police and newspaper offices during the seventy-day period of slaughter—confessions, taunts, threats, even verse, pouring in from all over England and beyond. Graphology, psychology, and just plain common sense indicate that the bulk of this correspondence was obviously the product of hoaxers and/or the mentally ill.

But how to explain the handwritten letter received by the Central News Agency on September 28 in which the writer promises that "the next job I do shall clip the lady's ears off and send them to the police officers"—and signs himself as "Jack the Ripper"?

What makes it interesting is that two days later the same pen pal sent a postcard warning, "You'll hear about Saucy Jack's work tomorrow. Double event this time…Had not time to get ears for the police." And it was on that date that the Ripper did indeed perform a "double event," which was not publicized in the press until the following day. The writer also offers his thanks for "keeping last

17

letter back until I got to work again"—a fact which only the writer of the first letter would know.

It has been argued that both letters were the work of a journalist bent on sensationalism to increase newspaper circulation, and that the second letter, dated September 30, might not have been mailed until the following day, at which time the press had news of the "double event."

But on October 16 another disturbing missive was received by George Lusk, head of the newly formed Whitechapel Vigilance Committee—enclosed in a parcel which contained "half the Kidne I took from one woman." The other half "I fried and ate it was very nise."

One of the "double event" victims was missing a kidney, and examination proved that the condition of the mailed fragment matched the kidney which remained, and had probably come from the same corpse. Very "nise" indeed.

So the letters, with their disguised handwriting, their seemingly contrived grammatical errors, their inconsistent misspelling and use of slang, cannot in these instances be arbitrarily dismissed as hoaxes.

The trouble is that none of them seem likely to be the work of the most popular suspects. It's hard to imagine a revenge-ridden doctor, a Russian secret agent, a royal personage, a classical tutor, or a barrister-turned-tutor managing to master colloquialisms correctly and employing elaborately disguised handwriting merely to mystify police. Nor does it explain the mysterious message chalked on a Whitechapel wall following the "double event." It read, "The Juwes are not the men that will be blamed for nothing," and if that sounds ambiguous it cannot be clarified by any handwriting analysis or comparison—because Sir Charles Warren, in charge of the investigation, rubbed it out before daylight permitted a photograph to be taken. He claimed he feared inciting anti-Semitic riots in Whitechapel, but whatever his reason, he destroyed a possibly important piece of evidence. Conceivably it could have been the work of someone trying to stir up dissension for political reasons, but if so, why didn't that person include inflammatory remarks in the two letters and postcard which seem genuine?

But these questions are merely samples of literally hundreds of puzzles, riddles, and mysteries-within-mysteries. Small wonder, then, that a century of controversy and conjecture has revolved around the Ripper's elusive identity.

From time to time the public has been enlightened by various self-styled "experts." Though particulars may differ, they all tell approximately the same story. Each one claims to have been the recipient of confidences from some highly placed member of the Metropolitan Police, Scotland Yard, or even the Home Office. This anonymous source assured them that of course the "authorities" knew exactly who Jack the Ripper really was—and knew it almost immediately after the time of the final slaying. In other words, although choosing not to name names, they had the correct answer and there was really no "mystery" left to solve.

But if the "authorities" really believed that Kosminski, Montague J. Druitt, or the Duke of Clarence or any of a dozen others was truly Jack the Ripper, then why were more than fifty extra plainclothes police officers still detailed to Whitechapel from other districts for over a full year after the 1888 murders?

I submit that they were still searching for Jack the Ripper.

And, a hundred years later, so are we.

Hence this book, this collection of fact and fancy, which may perhaps furnish clues with which you, the reader, can come up with a final solution. If so it would be a great victory, and I wish you luck in that endeavor.

Let's win this one for the Ripper!

—Robert Bloch

Yours Truly, Jack the Ripper

I looked at the stage Englishman. He looked at me.

"Sir Guy Hollis?" I asked.

"Indeed. Have I the pleasure of addressing John Carmody, the psychiatrist?"

I nodded. My eyes swept over the figure of my distinguished visitor. Tall, lean, sandy-haired—with the traditional tufted mustache. And the tweeds. I suspected a monocle concealed in a vest pocket, and wondered if he'd left his umbrella in the outer office.

But more than that, I wondered what the devil had impelled Sir Guy Hollis of the British Embassy to seek out a total stranger here in Chicago.

Sir Guy didn't help matters any as he sat down. He cleared his throat, glanced around nervously, tapped his pipe against the side of the desk. Then he opened his mouth.

"Mr. Carmody," he said, "have you ever heard of—Jack the Ripper?"

"The murderer?" I asked.

"Exactly. The greatest monster of them all. Worse than Springheel Jack or Crippen. Jack the Ripper. Red Jack."

"I've heard of him," I said.

"Do you know his history?"

"Listen, Sir Guy," I muttered. "I don't think we'll get any place swapping old wives' tales about famous crimes of history."

Another bull's-eye. He took a deep breath.

"This is no old wives' tale. It's a matter of life or death."

He was so wrapped up in his obsession he even talked that way. Well—I was willing to listen. We psychiatrists get paid for listening.

"Go ahead," I told him. "Let's have the story."

Sir Guy lit a cigarette and began to talk.

"London, 1888," he began. "Late summer and early fall. That was the time. Out of nowhere came the shadowy figure of Jack the Ripper—a stalking shadow with a knife, prowling through London's East End. Haunting the squalid dives of Whitechapel, Spitalfields. Where he came from no one knew. But he brought death. Death in a knife.

"Six times that knife descended to slash the throats and bodies of London's women. Drabs and alley sluts. August seventh was the date of the first butchery. They found her body lying there with thirty-nine stab wounds. A ghastly murder. On August thirty-first, another victim. The press became interested. The slum inhabitants were more deeply interested still.

"Who was this unknown killer who prowled in their midst and struck at will in the deserted alleyways of night-town? And what was more important—when would he strike again?

"September eighth was the date. Scotland Yard assigned special deputies. Rumors ran rampant. The atrocious nature of the slayings was the subject for shocking speculation.

"The killer used a knife—expertly. He cut throats and removed—certain portions—of the bodies after death. He chose victims and settings with a fiendish deliberation. No one saw him or heard him. But watchmen making their gray rounds in the dawn would stumble across the hacked and horrid thing that was the Ripper's handiwork.

"Who was he? What was he? A mad surgeon? A butcher? An insane scientist? A pathological degenerate escaped from an asylum? A deranged nobleman? A member of the London police?

"Then the poem appeared in the newspapers. The anonymous poem, designed to put a stop to speculations—but which only aroused public interest to a further frenzy. A mocking little stanza:

I'm not a butcher, I'm not a Yid
Nor yet a foreign skipper,
But I'm your own true loving friend,
Yours truly—Jack the Ripper.

"And on September thirtieth, two more throats were slashed open."

I interrupted Sir Guy for a moment. "Very interesting," I commented. I'm afraid a faint hint of sarcasm crept into my voice.

He winced, but didn't falter in his narrative.

"There was silence, then, in London for a time. Silence, and a nameless fear. When would Red Jack strike again? They waited through October. Every figment of fog concealed his phantom presence. Concealed it well—for nothing was learned of the Ripper's identity, or his purpose. The drabs of London shivered in the raw wind of early November. Shivered, and were thankful for the coming of each morning's sun.

"November ninth. They found her in her room. She lay there very quietly, limbs neatly arranged. And beside her, with equal neatness, were laid her head and heart. The Ripper had outdone himself in execution.

"Then, panic. But needless panic. For though press, police, and populace alike waited in sick dread, Jack the Ripper did not strike again.

"Months passed. A year. The immediate interest died, but not the memory. They said Jack had skipped to America. That he had committed suicide. They said—and they wrote. They've written ever since. Theories, hypotheses, arguments, treatises. But to this day no one knows who Jack the Ripper was. Or why he killed. Or why he stopped killing."

Sir Guy was silent. Obviously he expected some comment from me.

"You tell the story well," I remarked. "Though with a slight emotional bias."

"I've got all the documents," said Sir Guy Hollis. "I've made a collection of existing data and studied it."

I stood up. "Well," I yawned, in mock fatigue, "I've enjoyed your little bedtime story a great deal, Sir Guy. It was kind of you to abandon your duties at the British Embassy to drop in on a poor psychiatrist and regale him with your anecdotes."

Goading him always did the trick.

"I suppose you want to know why I'm interested?" he snapped.

"Yes. That's exactly what I'd like to know. Why are you interested?"

"Because," said Sir Guy Hollis, "I am on the trail of Jack the Ripper now. I think he's here—in Chicago!"

I sat down again. This time I did the blinking act.

"Say that again," I stuttered.

"Jack the Ripper is alive, in Chicago, and I'm out to find him."

"Wait a minute," I said. "Wait—a—minute!"

He wasn't smiling. It wasn't a joke.

"See here," I said. "What was the date of these murders?"

"August to November, 1888."

"1888? But if Jack the Ripper was an able-bodied man in 1888, he'd surely be dead today! Why, look, man—if he were merely born in that year, he'd be fifty-seven years old today!"

"Would he?" smiled Sir Guy Hollis. "Or should I say, 'Would she?' Because, Jack the Ripper may have been a woman. Or any number of things."

"Sir Guy," I said. "You came to the right person when you looked me up. You definitely need the services of a psychiatrist."

"Perhaps. Tell me, Mr. Carmody, do you think I'm crazy?"

I looked at him and shrugged. But I had to give him a truthful answer. "Frankly—no."

"Then you might listen to the reasons I believe Jack the Ripper is alive today."

"I might."

"I've studied these cases for thirty years. Been over the actual ground. Talked to officials. Talked to friends and acquaintances of the poor drabs who were killed. Visited with men and women in the neighborhood. Collected an entire library of material touching on Jack the Ripper. Studied all the wild theories or crazy notions.

"I learned a little. Not much, but a little. I won't bore you with my conclusions. But there was another branch of inquiry that yielded a more fruitful return. I have studied unsolved crimes. Murders.

"I could show you clippings from the papers of half the world's great cities. San Francisco. Shanghai. Calcutta. Omsk. Paris. Berlin. Pretoria. Cairo. Milan. Adelaide.

"The trail is there, the pattern. Unsolved crimes. Slashed throats of women. With the peculiar disfigurations and removals. Yes, I've followed a trail of blood. From New York westward across the continent. Then to the Pacific. From there to Africa. During the World War of 1914-18 it was Europe. After that, South America. And since 1930, the United States again. Eighty-seven such murders—and to the trained criminologist, all bear the stigma of the Ripper's handiwork.

"Recently there were the so-called Cleveland torso slayings. Remember? A shocking series. And finally, two recent deaths in Chicago. Within the past six months. One out on South Dearborn. The other somewhere up on Halsted. Same type of crime, same technique. I tell you, there are unmistakable indications in all these affairs—indications of the work of Jack the Ripper!"

I smiled. "A very tight theory," I said. "I'll not question your evidence at all, or the deductions you draw. You're the criminologist, and I'll take your word for it. Just one thing remains to be explained. A minor point, perhaps, but worth mentioning."

"And what is that?" asked Sir Guy.

"Just how could a man of, let us say, eighty-five years commit these crimes? For if Jack the Ripper was around thirty in 1888 and lived, he'd be eighty-five today."

Sir Guy Hollis was silent. I had him there. But—

"Suppose he didn't get any older?" whispered Sir Guy.

"What's that?"

"Suppose Jack the Ripper didn't grow old? Suppose he is still a young man today?"

"All right," I said. "I'll suppose for a moment. Then I'll stop supposing and call for my nurse to restrain you."

"I'm serious," said Sir Guy.

"They all are," I told him. "That's the pity of it all, isn't it? They know they hear voices and see demons. But we lock them up just the same."

It was cruel, but it got results. He rose and faced me.

"It's a crazy theory, I grant you," he said. "All the theories about the Ripper are crazy. The idea that he was a doctor. Or a maniac. Or a woman. The reasons advanced for such beliefs are flimsy enough. There's nothing to go by. So why should my notion be any worse?"

"Because people grow older," I reasoned with him. "Doctors, maniacs, and women alike."

"What about—*sorcerers?*"

"Sorcerers?"

"Necromancers. Wizards. Practicers of Black Magic?"

"What's the point?"

"I studied," said Sir Guy. "I studied everything. After a while I began to study the dates of the murders. The pattern those dates formed. The rhythm. The solar, lunar, stellar rhythm. The sidereal aspect. The astrological significance."

He was crazy. But I still listened.

"Suppose Jack the Ripper didn't murder for murder's sake alone? Suppose he wanted to make—a sacrifice?"

"What kind of sacrifice?"

Sir Guy shrugged. "It is said that if you offer blood to the dark gods that they grant boons. Yes, if a blood offering is made at the

25

proper time—when the moon and the stars are right—and with the proper ceremonies—they grant boons. Boons of youth. Eternal youth."

"But that's nonsense!"

"No. That's—Jack the Ripper."

I stood up. "A most interesting theory," I told him. "But Sir Guy—there's just one thing I'm interested in. Why do you come here and tell it to me? I'm not an authority on witchcraft. I'm not a police official or criminologist. I'm a practicing psychiatrist. What's the connection?"

Sir Guy smiled. "You are interested, then?"

"Well, yes. There must be some point."

"There is. But I wished to be assured of your interest first. Now I can tell you my plan."

"And just what is that plan?"

Sir Guy gave me a long look. Then he spoke.

"John Carmody," he said, "you and I are going to capture Jack the Ripper."

● ● ●

That's the way it happened. I've given the gist of that first interview in all its intricate and somewhat boring detail, because I think it's important. It helps to throw some light on Sir Guy's character and attitude. And in view of what happened after that—

But I'm coming to those matters.

Sir Guy's thought was simple. It wasn't even a thought, just a hunch.

"You know the people here," he told me. "I've inquired. That's why I came to you as the ideal man for my purpose. You number among your acquaintances many writers, painters, poets. The so-called intelligentsia. The Bohemians. The lunatic fringe from the Near North Side.

"For certain reasons—never mind what they are—my clues lead me to infer that Jack the Ripper is a member of that element. He chooses to pose as an eccentric. I've a feeling that with you to take me around and introduce me to your set, I might hit upon the right person."

"It's all right with me," I said. "But just how are you going to look for him? As you say, he might be anybody, anywhere. And you have no idea what he looks like. He might be young or old. Jack the Ripper—a Jack of all trades? Rich man, poor man, beggar man, thief, doctor, lawyer—how will you know?"

"We shall see." Sir Guy sighed heavily. "But I must find him. At once."

"Why the hurry?"

Sir Guy sighed again. "Because in two days he will kill again."

"Are you sure?"

"Sure as the stars. I've plotted this chart, you see. All of the murders correspond to certain astrological rhythm patterns. If, as I suspect, he makes a blood sacrifice to renew his youth, he must murder within two days. Notice the pattern of his first crimes in London. August seventh. Then August thirty-first. September eighth. September thirtieth. November ninth. Intervals of twenty-four days, nine days, twenty-two days—he killed two this time—and then forty days. Of course there were crimes in between. There had to be. But they weren't discovered and pinned on him.

"At any rate, I've worked out a pattern for him, based on all my data. And I say that within the next two days he kills. So I must seek him out, somehow, before then."

"And I'm still asking you what you want me to do."

"Take me out," said Sir Guy. "Introduce me to your friends. Take me to parties."

"But where do I begin? As far as I know, my artistic friends, despite their eccentricities, are all normal people."

"So is the Ripper. Perfectly normal. Except on certain nights." Again that faraway look in Sir Guy's eyes. "Then he becomes an ageless pathological monster, crouching to kill, on evenings when the stars blaze down in the blazing patterns of death."

"All right," I said. "All right. I'll take you to parties, Sir Guy. I want to go myself, anyway. I need the drinks they'll serve there, after listening to your kind of talk."

We made our plans. And that evening I took him over to Lester Baston's studio.

As we ascended to the penthouse roof in the elevator I took the opportunity to warn Sir Guy.

"Baston's a real screwball," I cautioned him. "So are his guests. Be prepared for anything and everything."

"I am." Sir Guy Hollis was perfectly serious. He put his hand in his trousers pocket and pulled out a gun.

"What the—" I began.

"If I see him I'll be ready," Sir Guy said. He didn't smile, either.

"But you can't go running around at a party with a loaded revolver in your pocket, man!"

"Don't worry, I won't behave foolishly."

I wondered. Sir Guy Hollis was not, to my way of thinking, a normal man.

We stepped out of the elevator, went toward Baston's apartment door.

"By the way," I murmured, "just how do you wish to be introduced? Shall I tell them who you are and what you are looking for?"

"I don't care. Perhaps it would be best to be frank."

"But don't you think that the Ripper—if by some miracle he or she is present—will immediately get the wind up and take cover?"

"I think the shock of the announcement that I am hunting the Ripper would provoke some kind of betraying gesture on his part," said Sir Guy.

"You'd make a pretty good psychiatrist yourself," I conceded. "It's a fine theory. But I warn you, you're going to be in for a lot of ribbing. This is a wild bunch."

Sir Guy smiled. "I'm ready," he announced. "I have a little plan of my own. Don't be shocked at anything I do," he warned me.

I nodded and knocked on the door.

Baston opened it and poured out into the hall. His eyes were as red as the maraschino cherries in his Manhattan. He teetered back and forth regarding us very gravely. He squinted at my square-cut Homburg hat and Sir Guy's mustache.

"Aha," he intoned. "The Walrus and the Carpenter."

I introduced Sir Guy.

"Welcome," said Baston, gesturing us inside with over-elaborate courtesy. He stumbled after us into the garish parlor.

I stared at the crowd that moved restlessly through the fog of cigarette smoke.

It was the shank of the evening for this mob. Every hand held a drink. Every face held a slightly hectic flush. Over in one corner the piano was going full blast, but the imperious strains of the March from *The Love for Three Oranges* couldn't drown out the profanity from the crap game in the other corner.

Prokofiev had no chance against African polo, and one set of ivories rattled louder than the other.

Sir Guy got a monocleful right away. He saw LaVern Gonnister, the poetess, hit Hymie Kralik in the eye. He saw Hymie sit down on the floor and cry until Dick Pool accidentally stepped on his stomach as he walked through to the dining room for a drink.

He heard Nadia Vilinoff, the commercial artist, tell Johnny Odcutt that she thought his tattooing was in dreadful taste and he saw Barclay Melton crawl under the dining room table with Johnny Odcutt's wife.

His zoological observations might have continued indefinitely if Lester Baston hadn't stepped to the center of the room and called for silence by dropping a vase on the floor.

"We have distinguished visitors in our midst," bawled Lester, waving his empty glass in our direction. "None other than the Walrus and the Carpenter. The Walrus is Sir Guy Hollis, a something-or-other from the British Embassy. The Carpenter, as you all know, is our own John Carmody, the prominent dispenser of libido liniment."

He turned and grabbed Sir Guy by the arm, dragging him to the middle of the carpet. For a moment I thought Hollis might object, but a quick wink reassured me. He was prepared for this.

"It is our custom, Sir Guy," said Baston loudly, "to subject our new friends to a little cross-examination. Just a little formality at these formal gatherings, you understand. Are you prepared to answer questions?"

Sir Guy nodded and grinned.

"Very well," Baston muttered. "Friends—I give you this bundle from Britain. Your witness."

Then the ribbing started. I meant to listen, but at that moment Lydia Dare saw me and dragged me off into the vestibule for one of those Darling-I-waited-for-your-call-all-day routines.

By the time I got rid of her and went back, the impromptu quiz session was in full swing. From the attitude of the crowd, I gathered that Sir Guy was doing all right for himself.

Then Baston himself interjected a question that upset the applecart.

"And what, may I ask, brings you to our midst tonight? What is your mission, O Walrus?"

"I'm looking for Jack the Ripper." Nobody laughed.

Perhaps it struck them all the way it did me. I glanced at my neighbors and began to *wonder*.

LaVerne Gonnister. Hymie Kralik. Harmless. Dick Pool. Nadia Vilinoff. Johnny Odcutt and his wife. Barclay Melton. Lydia Dare. All harmless.

But what a forced smile on Dick Pool's face! And that sly, self-conscious smirk that Barclay Melton wore!

Oh, it was absurd, I grant you. But for the first time I saw these people in a new light. I wondered about their lives—their secret lives beyond the scenes of parties.

How many of them were playing a part, concealing something?

Who here would worship Hecate and grant that horrid goddess the dark boon of blood?

Even Lester Baston might be masquerading.

The mood was upon us all, for a moment. I saw questions flicker in the circle of eyes around the room.

Sir Guy stood there, and I could swear he was fully conscious of the situation he'd created, and enjoyed it.

I wondered idly just what was *really* wrong with him. Why he had this odd fixation concerning Jack the Ripper. Maybe he was hiding secrets, too....

Baston, as usual, broke the mood. He burlesqued it.

"The Walrus isn't kidding, friends," he said. He slapped Sir Guy on the back and put his arm around him as he orated. "Our English cousin is really on the trail of the fabulous Jack the Ripper. You all remember Jack the Ripper, I presume? Quite a cutup in the old days, as I recall. Really had some ripping good times when he went out on a tear.

"The Walrus has some idea that the Ripper is still alive, probably prowling around Chicago with a Boy Scout knife. In fact"— Baston paused impressively and shot it out in a rasping stage whisper—"in fact, he has reason to believe that Jack the Ripper might even be right here in our midst tonight."

There was the expected reaction of giggles and grins. Baston eyed Lydia Dare reprovingly. "You girls needn't laugh," he smirked. "Jack the Ripper might be a woman, too, you know. Sort of a Jill the Ripper."

"You mean you actually suspect one of us?" shrieked LaVerne Gonnister, simpering up to Sir Guy. "But that Jack the Ripper person disappeared ages ago, didn't he? In 1888?"

"Aha!" interrupted Baston. "How do you know so much about it, young lady? Sounds suspicious! Watch her, Sir Guy—she may not be as young as she appears. These lady poets have dark pasts."

The tension was gone, the mood was shattered, and the whole thing was beginning to degenerate into a trivial party joke. The man who had played the March was eyeing the piano with a *Scherzo* gleam in his eye that augured ill for Prokofiev. Lydia Dare was glancing at the kitchen, waiting to make a break for another drink.

Then Baston caught it. "Guess what?" he yelled. "The Walrus has a gun."

His embracing arm had slipped and encountered the hard outline of the gun in Sir Guy's pocket. He snatched it out before Hollis had the opportunity to protest.

I stared hard at Sir Guy, wondering if this thing had carried far enough. But he flicked a wink my way and I remembered he had told me not to be alarmed.

So I waited as Baston broached a drunken inspiration.

"Let's play fair with our friend the Walrus," he cried. "He came all the way from England to our party on this mission. If none of you is willing to confess, I suggest we give him a chance to find out—the hard way."

"What's up?" asked Johnny Odcutt.

"I'll turn out the lights for one minute. Sir Guy can stand here with his gun. If anyone in this room is the Ripper he can either run for it or take the opportunity to—well, eradicate his pursuer. Fair enough?"

It was even sillier than it sounds, but it caught the popular fancy. Sir Guy's protests went unheard in the ensuing babble.

And before I could stride over and put in my two cents' worth, Lester Baston had reached the light switch.

"Don't anybody move," he announced, with fake solemnity. "For one minute we will remain in darkness—perhaps at the mercy of a killer. At the end of that time, I'll turn up the lights again and look for bodies. Choose your partners, ladies and gentlemen."

The lights went out.

Somebody giggled.

I heard footsteps in the darkness. Mutterings.

A hand brushed my face.

The watch on my wrist ticked violently. But even louder, rising above it, I heard another thumping. The beating of my heart.

Absurd. Standing in the dark with a group of tipsy fools And yet there was real terror lurking here, rustling through the velvet blackness.

Jack the Ripper prowled in darkness like this. And Jack the Ripper had a knife. Jack the Ripper had a madman's brain and a madman's purpose.

But Jack the Ripper was dead, dead and dust these many years— by every human law.

Only there are no human laws when you feel yourself in the darkness, when the darkness hides and protects and the outer mask slips off your face and you feel something welling up within you, a brooding shapeless purpose that is brother to the blackness.

Sir Guy Hollis shrieked.

There was a grisly thud.

Baston had the lights on.

Everybody screamed.

Sir Guy Hollis lay sprawled on the floor in the center of the room. The gun was still clutched in his hand.

I glanced at the faces, marveling at the variety of expressions human beings can assume when confronting horror.

All the faces were present in the circle. Nobody had fled. And yet Sir Guy Hollis lay there....

LaVerne Gonnister was wailing and hiding her face.

"All right." Sir Guy rolled over and jumped to his feet. He was smiling. "Just an experiment, eh? If Jack the Ripper *were* among those present, and thought I had been murdered, he would have betrayed himself in some way when the lights went on and he saw me lying there.

"I am convinced of your individual and collective innocence. Just a gentle spoof, my friends."

Hollis stared at the goggling Baston and the rest of them crowding in behind him.

"Shall we leave, John?" he called to me. "It's getting late, I think."

Turning, he headed for the closet. I followed him. Nobody said a word.

It was a pretty dull party after that.

• • •

I met Sir Guy the following evening as we agreed, on the corner of Twenty-ninth and South Halsted.

After what had happened the night before, I was prepared for almost anything. But Sir Guy seemed matter-of-fact enough as he stood huddled against a grimy doorway and waited for me to appear.

"Boo!" I said, jumping out suddenly. He smiled. Only the betraying gesture of his left hand indicated that he'd instinctively reached for his gun when I startled him.

"All ready for our wild-goose chase?" I asked.

"Yes." He nodded. "I'm glad that you agreed to meet me without asking questions," he told me. "It shows you trust my judgment."

He took my arm and edged me along the street slowly.

"It's foggy tonight, John," said Sir Guy Hollis. "Like London."

I nodded.

"Cold, too, for November."

I nodded again and half shivered my agreement.

"Curious," mused Sir Guy. "London fog and November. The place and the time of the Ripper murders."

I grinned through darkness. "Let me remind you, Sir Guy, that this isn't London, but Chicago. And it isn't November, 1888. It's over fifty years later."

Sir Guy returned my grin, but without mirth. "I'm not so sure, at that," he murmured. "Look about you. These tangled alleys and twisted streets. They're like the East End. Mitre Square. And surely they are as ancient as fifty years, at least."

"You're in the colored neighborhood off South Clark Street," I said shortly. "And why you dragged me down here I still don't know."

"It's a hunch," Sir Guy admitted. "Just a hunch on my part, John. I want to wander around down here. There's the same geographical conformation in these streets as in those courts where the Ripper roamed and slew. That's where we'll find him, John. Not in the bright lights of the Bohemian neighborhood, but down here in the darkness. The darkness where he waits and crouches."

"Is that why you brought a gun?" I asked. I was unable to keep a trace of sarcastic nervousness from my voice. All of this talk, this incessant obsession with Jack the Ripper, got on my nerves more than I cared to admit.

"We may need a gun," said Sir Guy, gravely. "After all, tonight is the appointed night."

I sighed. We wandered on through the foggy, deserted streets. Here and there a dim light burned above a gin-mill doorway. Otherwise, all was darkness and shadow. Deep, gaping alleyways loomed as we proceeded down a slanting side street.

We crawled through that fog, alone and silent, like two tiny maggots floundering within a shroud.

When that thought hit me, I winced. The atmosphere was beginning to get *me*, too. If I didn't watch my step I'd go as loony as Sir Guy.

"Can't you see there's not a soul around these streets?" I said, tugging at his coat impatiently.

"He's bound to come," said Sir Guy. "He'll be drawn here. This is what I've been looking for. A *genius loci*. An evil spot that attracts evil. Always, when he slays, it's in the slums.

"You see, that must be one of his weaknesses. He has a fascination for squalor. Besides, the women he needs for sacrifice are more easily found in the dives and stewpots of a great city."

I smiled. "Well, let's go into one of the dives or stewpots," I suggested. "I'm cold. Need a drink. This damned fog gets into your bones. You Britishers can stand it, but I like warmth and dry heat."

We emerged from our side street and stood upon the threshold of an alley.

Through the white clouds of mist ahead, I discerned a dim, blue light, a naked bulb dangling from a beer sign above an alley tavern.

"Let's take a chance," I said. "I'm beginning to shiver."

"Lead the way," said Sir Guy.

I led him down the alley passage. We halted before the door of the dive.

"What are you waiting for?" he asked.

"Just looking in," I told him. "This is a tough neighborhood, Sir Guy. Never know what you're liable to run into. And I'd prefer we didn't get into the wrong company. Some of these Negro places resent white customers."

"Good idea, John."

I finished my inspection through the doorway. "Looks deserted," I murmured. "Let's try it." We entered a dingy bar. A feeble light flickered above the counter and railing, but failed to penetrate the further gloom of the back booths.

A gigantic Negro lolled across the bar—a black giant with prognathous jaw and apelike torso. He scarcely stirred as we came in, but his eyes flicked open quite suddenly and I knew he noted our presence and was judging us.

"Evening," I said.

He took his time before replying. Still sizing us up. Then, he grinned. "Evening, gents. What's your pleasure?"

"Gin," I said. "Two gins. It's a cold night."

"That's right, gents."

He poured, I paid, and took the glasses over to one of the booths. We wasted no time in emptying them. The fiery liquor warmed.

I went over to the bar and got the bottle. Sir Guy and I poured ourselves another drink. The big Negro went back into his doze, with one wary eye half-open against any sudden activity.

The clock over the bar ticked on. The wind was rising outside, tearing the shroud of fog to ragged shreds. Sir Guy and I sat in the warm booth and drank our gin.

He began to talk, and the shadows crept up about to listen.

He rambled a great deal. He went over everything he'd said in the office when I met him, just as though I hadn't heard it before. The poor devils with obsessions are like that.

I listened very patiently. I poured Sir Guy another drink. And another.

But the liquor only made him more talkative. How he did run on! About ritual killings and prolonging the life unnaturally—the whole fantastic tale came out again. And of course, he maintained his unyielding conviction that the Ripper was abroad tonight.

I suppose I was guilty of goading him.

"Very well," I said, unable to keep the impatience from my voice. "Let us say that your theory is correct—even though we must overlook every natural law and swallow a lot of superstition to give it any credence.

"But let us say, for the sake of argument, that you are right. Jack the Ripper was a man who discovered how to prolong his own life through making human sacrifices. He did travel around the world as you believe. He is in Chicago now and he is planning to kill. In other words, let us suppose that everything you claim is gospel truth. So what?"

"What do you mean, 'so what'?" said Sir Guy.

"I mean—so what?" I answered. "If all this is true, it still doesn't prove that by sitting down in a dingy gin mill on the South Side, Jack the Ripper is going to walk in here and let you kill him or turn him over to the police. And come to think of it, I don't even know now just what you intend to *do* with him if you ever did find him."

Sir Guy gulped his gin. "I'd capture the bloody swine," he said. "Capture him and turn him over to the government, together with all the papers and documentary evidence I've collected against him over a period of many years. I've spent a fortune investigating this affair, I tell you, a fortune! His capture will mean the solution of hundreds of unsolved crimes, of that I am convinced.

"I tell you, a mad beast is loose on this world! An ageless, eternal beast, sacrificing to Hecate and the dark gods!"

In vino Veritas. Or was all this babbling the result of too much gin? It didn't matter. Sir Guy Hollis had another. I sat there and wondered what to do with him. The man was rapidly working up to a climax of hysterical drunkenness.

"One other point," I said, more for the sake of conversion than in any hopes of obtaining information. "You still don't explain how it is that you hope to just blunder into the Ripper."

"He'll be around," said Sir Guy. "I'm psychic. I know." Sir Guy wasn't psychic. He was maudlin.

The whole business was beginning to infuriate me. We'd been sitting here an hour and during all this time I'd been forced to play nursemaid and audience to a babbling idiot After all, he wasn't a regular patient of mine.

"That's enough," I said, putting out my hand as Sir Guy reached for the half-emptied bottle again. "You've had plenty. Now I've got a suggestion to make. Let's call a cab and get out of here. It's getting late and it doesn't look as though your elusive friend is going to put in his appearance. Tomorrow, if I were you, I'd plan to turn all those papers and documents over to the FBI. If you're so convinced of the truth of your wild theory, they are competent to make a very thorough investigation, and find your man."

"No." Sir Guy was drunkenly obstinate. "No cab."

"But let's get out of here anyway," I said, glancing at watch. "It's past midnight."

He sighed, shrugged, and rose unsteadily. As he started for the door, he tugged the gun free from his pocket.

"Here, give me that!" I whispered. "You can't walk around the street brandishing that thing."

I took the gun and slipped it inside my coat. Then I got hold of his right arm and steered him out of the door. The black man didn't look up as we departed.

We stood shivering in the alleyway. The fog had increased. I couldn't see either end of the alley where we stood. It was cold. Damp. Dark. Fog or no fog, a little wind was whispering secrets to the shadows at our backs.

The fresh air hit Sir Guy just as I expected it would. Fog and gin fumes don't mingle very well. He lurched as I guided him slowly through the mist.

Sir Guy, despite his incapacity, still stared apprehensively at the alley, as though he expected to see a figure approaching.

Disgust got the better of me. "Childish foolishness," I snorted. "Jack the Ripper, indeed! I call this carrying a hobby too far."

"Hobby?" He faced me. Through the fog I could see his distorted face. "You call this a hobby?"

"Well, what is it?" I grumbled. "Just why else are you so interested in tracking down this mythical killer?"

My arm held his. But his stare held me.

"In London," he whispered. "In 1888—one of those nameless drabs the Ripper slew—was my mother."

"What?"

"Later I was recognized by my father, and legitimatized. We swore to give our lives to find the Ripper. My father was the first to search. He died in Hollywood in 1926—on the trail of the Ripper. They said he was stabbed by an unknown assailant in a brawl. But I know who that assailant was.

"So I've taken up his work, do you see, John? I've carried on. And I will carry on until I do find him and kill him with my own hands.

"He took my mother's life and the lives of hundreds to keep his own hellish being alive. Like a vampire, he battens on blood. Like a ghoul, he is nourished by death. Like a fiend, he stalks the world to kill. He is cunning, devilishly cunning. But I'll never rest until I find him, never!"

I believed him then. He wouldn't give up. He wasn't just a drunken babbler anymore. He was as determined, as relentless as the Ripper himself.

Tomorrow he'd be sober. He'd continue the search. Perhaps he'd turn those papers over to the FBI. Sooner or later, with such persistence—and with his motive—he'd be successful. I'd always known he had a motive.

"Let's go," I said, steering him down the alley.

"Wait a minute," said Sir Guy. "Give me back my gun." He lurched a little. "I'd feel better with the gun on me."

He pressed me into the dark shadows of a little recess.

I tried to shrug him off, but he was insistent.

"Let me carry the gun, now, John," he mumbled.

"All right," I said.

I reached into my coat, brought my hand out.

"But that's not a gun," he protested. "That's a knife."

"I know."

I bore down on him swiftly.

"John!" he screamed.

"Never mind the 'John,'" I whispered, raising the knife. "Just call me—Jack."

A Most Unusual Murder

Only the dead know Brooklyn.

Thomas Wolfe said that, and he's dead now, so he ought to know. London, of course, is a different story.

At least that's the way Hilary Kane thought of it. Not as a story, perhaps, but rather as an old-fashioned, outsize picaresque novel in which every street was a chapter crammed with characters and incidents of its own. Each block a page, each structure a separate paragraph unto itself within the sprawling, tangled plot—such was Hilary Kane's concept of the city, and he knew it well.

Over the years he strolled the pavements, reading the city sentence by sentence until every line was familiar; he'd learned London by heart.

And that's why he was so startled when, one bleak afternoon late in November, he discovered the shop in Saxe-Coburg Square.

"I'll be damned!" he said.

"Probably." Lester Woods, his companion, took the edge off the affirmation with an indulgent smile. "What's the problem?"

"This." Kane gestured toward the tiny window of the establishment nestled inconspicuously between two residential relics of Victoria's day.

"An antique place." Woods nodded. "At the rate they're springing up there must be at least one for every tourist in London."

"But not here." Kane frowned. "I happen to have come by this way less than a week ago, and I'd swear there was no shop in the Square."

"Then it must have opened since." The two men moved up to the entrance, glancing through the display window in passing.

Kane's frown deepened. "You call this new? Look at the dust on those goblets."

"Playing detective again, eh?" Woods shook his head. "Trouble with you, Hilary, is that you have too many hobbies." He glanced across the Square as a chill wind heralded the coming of twilight. "Getting late—we'd better move along."

"Not until I find out about this."

Kane was already opening the door and Woods sighed. "The game is afoot, I suppose. All right, let's get it over with."

The shop-bell tinkled and the two men stepped inside. The door closed, the tinkling stopped, and they stood in the shadows and the silence.

But one of the shadows was not silent. It rose from behind the single counter in the small space before the rear wall.

"Good afternoon, gentlemen," said the shadow. And switched on an overhead light. It cast a dim nimbus over the countertop and gave dimension to the shadow, revealing the substance of a diminutive figure with an unremarkable face beneath a balding brow.

Kane addressed the proprietor. "Mind if we have a look?"

"Is there any special area of interest?" The proprietor gestured toward the shelves lining the wall behind him. "Books, maps, china, crystal?"

"Not really," Kane said. "It's just that I'm always curious about a new shop of this sort—"

The proprietor shook his head. "Begging your pardon, but it's hardly new."

Woods glanced at his friend with a barely suppressed smile, but Kane ignored it.

"Odd," Kane said. "I've never noticed this place before."

"Quite so. I've been in business a good many years, but this *is* a new location."

Now it was Kane's turn to glance quickly at Woods, and his smile was not suppressed. But Woods was already eyeing the artifacts on display, and after a moment Kane began his own inspection.

Peering at the shelving beneath the glass counter, he made a rapid inventory. He noted a boudoir lamp with a beaded fringe, a lavalier, a tray of pearly buttons, a durbar souvenir programme, and a framed and inscribed photograph of Matilda Alice Victoria Wood *aka* Bella Delmare *aka* Marie Lloyd. There was a miscellany of old jewelry, hunting-watches, pewter mugs, napkin rings, a toy bank in the shape of a miniature Crystal Palace, and a display poster of a formidably mustached Lord Kitchener with his gloved finger extended in a gesture of imperious command.

It was, he decided, the mixture as before. Nothing unusual, and most of it—like the Kitchener poster—not even properly antique but merely outmoded. Those fans on the bottom shelf, for example, and the silk toppers, the opera glasses, the black bag in the far corner covered with what was once called "American cloth."

Something about the phrase caused Kane to stoop and make a closer inspection. *American cloth.* Dusty now, but once shiny, like the tarnished silver nameplate identifying its owner. He read the inscription.

J. Ridley, M.D.

Kane looked up, striving to conceal his sudden surge of excitement.

Impossible! It couldn't be—and yet it was. Keeping his voice and gesture carefully casual, he indicated the bag to the proprietor.

"A medical kit?"

"Yes, I imagine so."

"Might I ask where you acquired it?"

The little man shrugged. "Hard to remember. In this line one picks up the odd item here and there over the years."

"Might I have a look at it, please?"

The elderly proprietor lifted the bag to the countertop. Woods stared at it, puzzled, but Kane ignored him, his gaze intent on the nameplate below the lock. "Would you mind opening it?" he said.

"I'm afraid I don't have a key."

Kane reached out and pressed the lock; it was rusted, but firmly fixed. Frowning, he lifted the bag and shook it gently.

Something jiggled inside, and as he heard the click of metal against metal his elation peaked. Somehow he suppressed it as he spoke.

"How much are you asking?"

The proprietor was equally emotionless. "Not for sale."

"But—"

"Sorry, sir. It's against my policy to dispose of blind items. And since there's no telling what's inside—"

"Look, it's only an old medical bag. I hardly imagine it contains the Crown jewels."

In the background Woods snickered, but the proprietor ignored him. "Granted," he said. "But one can't be certain of the contents."

Now the little man lifted the bag and once again there was a clicking sound. "Coins, perhaps."

"Probably just surgical instruments," Kane said impatiently. "Why don't you force the lock and settle the matter?"

"Oh, I couldn't do that. It would destroy its value."

"What value?" Kane's guard was down now; he knew he'd made a tactical error but he couldn't help himself.

The proprietor smiled. "I told you the bag is not for sale."

"Everything has its price."

Kane's statement was a challenge, and the proprietor's smile broadened as he met it. "One hundred pounds."

"A hundred pounds for *that*?" Woods grinned—then gaped at Kane's response.

"Done and done."

"But, sir—"

For answer Kane drew out his wallet and extracted five twenty-pound notes. Placing them on the countertop, he lifted the bag and moved toward the door. Woods followed hastily, turning to close the door behind him. The proprietor gestured. "Wait—come back—" But Kane was already hurrying down the street, clutching the black bag under his arm.

• • •

He was still clutching it half an hour later as Woods moved with him into the spacious study of Kane's flat overlooking the verdant vista of Cadogan Square. Dappled splotches of sunlight reflected from the gleaming oilcloth as Kane set the bag on the table and carefully wiped away the film of dust with a dampened rag. He smiled triumphantly at Woods.

"Looks a bit better now, don't you think?"

"I don't think anything." Woods shook his head. "A hundred pounds for an old medical kit—"

"A *very* old medical kit," said Kane. "Dates back to the eighties, if I'm not mistaken."

"Even so, I hardly see—"

"Of course you wouldn't! I doubt if anyone besides myself would attach much significance to the name of J. Ridley, M.D."

"Never heard of him."

"That's understandable." Kane smiled. "He preferred to call himself Jack the Ripper."

"Jack the Ripper?"

"Surely you know the case. Whitechapel, 1888—the savage slaying and mutilation of prostitutes by a cunning mass-murderer who taunted the police—a shadow, stalking his prey in the streets."

Woods frowned. "But he was never caught, was he? Not even identified."

"In that you're mistaken. No murderer has been identified quite as frequently as Red Jack. At the time of the crimes and over the years since, a score of suspects were named. A prime candidate was the Pole, Klosowski, alias George Chapman, who killed several wives—but poison was his method and gain his motive whereas the Ripper's victims were all penniless prostitutes who died under the knife. Another convicted murderer, Neil Cream, even openly proclaimed he was the Ripper—"

"Wouldn't that be the answer, then?"

Kane shrugged. "Unfortunately, Cream happened to be in America at the time of the Ripper murders. Egomania prompted his false confession." He shook his head. "Then there was John Pizer, a bookbinder known by the nickname of 'Leather Apron'—he was actually arrested, but quickly cleared and released. Some think the killings were the work of a Russian called Knovalov who also went by the name of Pedachenko and worked as a barber's surgeon; supposedly he was a Tsarist secret agent who perpetrated the slayings to discredit the British police."

"Sounds pretty far-fetched if you ask me."

"Exactly." Kane smiled. "But there are other candidates, equally improbable. Montague John Druitt for one, a barrister of unsound mind who drowned himself in the Thames shortly after the last Ripper murder. Unfortunately, it has been established that he was living in Bournemouth, and on the days before and after the final slaying he was there, playing cricket. Then there was the Duke of Clarence—"

"Who?"

"Queen Victoria's grandson in direct line of succession to the throne."

"Surely you're not serious?"

"No, but others are. It has been asserted that Clarence was a known deviate who suffered from insanity as the result of venereal infection, and that his death in 1892 was actually due to the ravages of his disease."

"But that doesn't prove him to be the Ripper."

"Quite so. It hardly seems possible that he could write the letters filled with American slang and crude errors in grammar and spelling which the Ripper sent to the authorities; letters containing information which could be known only by the murderer and the police. More to the point, Clarence was in Scotland at the time of one of the killings and at Sandringham when others took place. And there are equally firm reasons for exonerating suggested suspects close to him—his friend James Stephen and his physician, Sir William Gull."

"You've really studied up on this," Woods murmured. "I'd no idea you were so keen on it."

"And for good reason. I wasn't about to make a fool of myself by advancing an untenable notion. I don't believe the Ripper was a seaman, as some surmise, for there's not a scintilla of evidence to back the theory. Nor do I think the Ripper was a slaughterhouse worker, a midwife, a man disguised as a woman, or a London bobby. And I doubt the existence of a mysterious physician named Dr. Stanley, out to avenge himself against the woman who had infected him, or his son."

"But there do seem to be a great number of medical men amongst the suspects," Woods said.

"Right you are, and for good reason. Consider the nature of the crimes—the swift and skillful removal of vital organs, accomplished in the darkness of the streets under constant danger of imminent discovery. All this implies the discipline of someone versed in anatomy, someone with the cool nerves of a practicing surgeon. Then too there's the matter of escaping detection. The Ripper obviously knew the alleys and byways of the East End so thoroughly that he could slip through police cordons and patrols without discovery. But if seen, who would have a better alibi than a respectable physician, carrying a medical bag on an emergency call late at night?

"With that in mind, I set about my search, examining the rolls of London Hospital in Whitechapel Road. I went over the names of physicians and surgeons listed in the Medical Registry for that period."

"All of them?"

"It wasn't necessary. I knew what I was looking for—a surgeon who lived and practiced in the immediate Whitechapel area. Whenever possible, I followed up with a further investigation of my suspects' histories—researching hospital and clinic affiliations, even hobbies and background activities from medical journals, press reports, and family records. Of course, all this takes a great deal of time and patience. I must have been tilting at this windmill for a good five years before I found my man."

Woods glanced at the nameplate on the bag. "J. Ridley, M.D.?"

"John Ridley. *Jack,* to his friends—if he had any." Kane paused, thoughtful. "But that's just the point. Ridley appears to have had no friends, and no family. An orphan, he received his degree from Edinburgh in 1878, ten years before the date of the murders. He set up private practice here in London, but there is no office address listed. Nor is there any further information to be found concerning him; it's as though he took particular care to suppress every detail of his personal and private life. This, of course, is what roused my suspicions. For an entire decade J. Ridley lived and practiced in the East End without a single mention of his name anywhere in print, except for his Registry listing. And after 1888, even *that* disappeared."

"Suppose he died?"

"There's no obituary on record."

Woods shrugged. "Perhaps he moved, emigrated, took sick, abandoned practice?"

"Then why the secrecy? Why conceal his whereabouts? Don't you see—it's the very lack of such ordinary details which leads me to suspect the extraordinary."

"But that's not evidence. There's no proof that your Dr. Ridley was the Ripper."

"That's why this is so important." Kane indicated the bag on the tabletop. "If we knew its history, where it came from—"

As he spoke, Kane reached down and picked up a brass letter-opener from the table, then moved to the bag.

"Wait." Woods put a restraining hand on Kane's shoulder. "That may not be necessary."

"What do you mean?"

"I think the shopkeeper was lying. He knew what the bag contains—he had to, or else why did he fix such a ridiculous price? He never dreamed you'd take him up on it, of course. But there's no need for you to force the lock any more than there was for him to do so. My guess is that he has a key."

"You're right." Kane set the letter-opener down. "I should have realized, if I'd taken the time to consider his reluctance. He must have the key." He lifted the shiny bag and turned. "Come along— let's get back to him before the shop closes. And this time we won't be put off by any excuses."

• • •

Dusk had descended as Kane and his companion hastened through the streets, and darkness was creeping across the deserted silence of Saxe-Coburg Square when they arrived.

They halted then, staring into the shadows, seeking the spot where the shop nestled between the residences looming on either side. The shadows were deeper here and they moved closer, only to stare again at the empty gap between the two buildings.

The shop was gone.

Woods blinked, then turned and gestured to Kane. "But we were here—we saw it—"

Kane didn't reply. He was staring at the dusty, rubble-strewn surface of the space between the structures; at the weeds which sprouted from the bare ground beneath. A chill night wind echoed through the emptiness. Kane stooped and sifted a pinch of dust between his fingers. The dust was cold, like the wind that whirled the fine grains from his hand and blew them away into the darkness.

"What happened?" Woods was murmuring. "Could we both have dreamed—"

Kane stood erect, facing his friend. "This isn't a dream," he said, gripping the black bag.

"Then what's the answer?"

"I don't know." Kane frowned thoughtfully. "But there's only one place where we can possibly find it."

"Where?"

"The 1888 Medical Registry lists the address of John Ridley as Number 17 Dorcas Lane."

• • •

The cab which brought them to Dorcas Lane could not enter its narrow accessway. The dim alley beyond was silent and empty, but Kane plunged into it without hesitation, moving along the dark passage between solid rows of grimy brick. Treading over the cobblestones, it seemed to Woods that he was being led into another era, yet Kane's progress was swift and unfaltering.

"You've been here before?" Woods said.

"Of course." Kane halted before the unlighted entrance to Number 17, then knocked.

The door opened—not fully, but just enough to permit the figure behind it to peer out at them. Both glance and greeting were guarded.

"Whatcherwant?"

Kane stepped into the fan of light from the partial opening. "Good evening. Remember me?"

"Yes." The door opened wider and Woods could see the squat shadow of the middle-aged woman who nodded up at his companion. "Yer the one what rented the back vacancy last Bank 'oliday, ain'tcher?"

"Right. I was wondering if I might have it again."

"I dunno." The woman glanced at Woods.

"Only for a few hours." Kane reached for his wallet. "My friend and I have a business matter to discuss."

"Business, eh?" Woods felt the unflattering appraisal of the landlady's beady eyes. "Cost you a fiver."

"Here you are."

A hand extended to grasp the note. Then the door opened fully, revealing the dingy hall and the stairs beyond. "Mind the steps now," the landlady said.

The stairs were steep and the woman was puffing as they reached the upper landing. She led them along the creaking corridor to the door at the rear, fumbling for the keys in her apron.

"'Ere we are."

The door opened on musty darkness, scarcely dispelled by the faint illumination of the overhead fixture as she switched it on. The landlady nodded at Kane. "I don't rent this for lodgings no more—it ain't properly made up."

"Quite all right." Kane smiled, his hand on the door.

"If there's anything you'll be needing, best tell me now. I've got to run over to the neighbor for a bit—she's been took ill."

"I'm sure we'll manage." Kane closed the door, then listened for a moment as the landlady's footsteps receded down the hall.

"Well," he said. "What do you think?"

Woods surveyed the shabby room with its single window framed by yellowing curtains. He noted the faded carpet with its pattern well-nigh worn away, the marred and chipped surfaces of the massive old bureau and heavy morris chair, the brass bed covered with a much-mended spread, the ancient gas log in the fireplace framed by a cracked marble mantelpiece, and the equally cracked washstand fixture in the corner.

"I think you're out of your mind," Woods said. "Did I understand correctly that you've been here before?"

"Exactly. I came several months ago, as soon as I found the address in the Registry. I wanted a look around."

Woods wrinkled his nose. "More to smell than there is to see."

"Use your imagination, man! Doesn't it mean anything to you that you're standing in the very room once occupied by Jack the Ripper?"

Woods shook his head. "There must be a dozen rooms to let in this old barn. What makes you think this is the right one?"

"The Registry entry specified 'rear.' And there are no rear accommodations downstairs—that's where the kitchen is located. So this has to be the place."

Kane gestured. "Think of it—you may be looking at the very sink where the Ripper washed away the traces of his butchery, the bed in which he slept after his dark deeds were performed! Who knows what sights this room has seen and heard—the voice crying out in a tormented nightmare—"

"Come off it, Hilary!" Woods grimaced impatiently. "It's one thing to use your imagination, but quite another to let your imagination use you."

"Look." Kane pointed to the far corner of the room. "Do you see those indentations in the carpet? I noticed them when I examined this room on my previous visit. What do they suggest to you?"

Woods peered dutifully at the worn surface of the carpet, noting the four round, evenly spaced marks. "Must have been another piece of furniture in that corner. Something heavy, I'd say."

"But what sort of furniture?"

"Well—" Woods considered. "Judging from the space, it wasn't a sofa or chair. Could have been a cabinet, perhaps a large desk—"

"Exactly. A rolltop desk. Every doctor had one in those days." Kane sighed. "I'd give a pretty penny to know what became of that item. It might have held the answer to all our questions."

"After all these years? Not bloody likely." Woods glanced away. "Didn't find anything else, did you?"

"I'm afraid not. As you say, it's been a long time since the Ripper stayed here."

"I didn't say that." Woods shook his head. "You may be right about the desk. And no doubt the Medical Registry gives a correct address. But all it means is that this room may once have been rented by a Dr. John Ridley. You've already inspected it once—why bother to come back?"

"Because now I have this." Kane placed the black bag on the bed. "And this." He produced a pocket-knife.

"You intend to force the lock after all?"

"In the absence of a key I have no alternative." Kane wedged the blade under the metal guard and began to pry upwards. "It's important that the bag be opened here. Something it contains may very well be associated with this room. If we recognize the connection we might have an additional clue, a conclusive link—"

The lock snapped.

As the bag sprang open, the two men stared down at its contents—the jumble of vials and pillboxes, the clumsy old-style stethoscope, the probes and tweezers, the roll of gauze. And, resting atop it, the scalpel with the steel-tipped surface encrusted with brownish stains.

They were still staring as the door opened quietly behind them and the balding, elderly little man entered the room.

"I see my guess was correct, gentlemen. You too have read the Medical Registry." He nodded. "I was hoping I'd find you here."

Kane frowned. "What do you want?"

"I'm afraid I must trouble you for my bag."

"But it's my property now—I bought it."

The little man sighed. "Yes, and I was a fool to permit it. I thought putting on that price would dissuade you. How was I to know you were a collector like myself?"

"Collector?"

"Of curiosa pertaining to murder." The little man smiled. "A pity you cannot see some of the memorabilia I've acquired. Not the commonplace items associated with your so-called Black Museum in Scotland Yard, but true rarities with historical significance." He gestured. "The silver jar in which the notorious French sorceress, La Voisin, kept her poisonous ointments, the actual dirks which dispatched the unfortunate nephews of Richard III in the Tower—yes, even the poker responsible for the atrocious demise of Edward II at Berkeley Castle on the night of September 21, 1327. I had quite a bit of trouble locating it until I realized the date was reckoned according to the old Julian calendar."

Kane frowned impatiently. "Who are you? What happened to that shop of yours?"

"My name would mean nothing to you. As for the shop, let us say that it exists spatially and temporally as I do—when and where necessary for my purposes. By your current and limited understanding, you might call it a sort of time machine."

Woods shook his head. "You're not making sense."

"Ah, but I am, and very good sense too. How else do you think I could pursue my interests so successfully unless I were free to travel in time? It is my particular pleasure to return to certain eras in this primitive past of yours, visiting the scenes of famous and infamous crimes and locating trophies for my collection.

"The shop, of course, is just something I used as a blind for this particular mission. It's gone now, and I shall be going too, just as soon as I retrieve my property. It happens to be the souvenir of a most unusual murder."

"You see?" Kane nodded at Woods. "I told you this bag belonged to Jack the Ripper!"

"Not so," said the little man. "I already have the Ripper's murder weapon, which I retrieved directly after the slaying of his final victim on November 9th, 1888. And I can assure you that your Dr. Ridley was not Jack the Ripper but merely and simply an eccentric surgeon—" As he spoke, he edged toward the bed.

"No you don't!" Kane turned to intercept him, but he was already reaching for the bag.

"Let go of that!" Kane shouted.

The little man tried to pull away, but Kane's hand swooped down frantically into the open bag and clawed. Then it rose, gripping the scalpel.

The little man yanked the bag away. Clutching it, he retreated as Kane bore down upon him furiously.

"Stop!" Woods cried. Hurling himself forward, he stepped between the two men, directly into the orbit of the descending blade.

There was a gurgle, then a thud, as he fell.

The scalpel clattered to the floor, slipping from Kane's nerveless fingers and coming to rest amidst the crimson stain that seeped and spread.

The little man stooped and picked up the scalpel. "Thank you," he said softly. "You have given me what I came for." He dropped the weapon into the bag.

Then he shimmered.

Shimmered—and disappeared.

But Woods' body didn't disappear. Kane stared down at it—at the throat ripped open from ear to ear.

He was still staring when they came and took him away.

The trial, of course, was a sensation. It wasn't so much the crazy story Kane told as the fact that nobody could ever find the fatal weapon.

It was a most unusual murder....

A Toy For Juliette

Juliette entered her bedroom, smiling, and a thousand Juliettes smiled at her. For all the walls were paneled with mirrors, and the ceiling was set with inlaid panes that reflected her image.

Wherever she glanced she could see the blonde curls framing the sensitive features of a face that was a radiant amalgam of both child and angel; a striking contrast to the rich, ripe revelation of her body in the filmy robe. But Juliette wasn't smiling at herself. She smiled because she knew that Grandfather was back, and he'd brought her another toy. In just a few moments it would be decontaminated and delivered, and she wanted to be ready.

Juliette turned the ring on her finger and the mirrors dimmed. Another turn would darken the room entirely; a twist in the opposite direction would bring them blazing into brilliance. It was all a matter of choice—but then, that was the secret of life. To choose, for pleasure. And what was her pleasure tonight?

Juliette advanced to one of the mirror panels and passed her hand before it. The glass slid to one side, revealing the niche behind it; the coffin-shaped opening in the solid rock, with the boot and thumbscrews set at the proper heights.

For a moment she hesitated; she hadn't played *that* game in years. Another time, perhaps. Juliette waved her hand and the mirror moved to cover the opening again.

She wandered along the row of panels, gesturing as she walked, pausing to inspect what was behind each mirror in turn. Here was the rack, there the stocks with the barbed whips resting against the

51

dark-stained wood. And here was the dissecting table, hundreds of years old, with its quaint instruments behind the next panel, the electrical prods and wires that produced such weird grimaces and contortions of agony, to say nothing of screams. Of course the screams didn't matter in a soundproofed room.

Juliette moved to the side wall and waved her hand again; the obedient glass slid away and she stared at a plaything she'd almost forgotten. It was one of the first things Grandfather had ever given her, and it was very old, almost like a mummy case. What had he called it? The Iron Maiden of Nuremberg, that was it—with the sharpened steel spikes set inside the lid. You chained a man inside, and you turned the little crank that closed the lid, ever so slowly, and the spikes pierced the wrists and the elbows, the ankles and the knees, the groin and the eyes. You had to be careful not to get excited and turn too quickly, or you'd spoil the fun.

Grandfather had shown her how it worked, the first time he brought her a real *live* toy. But then, Grandfather had shown her everything. He'd taught her all she knew, for he was very wise. He'd even given her her name—Juliette—from one of the old-fashioned printed books he'd discovered by the philosopher, de Sade.

Grandfather had brought the books from the Past, just as he'd brought the playthings for her. He was the only one who had access to the Past, because he owned the Traveler.

The Traveler was a very ingenious mechanism, capable of attaining vibrational frequencies which freed it from the time-bind. At rest, it was just a big square boxlike shape, the size of a small room. But when Grandfather took over the controls and the oscillation started, the box would blur and disappear. It was still there, Grandfather said—at least, the *matrix* remained as a fixed point in space and time—but anything or anyone within the square could move freely into the Past to wherever the controls were programmed. Of course they would be invisible when they arrived, but that was actually an advantage, particularly when it came to finding things and bringing them back. Grandfather had brought back some very interesting objects from almost mythical places—the great Library of Alexandria, the Pyramid of Cheops, the Kremlin, the Vatican, Fort Knox—all the storehouses of treasure and knowledge which existed thousands of years ago. He liked to go to *that* part of the Past, the period before the thermonuclear wars and the robotic ages, and collect things. Of course books and jewels and metals were useless, except to an antiquarian, but Grandfather was a romanticist and loved the olden times.

It was strange to think of him owning the Traveler, but of course he hadn't actually created it. Juliette's father was really the one who built it, and Grandfather took possession of it after her father died. Juliette suspected Grandfather had killed her father and mother when she was just a baby, but she could never be sure. Not that it mattered; Grandfather was always good to her, and besides, soon he would die and she'd own the Traveler herself.

They used to joke about it frequently. "I've made you into a monster," he'd say. "And someday you'll end up by destroying me. After which, of course, you'll go on to destroy the entire world—or what little remains of it."

"Aren't you afraid?" she'd tease.

"Certainly not. That's my dream—the destruction of every-thing. An end to all this sterile decadence. Do you realize that at one time there were more than three billion inhabitants on this planet? And now, less that three thousand! Less than three thousand, shut up inside these Domes, prisoners of themselves and sealed away forever, thanks to the sins of the fathers who poisoned not only the outside world but outer space by meddling with the atomic order of the universe. Humanity is virtually extinct already; you will merely hasten the finale."

"But couldn't we all go back to another time, in the Traveler?" she asked.

"Back to *what* time? The continuum is changeless; one event leads inexorably to another, all links in a chain which binds us to the pres-ent and its inevitable end in destruction. We'd have temporary indi-vidual survival, yes, but to no purpose. And none of us are fitted to survive in a more primitive environment. So let us stay here and take what pleasure we can from the moment. *My* pleasure is to be the sole user and possessor of the Traveler. And yours, Juliette—"

Grandfather laughed then. They both laughed, because they knew what *her* pleasure was.

Juliette killed her first toy when she was eleven—a little boy. It had been brought to her as a special gift from Grandfather, from somewhere in the Past, for elementary sex-play. But it wouldn't cooperate, and she lost her temper and beat it to death with a steel rod. So Grandfather brought her an older toy, with brown skin, and it cooperated very well, but in the end she tired of it and one day when it was sleeping in her bed she tied it down and found a knife.

Experimenting a little before it died, Juliette discovered new sources of pleasure, and of course Grandfather found out. That's when he'd christened her "Juliette." He seemed to approve most highly, and from then on he brought her the playthings she kept behind the mirrors in her bedroom, and on his restless rovings into the Past he brought her new toys.

Being invisible, he could find them for her almost anywhere on his travels—all he did was to use a stunner and transport them when he returned. Of course each toy had to be very carefully decontaminated; the Past was teeming with strange microorganisms. But once the toys were properly antiseptic they were turned over to Juliette for her pleasure, and during the past seven years she had enjoyed herself.

It was always delicious, this moment of anticipation before a new toy arrived. What would it be like? Grandfather was most considerate; mainly, he made sure that the toys he brought her could speak and understand Anglish—or "English," as they used to call it in the Past. Verbal communication was often important, particularly if Juliette wanted to follow the precepts of the philosopher de Sade and enjoy some form of sex relation before going on to keener pleasures.

But there was still the guessing beforehand. Would this toy be young or old, wild or tame, male or female? She'd had all kinds, and every possible combination. Sometimes she kept them alive for days before tiring of them—or before the subtleties of which she was capable caused them to expire. At other times she wanted it to happen quickly; tonight, for example, she knew she could be soothed only by the most primitive and direct action.

Once Juliette realized this, she stopped playing with her mirror panels and went directly to the big bed. She pulled back the coverlet, groped under the pillow until she felt it. Yes, it was still there—the big knife, with the long, cruel blade. She knew what she would do now; take the toy to bed with her and then, at precisely the proper moment, combine her pleasures. If she could time her knife-thrust—

She shivered with anticipation, then with impatience.

What kind of toy would it be? She remembered the suave, cool one—Benjamin Bathurst was his name, an English diplomat from the time of what Grandfather called the Napoleonic Wars. Oh, he'd been suave and cool enough, until she beguiled him with her body, into the bed. And there'd been that American aviatrix from slightly later on in the Past, and once, as a very special treat, the entire crew of a sailing vessel called the *Marie Celeste*. They had lasted for *weeks!*

Strangely enough, she'd even read about some of her toys afterward. Because when Grandfather approached them with his stunner and brought them here, they disappeared forever from the Past, and if they were in any way known or important in their time, such disappearances were noted. And some of Grandfather's books had accounts of the "mysterious vanishing" which took place and was, of course, never explained. How delicious it all was!

Juliette patted the pillow back into place and slid the knife under it. She couldn't wait, now; what was delaying things?

She forced herself to move to a vent and depress the sprayer, shedding her robe as the perfumed mist bathed her body. It was the final allurement—but why didn't her toy arrive?

Suddenly Grandfather's voice came over the auditor.

"I'm sending you a little surprise, dearest."

That's what he always said; it was part of the game.

Juliette depressed the communicator toggle. "Don't tease," she begged. "Tell me what it's like."

"An Englishman. Late Victorian era. Very prim and proper, by the look of him."

"Young? Handsome?"

"Passable." Grandfather chuckled. "Your appetites betray you, dearest."

"Who is it—someone from the books?"

"I wouldn't know the name. We found no identification during the decontamination. But from his dress and manner, and the little black bag he carried when I discovered him so early in the morning, I'd judge him to be a physician returning from an emergency call."

Juliette knew about "physicians" from her reading, of course; just as she knew what "Victorian" meant. Somehow the combination seemed exactly right.

"Prim and proper?" She giggled. "Then I'm afraid it's due for a shock."

Grandfather laughed. "You have something in mind, I take it."

"Yes."

"Can I watch?"

"Please—not this time."

"Very well."

"Don't be mad, darling. I love you."

Juliette switched off. Just in time, too, because the door was opening and the toy came in.

She stared at it, realizing that Grandfather had told the truth. The toy was male of thirty-odd years, attractive but by no means handsome. It couldn't be, in that dark garb and those ridiculous side whiskers. There was something almost depressingly refined and mannered about it, an air of embarrassed repression.

And of course, when it caught sight of Juliette in her revealing robe, and the bed surrounded by mirrors, it actually began to *blush*.

That reaction won Juliette completely. A blushing Victorian, with the build of a bull—and unaware that this was the slaughterhouse!

It was so amusing she couldn't restrain herself; she moved forward at once and put her arms around it.

"Who—who are you? Where am I?"

The usual questions, voiced in the usual way. Ordinarily, Juliette would have amused herself by parrying with answers designed to tantalize and titillate her victim. But tonight she felt an urgency which only increased as she embraced the toy and pressed it back toward the waiting bed.

The toy began to breathe heavily, responding. But it was still bewildered. "Tell me—I don't understand. Am I alive? Or is this heaven?"

Juliette's robe fell open as she lay back. "You're alive, darling," she murmured. "Wonderfully alive." She laughed as she began to prove the statement. "But closer to heaven than you think."

And to prove *that* statement, her free hand slid under the pillow and groped for the waiting knife.

But the knife wasn't there any more. Somehow it had already found its way into the toy's hand. And the toy wasn't prim and proper any longer, its face was something glimpsed in nightmare. Just a glimpse, before the blinding blur of the knife-blade, as it came down, again and again and again—

The room, of course, was soundproof, and there was plenty of time. They didn't discover what was left of Juliette's body for several days.

Back in London, after the final mysterious murder in the early morning hours, they never did find Jack the Ripper....

The Night of the Ripper

This book is for those two
illiterates, Zan and Beau,
and for their nephew, Dickens.

CHAPTER ONE

On the night of August 5, 1888, Eva Sloane stepped out of the Paragon Music Hall and emerged in Hell.

Hell is murky.

That's what Shakespeare wrote, long ago, but he might have used the same words to describe London.

Beneath the black pall of smoke shrouding the city the gaslights flared and flamed as the lost souls stumbled down the shadowy streets of Inferno.

Demons dwelt here—drunken navvies reeling into suckcribs, mucksnipes lurking before netherskens, square-rigged swells prowling in search of buors.

Eva wondered what Papa would say if she told him. A respectable country vicar wasn't likely to know that a "suckcrib" was a beer-shop, that "mucksnipes" were down-and-outers, "netherskens" were cheap lodgings, and "square-rigged" swells seeking "buors" were well-dressed dandies looking for prostitutes.

But after these months in the city she'd learned the language of the streets, and visiting music halls added to her education.

Papa didn't approve of music halls. For that matter, he didn't approve of London. And he knew nothing of Hell, though he preached against it every Sunday. How he'd shudder if he could see the reality through her eyes!

Now Eva kept her own gaze discreetly lowered as she hurried along the pavement. Experience had taught her it was best to remain inconspicuous and avoid chance encounters with strangers here. Perhaps she should have hailed a hansom when she left the Paragon but it was too late now and all the cabs were taken. The only sensible thing was to make her way as quickly as possible.

Passing an alleyway she was startled by a sudden burst of sound from a barrel organ, blaring out a tune she'd just heard in the music hall. She remembered the words of the song.

Every Saturday afternoon we likes to drown our sorrers
So we all goes orf to the Waxworks
And we sits in the Chamber of 'Orrors.
There's a beautiful statue of Mother there—
Is it like the old girl? Rawther!
There's the same old smile on 'er comical dial
As the night she strangled Father!

Eva had laughed with the rest of the audience when the song was sung but she found no reason for amusement now. Laughter had little place in the streets of Whitechapel with its teeming tenements, filthy courtyards reeking of sweat and sewage. Instead one heard the endless echo of sobs and curses, the voices, the poverty and pain. Not everyone could afford to drown sorrow with a trip to the Waxworks; alcohol was the cheaper solution. Here even infants were put to sleep with a nip of gin.

But not all infants were so fortunate. As Eva moved on, a small figure stepped out of a doorway—a thin-faced, straggly-haired little girl, barefoot and clad in a patched hand-me-down dress. Cradled in her arms was a crying baby.

The girl herself made no sound, and Eva was silent as she reached into her purse and proffered a penny. The child took it and turned away, bearing her squalling burden.

Eva sighed, wondering if she should have spoken, told the youngster she was wise to her dodge—the beggar's trick of sticking the baby with a pin to make it cry. Like the pet-shop owners here, who used pins to pierce the eyes of canaries on the theory that blind birds make better singers.

"Chamber of 'Orrors"?

This was the real chamber of horrors, for birds and babies and little girls alike. No point in condemning the child; she'd already been condemned at birth to a life sentence of imprisonment in the slums. There was no escape from the tiny overcrowded lodgings where often a family of a half-dozen or more shivered through winters and sweltered through summers in a single squalid room. The girl was born to endure disease and malnutrition, raised in risk of rape by a drunken father or sale to a house of assignation where jaded gentlemen came in search of "unripe fruit." And if she was somehow spared such a fate, it would be only to join the ranks of the miserable menials who slaved as servants, nursemaids or factory workers, underpaid and underfed, who offered themselves for pennies on the streets. No wonder Mother smiled when she strangled Father!

Eva counted herself fortunate. Though her mother died in childbirth, her father and a maiden aunt saw to it that she had a good country upbringing and decent schooling in Reading. But continuing her education had been her own idea—one which Papa didn't approve. He held fast to the notion that a woman's place was in the home, and why would any decent female seek a life in London? Even Victoria preferred the quiet seclusion of Sandringham or faraway Scottish estates. *God Save Our Noble Queen*—and protect her from the violence of these savage streets!

Now a young man in a deerstalker cap sauntered by, winking at her as he passed. Eva averted her eyes and moved forward before he could speak, but the coincidence startled her. Here she'd been thinking of the Queen and this well-dressed, mustached stranger looked exactly like the pictures she's seen of Victoria's grandson, the Duke of Clarence. Prince Eddy, that's what they called him in the penny press—but what would he be doing here on an East End street at midnight? Still, the resemblance was unnerving.

Eva hastened on and the distant din of the barrel organ was lost in the surging sound of raucous voices as a tipsy troupe of costers in pearl-studded costumes lurched by to her left.

Suddenly another sound rose from the right. The deep growl echoed and Eva turned to confront the shape of nightmare. Something huge and black and menacing towered before her, its red eyes glaring, its cruel claws raised to rake and rend.

The dancing bear reared up on its hind legs, mouth muzzled and neck securely collared and leashed with a stout chain held by a long-haired gypsy carrying a sharp-pointed pole. Now he yanked the beast back, brandishing his weapon. Pawing at the pole in sullen defiance, the beast hunkered down and its master grinned at Eva, his smile serrated by a mouthful of stained and rotting teeth.

Passersby joined in his amusement but she moved on quickly, shaken by the instant intrusion of possible peril.

The black beast was the very symbol of the violence hovering here. Leashed and muzzled, perhaps, but there'd be no restraint once it got free. And what violence hid behind the gypsy's jagged smile, what anger was buried beneath the drunken oaths and leering laughter of poverty's prisoners? And was poverty alone to blame? Doesn't a portion of that rage reside in all of us? Conceal it though we may, the beast is always there, waiting to escape. And once the violence is unleashed, once the lurking lust is loosed—

Eva shook her head, shedding the thought. The bear was an animal, nothing more. And the grimacing roisterers under the gaslight were merely giving vent to their animal spirits, in anticipation of tomorrow's Bank Holiday.

Still, she was relieved to turn away from the turmoil, heading right into the deserted silence of Brady Street.

The light was dimmer but she welcomed both darkness and solitude. Here, only a stone's throw from the thronging thoroughfare, was a haven of security, a link to quieter ways of life.

Or was it life?

She glanced to her right, where iron railings loomed before the expanse of a graveyard.

In the gloom she could see the outlines of marble vaults, several with gateways guarded by bars against the intrusion of bodysnatchers who had once prowled these purlieus. Closer by, surfacing in all directions, were the mounds heaped over the remains of the poor and humble. Some boasted headstones or markers, but none had crosses, for this was the Jews' Cemetery.

There were many Jews in Whitechapel, Eva knew, immigrants from Poland, Russia and the Balkans. The fortunate few owned shops or small businesses, and it was for them that the vaults had been erected to preserve their final resting places. Beneath the massed mounds reposed the bodies of toilers in the sweatshops, the hawkers and street vendors, the porters, dockhands and slaughterhouse workers. Cramped and crowded together in life, their confines were no less narrow in death.

There was a miasma, a haze of fog, shrouding the vaults and hovering over the mounds. Hovering—or rising from them? *The aura of death.*

Not that she was afraid of death; she was familiar with its presence after all these months of work here and its image held no terrors for her. It was what lay beyond that Eva feared.

Papa preached of Heaven and Hell, but when he stepped down from the pulpit and removed his robes he was only a man. Perhaps he truly believed in the hereafter, but he didn't *know*. Only the dead knew what death was like.

Eternal bliss or eternal damnation? Was it merely an endless, dreamless sleep or did awareness remain, trapped within a body rotting in the grave? Could restless spirits wander the earth as phantom presences?

Unscientific, Eva told herself. One must face the unknown, not fear it.

But when she heard the first hint of sound in the distance her pulse and pace quickened, her footsteps echoing in the night. Echo? No, it couldn't be—the tempo was different. Someone else was here, moving in the darkness.

In spite of herself, Eva sought and searched the foggy fastness of the graveyard, knowing as she did so that the effort was absurd. There are no ghosts. And even if there were, phantom footsteps make no sound.

Eva started to glance over her shoulder, then realized the noise was growing louder; now it seemed to come not from behind her but from the street ahead. Suddenly the cobblestones were shaken with a clatter, a clatter that rose to a rumbling roar mingled with a hoarse bellowing.

Looking up toward the intersection before her she saw the source.

Curling around the corner came a plunging mass of monstrous figures, horned and hooved like the hordes of Hell. The bulk of their bodies filled the street as the surging shapes thundered toward her.

For a moment she stood transfixed, then recognized the reality. The creatures were cattle, not demons; cattle stampeding from the pens of the slaughterhouse beyond in Whitechapel Road. Somehow they'd burst their barriers to run rampant, wild-eyed with terror of impending doom.

And it was doom they were bringing now—blanketing the street and the walks on either side as they bore down upon her, braying in mindless panic; heads lowered, curved horns hooking, heavy hooves pounding to crush all that lay in their path.

Eva turned to run but they were already upon her, mouths foaming, red eyes glaring, and there was nowhere to flee, no escape—

Then, out of nowhere, a hand gripped her upper arm, tightened, yanked her back against the iron railing of the graveyard. Legs buckling, she shrank against the bars as the maddened beasts thudded by. Running behind them, a half-dozen drovers cursed and shouted, brandishing whips and staves.

Eva's gaze blurred momentarily; fighting the weakness invading her, she clung to the rails until the frantic flow vanished and the drumming din died away in the night beyond. Only then was she conscious of escape, and with it came the realization that her arm was no longer being held.

Now she turned to face her rescuer, but too late. As vision cleared she caught only a momentary sidelong glance of the figure disappearing into the fog—the distant figure of a mustached man in dark clothing, wearing a deerstalker cap.

CHAPTER TWO

Promptly at midnight on August 6 the bells of St. Jude's tolled an end to Bank Holiday.

No one heard them in the Angel and Crown Public House. Here the chimes were only a faint counterpoint to the chorus of "What Cheer, 'Ria?" as a dozen revelers grouped around a huge table competed with the clamor of the crowd. Market porters, slaughterhouse workers, sailors and soldiers from the garrison at the Tower of London thronged before the bar or paired off at tables with street women flaunting their bedraggled Sunday best.

Seated at a smaller table in the far corner, Dr. Albert Trebor studied the scene, gray-green eyes mirroring a mixture of interest both clinical and cynical. Although well past his middle years, the tall, thin physician still served as a consultant on the staff of nearby London Hospital, but that seemed his only apparent link with the customers here. His quiet dress and demeanor marked him as a toff, as was the young man sitting across the table with a deerstalker cap pushed back over a broad forehead.

Trebor's gaze shifted to his companion. "Well now," he said. "What do you make of it, Mark?"

Mark Robinson shrugged. "Hard to say. It's all still so new to me."

"Nothing like this in your Wild West, eh?"

"Michigan is neither wild nor western." Mark tweaked the corner of his mustache. "But you're right, there's nothing quite like this in Ann Arbor." He smiled at Trebor. "It's good of you to look after me like this—the sightseeing, a night on the town—"

"Nonsense, my boy. You came over here to study our professional procedure, but there's more to it than just observing hospital routine. Consider this part of your education." Trebor sipped his beer. "I've been in practice for almost forty years now and I'm still learning."

"What was it like when you started?"

"Quite primitive, really. Surgical techniques were crude, no anesthesia, no qualified assistants or female nurses, just mucking about in a bloody butcher shop. Not like London Hospital today. Think of what we do there—four hundred outpatients treated daily, seven thousand bed cases a year—"

"Everything changes," Mark said.

"Perhaps." Trebor glanced toward the carousing crowd gathered before the bar. "But Whitechapel hasn't changed all that much since Mr. Dickens wrote about life in the streets. Oh, we've had a go at reform movements, but laborers still live in squalor, the serving class is pitifully underpaid, our prisons and workhouses and asylums are hellholes." He frowned. "We used to think progress would take care of conditions—steam engines, machinery, the telegraph, that sort of thing. It didn't work out that way. Now we have eleven postal deliveries a day here in London alone, but what's the good of it when the majority of our population can't read or write a proper sentence? What point in an Education Act when children begin slaving in sweatshops and factories almost as soon as they learn to walk?"

"It's almost as bad in America." Mark nodded. "That's one reason I entered medicine, to help relieve some of the suffering—"

"There's more to medicine than alleviating physical pain," Trebor said. "Mental anguish, that's the real problem. Work that cripples bodies also cripples the mind and spirit. The trouble with our profession lies in thinking we're only dealing with patients. We forget that patients are human beings. Now that I've retired to a consultant's post I've shifted my attention from the study of patients to the study of people."

He gestured toward the bar. "That's why I take time to fre-
quent places like this. Not for amusement—who can enjoy the
spectacle of misery drowning its sorrows in drink and debauchery?—but to learn the real causes of distress rooted in the human
condition."

"You sound like a philosopher," Mark told him.

"Or an idiot." Trebor gulped his beer. "If there's any distinction
between the two."

"Damn your eyes!" This from the group at the large table, now
chanting the refrain of *Samuel Hall.*

"Well said," Trebor murmured. "But we're neglecting your
education." He smiled at his companion. "If you intend to admin-
ister treatment to these people you'll have to learn their language.
I suggest a few lessons in vocabulary."

"But I speak English," Mark said.

"Do you?" Trebor's tone was quizzical. "Then suppose you try
your hand at identifying the occupations of some of the patrons as
I point them out to you." He jabbed a finger in the direction of a
sooty-faced man wearing smudged coveralls and high boots who
stood at the end of the bar. "What does he do for a living?"

"I'd say he's a chimney sweep." Mark grinned. "And a drunken
one, at that."

"A flue-faker." Trebor smiled. "As for his condition, he'd gener-
ally be referred to as a lushington. Note the heavy side-whiskers?
They're called Newgate knockers hereabouts."

He pointed to a dark-skinned man in a pea jacket and stocking
cap, clinging to the bartop for dear life. "What about this fellow?"

"That's easy—a merchant seaman. And Asiatic, from the looks
of him. You call them Lascars, I believe."

"Full marks." Trebor's eyes narrowed. "But notice his friend.
While pretending to hold him up, his free hand is groping into his
companion's jacket."

"A pickpocket!"

"Better known as a mutcher. A drunken-roller." Trebor swiv-
eled in his seat. "How about that chap in the far corner, with the
portable grindstone beside his chair?"

"A knife grinder, obviously."

"Chiv sharpener is the preferred description. The lady he's
buying drinks for is a trooper—a polite euphemism for prostitute.
But he can afford the treat. Chiv sharpening is a lucrative profession, what with all the sailors, leather cutters, market porters and

slaughterhouse men using knives in their work. Some of them could teach us a bit about surgery and dissection, I fancy."

A fat waiter in a soiled apron waddled up to their table. "Your pleasure, gents? Another round o' gatter?"

"Why not?" Trebor nodded at him. "In for a penny, in for a pound." As the waiter moved away the older man reached into his pocket and pulled out a handful of coins. "Which reminds me," he said. "While we're at it, I'd best give you a lesson in arithmetic."

He spread the loose change on the tabletop before him, indicating each coin in turn with a thrust of his forefinger. "This ha'penny piece is called a Hatch. And here's a yennap—a penny, pronounced backward. The tuppence is a deuce. A sixpence is a sprat, the shilling is a deaner, the half-crown's an alderman—"

"What cheer, luv?"

Trebor glanced up quickly at the interruption. A plump double-chinned woman wearing a frayed jacket and brown skirt lurched unsteadily beside him, her bleary eyes blinking at the row of coins. At a table directly behind her, two bearded soldiers stared sullenly as another woman rose to join her intoxicated companion. She moved up to Mark, a tall imposing presence in her huge plumed hat and pearl-buttoned dress, then offered him a gold-toothed simulacrum of a smile and placed a hand on his shoulder. "Are you goodnatured, dearie?" she said.

Trebor scowled and shook his head. "Clear off," he muttered.

The pearl-festooned woman drew herself up with a look of injured innocence. "No need to jump down me throat! 'Ere we are, wantin' to be sociable-like—"

Trebor's scowl and voice deepened. "Mind what I said. Clear off, both of you!"

The tall woman turned to her matronly companion without replying. "Come along, Martha. To hell with these bloody buggers— let's go back to the sodgers."

As the two started away, Trebor relaxed, nodding at Mark. "Good riddance."

Mark shifted uneasily in his chair. "Weren't you a bit short with them?"

"One needs firmness. It's the only thing they can understand." The older doctor pushed the coins together as he spoke. "Thousands of them about, drunken and raddled with disease, spreading infection every time they spread their legs."

Mark nodded. "Still, they've got to live."

"Do they?" Trebor glanced over at the table occupied by the two whores and the pair of bearded ruffians in uniform. One soldier was pinching the tall woman's breasts while the other's hand crept up beneath the brown skirt of her drunken companion. "Disgusting," he said. "Animals prowling our streets. Thank heaven they're leaving."

Mark followed Trebor's gaze as the soldiers rose, yanking the women to their feet. The pudgy one stumbled and her escort cursed, cuffing her cheek with a meaty fist. Then they staggered off.

"Where are they going?" Mark asked.

"Does it matter?" Trebor shrugged. "Tarts like that will raise their skirts anywhere—in alleys, courtyards, or up against a wall. There's nothing too low for their tastes, no act too perverted for them to perform. And all for want of a sixpence to pay for a night's kip in a public lodging house."

Mark stared at him. "You mean to say we could have prevented this if we'd only given them a few pennies?"

"I dare say." Trebor nodded indifferently, then looked up as Mark pushed his chair back and started to rise. "Where are you off to? Our drinks are coming—"

The younger man didn't reply. His eyes were fixed firmly on the two couples as they weaved to the swinging door and reeled out into the street.

"Hold on," Trebor said. "Don't be a fool—"

But Mark was already striding to the doorway and now he too moved past it and disappeared in the night beyond.

For a moment Trebor remained seated, his jaw tightening as anger overcame him. "Filthy sluts," he murmured. Scooping up the coins from the tabletop, he thrust them into his pocket.

Then he rose, lifting his brown surgical bag from underneath the table, and hurried toward the door.

CHAPTER THREE

It was still dark when John Reeves stumbled down the steps of his lodgings in the George Yard buildings early on the following morning.

Early? Five o' bloody clock it was, and him off to the bleeding market without so much as a wash or a cuppa tea.

The stale reek of fried fish filled the hallway and through the thin walls he could hear the sound of snoring from the tiny rooms on either side; their occupants were sleeping off the aftereffects of Bank Holiday celebrations.

No sleep for Johnny Reeves, worse luck. No sleep, nor even a taste of kipper—though the notion fair put him off this morning, seeing what lay in his gut from last night.

Just putting one foot before the other was a bit of a rum go, let alone dodging through the dark like this. Johnny started down the stone staircase and almost went arse-over-teakettle as he slipped on a spot of wet at the first-floor landing.

What the flaming hell was this? Most likely some drunken sod who couldn't wait to get rid of his gatter, using the stairs for a muzzpot. What a stink!

But not the smell of piss. And now, as he blinked down in the dim dawn light, not the look of it either.

His eyes widened as he stared at the dark design staining the stone.

Then he saw what lay huddled against the wall beyond—the body of a woman, with blood oozing in rivulets of red from under her upraised brown skirt.

CHAPTER FOUR

Egypt, 2300 B.C. *In addition to the usual tortures—scourging and mutilation—and execution by strangling, impaling, or burning—the ultimate punishment was to be embalmed alive coated with corrosive natron, which slowly ate through the flesh.*

● ● ●

Shortly past noon on the following Thursday, Eva Sloane climbed the dim stairwell of the new Whitechapel Underground Station and found herself in the hazy sunlight of the street.

Threading her way among dogcarts, traps and wagonettes jamming the thoroughfare, she crossed to the opposite side and made her way up the walk and through the doors of London Hospital. Pausing for a moment, she loosened her bonnet, freeing the mass of auburn curls beneath.

Now, as she moved into the round front lobby, the porter faced her in his longskirted blue uniform and touched a finger to his cap.

"Good afternoon, miss."

"Thank you, Jenkins." She nodded, blue eyes peering up inquiringly. "Would you happen to know if the lecture has started yet?"

"Most likely it did," the porter told her. "I saw Dr. Hume come in about ten minutes ago."

"Then I'm late."

Quickening her pace, Eva crossed before the front reception desk and approached the corridors beyond. The one at her right led to the medical wards; the left would bring her to the surgical section.

It was in this direction that she turned now, moving through the narrow confines of a long hall. The inner wall was lined with consultation room doors, each bearing the name of the physician or surgeon occupying the premises. The outer wall loomed above a row of black benches on which outpatients waited to be summoned for examination and treatment.

They were a mixed bag, as always; a few elderly men in grimy, sweatstained work clothes and a far greater number of drably dressed women, many carrying infants or clutching the hands of small children. Aside from the occasional echo of consumptive coughing there was no sound to indicate the presence of those assembled here. The men sat motionless, lips compressed, and the women did not speak. Even the children sat strangely silent as they stared at the brown doors opposite.

Behind their silence Eva sensed the dread. All of these unfortunates were pondering what awaited them in the rooms beyond— the peering and the probing, the mysterious medication, the jabbing of the needle or even the horror of the surgeon's knife. And for some there was a prospect even more ghastly; the shrug of resignation, a few words of meaningless consolation, then the curt dismissal which indicated there was neither treatment nor hope to be had for their affliction. Fear was almost a palpable presence here—the fear of pain, the fear of death.

Eva passed by quickly and parted the swinging double doors at the end of the hall which brought her into the glass-roofed outpatients' surgery. It was unoccupied at the moment, and she crossed the room to open the door at the far side which led to the operating theater.

Lining the green walls of the chamber were frosted windows reflecting the glitter of gas jets. Below the translucent panes a semicircle of benches held an audience of onlookers. Eva halted for a moment as she scanned their ranks—nursing sisters in blue uniforms, probationers in stripes and white caps, young students clad in street clothing, older men wearing the frock coats of practicing physicians.

In the central area before them was the operating table, surrounded by smaller tables displaying an array of scalpels, probes, forceps and other medical instruments along with vials of chloroform, bowls of hot water, rolls of cloth bandages, bundles of sutures and clumps of sponges ready for use. Posted behind them, several house surgeons stood waiting, easily identifiable in their white aprons and sleeve-covers. At the head of the table a student adjusted the nozzle of a carbolic spray pump—Dr. Lister's innovation, used to sterilize instruments, the patient's wound and even the hands of the surgeon, should he happen to believe in the controversial new theory of germs and antisepsis.

On the table itself, lower limbs decorously draped with a white sheet, was the patient, a corpulent middle-aged man with a swollen belly. Chloroform had already done its work and he lay quietly, eyes closed, fat stomach rising and falling to the accompaniment of his stertorous snores.

The operating surgeon bent over him, scalpel poised in his hairy left hand. That, plus the sight of his florid face with its bristling mustache surmounted by a bulbous nose and slightly slanted eyes, served to identify Dr. Jeremy Hume.

Frowning, Eva hesitated. Had she known Hume was operating she wouldn't have made such an effort to attend. There was something about him that disturbed her—not his appearance, but his manner. He'd never been brusque; on the contrary he seemed almost effusively cordial and eager to acknowledge her presence. On reflection perhaps it was his appearance after all; the way she'd caught him staring through those slitted eyes, as though he were studying her with a kind of mocking amusement.

Silly goose. Eva told herself. No sense imagining things. Resolutely she moved forward to a bench just left of the doorway and seated herself on the end.

Certainly Dr. Hume wasn't staring at her now. His attention was directed at the patient—or, more accurately, to the gleaming tip of the scalpel poised above the recumbent figure as, with a self-assured smile, he brought it down to incise the exposed abdomen, deftly slicing through a layer of fatty subcutaneous tissue.

The blood gushed forth and one of the house surgeons stepped forward, gripping a sponge with which he swabbed the outer edges of the incision.

Nodding, Dr. Hume gestured him back and parted the flaps of skin on either side of the opening, then bent forward to insert the tip of his scalpel into the cavity. His eyes were intent on the task before him but he was still smiling; to Eva came the realization that he actually seemed to be enjoying himself. Not so the man seated beside her.

He squirmed uneasily on the bench, and as Eva glanced at him she was startled to see that he'd closed his eyes.

There was something else about his appearance which disturbed her—the pale face with its heavy brows and thin mustache looked oddly familiar. In her mind's eye Eva tried to picture his profile, but the image was blurred, as though by fog.

Fog.

That was it. Fog, and the deerstalker cap. This was the stranger who'd come to her rescue the other night.

Now he seemed to be the one who needed rescuing. Eyes averted, he lurched up and stumbled past her, groping for the door which led back into the deserted outpatients' surgery.

No one else seemed to note his departure; all attention focused on Dr. Hume as he interrupted his procedure, scalpel in hand, and glanced up to address the assemblage.

"What we have here is an acute inflammation of the vermiform appendix, characterized by the usual edema and consequent sensitivity in the lower abdominal area—"

The sound of his voice was cut off by the closing of the door after Eva rose and followed the young man.

She found him standing before an open window, breathing deeply, his lips compressed and fists clenched. But now he turned at the sound of her approaching footsteps and his brown eyes widened in surprised recognition.

"You?"

Eva nodded.

He stared at her. "I don't understand. How did you know where to find me—?"

"I didn't." She smiled. "I came for the lecture."

"You're a medical student?"

"No, a probationer here at the hospital. I was away this morning and didn't have time to change into my uniform before the demonstration." Still smiling, she held out her hand. "My name is Eva Sloane."

He accepted the greeting; his fingers were ice-cold. "Mark Robinson," he said. "Pleased to meet you."

"Not nearly as pleased as I was the other evening. I wanted to thank you then but you disappeared so quickly—"

"Sorry. Emergency. I was on my way to a patient."

"Are you on the staff here?"

"Just as an observer, though I do lend a hand in assisting from time to time. The patient I attended the other night was Dr. Trebor's case." The young man's voice softened, his features relaxing. "Actually, I'm from the States."

"I should have guessed because of your accent," Eva told him "But you are a physician?"

"Not much of a one, I'm afraid." He smiled ruefully. "What do you make of a doctor who hates the sight of blood?"

"We all go through that phase, don't we?" Eva said. "I remember feeling quite giddy the first time I assisted. Of course I got used to it."

"That's just the point," he said. "I never did. When I studied for my degree at the University of Michigan I witnessed my first dissection. Somehow I got through it, but immediately after the session I fainted dead away. Luckily the instructor had already left, and Herman managed to drag me out before anyone noticed."

"Herman?"

"One of my fellow students, Herman Mudgett. Now there was a cool one for you—he could carve up a cadaver with a dull butter knife and never turn a hair." Mark Robinson sighed. "I often wonder what became of him; he's probably enjoying a brilliant career as a surgeon right now."

"I take it you don't intend to specialize in that field?"

"Correct. I find myself more interested in the study of mental disorders."

"Psychology?"

"It's still more a matter of theory than actual practice, but I've a hunch it's the coming thing. Once we start to learn the secrets of the human mind we can extend the boundaries of medical knowledge—" He broke off abruptly. "I'm boring you," he said.

"Not at all. It's quite fascinating, really. I'd like to hear more about it, but—"

"But what?"

Eva glanced at the wall clock. "It's past two," she said. "I'm on ward duty within the hour."

The young man nodded. "Well, then, suppose we continue my lecture over dinner the next time you're free?"

"Sorry." Eva shook her head. "I'm leaving on holiday tomorrow evening. I'll be visiting my father in Reading until the end of the month."

"When you return, then."

"Perhaps." She hesitated. "But I won't be staying in quarters here at the hospital. The probationers' dormitory is quite wretched, really—we sleep in shifts and there's no such thing as privacy. I've just arranged for lodgings over on Old Montague Street, at Number Seven. It's only a single room, but at least one can have a quiet moment there."

"You say you'll be back on the thirty-first," he murmured. "Suppose we dine that evening, at seven?"

"Very well, Mr. Robinson." Eva paused. "Or should I address you as Dr. Robinson?"

"Mark will do nicely, thank you."

"As you wish." She turned with a smile and crossed to the door leading back into the outpatients' hall. As she reached it he called after her.

"Have a pleasant holiday."

Eva didn't reply, but when she moved through the doorway her smile had faded.

Papa didn't approve of holidays. And whatever awaited her in Reading, it would not be pleasant.

CHAPTER FIVE

Assyria, 850 B.C. *King Ashurnasirpal declared, "All the chiefs who revolted against me I flayed alive. With their skins I covered the pillars. These warriors who had sinned against me—from their hostile mouths I tore their tongues and I have compassed their destruction. As for the others, who remain alive, their lacerated members I have given to the dogs, the swine, the wolves."*

• • •

Mark was still staring at the door through which Eva had made her exit when it reopened abruptly and Dr. Trebor came into the room.

"There you are," he said. "I was hoping to find you here. Is the lecture over?"

"No. I stepped out for a moment to speak with Miss Sloane."

"Ah yes—I saw her passing by in the hall just now. Bright girl, Eva. She should make an excellent nurse." Trebor smiled. "But I take it your interest isn't necessarily professional."

"Not entirely." Mark avoided the doctor's inquisitive eyes.

"Well, no matter," Trebor said. "There's something I'd like to discuss with you. I've just come from seeing a friend of yours— Martha Tabram, or Turner, as she calls herself."

"Who?"

"The woman who offered you the privilege of her person the other evening at the Angel and Crown."

Mark paled. "You spoke to her?"

"Hardly that. Despite the claims of spiritualists, there is no way to communicate with the dead."

"Dead?"

Trebor nodded. "Murdered. I've just come from the inquest. She was stabbed—thirty-three times.

CHAPTER SIX

Persia, 500 B.C. *Special prisoners received a special punishment. The victim was placed between two small boards fitted together with openings for the head, hands, and feet. By keeping his face to the sun it attracted insects and was soon covered with a swarm of hungry flies. Sometimes it took several weeks before the release of death.*

• • •

"You didn't know?" Trebor said.

Mark shook his head. "How did it happen?"

"Come along and I'll tell you about it." Trebor led the way and the two men left the room together, moving past medical wards and into the quiet confines of the hospital library.

"Here, sit down and make yourself comfortable." As Mark sank into a leatherbacked chair in the corner, Trebor turned to the wall buffet's display of carafes and glassware. "Care for a spot of port?"

"No, thank you. I'm all right."

"As you wish." The older man filled a glass and carried it over to a chair opposite Mark, seating himself with a sigh of satisfaction, long legs sprawled before him. "That's better. At least we can have privacy here." He peered up at the portraits of long-deceased medical practitioners which lined the walls above the rows of bookshelves. "That's one of the chief virtues of the dead—they may listen, but they never interrupt."

Mark stared at him impatiently. "The inquest," he said. "Why were you attending?"

"There were newspaper reports of the crime. The moment I read them I connected the circumstances with that little episode at the public house on Bank Holiday night, but I couldn't be entirely sure. So when I saw the notice regarding today's proceedings I made it a point to be present."

Mark leaned forward. "What took place?"

"The usual formalities." Trebor sipped his wine. "George Collier presided. Sound man, no nonsense. According to him the Tabram woman was only thirty-five. I'd have guessed her to be a good bit older, but of course one must make allowances for the sort of life she led. Drink and disease—"

The younger man nodded quickly. "The murder," he said. "How did it happen?"

"Ah yes." Trebor nodded. "The woman had nine wounds in the region of the throat, eleven in her breasts and thirteen in the abdomen and pelvic girdle, almost any one of which could have proved fatal. Quite obviously her assailant continued his attack long after realizing she was dead. And the nature of the incisions indicated that two weapons were employed—one a dagger and the other a much longer and broader instrument."

"What sort of instrument?"

"Perhaps a soldier's bayonet." Trebor twirled his glass "Tabram's companion—Pearly Poll she calls herself, though her real name is Mary Ann Connelly—took the stand. She said that when the two left with the soldiers they paired off. Pearly Poll and her corporal did their business in a close called Angel Alley. Martha Tabram and the other soldier headed for the George Yard buildings down the street. That was the last she saw of them."

Mark tugged at his mustache. "Did they identify the soldier?"

"I was about to tell you. Inspector Reid of Scotland Yard escorted Pearly Poll to the Tower of London. Everyone in the garrison who'd had leave on Bank Holiday night was lined up on parade for her to inspect, but she couldn't recognize the man, or even her own client."

Mark frowned. "She must have been lying."

"So they believed." Trebor finished his wine and set the glass down on the table beside him. "But to give her the benefit of the doubt, they went through a similar inspection at Wellington Barracks, this time with the Coldstream Guards. And this time she immediately indicated two men—one a corporal and the other a private—and accused them."

"Thank goodness." Mark nodded and leaned back in his chair.

"Save your gratitude," Trebor murmured. "Further inquiries disclosed that the corporal had been home with his wife all evening, and the other guardsman returned to barracks at ten o'clock."

Mark's hand went to his mustache again. "But if it wasn't a soldier, then who—?"

"The verdict of the coroner's jury was murder by person or persons unknown."

For a moment Mark glanced away, meeting the silent stare of the portraits on the wall. Then he faced Trebor again and when he found his voice the words were scarcely audible.

"My fault," he said.

"What do you mean?"

"I should have spoken to the woman. I fully intended to. That's why I left so abruptly. After what you told me about their circumstances I meant to give both of them some money, enough for a decent night's lodging. But when I got outside and saw them going off with those drunken brutes I lost my nerve. And my dinner."

"You were ill?" Trebor said.

"Yes. That's why I didn't come back to the pub."

"Where did you go?"

"To my rooms. I would have apologized to you next morning but you weren't here."

"Business took me out of the city," said Trebor. "I just returned last night. When I read about the inquest it occurred to me that perhaps I could give testimony."

Mark swallowed quickly. "You didn't tell me that."

"No need. After hearing the proceedings I thought the better of it. All I could have done was corroborate the victim's presence at the pub and this had already been established by others. No point bringing myself into the picture. Or you."

Mark nodded. "Just as well. Let sleeping dogs lie." Then he shook his head quickly. "I shouldn't say that. She wasn't a dog—she was a human being."

"Whoever killed her didn't think so." Trebor spoke slowly. "Over thirty stab wounds. Not just murder, but the savage mutilation of a corpse after her death agonies in the dark. The work of a maniac."

"Yes. it must have been." Mark rose, his face pallid in the wan light from the window as he turned and started for the door. "We must talk further. But it's time for me to make my rounds. If I can be excused—"

"Of course."

Mark moved away and the door closed behind him, leaving Trebor alone in the gathering twilight. Only the eyes in the portraits saw his troubled frown.

CHAPTER SEVEN

Rome, A.D. 85 *A robber was crucified in the arena. He did not die quickly enough to please the crowd, so a bear was set loose to eat him as he writhed upon the cross.*

• • •

Bracing herself against the worn seat-cushion of the swaying hansom, Eva stared out at the gathering fog.

Over the clop of the horse's hooves and the rattle of revolving wheels, the bells of St. Mary's Whitechapel sounded seven times, marking the hour and the end of her holiday.

Eva's sigh held no regret, only relief. The fortnight with Papa had been more of an ordeal than she'd anticipated, though she might have known what to expect. Papa was an old man, and his retirement offered him nothing but poverty and loneliness. Worst of all, after a lifetime in the pulpit, now he had no one to preach to.

But why must he preach to me? Eva frowned at the thought, hastily summoning excuses. Papa was getting senile, didn't understand that things have changed, he was afraid of dying.

True enough, yet hardly consolation against his constant whining and complaining. He exaggerated on his age and infirmities to gain sympathy, still trying to wheedle her into returning home.

But even if she wanted to, that was impossible now. Times had changed. She had changed—the last six months proved that. The things she'd learned about the world, the things she'd learned about herself, had taught her there could be no turning back. This time Eva saw Papa through different eyes; a selfish old man whose thoughts dwelled only on death and suffering.

Suffering? Eva glanced up at the sudden sound of a whip-crack and the curse of the cabbie as he lashed the horse forward around a corner. Cruelty and suffering were everywhere; she didn't need Papa to remind her of the presence of pain. And if she tried to tell him that pain had its uses he'd never understand. The idea of taking a whip to the cabdriver and teaching him a lesson would horrify Papa; he believed that punishment must come only from God.

Eva sighed again. Perhaps he was right. At least she had no intention of carrying out her thought as the hansom pulled to a halt at the curb.

The cabbie climbed down from his perch and came around to open the door. "'Ere we are, Miss. Number Seven, Old Montague Street."

She opened her purse as he helped her out, extending the fare with her face turned away to avoid his beery breath.

"Want me ter give you a hand with yer bag?" he said.

"No, thank you. I can manage." Eva reached in and grasped the portmanteau resting on the hansom seat.

As the cab rolled off she moved up the walk. The streetlamp at the corner was unlit and no light was visible in the windows of Number Seven. Through the twilight fog the bleak bulk of the building loomed above her.

So did the figure.

A dark shadow rose swiftly from the stairwell beside the entrance. It swooped forward, hand extended, grasping her arm. The shadow had substance. And a voice. "Miss Sloane?"

Eva blinked up toward the dim outline of the face before her, then relaxed as recognition came.

"I've been waiting for you," Mark Robinson said.

"Sorry. My train was late."

The mustached mouth formed a smile. "That's quite all right. I was beginning to think you'd forgotten our dinner engagement."

"Oh no—!" Eva shook her head. "As a matter of fact, I did. Please forgive me, I feel like such an idiot—"

"No matter, you're here now."

"But you don't understand. I can't dine out this evening. Not after the train trip. I'm due to report for duty at six tomorrow morning, and I've still not settled in my new quarters here—" As she spoke Eva realized that she *did* feel like an idiot, but there was no help for it. "Really, I'm so embarrassed—if you could possibly postpone your plans until—"

But she was talking to herself.

Mark had already turned abruptly and now, as Eva watched, the figure of the man in the deerstalker cap vanished in the night.

CHAPTER EIGHT

Rome, A.D. 265 *The historian Eusebius writes of the persecution and punishment of Christians in his Ecclesiastical History. "The flesh was flogged from their bones or scraped to the bone with shells, and salt and vinegar poured on the wounds. Others had molten lead poured down their throats or were tied to the bent branches of two trees which, when released, sprang back apart to tear them asunder."*

• • •

Gaslight cast a ghostly glow over the walls of the medical laboratory, flickering faintly in sinister silence.

And there was something sinister about the silent man who crouched before the clutter of chemical retorts on the tabletop, glancing about furtively to make sure he was not observed. His normally composed face was haggard now, his trembling hand tensing with an effort at control as he carefully measured off a few drops from a retort and poured the colorless concoction into a beaker. The liquid bubbled and foamed. Raising the fuming vessel to his lips he drained its contents at a single gulp, then stood swaying as the beaker fell from nerveless fingers.

Clutching his throat, face contorted with agony and anguish, he gasped, staggered, and fell behind the table.

For a moment all was still.

Then the silence was broken by the sound of panting as he rose slowly to face the light.

But now his features were changed. The pale aristocratic countenance had disappeared; in its place was the hairy bestial visage of a monster. Glaring wildly, the beast-man turned toward the door at the sound of a knock and a muffled voice crying out.

"Dr. Jekyll—Dr. Jekyll—are you there?"

Spontaneous applause resounded, drowning out Richard Mansfield's reply. The Royal Lyceum Theatre audience was completely captivated by his performance in *Dr. Jekyll and Mr. Hyde*.

Or almost completely.

Trebor, seated in the stalls beside Mark, observed the ovation without emotion. And when the curtain fell for the interval, he led Mark through the jostling, murmuring mob thronging the foyer, and ordered two whiskies at the bar.

As the drinks arrived the younger man's hand moved toward his breast pocket but Trebor restrained him. "My treat," he said. "You paid for the tickets."

Mark lifted his glass. "I'm glad you came," he said. "Seeing as how it was a last-minute invitation."

Trebor nodded. "Stood you up, eh?"

"What do you mean?"

"The young lady." He smiled. "Obviously, since you booked seats in advance, you must have counted on more pleasant companionship." Trebor caught himself quickly. "None of my business, really. Her loss is my gain."

Mark downed his drink, making no reply. Still Trebor couldn't help wondering. The lady in question—who might she be?

But now it was Mark's question he must answer; the sound of his voice registered over Trebor's thought. "Well, what do you think of it?"

"The play?" Trebor set his glass on the bar as he resolved his reply. "Mansfield is a consummate actor, no doubt about that. But the premise is utterly absurd."

"Do you really think so?" Mark's eyes were thoughtful. "Of course the device is childish. I realize there's no chemical agency which could bring about such a drastic, instantaneous transformation. But we both know that seemingly normal personalities are capable of a sudden change."

"Granted." Trebor shrugged. "In this instance I must admit that bad science can also make for good melodrama."

He turned to return a nod of greeting from a tall man striding past, monocle glinting from one scowling eye. His close-cropped hair, downpointed mustache and stiff bearing seemed better suited to a uniform than evening clothes.

Mark glanced at him. "Friend of yours?"

"Sir Charles Warren. He's the commissioner of the Metropolitan Police."

"Sounds important."

"That he is, and he'd be the first to tell you so. Warren was Major General of the Royal Engineers when they put down the Bantu tribes in Griqualand West, then commanded them again at Suakin. Quite the heroic figure, but not exactly an endearing one. When he took over as commissioner last year he called out the troops to fire on demonstrators in Trafalgar Square. 'Bloody Sunday,' they call it." Trebor shook his head. "I'd be hard put to find many who'd count Sir Charles Warren a friend."

Now the warning buzzer sounded and they returned to their seats. As the curtain rose again Trebor noted Mark's total absorption in the drama. Strange that he should be so completely captivated by such claptrap. The play was quite obviously the product of a morbid imagination—and morbid anatomy. Trebor recalled that the author of the story, Robert Louis Stevenson, was known to suffer from phthisis, and no doubt the disease exerted an influence over his mind as well as his body. But the work had power, and at its conclusion the audience clamored its approval. Curtain calls were still continuing when Trebor and Mark made their way through the lobby, glancing appreciatively at the new display of electrical lighting.

Its dazzle formed quite a contrast to the fog they found in the street. Here in the gathering gloom artificial light gave way to a darker reality.

As they strolled, Mark murmured softly, almost to himself. "It could be true, you know."

"The play?"

"Just the idea behind it. An ordinary man turning into a monster."

"Medically impossible," Trebor said. "There are no such chemicals."

"I'm not thinking about a physical change. But suppose there's something inside the brain itself that can sometimes be summoned to take control. Perhaps we all have a monster hidden inside us."

"Nothing's hidden inside me that I know of except the need for a stiff drink." Trebor shivered in the chill of the damp street. "What say we stop for a nightcap?"

Mark shook his head. "If you don't mind, I'll just go on to my lodgings."

"Suit yourself. Personally, I've no taste for this weather."

"I rather like it," Mark said.

"You'd be better off to hail a cab—"

Trebor's voice trailed off as he realized the young man wasn't listening. With a gesture of farewell, Mark turned the corner and the fog swallowed him.

For a moment Trebor considered following, but then a stronger impulse inclined him in the direction of the public house directly across the street. Its brightly lit windows blazed a promise of warm delights within.

Strange that the notion had taken him so suddenly. How many times had he told himself that a man his age must put aside the pleasures of the flesh? But the urge was always there, buried somewhere inside him, and now he felt it emerging like the monster Mansfield played. Suppose that another drama was about to unfold—*Dr. Trebor and Mr. Hyde?*

Hurrying toward the entrance of the public house he shrugged the thought away.

There was nothing monstrous about wanting a woman....

CHAPTER NINE

Egypt, A.D. 1010 *Caliph Hakim was a madman who killed passing slaves in the street and ripped out their entrails with his bare hands. In his palace garden was a pool on which floated a piece of wood. As a joke he dared visitors to jump on it, a challenge which could not be politely refused. When the unsuspecting guest leaped into the water, the floating wood was knocked aside and the poor wretch was skewered on an up-thrust spear which had been hidden beneath. Later Hakim proclaimed himself the Messiah.*

• • •

Early morning sunshine faded behind him as Detective Inspector Frederick Abberline passed through the doorway of Number Four, Whitehall Place and moved into the darker domain of Scotland Yard. Portly, plump and proper, he plodded down the hall, acknowledging the greetings of passersby in the busy corridors.

But his smile of salutation concealed concern. Did anyone suspect? His mission here today called for all the poise he could muster, and nothing upset dignity more than the rumble of an upset stomach.

Entering the reception room at the end of the hall, Abberline breathed a silent prayer that his queasiness would quiet. James Monro, assistant commissioner and head of the C.I.D., regarded any infirmity in an underling as insubordination; every member of the force was expected to be physically and mentally fit at all times. Still, he had respect for his people, which was more than could be said for a bully like Warren.

Bracing himself for the ordeal ahead, Abberline stated his errand to the duty officer at the outer desk.

The uniformed man shook his head. "Sorry, Inspector. He's not in."

"But he's expecting me. We have an appointment."

Abberline paused as the door behind the desk opened abruptly and a frowning face peered out.

Sir Charles Warren! His stomach churned as he recognized the familiar features. *Speak of the devil—*

"Here now, what's all this?" Eyeing the intruder, Warren's frown relaxed but did not fade fully. "Oh, it's you, Abberline. And what brings you here, might I ask?"

"Official business, sir. I'm to meet with Mr. Monro."

"Indeed." Warren's tone was curt. "Then I'd best have a word with you." Turning, he glanced back impatiently over his shoulder. "Come along, man. I've no time for dilly-dallying."

A twinge of heartburn erupted beneath Abberline's vest as he followed Sir Charles into the private office. Warren shut the door firmly and seated himself behind an ornate desk littered with papers and leatherbound file folders. Several chairs were grouped in a semicircle before it, but he did not invite his visitor to sit down.

Abberline stood stiffly, conscious of the sour taste at the base of his mouth. *Bloaters, that's what did it—might have known better than to risk bloaters for breakfast—*

"Well now." Warren affixed his monocle and squinted up at him. "I don't have all day. Suppose you get on with your business."

"Sorry, Sir Charles." The Inspector shifted his weight, avoiding the monocular stare. "It's a matter that concerns Mr. Monro. Hadn't we better wait until he arrives?"

"I doubt he'd be interested." Warren glanced toward the door, his voice lowering. "There's been no announcement yet but you'll know soon enough. Monro resigned his post last night."

"Resigned?" Abberline bit his lip.

"We had a difference of opinion regarding his conduct of the Tabram case. I suppose you're aware of the matter?"

Abberline nodded. "That's why I'm here. There's new evidence bearing on the affair. If you'll hear me out—"

"I've no time for that now." Warren shook his head quickly. "The case will come under the jurisdiction of the new assistant commissioner."

"Who might that be, sir?"

"Robert Anderson. He's already notified his acceptance of the appointment."

"Then perhaps I can see him."

"I'm afraid that's impossible. He's not in the best of health at the moment and is seeing no one. I dare say your findings can wait until he feels fit again."

And what about my health? Irritation rose on a gaseous wave from the pit of Abberline's stomach. He did his best to force it down as he spoke.

"With all due respect, sir, the present situation in Whitechapel is too touchy for delay. Ever since the Tabram murder rumors have been going around that other killings—Emma Smith's, for one— were the work of the same man. So far it's only hearsay, but if what they say is true—"

"Balderdash!" Warren's fist thumped the desktop. "Pure rubbish!" He jerked the monocle from his eye and fixed Abberline with a naked glare. "No need to get the wind up just because a few buors come to a bad end. Women of that sort always do—sooner or later they're random victims of the law of averages. Any talk of a mass murderer on the loose is ruddy nonsense!"

Warren jerked his head around as the office door opened and the uniformed duty officer hurried forward into the room.

"Excuse me, Sir Charles—the news just came in and I thought you'd want to know—"

"What are you babbling about?"

"The report from Bethnal Green Station, sir. It's happened again. They found a woman with her throat cut, over at Buck's Row."

CHAPTER TEN

Egypt, A.D. 1250 *Joinville writes of Saracen punishment: "The bernicles are the cruelest torture that anyone can suffer. They are made of pieces of pliable wood, notched at the ends with strong teeth that eat into one another, and bound together with strips of oxhide. When the Saracens want to set people therein they lay them on their side and put their legs between the teeth; then they cause a heavy man to sit on the pieces of wood. And it so happens that not an inch of bone remains uncrushed in either leg. And at the end of three days, they put them in the bernicles and crush them again."*

• • •

Abberline's abdominal distress did not ease in the week that followed. But it wasn't personal pain that brought him to London Hospital on Friday afternoon.

His appearance in the library was a matter of official business, and he lost no time in stating as much to the surgeons assembled there. Standing before the long table he surveyed the faces of the medical men seated before him. Some, like Dr. Trebor and Dr. Hume, were already familiar; others he recognized by name as they introduced themselves. Young Mark Robinson was a total stranger, but that wasn't surprising, since he'd just recently come over from America.

America. Must look into that. Abberline made a mental note, filing it away quickly behind his smile of greeting as he spoke.

"First off, I want to thank you for coming here. I know you're busy and haven't much time to spare, so I appreciate your cooperation."

Enough of the soft-soap. Get down to business.

"Before we begin, let me assure you that this meeting is off the record. Anything said here today will be considered as privileged information; you have my word on that.

"In exchange, I'm going to ask you to keep silent regarding the matters I present to you. Consider this a confidential consultation on a medical problem. What I want from you is your professional opinion—perhaps a diagnosis."

Abberline paused just long enough to confirm that his audience was smiling. *Good enough,* he told himself. *Now let's wipe the grin off their mugs.*

"I'm sure you're all aware of the murder of Mary Ann Nicholls on Monday last, thanks to the attention given it in the public press. Some of the accounts identified her as Polly, but that's not important." He paused again, then spoke softly. "What is important is that the woman was murdered in Buck's Row—only a square away from this hospital."

Once more Abberline hesitated, scanning the faces before him. The smiles had disappeared, just as he'd expected, and now he took quick inventory of assorted frowns, shocked glances and murmurs of agitation.

Mustn't stare, he reminded himself. Best they didn't know he was studying their reactions. And it wouldn't do if they realized he knew more about them than they might imagine. Before coming here today he'd made a point of checking into the backgrounds of some of these fine gentlemen. Respectable citizens, one and all, reputations solid as a rock. But turn over the rock and you'd be surprised what might come crawling out from under—

"Let me tell you about the deceased," Abberline said. "Forty-two years old, married, but separated from her husband and children. Last known address, a doss-house lodging at Number Eighteen, Thrawl Street. Shabbily dressed, with clothing including two flannel petticoats stenciled with the mark of Lambeth Workhouse, but she did have a new black bonnet. Last seen alive at two-thirty Monday morning, on the corner of Osborn Street and Whitechapel Road.'"

He was reading now from the notebook he'd pulled from his pocket. "The witness who saw her, Emily Holland, testified that Nicholls was intoxicated and said she'd been turned out of lodgings because she had no money, but intended to get more shortly.

"A little more than an hour later her body was found in Buck's Row by two men—William Cross, a carter on his way to work, and Robert Paul, a carman. Nicholls was lying on her back at the footway before the gates of a stableyard, and they assumed she was drunk. But when the two tried to raise her up they realized her head had almost been severed from her neck."

Ignoring the low murmur from the group before him, the inspector riffled through the pages of the notebook, muttering to himself. "Run down street—meet Police Constable Haines on patrol—summon Officer Mizen—Constable Neill on scene—Dr. Ralph Llewellyn summoned from residence nearby, takes pulse, doesn't examine body—police ambulance to workhouse mortuary—stomach wounds discovered there—Dr. Llewellyn returns—ah, here we are!"

He glanced up, nodding. "Your attention please, gentlemen. I'd like to read you the postmortem findings reported at the coroner's inquest. Here's Dr. Llewellyn's testimony:

"'I was called by the police at about four o'clock. When I arrived the woman had apparently been dead for about half an hour. Her throat was deeply cut. About an hour afterward I was sent for again by the police and upon going to the mortuary where the body had been carried, I found the most extensive injuries to the abdomen. At ten o'clock the following morning I carried out a postmortem. On the right side of the face there was a recent and strongly marked bruise, caused by a blow from a fist or the pressure of a thumb. On the left side a circular bruise might have been produced by the pressure of the fingers. There were two cuts in the throat, one four inches long, the other eight. The large vessels of the neck on both sides were severed. The incisions also completely severed all the tissues down to the vertebrae which had also been penetrated. These wounds must have been caused by a long-bladed knife, moderately sharp and used with great violence. Then in the lower part of the abdomen—two or three inches from the left side—was a wound running in a jagged manner. It was a very deep wound and tissues were cut through. There were several incisions running across the abdomen. On the right side there were also three or four similar cuts running downward. As far as the throat is concerned the weapon appeared to have been held in the left hand of the person who used it. Similarly the wounds in the abdomen ran from left to right and might have been done by a left-handed person. The murderer must also have had some rough anatomical knowledge. He seems to have attacked all the vital parts. I would say the murder might have occupied four or five minutes.'"

Abberline flipped a page. "That's the official testimony," he said "But there's a bit more you might consider. The omentum—do I pronounce that right?—was cut in several places. And two of those stab wounds were in the vagina."

He paused just long enough to note the effect on his auditors. "Mutilations, gentlemen. Four or five minutes of mutilations which may have occurred while the victim was still alive. Because—in Dr. Llewellyn's opinion—the abdomen was torn open *before* the throat was cut."

No question about the effect of his words now; the excited murmur of voices rose from the semicircle but this time he ignored them. Bending below the table the inspector lifted a leather bag and placed it before him, unlocking it as he spoke.

"There you have the nature of the wounds and the way they were inflicted. I want you to consider this testimony very carefully in the light of your professional experience. Because the question I put to you now is the important one. What was the weapon?"

Opening the bag, Abberline reached inside and pulled out a pearl-handled dagger with a sharp point, then held it up against the light. "Would it be something like this?"

"No." The answer came quickly from a bespectacled man in a frockcoat whom he recognized as Dr. Reid, one of the surgical staff members. "It could be used for penetration only, not for slicing."

Amid nods and murmurs of confirmation, Abberline put the dagger down and dipped into the bag again. This time he brought out a short thick-handled cutting tool with a curving blade.

"What about this one?"

"A cork-cutter's knife, isn't it?" Again it was Dr. Reid who spoke.

Abberline nodded. "There's also a cobbler's knife, very similar, almost the same shape. Could either one of them do the job?"

"I doubt it." Dr. Trebor was answering him now. "The findings indicate a longer blade was employed."

"There's word going around about a shoemaker," the Inspector said. "Someone nicknamed 'Leather Apron' who is said to have threatened several women in the district over the past weeks. He's done a bunk since the killings, but we're on the lookout for him now. Are you sure this type of weapon wasn't responsible?"

"Almost positive." Trebor hesitated. "Of course that doesn't rule out your suspect. He could have used something besides his work tool."

"Like this?"

Abberline took a sailor's jackknife from the bag but the muttered reaction from the group was almost instantaneous and entirely negative. Now he withdrew a long thick-bladed knife with a double-edged point. "Or this?" he said.

For a moment no one answered. Then a doctor seated next to Trebor voiced the general puzzlement. "I'm not familiar with this. What's it used for?"

Before Abberline could reply, an answer came. "A hunting knife—looks like a Bowie. Very common in our western states."

It was Mark Robinson who'd spoken. Abberline glanced at him quickly. "Right you are," he said. "An American knife. And do you believe it could inflict such wounds?"

"Perhaps." The young man nodded. "We use them to gut deer."

"We?" Abberline faced him. "Have you had personal experience with this sort of weapon? Do you own one?"

Mark Robinson flushed. "Hold on, Inspector. I came here to study surgical techniques and this is hardly the kind of instrument a doctor would need for that."

"Exactly." Once more Abberline's hand descended into the bag and emerged holding a long thin glittering blade. "You'd probably use one of these."

Dead silence greeted his words. The inspector brandished the blade. "A surgical scalpel. You're all familiar with it. You all are skilled in its use."

"Just what are you insinuating?" Dr. Hume was speaking now, his slant-eyes constricting in an accusing scowl. "Do you think one of us is responsible for this abominable deed?"

"What I think isn't important." Abberline shrugged. "But if you must know, we've heard talk of a surgeon as a likely suspect."

"Preposterous!" Hume's voice rose indignantly. "You're grasping at straws."

"That's our job," the inspector said. "To grasp at straws until we find the needle in the haystack. Or the scalpel."

He met Hume's accusing stare. "Consider the circumstances. Whoever committed this crime got clean away in a matter of minutes without anyone setting eyes on him. Why? Because he knows the district, knows it well enough to choose a route where he'll escape detection. And who knows the area better than a local doctor, practicing here—perhaps in a place like this hospital?"

"Not so fast." Trebor shook his head. "Thousands of people live and work in Whitechapel. Many of them are as familiar with it as we are. Why make us the target of your suspicions?"

"Because nobody would take notice of you."

"That doesn't make sense."

"I think it does. As you say, the people who work here are familiar with the district. But they also know each other. If they saw a friend or neighbor out on the street in the middle of the night they'd wonder why, and they'd remember. Of course there are some who wouldn't attract attention—market porters or slaughterhouse men on their way to work before dawn, for example. Or a doctor called out on emergency, carrying a medical bag filled with surgical scalpels—"

Dr. Hume was on his feet. "Have you gone mad?" he shouted. "My colleagues and I are respectable members of our profession. How dare you accuse us of criminal behavior, without a scintilla of evidence to go on?"

Abberline felt a smoldering sensation in his stomach. "Believe me, I'm not accusing you. I'm only asking your opinions, your cooperation."

"Cooperation be damned! Why don't you clear out of here?" Dr. Hume took a step forward, his voice strident. "Clear out and take your bloody butcher knives with you!"

Murmurs of angry assent came from the group seated behind him, muffling Abberline's sigh. As the others began to rise and follow Hume from the room the inspector turned and replaced his assortment of weapons in the bag. No point trying to say any more, no point trying to stop them; at the moment there was only one thing claiming Abberline's complete attention.

His stomach was on fire.

CHAPTER ELEVEN

England, A.D. 1290 *Outlaw Thomas Dun was captured and executed at Redford before a large crowd. Using jagged knives, the executioners cut off both his arms below the elbows, and then the upper arms to his shoulders. Next they sawed off his feet below the ankles, then lopped off his legs at the knees. The thighs were then cut off just below the trunk. Then they cut off his head and boned the torso. The amputated remains were hung for display until they rotted.*

• • •

The corridor outside the library echoed with the sound of righteous indignation as the staff members departed to resume their rounds.

Trebor lagged behind, and Mark halted beside him. "What are you waiting for?" he asked.

"Abberline." Trebor turned as the inspector emerged from the doorway, carrying his bag. "A word with you, sir?"

Abberline nodded. He seemed drawn and spent, poor devil; no wonder, after the dressing-down Hume had given him.

"Sorry about what happened in there," Trebor told him. "Speaking for myself I want to apologize—"

"Not necessary." But the inspector's glance was grateful. "It's my fault for getting carried away. Reckon I should have been a bit more tactful."

"All you did was express your opinion."

"Which nobody wants to hear." Abberline shook his head. "They can't afford to admit the case was bungled from the start."

"How so?"

"To begin with, they sent a telegram round to my home that morning informing me of the affair. I went straightaway to Buck's Row but the body had already been removed. And the bloodstains on the pavement were scrubbed clean with a bucket of water on Constable Neill's orders. If the fool had left well enough alone the pattern of those stains might have told us something about the murder methods. As it is we've got nothing to go on but the bruises of the jaw and side of the victim's face, which indicate strangulation by someone approaching her from behind."

"You're sure about that?" Mark said.

"I'm not sure of anything, after the way they mucked about with the corpse at the mortuary."

Trebor looked puzzled. "But you told us that Dr. Llewellyn examined the body there."

"Not until after it was stripped. Two workhouse inmates—one of them a bloody halfwit, mind you—had already removed the clothing, even cut some of it off. And then those idiots washed the body."

"By whose orders?"

"I can't get a straight answer on that. No one admits responsibility."

Trebor nodded. "So you came here hoping for a further medical opinion."

"Not entirely. I scarcely counted on any doctor coming up with fresh clues without even seeing the corpse." Abberline paused. "Just between us, what I had in mind was more of a fishing expedition, you might say."

Trebor nodded again. "Then asking questions and exhibiting those knives was merely a charade. The whole business was designed to test our reactions by showing us that scalpel." He smiled. "I'm afraid I underestimated you, Inspector. You play a good game."

Abberline shrugged. "It's no game. In my opinion the murder weapon had to be a scalpel. And a doctor may be the man who used it."

Trebor met his gaze. "Which one of us do you suspect?"

"I can't answer that now."

"And if you could, you wouldn't."

"Not without further investigation. I'm still looking for more information."

"Perhaps we can help you," Mark said. Trebor glanced at him in surprise as he continued. "If there's any way we could be of assistance—"

"Perhaps you can. I need to know more about some of your colleagues. Dr. Reid, for example. I've heard from reliable sources that he's rather keen on using the knife."

"You're speaking of his operating procedures, of course." Trebor chose his words carefully. "Reid's a sound man. I know there are those who think he's too quick with a diagnosis, too eager to perform surgery rather than suggest other procedures. But you've got to understand his position. With the volume of patients we handle here daily there's neither time nor staff enough for prolonged treatment. In case of doubt, surgery is the sensible solution. I don't believe Dr. Reid does any cutting just for cutting's sake."

"What about Hume?"

Trebor hesitated. "Hard to say. He's inclined to be a bit conservative in his views—one of the old school of practitioners who still believe in laudanum and laudable pus."

"I take it you don't much care for him."

"I don't really know the man."

"Suppose I tell you that he spends a good deal of his spare time in the local slaughterhouses watching the butchers at their work?"

"That's quite possible," Trebor said. "But it doesn't necessarily indicate he's a murderer." He smiled. "No, I'm afraid you'll have to do better than that."

"Very well, then. What about you?"

The question came quickly, catching Trebor off guard. "Really, Inspector—can you offer any evidence for such an accusation?"

"Only circumstantial," Abberline said. "Take the matter of your prolonged absences from duty here. Most of the doctors work regular shifts, but you seem to come and go as you please."

"That's because I serve only in the capacity of a voluntary consultant," Trebor told him. "I'm privileged to keep my own hours."

"So you have time to attend inquests." Abberline spoke slowly. "Martha Tabram's, for one. And Polly Nicholls'." He stared at the doctor. "You didn't mention your attendance the other day, but I saw you there."

"As one of fifty spectators," Trebor said. "If mere presence is an indication of possible guilt, you've got forty-nine other suspects to question."

"Right now I'm questioning you."

"And I'm ready to answer." Trebor took a deep breath. "First off, I agree with you—inquiries on both the Tabram and Nicholls cases were botched. As a result all sorts of wild rumors are making the rounds, including this gossip about the killer being a doctor. We already have problems here at the hospital because patients fear our surgeons and the knife. The last thing we need is an accusation of murder. That's why I've followed the autopsy proceedings. I keep hoping to hit upon some clue that might help resolve matters once and for all."

Abberline nodded. "Then I can count on you if I need medical information?"

"By all means." It was Mark who answered. "If anything turns up, please let us know."

"I'll be in touch." The inspector turned and moved down the hall, the sound of his footsteps mingling with the faint clank of metal from inside his bag.

Trebor waited until he disappeared around the corner at the far end, then turned to Mark. "Why did you volunteer?"

"For the same reason you did. I want to help."

"That may not be wise."

"How so?"

"Consider the circumstances. All this unrest here in White-chapel, fears of a mass murderer roaming the district, suspects being mobbed in the streets. Every foreigner is under suspicion—Jews, Poles, Russian anarchists—even Americans."

"But that's ridiculous. No one would accuse me."

"Don't be too sure," Trebor said. "Suppose someone asked you where you were on the night of the last murder?"

"I'd refer them to you. We were at the theater together—"

"And afterward you took off alone."

"I went to my lodgings."

"So you said. But can you prove that? Did anyone see you there?"

Mark stiffened, eyes wary. "What are you driving at? Do you think I killed those poor unfortunates?"

"Others might." Trebor nodded. "So it's best not to get involved." He reached into his vest pocket and consulted his watch with a frown. "Past three—I must be on my way. We'll discuss this later."

He started down the corridor, leaving the younger man behind. As he turned he glanced back and saw that Mark was no longer alone. Now he stood deep in conversation with a young woman in a probationer's uniform. As she raised her face to the light he recognized Eva Sloane.

CHAPTER TWELVE

Milan, A.D. 1354 *Bernabò Visconti, ruler of Milan, disposed of prisoners he considered criminals against the state in tortures prolonged for forty days. On the forty-first day the victim, completely disabled and dismembered, was torn with pincers and then broken upon the wheel.*

• • •

Eva had taken a shortcut through the library on her way to the infirmary. When she opened the door to the hall she saw Mark Robinson standing before her.

"Miss Sloane!" he said. "I've been hoping to run into you. Where've you been keeping yourself all week?"

"They posted me for infirmary duty."

"So that's it." He smiled. "Well, no matter. You're here now and I'm taking you up on your promise."

"Promise?"

"Don't you remember? When you postponed our dinner together you said you'd be available later. What do you say we dine this evening?"

Eva avoided his gaze. "I'm afraid that won't be possible."

"You've made other plans?"

"Yes." She spoke rapidly. "As a matter of fact my time is not my own."

"But I don't understand. Is there some reason for you to keep putting me off like this?"

"A very good reason." Now she hesitated, then took the plunge. "If you must know, I'm already spoken for."

"Spoken for." Mark's smile faded. "You mean you're engaged?"

"That's right." Eva forced herself to meet his glance. "It's my fault, I should have made that plain to you from the beginning—"

"Indeed you should."

"I'm sorry, truly I am. I oughtn't to have led you on this way."

"But you did." Mark's voice was strained. "Who is this fiancé of yours? Do I know him?"

"I don't think so." Eva took a step forward. "Really, there's no point discussing it any further."

"That's for me to decide," Mark said. "Forgive me for reminding you, but I did you a service."

"For which I'm grateful. But that doesn't entitle you to pry into my affairs."

"Maybe it does." Oddly enough Mark didn't seem angry now; his tone was thoughtful. "The Chinese believe that if you save someone's life you then become responsible for their welfare. I have a feeling they're right."

Eva shook her head. "I must say you're a strange one." She softened her words with a smile. "But I'm truly sorry. If only—"

"Yes?"

"Not now." She turned away quickly. "Please, I have to go or I'll be late."

Mark didn't reply; he stood staring silently, and no hint of any reaction was visible in his intent eyes.

But as Eva hastened off down the corridor she could feel those eyes boring into her back.

CHAPTER THIRTEEN

Romania, A.D. 1462 *Vlad Tepes (Vlad the Impaler) had a somewhat special sense of humor. When oriental visitors to his court refused to doff their headgear in his presence, Vlad ordered that their turbans be nailed to their heads—with short nails, so as not to kill them instantly. He often dined while surrounded by his victims impaled on blunt stakes to prolong their agonies. When a guest complained of the stench, Vlad thoughtfully impaled him on a higher stake, above the source of the odors.*

• • •

The lamplighter had just completed his task as Mark rounded the corner and stepped into the circle of golden glow.

He paused momentarily, staring down the street into the darkness beyond. The gas flame flickering above him lent luminance, not heat, but the illusion of warmth was there and he welcomed it.
Illusion.

Why do we seek light and shun the dark? Is it because our primitive ancestors huddled around fires in their caves as a protection against peril prowling the night? Light lends us security.

Mark shrugged. *Security is an illusion too,* he told himself. There never was a time when we were really secure, not in the rocky refuges of the past or the stone streets of today. Sunshine still gives way to darkness and in that darkness the beasts still prowl. Only now it's the human beasts we fear.

Perhaps our longing for light is just an instinctive reaction. But what is instinct? Trepan the skull, then open it fully and examine the gray glob within; you won't locate the seat of instinctual reaction there, any more than you'll find the source of what we call the soul. Our sophisticated labels are no more exact than the fantasies of the phrenologists.

That much I've learned, Mark reflected. He'd come here hoping to master his physical repulsion at the sight of blood, the first requisite for objectivity in medical research. But the mechanics of surgery would never reveal what he sought; the brain could be dissected yet the mind withholds its secrets.

Mark moved forward into the shadowed street, his thoughts still churning. *Secrets.* Our loves, our hates, our dreams and desires— how are they formed and why does what we call intelligence give way to animal impulse? The human beasts out there in the night— what drives them to rend and tear and raven for the sight of blood which he so dreaded?

You're a strange one. Now Eva's words echoed in his ears. She was right, of course, but then all of us are strange, even to ourselves. Strange because all of us harbor secrets we cannot comprehend.

He thought of what he'd learned earlier in the day; of Dr. Hume haunting the shambles of the slaughterhouse and Trebor perching like a vulture over the lifeless flesh of those corpses at the inquests. Was it really the quest for knowledge that concerned them or were they prompted by darker needs? Strange ones indeed.

And Eva. She too was a strange one. He could have sworn she felt attracted to him from the first, just as he was to her, but now came this abrupt dismissal. She said she had a fiancé, but was she telling the truth? Behind her words he'd sensed a deeper import; it was almost as though she'd been afraid to reveal the real reason for rejection. If so, what did she fear? That was her secret.

And what is yours? Why do you walk the night?

Mark blinked as he found himself halting in the dark midway down the street. *Old Montague Street.* Wandering aimlessly, his thoughts a million miles away, something had guided his footsteps to this spot directly across from Eva's lodgings. There again, the secrets of the human mind—

The sudden sound of a carriage in motion claimed his attention.

He turned and watched as it came to a stop before the building across the way. And now, coming out of the entrance, he saw Eva.

The door of the waiting vehicle opened and a man emerged. Stepping to one side, he grasped Eva's arm, assisting her into the carriage.

Turning, he climbed in after her, and Mark glanced quickly at the profile of his mustached face surmounted by a peaked cap very much like his own. Then the door closed. Mark stepped back into the concealment of the shadows as the carriage started off down the street.

Once again he was alone in the night, but not entirely so.

Something else lay hidden in the darkness ahead. Perhaps, if he dared venture into that darkness now, he might find other secrets waiting there.

CHAPTER FOURTEEN

Germany, A.D. 1490 *In the castle of Nuremberg some of the torture devices were later exhibited. Prisoners were crushed to death against stones, their limbs dislocated on the rack, their feet seared by fire. Some were confined in sharp iron cages in which it was impossible to sit or lie down. The infamous "Iron Maiden" closed and crushed a victim against its spikes, then released him to fall into a pit of pointed stakes and revolving knives.*

• • •

Slowly Mark moved through moonless midnight. The alleyway was steeped in shadow but light flared from the open doorway of the abattoir ahead.

As he approached the entrance the scent of blood was strong and for a moment he paused, dreading the sight of its source. But the light lured him forward again, even when he heard the sounds and saw the shapes through the open doorway.

Where had he heard those sounds before? Mark remembered that night, weeks ago, when he'd first seen Eva, the night when the cattle stampeded from the slaughterhouse.

Now they were in the slaughterhouse, and this time there was no escape.

No escape from the terror, no escape from the *shocets*. Clad in leather aprons, the slaughtermen were everywhere, hobbling the

legs of their fear-crazed victims in preparation for the rite pre-
scribed by ancient Talmudic law—*shechita*, the draining of blood
from the body of the beast.

Long knives raised, they muttered the sacred benediction, then
slashed the throat to the bone in two quick strokes, moving back
quickly to avoid the crimson cascade spurting forth over the saw-
dust shambles. The red-stained blades rose and fell again, first ripping open the breast and then the stomach, revealing the inner
organs for ritual inspection of the remains. The slaughtermen
worked swiftly, expertly, oblivious to the bellowing of the brutes
they butchered and the bright bubbling of their blood.

That was the worst of it, Mark reasoned, scanning the faces of
those who dealt in death; their eyes were empty, their frozen features
betrayed no hint of any emotion.

But as he stared a greater horror assailed him—the horror of
familiarity. He *knew* these men!

The fat fiend with the pince-nez perched incongruously on
a snouted nose was Dr. Reid. The slant-eyed monster with the
dripping knife was Dr. Hume. And the tall thin throat-slasher
was Trebor.

Why were they here? How could they kill so callously, go on killing without heeding the moans of agony, the cries of their victims?

He watched as they dragged another helpless hobbled figure forward, flinging it down beneath the upraised knives. Threshing, the
creature turned its face to the light, and this was the ultimate horror.

The body beneath the blades was that of a beast, but it had a
human face.

A woman's face, contorted in fear, mouth opening wide in a
scream—

"Murder!"

Perspiration pouring from his fevered forehead, Mark jerked
bolt upright in the sunlight blazing through the window beside
his bed.

His eyes opened and for a moment he gave thanks for the safety
which surrounded him, the reality of his own room, the knowledge
that he'd escaped from a nightmare.

But only for a moment.

"Murder!"

Now the cry sounded again, and this time he found its source—
not in the darkness of a dream but in the dazzling sunlight of the
street below.

Peering down he saw the canvas-aproned figure of the newsboy hawking papers. And heard his shout.

"*Murder—read all about it! New slaying in Whitechapel!*"

CHAPTER FIFTEEN

Mexico, A.D. 1500 In order to secure enough victims for sacrifice, the Aztecs fought prearranged combats between cities just to obtain captives for their religious ceremonies. These, plus slaves, were ritually slain on the feast days of various gods, held eighteen times a year. Others died daily as offerings to Huitzilopochtli, who demanded human blood and hearts in tribute for his offices when restoring the sun each day. Children were butchered to please Tlaloc, the god of rain, adults burned alive for the god of the harvest, hearts ripped from the bodies of living victims. Others were flayed alive; the priests of Tlaloc wrapped themselves in the bloody skins and danced to the throbbing drums and shrill flutes which joyously sounded a public holiday.

● ● ●

Mark wasn't the only one who saw the paper. All London was reading the news.

Inspector Joseph Chandler read it with particular interest, because of his own involvement.

At six in the morning he was walking down Commercial Street on his way to the police station when two workmen accosted him. They'd been hailed by an elderly market porter who'd found a dead body lying in the backyard of his lodgings at 29 Hanbury Street.

By the time Chandler arrived there a crowd had already gathered before the house; he fought his way through and ordered his men to keep the yard clear. Then he saw the corpse. He saw it then, he saw it now, and he knew he would see it again in his troubled dreams.

The middle-aged woman with dark brown hair was sprawled before the steps of a passage leading into the yard beside a fence. The victim lay on her back, legs parted in an obscene parody of invitation. Her stomach gaped, open and disemboweled; the intestines were drawn up on her right shoulder, still connected by a cord dangling from her abdomen. Two flaps of lower abdominal skin rested above her left shoulder in a pool of blood. Her throat had been cut from behind in a jagged wound that encircled the neck. She wore a handkerchief as a scarf, but that had not protected her from what amounted to partial decapitation.

Chandler couldn't forget the first sight of that bruised and bloody face, the bulging eyes, the swollen tongue protruding from between yellowed teeth. Thank God the newspapers hadn't printed the details!

At his orders a constable obtained a piece of canvas from a neighbor and covered the body. Help was summoned, Inspector Abberline was notified, and then he waited.

But not in idleness. Chandler searched the yard. It was unpaved, but he saw no footprints, nor any indentations indicating signs of a struggle. The woman must have been suffocated, then lowered to the ground before the knife was used. He'd found patches of blood, some as large as a sixpence and others mere pinpoint drops, and there were smears on the fence about a foot above the ground. Under the circumstances this was understandable; the puzzle lay elsewhere.

It lay beside the body in the shape of a bit of muslin cloth, possibly a handkerchief, resting next to a comb and a paper case which must have come from the slashed-open pocket under her skirt. It lay beside her feet; the two brass rings torn from her fingers, a few pennies and a couple of new farthings placed there as though in mocking payment for services rendered. It lay at her head as a piece of paper wrapped around two pills, and as part of an envelope. On the back of the envelope was the seal of a Sussex regiment, and on the other side was a London postmark dated August 28th. It lay near the water-tap across the way in the form of a wet leather apron. Pieces of a puzzle, all of them; pieces that made no more sense than the pieces of bloody flesh and internal organs that Chandler would hide from sight but not from the eyes of memory.

When the stretcher arrived the body was carried away to the mortuary by two constables and after that Abberline took charge. Reading about it now, Chandler gave thanks that his role in the affair was ended. Let Dr. Phillips fit these pieces together, or take them apart in his autopsy....

Dr. George Bagster Phillips was too busy to read anything in the papers. Too busy, and too angry.

The whole affair was disgraceful, no other word for it. Twenty-three years as a divisional surgeon of police, and still no adequate provision had been made for him to carry out his duties. How did they expect him to perform a decent examination under conditions like this?

It was bad enough that the borough didn't have a proper public mortuary; instead he was forced to conduct his autopsy in a make-do shed, with incompetent assistance.

Incompetent? What they did before his arrival was almost criminal. Two nurses had stripped and washed the corpse, just as in the Nicholls affair. He raised a devil of a row with the clerk in charge but there was no help for it now and all he could do was set to work as best he could.

And wicked work it was. The nurses had left one article of apparel untouched—the handkerchief around the neck of the cadaver. Now, when he removed it, the head nearly came clean away. Whoever used the knife had almost succeeded in cutting through the spine.

The murderer had done a more thorough job below. The abdomen had been entirely laid open and the small intestines severed from their mesenteric attachments before being placed on the corpse's shoulder. But the greatest damage was in the pelvic area; the uterus and its appendages, along with the upper portion of the vagina and the posterior two-thirds of the bladder, had been entirely removed.

Obviously it was the work of someone who had enough knowledge of anatomy to secure the pelvic organs with one sweep of the knife.

As for the knife itself, Dr. Phillips fancied it had to be extremely sharp; not a bayonet or an ordinary butcher's tool. His findings indicated the use of a thin, narrow blade, probably six to eight inches long. An expert's weapon, an expert's skill, but a madman's deed.

Dr. Phillips made careful notes of his discoveries for future publication in *The Lancet*. That's where such information belonged, in a medical journal, not the popular press. Matters were already bad enough without stirring up morbid imaginations....

But the stirring had already started.

In the smoky confines of the Coach and Four Public House barflies buzzed over the latest news. From early morning on patrons had stopped by to contribute gossip and theory about the "'Anbury Street 'Orror." Some had actually been spectators at the scene, and several already identified the victim as Annie Chapman.

"Dark Annie" they called her, or "Annie Sievey," seeing as how her husband, the late-lamented, had been a maker of iron sieves. No better than she should be, perhaps, but what's a poor widow woman to do? A bit long in the tooth for going on the game, and in and out of the infirmary as well, worse luck.

Tim Donovan said he saw her in the kitchen of the Dorset Street lodging house at two in the morning; skint, she told him, but would he hold a bed for her until she went out and found some nicker for the night? A little the worse for drink, he reckoned, but still walking straight enough as she went off.

And Mrs. Long caught sight of her as late as five-thirty. On her way to Spitalfields Market she was, when the brewer's clock struck, so no doubt about the time. And no doubt about the man and woman she saw talking on the pavement just outside 29 'Anbury Street. She'd paid a special visit to the mortuary since, just to 'ave a look-see; the deceased was the same woman and no mistake. Too bad she didn't give much heed to the man, but she did catch a smidge of their words as she passed by. He said, "Will you?" and she said, "Yes." No need to be an Oxford graduate to guess what they was up to, but it was none of her affair and she went on down the street. Just to think, if Annie copped it 'arf-and-'our later like the papers said, then she was most likely the last one to set eyes on the pore thing, outside of the murderer. God knows what the dirty devil did to her in the back yard there on 'Anbury Street!

God, and Jerry the publican. He knew because he'd put together all he heard, confiding it to his eager customers.

"They say 'er 'ead was cut clean orf 'er body." He lowered his voice to a whisper. "And 'er female orgerns was removed...."

The young man in the frogged morning jacket read the first accounts of the crime while seated over breakfast in the subdued silence of the drawing room. As he scanned the report the thin mouth beneath his mustache twitched and his hands trembled.

Stop it, he told himself. *You're not a child. No reason to act the fool over a newspaper story.*

But he took pains to hide the paper in his lap when Watkins brought the tea tray, and he busied himself with a silver crumb-scoop until the butler left. Thank heaven the old fool hadn't noticed the newspaper; no one must know he read such trash, not Mama or Papa, and certainly not Grandmother. They thought they were shielding him from that sort of thing. No wonder he had to keep reminding himself he wasn't a child—they still treated him like one.

If so, then why hadn't they protected him better? Sending him off on that bloody cruise when he was only fifteen, and little George as well, even younger. They had been responsible.

Thinking about the cruise he found himself atremble again, but this time in anger rather than fear. Couldn't they have foreseen what would happen? The *H.M.S. Bacchante*—the very name of the vessel was an omen. Warm tropical nights in the West Indies, and his shipmates all tiddly, urging him on.

"Drink up," they said. "Be a man." And from that to the inevitable. "You're not a man until you've had a woman."

Well, he'd had his woman. It was only a lark, slipping ashore after a word with the watch; they'd made all the arrangements in advance. Just a bit of slap-and-tickle, they said, and no harm done.

But harm it was. They didn't know how he hated it, hated the dark woman in the dark room, hated the dark eyes laughing at him as he fumbled to perform the dark deed. And they didn't know about the rash.

Only the doctor ever learned about the rash, and he'd kept his secret well. Only the doctor understood what it was like to fall prey to such a horror, to endure the ravages of a vile disease. Sometimes he thought he might go mad, sometimes he thought he *was* mad, but there was no help for it, one had to keep up appearances.

And it wasn't hypocrisy to do so. It was they who were the hypocrites, all of them, pretending such things didn't exist. As if everyone didn't know about Papa and his women! Not just the actresses, or even the wives of his dearest friends—he did the deed with common courtesans in Paris and all over the Continent. What a farce! How could Papa lower himself like that? The deed itself was loathsome, and the creatures one coupled with were disgusting.

James was the only one who understood. Dear James, so much more than a tutor, so much more than a friend. It was he who helped him find a new life with the artists and free spirits who shared his feelings and his tastes. James was the one who'd made it possible for him to slip away for a night on the town, taught him to dress discreetly—dark clothing, a fore-and-aft cap like the ones so many chaps wore nowadays. Discretion, that was the ticket, not to attract attention like a swell on the randy.

What jolly times they'd had together! Oh, once or twice there'd been a bit of a near thing—that raid on the house in Cleveland Street, for example. One of the lads had blabbed but they managed to hush it up nicely. If only poor James hadn't suffered that dreadful accident two years ago! Brain injury, they said; laid him up for months.

It was then that he'd started going out on his own, quite alone. It was then that he'd really discovered the East End with all its delicious diversions, its perils and pitfalls, trollops and tarts.

Those damned whores were the worst. Taunting him, baiting him, because somehow they seemed to know what he was after. "Not good enough for the likes of you, eh, dearie? You're the sort who prefers a touch of backgammon."

Backgammon. A filthy term from a filthy mouth. What right did scum like these have, mocking him? No wonder he suffered seizures; it was enough to enrage anyone.

But now, after all that had happened, it was time to lay doggo, at least for a while. Presently he might go again, might have to go, just to put matters to the test for his own satisfaction. But he must be awfully, awfully careful lest someone—Mama, Papa, or even Grandmother—found him out.

And that would never do. Not for Albert Victor Christian Edward, Duke of Clarence, son of the Prince of Wales and grandson of Queen Victoria....

"God Save the Queen!" That's how George Lusk opened the meeting and that's how he ended it.

He wanted to make it perfectly clear; forming the Vigilance Committee was a patriotic duty. And by the morning of September 10th it had actually become a necessity. This panic in the district, the patrols searching everywhere, the wild accusations and arrests following Annie Chapman's death, all added up to one thing—the Jews were in danger.

So he summoned them, a group of loyal, innocent people like himself and the local vestrymen, and presented his proposal.

It was the only way, the only sensible way, to combat vicious prejudice. Form a committee of responsible residents, offer full cooperation to the police, make recommendations to the authorities for protection and precautions, arrange for decent private citizens to conduct inquiries on their own and report any and all evidence of suspicious behavior.

As a builder and a respectable member of the community he was willing to chair the Committee; that was a step in the right direction. And they agreed to a further proposal, the posting of a sizeable reward for information leading to the arrest and conviction of the murderer.

All in all it had been a good day's work, and George Lusk was satisfied. It was probably too much to hope for that the Committee would actually bring the killer to justice, but at least its formation might achieve his primary purpose and quiet this hysteria about the Jews.

Unless, of course, one of their own proved guilty of the crimes.

Lusk hadn't mentioned this last possibility to his associates nor did he dare tell anyone. But the hideous hypothesis haunted him, the more he read and heard, the more he wondered if the murderer could be the man whom the newspapers were accusing, a Jew nicknamed "Leather Apron"....

It was to laugh, this "Leather Apron" business. But John Pizer wasn't laughing.

Ever since they'd found that leather apron in the backyard where the *nafke* had been killed, there'd been a *tsimis* going on. At first they thought it belonged to a slaughterman, and then some troublemaker began telling tales, giving those journalists his name.

And for what?

Everyone knew he wasn't a slaughterman. He was a boot-finisher, that was a fact. Everyone in the trade wore such an apron, so why shouldn't he have one too? Just because he sometimes wore it on the street the *momsers* called him "Leather Apron"—but did this prove he was guilty?

They said he hated women, said he had cursed and threatened to attack them. As if that was any of their business what he felt about these *corvars* or what he did to them. And this they couldn't prove either.

But he'd guessed what they were thinking and his brother and sister were ready to swear he stayed inside the house with them. From Thursday night until Monday morning he stayed, and then the police came and arrested him.

Sergeant Thicke, he was the one who took him in. A good name for that *shmuck*—thick in the body, thick in the head. He searched the house and found five knives. *Nu*, so the knives were long, their blades were sharp; they had to be, for his line of work. Again this proved nothing.

At the Leman Street police station they made him stand in line with others they'd arrested. Then they brought in the stupid women who'd spread gossip about seeing the killer and his victim together and asked them to identify him. None of them could say for sure that he was the man they saw. A man, some crazy foreigner, told about seeing him quarrel with a woman in Hanbury Street before the murder, but even the police admitted he was *meshugga*.

At the inquest they found out about the leather apron lying in the back yard on the scene of the crime. It belonged to one of the lodgers, John Richardson his name was, and his mother had washed it and left it there.

After that they let him go. And now maybe the worst was over. Maybe he could even sue the newspapers for printing those stories about him. That would put a stop to all this "Leather Apron" foolishness. John Pizer always hated that part the worst. If he had to have a nickname, why couldn't they just call him "Jack"?

CHAPTER SIXTEEN

Hungary, A.D. 1514 *György Dózsa, leader of a revolt against the nobles, was captured and starved for two weeks, together with his accomplices. Then his captors tied him down on a red-hot throne, clapped a red-hot crown on his head, and thrust a red-hot scepter into his hand. As he roasted, he was eaten alive by his famished followers.*

• • •

Inspector Abberline wasn't sure.

Waiting in the anteroom of Sir Charles Warren's office he tried to find an answer. Could it be that meal at the Gravesend Inn, topped off by gooseberry fool? Maybe this was making his stomach growl.

The meal had been a mistake and the whole trip to Gravesend was a fiasco. They'd held a suspect for him there, and nothing would do but for him to jar his digestion with a long train ride to pick the man up. William Piggott was his name, and he'd been seen by the landlady of the Prince of Wales public house on the morning after Annie Chapman's murder, disheveled and with blood on his clothing.

The accused fitted the description, admitting he'd been in Whitechapel that morning and quarreled with a woman who bit his finger. Other than this he refused to speak on the journey back to London and seemed to be in a state bordering on delirium tremens. It all added up until they learned he'd slept in a lodging house straight through the time of the murder. The blood on his clothing probably came from the finger bitten during the quarrel after he awoke. And when Piggott was brought in neither the landlady nor any of the public house patrons could positively identify him. To top it off, the divisional surgeon who examined the man certified he was quite insane.

No wonder Abberline had a bad stomach. And when he finally found himself ushered into Sir Charles Warren's presence, matters only got worse.

Of course Warren knew about Piggott, and John Pizer, and another suspect—a barber's assistant named Ludwig—who'd been arrested and released. He'd read it all in the papers.

"That's what I want you to explain," Warren said. "How does all this twaddle get into the hands of the press?"

Abberline stood there, hat in hand, forcing himself to remain calm, but his fingers twisted the brim of his bowler.

"I'm afraid there's no help for it, sir. The way journalists keep swarming into Whitechapel asking questions they're bound to turn up information. We can't prevent that."

"Information?" Warren fixed the monocle to his bad eye and regarded him with a steely squint. "It's enough they know we've planted detectives working in the slaughterhouses, visiting all the butcher shops, questioning every lodging-house keeper in the district. Personally I think it a mistake to print such stories—they're bound to put the murderer on the *qui vive*—but at least it shows we're doing our duty." He picked up a morning paper from his desktop. "What I can't countenance is rot like this. Suggesting that whores should carry whistles and walk in couples, or that officers on patrol disguise themselves as common prostitutes!"

"I admit that isn't practical," Abberline said. "Speaking for my men I can vouch they'll do almost anything they're ordered to, but shaving off their mustaches is a bit much."

"Damn it, man, are you trying to make sport of this?" Warren's squint grew into a glare. "Leave the bad jokes to Fleet Street." He opened the newspaper, riffling through its pages. "There's more bilge here in the letter columns. Suggestions that we recruit prizefighters to dress as women. Or even enlisting effeminates to pose as street-walkers, giving them spiked steel collars to wear because the murderer first attacks the throat. I tell you the whole city has gone crazy."

"Agreed." Abberline nodded. "But it's a crazy man we're after. And we're bound to find him, sooner or later. I have some fresh leads—"

"Then go after them!" Warren's maniacal monocle glittered. "But mind you, not a word to the press. They're having a field day,

blowing this whole affair up out of all proportion, and I know why."
His mustache quivered as he spoke. "You can see the reason behind
this puffery, can't you? They're out to discredit me. Ever since those
infernal riots last year they've been after my blood. Well, let them
try and be damned to them!" Crumpling the paper, he threw it into
the wastebasket beside his desk. "I won't have it, do you hear? I
won't have it!"

A warning sounded in Abberline's stomach and he covered it
hastily, clearing his throat. No sense talking to Warren any further,
but there was another alternative.

"I appreciate your feelings in the matter, Sir Charles, and I'll
not trouble you about those leads. But I do want an official opinion
before I go ahead. Perhaps it would be best for me to discuss plans
with the assistant commissioner. If he's ready to assume charge of
the case now—"

"Anderson?" Warren offered him a surprised stare. "Haven't
you heard? He left here the day after the Chapman murder."

"Left?" It was Abberline's turn to display surprise.

"I told you he was feeling poorly. His physician recommended
a month's holiday abroad. Switzerland, I believe."

Something spasmed in Abberline's gut and he turned away
quickly without replying; a nod of farewell was all he could safely
venture as he put on his hat and left the office.

Only upon reaching the outer corridor beyond the anteroom
did he give voice to his reaction.

"Switzerland," Abberline muttered. "All hell breaks loose in
Whitechapel and he runs off to take a holiday." His stomach rumbled in counterpoint to his words. "No hard feelings, but I hope he
falls off an alp and breaks his bloody neck!"

CHAPTER SEVENTEEN

England, A.D. 1531 *Good King Henry VIII established a law to dis-
courage poisoners. They were boiled alive.*

• • •

All week long Mark avoided reading the papers.

After the shock of the murder report he'd come to a decision.
Following the accounts of the crime could only lead to troubled sleep

and worse waking moments. He made up his mind to concentrate on work.

But what a curious phrase—making up one's mind. Was it just a figure of speech? Or do we literally "make up" our minds? To what extent do we control our perception of reality; where does thought end and imagination begin?

The problem intrigued him. It would be helpful to discuss the subject with someone like Trebor, but he hadn't appeared at the hospital since the day before the murder.

Twice Mark had seen Eva going about her duties in the infirmary, but there had been no chance to speak with her. She was deliberately avoiding him, he knew, and sooner or later he intended to force the issue. The question was how to go about it.

He considered the matter again as he came out of the consultation room on Saturday noon. Surely she'd have some free time this weekend. Perhaps the best thing to do was go directly to her lodgings and insist on seeing her. Whatever Eva's feelings about him might be, she owed him that much.

"Dr. Robinson!"

Mark halted, recognizing the portly figure of Inspector Abberline as he approached.

"Sorry to bother you," Abberline said. "I've been trying to locate Dr. Trebor."

Mark shook his head. "I haven't seen him here all week."

"Neither has anyone in the administration office." Abberline pushed his bowler back to reveal a perspiring forehead. "They say he was called away on business. You wouldn't happen to know where he went, by any chance?"

"I'm afraid not."

"Odd he didn't leave word of his whereabouts." Abberline took a handkerchief from his vest pocket and blotted his brow with it. "You medicos are a closemouthed lot."

"I don't believe Dr. Trebor is required to account for his absence," Mark said. "He's only a voluntary consultant. And if he has business elsewhere—"

"Any idea what sort of business that might be? Or is that a professional secret?"

Mark felt a twinge of irritation. "I know nothing about his personal affairs."

"That's the point. Nobody seems to know where he goes and why."

"Is there any reason they should?" Even as he spoke Mark knew the answer and anticipated it. "Surely you don't suspect Dr. Trebor of any connection with what's been happening."

"That's not why I'm here." Abberline replaced the now-soggy handkerchief in his pocket. "You may recall he volunteered assistance if required. I was about to take him up on his offer."

Mark found himself hesitating before he replied. Despite his disclaimer Abberline might still suspect Trebor and probably suspected him as well. Like it or not, he was still involved, and the best course now was to cooperate.

"Could I be of any help?" he asked.

Abberline smiled. "Good of you to ask. If you're free for an hour or so you might take lunch with us."

"Us?"

"I've an appointment at the Duck and Drake for one o'clock. Chap named L. Forbes Winslow. Ever heard of him?"

"Can't say I have."

"No matter. Come along and form your own opinion. I fancy you may find him a bit of an odd fish."

And that was all Abberline would say. During the carriage ride to Wimpole Street both men confined themselves to silence. It wasn't until they entered the restaurant and made their way to a corner table that Mark learned anything more about the odd fish.

At first glance there was nothing either odd or piscatorial about the tall dignified man with muttonchop whiskers who rose to greet them. Much to Mark's surprise, L. Forbes Winslow was introduced as a doctor. And once they scanned the menu and gave their orders to the waiter, Dr. Forbes Winslow corroborated his professional status.

"Good of you to come," he said. "I welcome the support of a fellow physician." Forbes Winslow smiled at Abberline. "And you too, Inspector. As you know, my suggestions to the authorities have fallen on deaf ears. But we've no time to waste, with a diseased degenerate at large."

Abberline nodded to Mark. "Dr. Winslow has a theory about the recent murders," he said.

Forbes Winslow's smile disappeared. "I do not deal in theories. As an alienist, I state facts."

"Alienist?" Mark was intrigued. "I take it you've had some first-hand experience in the study of mental disorders?"

"Indeed I have." Forbes Winslow was beaming again. "After all, I grew up in a lunatic asylum."

Mark glanced at Abberline, seeking his reaction, but the inspector's face was impassive.

"My father was the resident physician at Hammersmith," Forbes Winslow continued. "I've studied lunacy all my life. That's why these crimes attracted my attention from the start. Although I conduct a practice here at Wimpole Street I've spent a great deal of time investigating the Whitechapel murders. The East End residents don't take kindly to the police, but they trust me. I've talked to the witnesses, the lodging-house keepers and those poor creatures of the streets. What I learned has been communicated to the press and to Sir Charles Warren himself. But no one listens, and the killings go on."

"That's why we're here," Abberline said. "Suppose you tell us your conclusions."

Dr. Forbes Winslow spoke slowly. "There are three possibilities. First, that the murderer is a monomaniac who labors under the belief that he is bringing the vengeance of God upon fallen women. This would account for his singling out prostitutes as his victims."

"We've thought of that," Abberline said. "It's an obvious motive. Trouble is, there's nothing to support the notion."

"Not as yet." Forbes Winslow leaned forward. "So let us consider the next alternative. Suppose the murderer is an epileptic? In that case he might kill and not even be aware of what he's done."

Abberline raised his eyebrows but Mark nodded to him quickly. "Dr. Forbes Winslow is talking about amnesia. Sufferers from epilepsy don't remember what occurs during a seizure. But we really can't say how these spells are brought about."

"Not so." Forbes Winslow shook his head. "From my long observation of the insane I'm convinced they are influenced by phases of the moon. Lunatic—the very term speaks for itself. Even our ancestors knew of the relationship between the moon and madness. Modern medicine would do well to heed ancient wisdom in this regard. And I've done so. These murders were committed either when the new moon rose or when it entered its last quarter."

He was interrupted by the arrival of their orders, and said no more until the waiter departed. Inspecting Abberline's luncheon choice, he nodded approvingly.

"Tea and biscuit. Very sensible. As you see, I confine my own midday repast to a fruit *compote*. I'm firmly convinced that many mental disorders are due to an excessive intake of food. My father placed his charges on a meat-free diet; no spices or condiments, no sweets, no alcohol." He surveyed Mark's plate with a frown. "But you, sir—steak-and-kidney pie—very dangerous. Very dangerous indeed."

"We tend to heavy meals where I come from." Mark smiled. "I can't say that Americans are any crazier as a result."

Forbes Winslow shrugged. "Read your history. You Yankees were always a violent people. Whiskey and wars, red meat and revolution."

"Interesting idea." Abberline cleared his throat. "But you were telling us why you thought the Whitechapel murderer is an epileptic."

"That was my second opinion. However, I find it unlikely."

"For what reason?"

"Because of the nature of the crimes. The severe mutilation and dissection of the corpses could not be performed by someone in the throes of violent physical spasms. The use of the knife indicates a steady hand and a calculated purpose."

"Someone has suggested that Chapman's uterus was removed for possible sale to a medical school." Abberline regarded his tea and biscuit with distasteful resignation. "We've checked into that, but no one admits to making such an offer. Besides, it wouldn't account for the other murders."

"Quite true." Forbes Winslow forked a piece of fruit. "And that brings me to the third possibility. The man we're looking for is a monster, possessing both shrewdness and intelligence. He's alert to the danger of detection and goes about his work with diabolical caution. I am not completely ruling out the presence of a delusion or lunar influence, or even an amnesia caused by something other than seizure, but his actual motivation for these crimes may be far worse."

"And what is that?" Abberline asked.

"Sexual mania." Forbes Winslow bit into a cherry. "A perversion of instinct in which physical gratification can be obtained only when accompanied by the infliction of pain and suffering. Sadism, if you will. But not the milder form—mere whipping or ordinary abuse of one's victim. This is a state of acute frenzy, a demented rage which finds satisfaction only in death and torment. Blood-lust, gentlemen. Sheer, hideous blood-lust."

For a moment his auditors were silent, but Abberline's frown was eloquent. Mark glanced down, avoiding Forbes Winslow's gaze. In so doing he discovered something about the man's attire which he hadn't noticed before. His spats and shoes were partially concealed by a pair of heavy brown rubbers.

The alienist followed Mark's stare, then nodded. "Ah yes, I see you're observing my rubbers. I make it a practice to wear them at all times as a precaution against sudden rainfall. It is my considered opinion that dampness is dangerous. Not only does it lay the body open to the onslaught of disease; it can also affect the orderly workings of the mind." He gestured hastily. "But that's of no bearing on our problem. What do you say to my conclusions?"

Now Mark's eyes met Abberline's. There was no doubt as to what the inspector was thinking, and he marveled at the mildness of his reply.

"You've given us a great deal to mull over. Your findings will be carefully considered."

Forbes Winslow smiled. "Thank you, sir. All I ask is that you maintain an open mind. And I trust you do agree that these murders are the work of one man."

"What makes you so sure?" Mark asked.

"In each instance witnesses have come forward to describe a suspect, and the descriptions tally."

"I haven't followed the last case," Mark said. "Did someone claim to have seen Chapman's killer too?"

Forbes Winslow nodded. "I spoke to Mrs. Long, who testified at the inquest. She saw the victim talking to a stranger in Hanbury Street, just before the time of the murder. Her companion was a mustached man who wore dark clothing and a brown deerstalker hat." The alienist jabbed his fork in Mark's direction. "In fact he looked very much like you."

CHAPTER EIGHTEEN

Brazil, A.D. 1550 *Colonists administered civilized punishment to barbaric natives: Sometimes Indians were tied to the mouths of cannon and blown to bits. Instead of tearing victims apart between wild horses, the Indian might be placed in the water of a river and bound between two canoes. The canoes were then paddled furiously in opposite directions. Justice—and waiting alligators—were equally served.*

• • •

"I should have known as much from what they told me," Abberline said. "But I had to be sure. The man's as mad as a hatter."

Hatter. The word echoed in the confines of the carriage moving between drays and barrows in the mid-afternoon sunlight of Aldgate High Road. Mark closed his eyes and the image of the man in the deerstalker hat appeared.

"Asleep, are you?" Abberline asked.

Mark blinked. "No, just thinking. Some of the things he said seemed to make sense."

"Not if you consider the source. I've talked to a dozen of these cranks and Forbes Winslow's the worst of the lot. All that tommyrot about the moon—sheer superstition, if you want my opinion."

"But his theory about sadism may hold water," said Mark. "When you come right down to it, we know very little about the impulses influencing human behavior. A German neurologist named Krafft-Ebing has published a book on the relationship between the sexual urge and cruelty. Rape, for example—"

"No mystery about that." Abberline loosened his vest as he spoke. "A drunken brute who wants a woman will take her by force if necessary. That business about blood-lust or whatever he called it is right out of the penny-dreadfuls. The chap we're after is clever, no doubt of it. But he's not Varney the Vampire or Sweeney Todd, the Demon Barber of Fleet Street."

"Then he said nothing you'd be willing to accept?"

"Only his description of the killer."

"Which fits me," Mark murmured.

"And thousands of others, any one of whom those witnesses might have seen." Abberline smiled bleakly. "I'm afraid I'd need a good deal more to go on before taking you in."

"That's a relief."

"Is it?" For a moment the inspector's eyes narrowed; then he shrugged as though dismissing some secret thought. "All I know is I'm back where I started." He glanced through the carriage window. "And so are you."

The hansom drew up before the entrance to London Hospital. Mark opened the door and climbed out, but Abberline remained seated.

"I'm off to the Yard," he said. "But thanks for your cooperation. And if you see Dr. Trebor, tell him I'll be in touch."

Mark nodded and turned away, hurrying through the entrance. As he passed along the outer lobby he consulted the wall clock. Almost four; he'd be on call again in a few minutes. But first there was a mission to perform. Eva would have to listen to him now if, as he hoped, she was still here.

Luck was with him and he found her in the outpatients' waiting hall; to be exact, in one of the consultation rooms, standing in attendance as Dr. Hume interviewed a patient.

The door was open and Mark halted before it for a moment, unwilling to intrude but trying to catch her eye. Like himself she was listening to the exchange between the slit-eyed surgeon and the dowdily-dressed middle-aged female who lay before him on the examination table. Her left sleeve had been rolled up, baring her arm to the elbow. Mark noted the edema extending from a deep laceration on her wrist; a mass of puffed angry reddish flesh striated with telltale blue-green discoloration. The woman was sobbing, and Hume frowned impatiently.

"Quit your blubbering," he said. "If you had any sense you'd have come sooner, instead of trying to doctor yourself with a poultice. Now it's too late."

"Please, sir." The woman's voice faltered, then rose in a despairing wail. "I don't wants ter be cut—"

"Nonsense." Dr. Hume shook his head. "I tell you the wound's gangrenous. That hand must come off."

"Oh no—"

Ignoring her, Hume turned to Eva. "I'm putting this patient into the receiving ward. Get over to surgery and find out how soon an amputation can be scheduled."

"Yes, Doctor."

Eva turned and moved into the hall.

As she started off, Mark moved out from beside the open door and took her arm.

"Eva—"

She glanced up, startled. "What are you doing here?"

"I must talk to you."

"Can't you see I'm on duty?"

"I know, but this can't wait."

Eva glanced back to make sure they were no longer visible from inside Hume's office, then faced Mark with a frown. "What's so important?"

"You recall the last time we spoke," said Mark. "You told me about your fiancé."

"So?"

"Is he the man you went out with that evening?"

"How would you know about that?"

"Because I saw you. It happened I was in the neighborhood—"

"Happened?" Eva's eyes accused. "You were spying on me!"

"Please, keep your voice down." Mark glanced at the row of patients seated on the benches lining the wall. "What I was doing doesn't matter now. All that's important is that you tell me the truth. The man I saw with you had a mustache. He wore a dark coat and a brown or black deerstalker hat."

"That's right—a fore-and-aft, they call it. But I fail to see why it's any of your concern."

"Don't you read the papers? Don't you know this is how witnesses have described the Whitechapel murderer?"

Mark saw Eva's eyes widen in sudden shock. Quite unwittingly she'd offered an explanation in her own words; she'd failed to see.

For a moment Mark found relief in her reaction, but now her reply dispelled it quickly.

"You're not making sense," she said. "Accusing someone you don't know just on the basis of the way they dress! Half the men in London have mustaches, and this season everyone seems to own one of those caps." She stared at him. "Yourself included."

"Are you accusing me of being the murderer?"

"I'm accusing no one. But when it comes down to that, I really know nothing about you. And I do know the man you suspect couldn't be guilty. On the night of the last killing he was with me."

Mark spoke softly. "All night?"

"Certainly not!" Eva crimsoned. "What right do you have to—"

"Please." Mark gestured in interruption. "I don't mean to offend you. It's just that I'm concerned. Perhaps I've gone overboard on this, but believe me, I'm only thinking of your welfare."

"I understand." Eva sighed, her voice softening. "And I'm not accusing you. But with all these rumors going around one can't help wondering."

Mark nodded. "Then you can realize why I asked about your fiancé. It would help put my mind at ease if you told me who he is, what you know about him."

Eva shook her head. "I can't talk now. I must go over to surgery.

"Later, then. Perhaps this evening."

"I'll be on duty until eleven." Eva smiled and put her hand on his arm. "I appreciate your concern, but I'm quite sure there's no danger."

"It's dangerous for any woman to go about alone at night."

"You needn't worry. Alan will look after me." Then she was gone.

Mark tugged at his mustache. *Alan.* Just who was he and what was his background? Eva was right—many men answered the description of the killer and there was no more reason to suspect Alan than to accuse himself. But that didn't answer his questions, and in spite of her assurance he felt a vague unease. All he could think of now was Forbes Winslow's words. *The man we're looking for is a monster....*

"Beggin' your pardon, sir." The soft voice sounded scarcely more than a whisper, but the words were clear. "I reckon I knows the one you're after."

CHAPTER NINETEEN

Russia, A.D. 1560 *Bored with watching captives turned slowly on a spit and roasted over a slow fire, Czar Ivan IV substituted a huge iron pan in which his victims were fried to death.*

• • •

Mark turned to confront the speaker.

She was one of the patients he'd noticed waiting for consultation, on a bench near the wall; a woman in her early forties, or so he judged, with dark hair and a pallid complexion. She wore a black crepe bonnet, a black skirt, and a black velveteen jacket trimmed with moth-eaten fur. A checkered scarf tied in a bowknot around her neck helped to conceal the telltale wrinkles at her throat. But when she opened her mouth nothing could disguise the gap between her lips; the upper teeth were missing.

The gap was clearly visible now as she spoke again. "I'm not one to pry, but I couldn't 'elp 'earing. That bloke you and the young lady was talking about—the one as did the dirty—"

"You say you know him?"

The woman nodded, her gray eyes furtively scanning the seated patients in the background. Moving closer to Mark, she lowered her voice. "That's for dead sure. I knows 'is name and I knows 'is game, the filthy sod."

Mark frowned. "Why haven't you given your information to the police?"

"Me blow to the crushers?" She shook her head indignantly. "I don't trust a one o' that lot."

"But it's your duty. Don't you want to see this man apprehended?"

"I wants to see 'im strung up by 'is bloody bollocks, if that's what you means." She nodded quickly. "Like you say, it's me duty. The thing of it is, if I go nosin' to the pigs they'd not believe me. But if a respectable gentleman like you was to speak out—"

"You want me to pass the information along, is that it?"

Again the gray eyes darted cautiously toward the patients on the benches behind. "If we can do a deal."

"You needn't worry about keeping your name out of this," Mark said. "I promise I won't reveal my source."

"Fair enough." The woman gave him a knowing smile. "That way you stands to make a packet."

"What do you mean?"

"No need to play the innercent with me. There's a lollopin' fat reward posted for the bugger, and you'll be in line to nab it all."

"If that's what worries you there's no problem," Mark told her. "You're perfectly welcome to the money, I give you my word on it."

"And oo's to say the rozzers don't diddle you out of their perishin' reward in the end?" Her lip curled in scorn above the gap. "So let's not 'ave no more muck about promises. What it comes to is this—you wants the gen on 'is nibs and I wants five couter, now."

"Five pounds?"

"Take it or leave it."

Mark hesitated. "Forgive my bluntness, but what assurance do I have that you'll be telling me the truth?"

The woman shrugged. "That's for you to decide when you 'ears it. If you reckon I'm codding you, there's no need to pay. But if you wants to lay 'ands on the one as did in those pore souls, you'd best listen."

"Very well, then." Mark made his decision. "If you'll come with me we can find a quiet place to talk—"

"Not 'ere!" She glanced around quickly. "Not now."

"Then where and when?"

"You knows the Coach and Four?"

"It's a public house, isn't it?"

"On Commercial Road. I'll be stopping by there tonight."

"I'm on call here until twelve."

"Shank of the evening." The gray eyes narrowed. "There's a room in back where's we can 'ave our privacy. I'll wait for you there."

"Who shall I ask for?"

"Tell Jerry behind the bar you come to see Annie Fitzgerald."

CHAPTER TWENTY

France, A.D. 1572 *During the St. Bartholomew's Day Massacre, the wounded Admiral Coligny was dragged from his bed, hacked to pieces, and pitched out an upstairs window. His head was cut off. Children then chopped off his hands, penis, and testicles, which were sold as souvenirs of the happy occasion. What remained of the corpse was hung from a public scaffold by the feet. Thirty thousand others were slaughtered thereafter in Paris and the provinces.*

• • •

It was just after ten o'clock when Eva finished changing into her street clothes and left the nurses' quarters of the hospital.

As she passed through the outer lobby she looked around quickly to make sure no one observed her departure, but the porter was gone and the clerk at the reception desk didn't bother to take his nose out of the shilling shocker which claimed his attention.

Eva sighed in relief. Telling Mark she wouldn't get off until eleven had been the only solution; had she told the truth he might very well plan to spy on her again, the way he did the other evening. And if so, he'd know she'd lied about being met and probably insist on escorting her home. Then there would be more questions. Eva resented the prospect, even though she realized his concern was prompted only by the best of intentions.

The road to Hell is paved with good intentions. There it was, Papa and his Hell again, but in this instance he was right. Her life was her own and she didn't need questions, no matter what intent lay behind them. Papa could never understand that, and neither would Mark.

Odd how her thoughts kept turning to Mark. Admittedly she found him attractive, yet there was something about him—was it his solicitude for her welfare?—which reminded her of Papa. Perhaps if she came to know him better she'd learn what it was; on the other hand it might be an unpleasant surprise. No, her decision to avoid him was for the best. She'd had enough surprises in her life, both pleasant and unpleasant.

But once outside the hospital, another surprise awaited her.

During the past few weeks Eva had passed by the row of shops across the way on Whitechapel Road without giving them a second glance. There was the inevitable pub near Whitechapel Station, a small confectionary, a dingy chophouse and a rundown storefront housing a waxworks exhibit, but none of these had ever attracted her attention.

Until now.

Now, as she beheld the painted banner emblazoned with blood red lettering. *"Horrible Whitechapel Murders—See the George Yard, Buck's Row, Hanbury Street victims!"*

Surprise number one.

"Shall we?"

She turned at the sound of the voice and confronted the familiar figure.

Surprise number two.

He stood before her, slant eyes inscrutable. "Dr. Hume—"

"Probationer Sloane." He smiled. "Miss Sloane, rather. We're both off duty, are we not?" Jeremy Hume nodded. "I note your interest in that rather garish exhibit over yonder, and I confess to a somewhat vulgar curiosity of my own. Hence my question. Shall we join forces and investigate?"

"Really, Dr. Hume—it's quite late, and I'm tired."

"All the more reason. A bit of relaxation will do you good." He took her arm. "Come along."

Before she could protest further Eva found herself moving with him across the street. Once beside the storefront entrance she managed to speak again. "If you don't mind, I'd prefer some other time."

"No time like the present. I'm quite sure its attractions won't detain you more than a few minutes." His smile was steady, and so was the pressure of his fingers on her arm.

Eva made a hasty decision. Why risk a scene? She must work side by side with this man every day, like it or not, and there was no point in antagonizing him. Besides, she *was* curious.

The elderly woman presiding over a counter inside the doorway offered Dr. Hume a perfunctory smile. Two shillings changed hands and then Eva and her companion were moving down a short corridor past the draped entryway to the chamber beyond.

Chamber. Eva recalled her evening at the music hall and a snatch of song emerged from memory.

….So we all goes orf to the Waxworks
And we sits in the Chamber of 'Orrors

But almost two months had passed since she'd heard those words; things were different now. The song was no longer amusing, and this chamber was real.

On the far side of the dimly-lit room a half-dozen men and their female companions were clustered before a platform against the wall. Obviously these patrons weren't local residents; their clothing identified them as West Enders, most probably down for a night of slumming in wicked Whitechapel. And the proprietor of the exhibit, a cottonhaired old man in a frayed frock coat, was doing his best to give them what they'd come for.

As Eva and Dr. Hume joined the group, the hoarse voice of the showman rasped through the confines of the small room.

"—and 'ere they are, lydies and gentlemen, just the syme as they appeared in life—the 'elpless innercent victims of a gharstly murderer—"

He gestured toward the platform, and over the shoulders of the spectators Eva saw the display.

Again the words of the song echoed. *There's a beautiful statue of Mother there—*

But the trio of figures lining the wall beneath the gaslight's glare were neither beautiful nor motherly. Each had been mounted against a bare wooden board, as though on separate mortuary slabs uptilted for inspection. The old man stood before them, warming to his work.

"—modeled exactically like they looked at the medical ortopsies—"

"Not really," Dr. Hume murmured. "More like a knacker's work don't you think?"

And indeed there was a harrowing resemblance to a butcher's handiwork in the mutilations inflicted on the effigies. Quite obviously they were not actual models of the victims; merely wax dummies that had been hastily bewigged and dressed to roughly resemble the three women, then gashed and daubed with crimson in simulation of their wounds. But even so, there was something unspeakably revolting about the sightless stare of the glassy eyes, the mouths gaping in soundless screams, the white bodies bespattered by a red rain.

The voice went grinding on. "A piterful sight, my friends! Three 'armless creatures, that they were—Martha Turner, struck down and stabbed thirty-nine times by a fiend in 'uman form—'ere in the throat, 'ere in the breast, and 'ere below—"

There were hushed murmurs from the onlookers as the old man continued. But following her initial reaction Eva found nothing disturbing about the dummies themselves; they were, after all, only waxworks, crudely made and clumsily disfigured for show. It was foolish to be moved by the death of what never was alive.

What did disturb her now was the living; the almost feverish intensity of excitement emanating from the spectators as their eyes fastened and feasted on the mock mutilations of the silent shapes before them.

"—Polly Nicholls, she as was done to death in Buck's Row larst month," the old man intoned. "They sy as 'ow 'er abdominabler parts was attacted before 'er throat was cut—"

Eva glanced at Dr. Hume, noting that he too was staring along with the rest, but not at the figures on the platform.

He was staring at her.

"Disgusting, isn't it?" he said. "One can almost feel the reality." Eva didn't reply, pretending to be absorbed by the words of the proprietor.

"—and ere we 'ave Annie Chapman, pore soul! The demon worked 'is will on 'er in 'Anbury Street and near sliced orf the 'ead. Then 'e savaged the body. Out of respect for the lydies present I will refryne from mention of the 'orrid details—"

But Jeremy Hume had no respect. The slant eyes stared and he bent to whisper in Eva's ear. "You know what he's referring to, of course—the excision of the uterus. It's highly probable that he had his way with her first; the sight of blood seems to intensify the venereal spasm."

"Please," Eva murmured.

Hume drew back, shaking his head. "No need to play coy with me. After all, we're both members of the same profession. We can face the truth without such hypocrisy."

"I don't know what you're talking about."

Eva started to step aside, but he gripped her shoulder, his eyes intent on hers. "Ah, but you do! Even the beasts in the slaughterhouse know. When the butchers begin their work the brutes begin to couple in one final frenzy. We're all animals, my dear; we know that death prompts desire. I feel its stirrings every time I take my knife in hand for surgery. You feel it too."

"Let me go—" She tried to break away but his fingers tightened.

"Stop playing the lady." His voice was hoarse. "I've been watching you while I worked, and the signs are there. The eyes grow bright, the respiration quickens. In the presence of death the body comes fully alive, ready for pleasure, just as you and I are ready now. And you *are* ready, aren't you? Your pulse is racing, your lips are moist and full, above and below. Come away with me, let me show you—"

Eva shut out the sound of his words but she couldn't blur her vision. And what she glimpsed in his slitted eyes prompted panic as she wrenched free.

Now his smile shattered into a gargoyle's grimace. He lunged forward, but it was too late. Turning, Eva ran blindly from the room, leaving Hume and the Chamber of 'Orrors behind. But there was no escape from the horror she carried with her—the horror behind Jeremy Hume's smile.

CHAPTER TWENTY-ONE

Germany, A.D. 1604 *A Leipzig professor boasted of signing twenty thousand death warrants for accused witches and wizards. A thousand were executed in a decade, including children between two and four years of age. A judge and jury drank seventeen cans of wine and twenty-six of beer while watching the torture of an eighty-year-old woman.*

• • •

It was well past midnight when Mark turned down Commercial Street. A light rain had just fallen and the cobbled pavements were still wet. Possibly the weather had dampened the spirits as well as the persons of East End pleasure seekers; whatever the reason, Mark encountered few pedestrians and the usual Saturday night carriage traffic had stilled its clamor here. In the distance he heard the ghostly echo of a train whistle rising from the London, Tilbury and Southend tracks, but the street itself stood silent.

Mark quickened his pace, searching for sight of his destination along the rows of darkened shops. It was his resolution, not his feet, which faltered now.

Was it wise to venture here alone? True, he'd given the Fitzgerald woman his word, but perhaps he should have told Abberline of his appointment. On the other hand there was no way of anticipating the inspector's reaction; if he insisted on coming his presence might frighten her away.

Once again Mark found himself regretting Dr. Trebor's absence. He'd know the right thing to do under these circumstances and his company would be welcome in the lonely night.

For a moment he wondered if he should turn back. Suppose it was all a fool's errand? The woman had seemed sincere, yet that proved nothing; even if she told the truth she could be mistaken. If only Trebor were here to advise him!

But Trebor wasn't here. And it was too late to abandon his mission now as the sign of the Coach and Four beckoned directly before him, swaying under a fan of gaslight.

Mark entered, grateful for sudden warmth and the muted murmur of voices; the mere presence of others was reassuring.

To his surprise he found the pub well patronized. Others seemingly shared a need for companionship, and a sizeable group had gathered at the bar. Obviously they were neighborhood residents; the billycock hats of shopkeepers bobbed between the peaked caps of manual laborers and the shawls and bonnets of their women. Conversation rose steadily but there was little laughter and none of the song he recalled from Bank Holiday night at the Angel and Crown.

Mark spied the moonshaped bald head of the publican bending over his taps at the center, and he moved to the bar before him. The moon rose. "Evenin', sir."

"Jerry?"

"That's me name." The bartender smiled, but his eyes were wary. "What's yer pleasure?"

"I'm looking for Annie Fitzgerald."

The smile faded but the eyes were intent. "You a crusher?"

"No, this has nothing to do with the police. I'm a friend of hers."

"Not bloody likely." Jerry's smile returned, but now it hinted of contempt. "Seein' as how you don't even know 'er rightful name"

"I don't understand. She said she'd be waiting. I was to ask for Annie Fitzgerald—"

The bartender nodded in sudden comprehension. "Now I sees the light. You come for a bit o' business, eh?"

"In a manner of speaking, yes."

"Well, then—yer in the right church but the wrong pew. She was 'ere a while back, but she did a bunk."

"How long ago did she leave?"

The bartender shrugged. "I disremember." He turned to address a dwarfish man wearing a soiled butcher's apron who nursed a beer beside Mark at the bar. "Shorty, old cock—the gent 'ere's inquirin' after Long Liz. You 'appen to take notice when she shoved off?"

The small man nodded. "Past 'arf an 'our ago, I makes it. I sawr 'er blabbin' wiv that foreign-lookin' chap what come in a while before. Figgered 'im for a masher, but 'e didn't seem to take 'er fancy, 'cause next I noticed she gives' im a shove and goes poppin' out the door. In one 'ell of a 'urry, too, like she was late for midnight mass."

"The man she was talking to," Mark said. "Where is he?"

The short customer squinted toward the line of patrons at the bar, then shook his head. "Don't see 'im. Must be 'e follered 'er."

Jerry glanced at Mark. "No 'arm done," he said. "Once she does 'er business she'll be back, most likely. What say you 'ave a lush while yer waitin'—"

But Mark was already heading for the door.

The night air was damp and he felt the sudden shock of cold wind against his cheeks as he scanned the empty shadows of the deserted street. The chill that rippled along his spine wasn't the work of the wind; it came from within, from the memory of the short man's words. *"A foreign-lookin' chap. Must be 'e follered 'er."*

Mark glanced to his left. That was the direction he'd come from, and he'd seen no sign of anyone then. So the woman had probably gone off to the right.

He started on that route, pausing at the next intersection, Backchurch Lane, to stare into the dark depths beyond. Nothing moved in the narrow passageway between the grimy walls of the huddled houses and the only sound he heard was the lonely keening of the wind.

Mark moved on quickly, but pace alone was not enough to account for the way his heart was pounding, and the cold not cause enough to set him trembling. Now it was the woman's voice that murmured in his ears. *"I reckon I knows the one you're after. I knows 'is name and I knows 'is game."*

He came to Berner Street and there the inner voice faded, drowned in sound that rose from his right. He peered through darkness and found its source; a cluster of shadowy shapes milling around the open wooden gateway beside a lighted house.

Mark hastened toward them and the babbling rose about him. Bearded men muttered to one another before the opening but their excited interchange, in German and Yiddish, told him nothing. It was only in their faces that he found a common language; eyes and expressions were eloquent with fear.

He pushed his way through the group before the gateway and blinked as lanternlight flared from the narrow courtyard beyond. More bearded figures moved within, but among them were several cleanshaven men in police uniforms. Now two of them approached, waving their bull's-eye lanterns.

"Clear out, the lot of you—out, you 'ear?"

The crowd retreated, murmuring in protest, and Mark fell back with the rest as the officers drew the double gates shut before them.

But as they did so he was given a final glimpse of what lay inside the courtyard—the body of a woman. He recognized the soiled black skirt and shabby velveteen jacket trimmed with moth-eaten fur, recognized the checkered scarf tied in a bowknot around her neck.

It was only the garments that identified her now, for the face leering up in the lanternlight had changed. The brown curls framing it were soaked with scarlet, the pale complexion was spattered with streaks of red, and from the slashed and severed throat a burst of blood flowed over the cobblestones.

Numb with nausea, Mark turned away. Now whistles screeched in the distance and a carriage jerked to a halt at the intersection. Its occupants emerged—two men in business suits and another wearing a frockcoat and carrying a medical bag. From the street beyond a group of police constables converged, moving toward the gate. It opened now to admit the party, but Mark didn't look back. He elbowed his way through the surging, jostling throng, sickened by the sound of voices shrilling and thrilling with eager expectation, and by the sight of faces grimacing in ghoulish glee.

Blood-lust. Dr. Forbes Winslow's words held a new meaning for him now. But his diagnosis didn't apply to the killer alone; the mob that hovered here was possessed by the same craving. Once the predator has struck, the vultures gather—

"Mark!"

The voice came from behind and he halted at the head of the street, glancing back at the figure advancing from the gateway as the wooden barrier swung shut. Now Dr. Trebor's face was discernible under the lamplight at the intersection.

"I thought I saw you in that crowd," Trebor said. "What brings you here?"

Quickly Mark told him of his errand and its consequences. The older man listened in silence, then nodded. "She must have been killed shortly after leaving the pub. Someone claims to have seen her with a man here in Berner Street only a short time before the body was discovered, or so they tell me."

Mark met his glance. "How did you happen to get inside the courtyard?"

"I was passing by on Commercial Street when I heard shouting. The body had just been discovered by a coster driving his barrow and pony into the yard. Apparently this man—Diemschutz, or some such name—is the steward of the International Working Men's Educational Club, which meets in the building on the right. It's one of those socialist groups."

"I noticed there were a lot of foreigners in the crowd," Mark said.

"Some of them live in the cottages along the street. They heard the commotion and came running out. I got there just as the first constable arrived. The corpse was still warm. The throat had been cut but I didn't note any further mutilations. Most likely the killer heard Diemschutz's cart in the street and took off unnoticed as he drove in."

"You didn't stay to examine the body further?"

Dr. Trebor shrugged. "They'd already sent for the police surgeons. As far as anyone knew, I was just another member of the crowd that got into the courtyard before the gates were closed. I saw no reason to get involved. It would only mean another night without sleep, and I'm exhausted enough, what with the long trip—"

"You were away all week?"

"That's right." Trebor spoke quickly. "A business matter. I just got into town before midnight."

Mark held silent for a moment, sorting his thoughts. The face in the lamplight seemed haggard indeed, but was fatigue the sole cause? And if he'd just returned from an extended journey, where was his luggage?

Trebor stared at him. "Is something wrong?"

"I was just wondering. About your bags—"

"They're at my digs. I meant to unpack, but I was too tired."

"Yet you went out again, at this hour?"

"I felt the need for a bit of food before retiring, since there was no dining car on the train." Trebor broke off, frowning. "But why all these questions? Surely you don't think—"

But I do think, Mark told himself. Perhaps Trebor was telling the truth; perhaps coincidence accounted for his presence here. Unless his presence had a purpose.

Suppose the murderer hadn't taken off when he was interrupted? Suppose there wasn't time to run, only moments enough to conceal himself somewhere in the courtyard and avoid discovery? Then, as the others arrived, he could step forth unnoticed as just another onlooker. An onlooker like Dr. Trebor—

"Answer me!" Trebor's voice was harsh. "Answer me!"

But the answer that came rose from another source. Both men turned at the sound of pounding feet against the pavement, both stared at the bowler-hatted intruder who ran past them into the crowd before the gates. And both men heard his hoarse cry echo through the night.

"Another one!" he shouted. "There's been another woman murdered in Mitre Square!"

CHAPTER TWENTY-TWO

New England, A.D. 1623 *Colonists reported that the Indians "tormente men in ye most bloodie maner that may be; fleaing some alive with ye shells of fishes, cutting off ye members and joynts of others by peesmeale, and broiling on ye coals, eat ye collops of their flesh in their sight whilst they live; with other cruelties horrible to be related."*

• • •

Police Constable Watkins found the body.

At one-thirty he'd passed through Mitre Square on patrol; the tea warehouses lining it on two sides were dark, the dwellings facing them were empty and the square itself was deserted. Fastening his lantern to his belt he continued on his rounds. Watkins kept his eyes and ears open as he walked but all was quiet. Nothing to see, nothing to hear, and the beat was a short one; fifteen minutes later he had already retraced his route and returned to the square.

It was then, as he entered, that he saw the woman lying on her back in the shadows of the southwest corner.

She wore a black straw bonnet over her dark auburn hair, a black cloth jacket, a thin white vest, a linsey-woolen skirt and a dark green print dress with a pattern of daisies beneath the outer clothing. Brown ribbed stockings and a pair of men's laced boots encased her feet, while a piece of a coarse white apron and a bit of ribbon were tied loosely around her neck. Obviously she'd taken precautions to protect herself from the chill of the night.

But nothing had protected her from the cold steel of the knife.

She lay on her back with both arms extended, the left leg straight and the right bent at the knee. Her upturned face was a Halloween horror; part of the nose had been cut off, the lobe of her right ear nearly severed and both lower eyelids were nicked. Her cheeks, jaw and lips were gashed, and the throat beneath opened in a yawning crimson cavity from ear to ear.

The knife had not halted there. Her upper garments bunched above her breasts to expose the naked flesh below. She'd been disemboweled; the intestines were pulled out and draped over her right shoulder, with a detached segment lying beside the left arm. The pavement beneath the body was bathed in blood.

Police Constable Watkins wasted no time. Remembering there was a night watchman on duty inside one of the tea warehouses he ran over and banged on the door, then pushed it open as the man appeared. "For God's sake, mate, come to my assistance," he cried. "There's another woman cut to pieces."

The Acting Police Commissioner for the City of London was Major Henry Smith. At two o'clock he was notified of the crime at the Cloak Lane station; by the time he arrived on the scene with three detectives and an inspector the hunt was under way. In the hours that followed a series of shocking discoveries were made.

The first surprise came when Smith viewed the corpse. In spite of the mutilations, detectives identified her as a woman who'd been found lying drunk in Aldgate Street earlier that evening and taken to the Bishopgate police station. Sober again shortly after midnight she was released from her cell and sent on her way. Sometime within the next forty-five minutes she'd met her murderer.

Major Smith took over. After Dr. Blackwell had arrived and examined the body, he ordered the corpse removed to the city mortuary. The contents of the victim's pockets offered no immediate clues, and Smith was much more interested now in tracing the killer's possible escape route. He sent his men off to search the surrounding area, knocking on doors and stopping every passerby in the streets.

One of the detectives made a discovery; he came rushing back and led Smith to confront surprise number two.

In a narrow close off Dorset Street a public sink bubbled with red-streaked water. A few telltale drops still remained when Smith reached it. "The murderer must have stopped here on the run to wash his hands," the detective said. "The way I see it—"

He was interrupted as another searcher came up to Major Smith.

"You're wanted over in Goulston Street, sir," he shouted. "Constable Long's just found something there."

What he'd found was a piece of the victim's white apron, soaked with blood. Dr. Blackwell had noticed that a piece had been missing, obviously hacked off by the killer's knife. And here it was, lying beside a passageway—surprise number three.

But as Major Smith appeared on the scene another surprise claimed his full attention.

Behind the spot where the bloodstained piece of apron lay, a dark doorway loomed. On its black dado wall were three lines scrawled in chalk. Smith stared at the message.

The Juwes are not the
men that will be blamed
for nothing.

The words were still there at five o'clock when Sir Charles Warren arrived. Major Smith waited for him with City Police Inspector MacWilliams and two detectives.

Warren studied the message through his monocle, then scowled. "Rub it out," he said.

Major Smith had suffered enough surprises over the past few hours, and this one was the final straw. "But Sir Charles—this is important evidence! I've ordered one of my men to fetch a camera, and as soon as it's daylight we'll photograph the writing—"

"Daylight be damned!" Warren plucked his monocle free and gestured with it. "We can't wait any longer. There's a Sunday morning market at Petticoat Lane, and the costers will be up and about in a few minutes now. If any of them catch sight of a message like this we'll have race riots on our hands."

"Might I make a suggestion, sir?" One of the detectives spoke softly. "If it's the Jews you're worried about, couldn't we just rub out the first line? Maybe only the one word—"

Warren shook his head. "I'll not take chances. Wipe it out, man—all of it!"

The detective hesitated and Major Smith stepped forward.

"Begging your pardon, Sir Charles, but I'm in charge here and I refuse to permit this."

"Blast your permission!" Warren roared. "You city police have authority over Mitre Square, but this street is under metropolitan jurisdiction. I give the orders here, and I want that writing removed—immediately!"

The detective glanced at his superior, but Major Smith made no sign. Warren turned to Inspector MacWilliams and the other detective; neither man moved.

"Insubordination, is it?" Warren's face was grim. "If that's your game, I'll wipe out the bloody thing myself!"

And he did.

But no one could wipe out the message published in the papers.

"TWO MORE EAST END ATROCITIES," was the headline in *The Daily Chronicle*. "HORRIBLE MURDER OF A WOMAN IN COMMERCIAL ROAD EAST. A WOMAN MURDERED AND MUTILATED IN ALDGATE. GREAT EXCITEMENT."

Among those excited was John Montague Druitt, a barrister who tutored at a boy's school in Blackheath. He also maintained chambers at King's Bench Walk in London, and frequently spent weekends there when not playing cricket. It was a healthful outdoor sport, beneficial to the mind and spirit, and the doctors recommended it as an excellent remedy for melancholia.

But what did they know of melancholia? What did they know about how it felt to fail at law, fail at teaching, fail even in normal relationships with the fair sex?

Druitt read the news and the morning sunlight disappeared as angry clouds of memory descended. He'd set up practice here with no success; he'd turned to teaching and that wasn't working out well either, not with those unkind rumors circulating about him and some of the younger boys. As for women, it was they who had failed him. The female is indeed deadlier than the male; he remembered the cutting remarks, the piercing laughter, the wounds of rejection. Even his own mother had failed him, for the recent news of her confinement in a mental institution was like the stab of a knife.

Sometimes he tried to put all this out of his mind, and lately it seemed to him that he'd succeeded only too well. There were gaps in his memory, whole days and nights he couldn't quite account for. Last night, for instance; where had he been last night?

Was it all a dream? Like the trip to Venice where the funeral barge floated on the water—a black gondola gliding through the oozing slime of the canal?

Melancholia. That was his mother's affliction, that's why they put her away, and now there were times when she couldn't remember. Was that to be his fate?

Somehow the accounts in the newspaper brought back the failures and the fears, but last night was still a blank. Why did he keep thinking about knives?

Reading about the murders, John Montague Druitt wondered if he was going mad....

A Polish refugee named Severin Klosowski read the paper too but he was not mad. To rise to the rank of *feldscher*, a doctor's assistant in the army of His Imperial Highness, Czar of Russia, calls for the keenest intelligence, and his was razor-sharp. Just because his command of English was not yet perfect, just because he'd been reduced to odd jobs of barbering, these stupid clods in Whitechapel took him for a fool; even the whores laughed at him. But there were ways to pay them back for their ridicule. They might mistrust his appearance, his bushy mustache and foreign dress, and make fun of his accent, but he knew a trick or two. Like the little one he played, showing them two polished farthings in the dark, which they mistook for sovereigns. In the end he always got what he was after; one way or another, he had his revenge.

No, he was not mad, merely clever. More clever than all the whores and all the police put together. It was just that these newspapers made trouble for him with their stories about suspicious foreigners. Perhaps the time had come to think about moving on. If he could speak the language better maybe he would change his name and go to America. He was already learning American slang and that would help. There were a few whores less in London now, but America was a different story—didn't they call it the Land of Opportunity?

Yes, a clever man could find opportunities there, of that he was certain. Meanwhile he must be careful. Careful and clever. No one would ever get the best of Severin Klosowski—not if he took pains to sharpen his wits the way a skillful *feldscher* sharpens his knife....

There were some who missed the morning newspapers because they slept. Dr. Trebor was one of them; he didn't get around to reading a report until late in the afternoon. And it was then, in the *Evening News*, that he read the story which sent him into shock.

"The Central News Agency gives us the following information, namely, that on Thursday last a letter bearing the EC postmark directed in red ink, was delivered at their agency.

September 25, 1888

Dear Boss,

I keep on hearing the police have caught me, but they won't fix me just yet. I have laughed when they look so clever and talk about being on the right track. That joke about Leather Apron gave me real fits. I am down on whores and I shan't quit ripping them till I do get buckled. Grand work the last job was. I gave the lady no time to squeal. How can they catch me now. I love my work and want to start again. You will soon hear of me and my funny little games. I saved some of the proper red stuff in a ginger beer bottle over the last job to write with but it went thick like glue and I can't use it. Red ink is fit enough I hope ha, ha, ha! The next job I do I shall clip the lady's ears and send them to the police officers just for jolly. Wouldn't you keep this letter back until I do a bit more work; then give it out straight. My knife is so nice and sharp, I want to get right to work if I get the chance. Good luck.

Yours truly,

Jack the Ripper

Don't mind me giving the trade name. Wasn't good enough to post this before I got all the red ink off my hands, curse it. They say I'm a doctor. Ha! ha! ha!

Dr. Trebor wasn't amused.

Neither was Mark, who read the same story in his own newspaper that evening. His dismay was not lessened as he scanned the rest of the account.

According to the story, another message—this time on a postcard bearing the cancellation stamp "London E. October 1," had been received today. It too had been written in red ink, in the same style of handwriting.

I was not codding, dear old Boss, when I gave you the tip. You'll hear about Saucy Jack's work tomorrow. Double event this time. Number One squealed a bit. Couldn't finish straight off. Had no time to get ears for police. Thanks for keeping the last letter back till I got to work again.

Jack the Ripper

Mark remembered last night only too well. It *had* been a "double event," just as the postcard promised. And the killer "couldn't finish" the disfigurement of the first victim. He "had no time to get ears for police"—but the paper stated that one of the second victim's ears was nearly cut off.

None of these details appeared in the morning press, but the card had already been mailed. Unless one of the police or onlookers was a practical joker, this message came from the murderer himself.

Jack the Ripper. So now they knew his name.

Mark shuddered....

Others saw the same story, but they didn't shudder.

Dr. Forbes Winslow prayed.

Sir Charles Warren cursed.

And Jeremy Hume laughed.

CHAPTER TWENTY-THREE

Hispaniola, A.D. 1630 *The buccaneers improvised new tortures by using whatever materials were at hand. A hemp caulking material called oakum was highly flammable; it could be stuffed into a prisoner's mouth or other bodily openings and then set afire.*

• • •

Sitting beside Dr. Trebor in the stuffy little room at the Guilders Green mortuary, Mark wondered if he was experiencing *déjà vu.* The inquest underway seemed familiar, as though he'd heard the same proceedings before.

That much was true. Only a few days ago he and Trebor were seated in a very similar chamber in Vestry Hall, attending the inquest of Elizabeth Stride.

This, it was disclosed, had been Annie Fitzgerald's real name. "Long Liz," the first victim of the double event, used an alias, like so many others plying her trade.

And just prior to the time of her murder, three witnesses, one of them a police constable, testified they'd seen her talking to a man in Berner Street. One took no notice of him at the time, but another said he was stout, dressed in a cutaway coat and a round peaked cap. The constable noted that he had carried a newspaper parcel about eighteen inches long and six inches wide, and wore a dark felt deerstalker hat.

The doctor in charge concluded that the killer probably caught his victim by her scarf, pulling it backwards and cutting her throat while she was falling or when she was on the ground, to avoid the spurting blood.

Now Mark was hearing it all again. The second victim had also used other names—Kate Kelly and Kate Conway—but here she was identified as Catherine Eddowes.

Once more there was a witness; this time a man named Joseph Lavende saw the deceased with a stranger just off Mitre Square shortly before her death. He said the woman's companion wore a cloth cap with a peak.

Again the doctors agreed that the mutilations occurred after death, with the victim on the ground so that there'd be less chance of staining the murderer's clothing with blood.

As the medical testimony droned on, Mark made a mental resolve to discard his deerstalker cap, and he wondered if Dr. Trebor had formed a similar resolution. But then he wondered about many other things concerning the older man. Since the night of the double slaying they had never discussed Trebor's mysterious absence during the previous week, nor his sudden reappearance at the scene of the first crime. Only one thing seemed certain; if Trebor had been at Berner Street when it occurred, he couldn't possibly be involved in what happened at Mitre Square a half-mile away.

But did Inspector Abberline know that?

Mark glanced toward the rotund figure seated on his right at the end of the row. Abberline was ignoring him; he seemed totally absorbed in listening as Dr. Brown, the police surgeon, answered the questions of Mr. Crawford.

"I understand you found certain portions of the body removed," Crawford said.

"Yes." Dr. Brown consulted his notes. "The uterus was cut away with the exception of a small portion, and the left kidney was cut out. Both these organs were absent and have not been found."

Over the murmurs of the coroner's jury, Mr. Crawford continued. "Would you consider that the person who inflicted the wounds possessed great anatomical skill?"

Dr. Brown nodded. "He must have had a good deal of knowledge as to the position of the abdominal organs and the way to remove them. The way in which the kidney was cut out showed that it was done by somebody who knew what he was about."

Mark stiffened. Out of the corner of his eye he saw Abberline's head turn swiftly; now the inspector was staring directly at him and Dr. Trebor.

And when the inquest concluded he was still staring. The coroner's verdict was a simple one: "Willful murder by some person unknown."

But the look in the inspector's eyes gave Mark the uneasy feeling that Abberline didn't agree.

CHAPTER TWENTY-FOUR

Turkey, A.D. 1635 *Murad IV, Sultan of the Ottoman Empire, had the royal privilege of killing ten innocent subjects a day. When riding abroad, he was accompanied by an executioner carrying clubs, knives, nails, and other useful implements of his trade. The Sultan himself bore a bow or an arquebus to shoot down anyone who crossed his path. He hated smoking and forbade it in public; anyone found disobeying could be executed. One of his wives and a gardener were discovered smoking. He had their legs chopped off in a public ceremony and let them bleed to death.*

• • •

Inspector Abberline's stomach was at it again, growling away like a dog worrying a bone.

Didn't it ever get tired? *He* was tired; weary of walking, fatigued by constant questioning, exhausted from scribbling notes and writing endless reports, but somehow his stomach found the strength to churn. His stomach and his brain, revolving over the events of the past few days.

The inquests had solved nothing. Nothing that would lead to the discovery of the murderer, nothing that would stop the clamor in the press and the turmoil in the streets.

How many suspects had been arrested since the night of the double killings—arrested to save them from angry mobs that recognized the Ripper every time they saw a suspicious-looking stranger? All were investigated and all were eventually released as innocent, but this didn't end the uproar.

How many rewards had been posted, how many petitions sent to the Prime Minister and the Queen herself? Nothing had come of that either, except more panic.

How many witnesses had offered tips which had to be checked out, wild rumors about crazy foreigners who muttered threats against prostitutes or staggered into pubs with blood on their hands? How many knives were found in the streets, only to be discarded as evidence because none of them matched medical testimony about the type of weapon used? How many false leads had he pursued? How many orders had he given to question local residents, search the premises of crowded doss-houses and deserted buildings?

Police procedure—what a farce! The whole system was hopelessly out-of-date. No wonder the murderer had slipped through their fingers. And speaking of fingers, why didn't they adopt this Frenchie's—Adolphe Bertillion's—new system of fingerprinting every suspect? A chap named Spearman had been trying to interest the Home Office in the idea, but of course nobody listened. All they did was keep lists of convicted criminals. Much good that was, with the files a bloody shambles. The Home Office was nine months behind in forwarding them to Scotland Yard, and when they came the physical descriptions were no damned use to anyone. How did it help to read that a missing suspect had "a scar on his cheek"? You had to know what kind of a scar, and which cheek it was on. Could be his bloody arse-cheek for all the good it did.

He was tired, dead tired of the whole business, and that went for the meetings as well. Meetings like this one here in Robert Anderson's office.

Abberline sighed and his stomach echoed agreement. He'd tried so long to see the new assistant commissioner, but now that he finally found himself in his presence it scarcely seemed worth the wait.

And Robert Anderson was tired too. He sat hunched over the desk, his face pale and his eyes staring blankly at the litter of documents heaped before him.

Only Sir Charles Warren maintained his customary vigor. Monocle glinting in the sunlight, he paced before the open window, a one-man parade.

"I tell you time is of the essence! The newspapers accuse us of incompetence, they call for a departmental investigation, they demand an inquiry in Parliament. Do you know what that means? It's our blood they're crying for now, not the killer's!"

Anderson sighed. "We're doing all we can. We've put out descriptions of the suspect and photographic reproductions of those letters. We've talked with scores of known prostitutes and informers. No possible source of information stands neglected. Police in other cities are cooperating. And we've requested the heads of every asylum in the country to furnish descriptions of violent patients who have been freed or escaped from custody at the time of the murders."

"All you're saying is that you're asking questions." Warren shook his head. "What do you intend to do—send a bloody questionnaire to everybody in London? It won't wash!"

"I have extra constabulary posted all over the district," Anderson said. "I've canceled leaves, redoubled patrols—"

"Much good that does us! We had virtually half the entire force on duty the night of the double event, but the cunning devil gave us the slip all the same."

Common sense told Abberline to keep silent but the stirring in his stomach prompted him to speak. "Maybe he didn't."

Warren glared at him but Abberline continued.

"I've a report from one of our men in Spitalfields," he said. "Police Constable Robert Spicer was on his beat there that night. Shortly before two o'clock he saw a prostitute named Rosy talking to a mustached man carrying a brown bag. He was well-dressed— fancy coat, high hat, gold watch and chain. He refused to give an account of himself, so Spicer took them both in to Commercial Street station. Mind you, we had eight inspectors on special duty there, and they had news of the two murders just a short time earlier. Spicer told them what he suspected but the man raised a row, said he was a doctor down from Brixton, and what right did they have to arrest a respectable physician just for standing on the pavement talking to a friend? The upshot of it was, they let him go. Let him go scot free, mind you, without even opening his bag—"

"Humbug!" Sir Charles Warren's glare intensified. "I happen to have heard that report myself and it's perfectly obvious what our fellow was up to. The whore said he gave her two shillings for her services and she had no complaints." He removed his monocle, its polished surface glittering in a gesturing hand. "You know my orders. It's up to the police to deal with those whose actions warrant suspicion. But on no account do I want them making trouble by molesting decent citizens."

Abberline faced him now. "But how do you expect us to tell the difference unless we investigate?"

"Blast your investigations! While your men were wasting time asking questions, that murdering lunatic was running loose. Now he's writing letters to the newspapers and cracking jokes, making the whole force look like a pack of fools. All the questions and all the patrols won't stop him if he decides to kill again. And mark my words—he will!"

"Gentlemen—" Anderson's interruption came quickly. "There's no point in crying over spilt milk, or spilt blood, if I may say so. We're here to decide upon a course of action." He glanced at Abberline. "Sir Charles has raised an issue we cannot afford to ignore. Do you agree that the murderer may commit further crimes of this nature?"

Abberline shifted uneasily in his chair. "Hard to say. On the basis of the threats in those two letters, it's a possibility."

"And one we can't afford to overlook." Robert Anderson nodded. "Now I put it to you—in the unfortunate event that another murder can be anticipated, just what steps do you propose to prevent it?"

"I'm not giving up hope yet, sir. There are still several lines of inquiry I'll be following up in the next few days. With any luck we may lay hands on our man before he strikes again."

"And if you're not successful?" Anderson pressed on without waiting for a reply. "What plans have you made to deal with the matter?"

Abberline shrugged. "It depends on circumstances. Rest assured we'll be taking every precaution."

"Not good enough." Warren shook his head. "Your methods have been flat-out failures. The time has come to try a new approach. And if there is another murder we must be prepared to apprehend the killer immediately. We must locate him while he's still in the vicinity of his crime, hunt him down before he can make another escape."

Anderson glanced at him, frowning. "But how do you intend to do that?"

Sir Charles Warren affixed the monocle to his eye. "The same way I'd track down any animal," he said. "I'll use bloodhounds."

CHAPTER TWENTY-FIVE

Germany, A.D. 1640 *From its inception in 1618, the Thirty Years' War grew to a point where it involved six armies of mercenaries bent on rape and plunder. Hundreds of towns and major cities were razed to the ground, their entire civilian population massacred to the last man, woman, and child. As the war dragged on, plague and famine decimated the peasantry. They ate their livestock, then their pets, and finally the very grass left unburned. Corpses were cut down from the gallows and bodies dug up from graves to be devoured, and a mother confessed that she had eaten her baby. The dogs of war were loosed; in the end, they were halted only by starvation.*

• • •

At seven o'clock on a foggy morning, Inspector Abberline stood shivering on a knoll in Regent's Park, cursing the London *Times*.

The newspaper was responsible for this, he was sure of it now. That's where Warren must have picked up his wild idea, from an editorial which told of using bloodhounds to track down a murderer at Blackburn twelve years ago. It had worked then, the paper remarked, so why not try the method now?

Because Blackburn isn't Whitechapel, that's why, Abberline told himself. Tracking a man in the countryside is one thing; trying to run him down in the streets of a swarming slum is quite another matter. He could have told them that, but they didn't ask. And they wouldn't listen. Once he'd proposed the notion Sir Charles Warren became a bit of a bloodhound himself, hot on the scent of favorable publicity. It was Warren who contacted a dog breeder in Scarborough and arranged for him to bring two of the beasts up to London for a trial run.

So here they were now; Sir Melville MacNaughten, Warren, and burly bewhiskered Brough the breeder with his hounds, out in the biting cold of the fogbound park at this ungodly hour.

Abberline stamped his feet against the hoar-frosted ground, his steaming breath mingling with swirls of fog. A few paces away the dogs strained at the leash, eager for freedom. They were formidable-looking creatures; Champion Barnaby's red eyes and yellowish, pointed fangs hinted at a disposition even more irascible than Warren's himself. And Burgho, the younger dog, was a huge black and tan specimen with a head at least a foot long, most of it running to muzzle.

MacNaughten, Warren and Brough stood behind them conversing in low tones. Abberline couldn't overhear what they were saying but he felt no desire to join them; the further he kept away from those animals the better. Home in bed was the best place to be right now, yet he had to come here. One must always allow for the off chance, and perhaps these monsters might prove of some use after all. Seeing them now, he could only pity the man they might succeed in hunting down.

But where was that man?

A figure emerged from the mist behind him and the inspector turned to see a uniformed constable approaching. He carried a jacket bundled under his arm and as he reached the group he unfolded it. For a moment Abberline thought he detected a fishy odor mingling with the damp chill of the fog; then, as he moved up to the others, confirmation came.

"Here it is, sir." The constable addressed Warren. "Straight from the fish market, just like you ordered. Fresh blood's still on it."

Sir Charles Warren's nostrils flared appreciatively, as though he were sniffing roses. "Excellent!" He turned to Brough. "Shall we let the dogs have a whiff of this?"

The trainer nodded and Warren gestured to the constable. Holding the reeking jacket at arm's length, the man made a gingerly approach to the two hounds. Quivering with excitement, the beasts snuffled, low growls rumbling deep within their throats. Brough's arms tensed with effort as he gripped the double leash to restrain them from leaping at the bloodstained coat. "Easy now, that'll be enough," he said. "They've got the scent."

The constable needed no further urging; he stepped back, glancing timorously at Warren.

"What next, sir? Shall I put it on?"

Abberline blinked at him. *Good God, don't tell me he's volunteering to let himself be tracked! The man's a fool—*

"Wait!" Sir Charles Warren gestured peremptorily. "It's my responsibility. I'll wear the jacket." And reaching for the garment he slipped his arms into the sleeves.

Abberline stared. So *he's* the fool! One had to admire his courage even while realizing it was prompted by a hunger for acclaim if the experiment succeeded.

"Very good, sir." Brough nodded at Warren. "Are you quite sure you know what to do?"

"Certainly. I'm to go off and find a suitable hiding place at the far end of the park. Give me a five minute start, then release your dogs. Mind you, stay as close to them as you can. I've no desire to be attacked by the brutes."

"No danger of that," Brough said. "I assure you they've been trained to stand at point once they have you at bay."

"Assurances be damned." Warren fumbled in his trouser pocket and produced an army revolver. "In case you've misled me, your beasts will have to answer to this."

He turned to MacNaughten. "Five minutes, now. I'll thank you to keep track of the time."

MacNaughten took a watch from his vest and consulted it. "Exactly seven-ten."

"Then I'm off."

"Good luck," Brough said.

"Good hunting." Sir Charles Warren tightened his chimney-pot hat against his forehead, then broke into a run as he started away down the slope. A moment later he disappeared into the gray silence.

Abberline stood beside MacNaughten, breathing deeply as the fish odor faded like the figure in the fog.

"What do you think?" he said. "Wouldn't it have been wiser to wait until this clears away?"

MacNaughten shrugged. "Might as well give it a real test. After all, the fog's likely to be just as thick some nights in Whitechapel this time of year."

"I still say they won't find him."

"Never fear." Brough glanced at the hounds as they tugged impatiently on leash. "These two are best of breed. I'll back them against all comers, even the Cubans trained for slave hunting." He nodded at the black and tan dog. "Look at that muzzle. You won't find such flews in your ordinary bloodhound. These specimens were bred for scenting power. Once they're turned loose at the scene of the crime, your Jack the Ripper won't stand a chance."

Abberline sighed. "I hope you're right. But Regent's Park's not exactly crowded this time of morning, and there's nothing to confuse the trail. The East End is packed with people every night, and what with fishmongers and butchers and slaughtermen wearing bloody clothing, it's likely your dogs could be confused."

Brough scowled. "Barnaby and Burgho never make mistakes. You'll see." He turned to MacNaughten. "How much longer to go?"

MacNaughten squinted at his watch. "Less than a minute. Get ready."

The trainer knelt and started to unbuckle the leash ends attached to the bloodhounds' collars. "Hold it now, lads," he murmured. "Ah, that's it, me hearties. Got the scent, have you? Then—off you go!"

And the dogs bounded forward with a rush that nearly tumbled Brough to the ground.

He rose, gesturing to his companions. "Come along, before we lose them!"

Abberline, MacNaughten and the constable started down the slope, trotting in the wake of the trainer, but their efforts were foredoomed. Within seconds the bloodhounds had vanished into the fog.

"Now what?" MacNaughten muttered. "You should have let them track on leash."

"Hardly a fair test, sir," said Brough. "Slows them down. Best to show you how quickly they work on their own." He gestured toward the white wall of mist ahead. "Carry on."

The trio stumbled down the frosty incline behind him. Brough set a fast pace, and Abberline found himself panting with unaccustomed exertion as he floundered amid a tangle of trees and shrubbery in their path. "Not so fast," he wheezed. "This damned fog's so thick we're likely to lose each other."

"Join hands," MacNaughten suggested.

It wasn't much help. The undergrowth impeded their progress and they had to break grip to circle the trees which appeared abruptly before them.

"Where are the dogs?" Abberline panted. "I don't hear them."

"You will, once they have the quarry at bay." Brough grasped his hand. "Stay with it, sir."

Their feet thudded across flatland now, and Abberline noted with grim satisfaction that the others were breathing heavily too.

"What's taking them so long?" he gasped.

Brough shrugged. "Not to worry. Remember, this is clean-shoe tracking—it makes for slower going to work by scent alone."

MacNaughten cast a dubious glance at the trainer. "I haven't the faintest idea where we are," he said. "Perhaps the dogs are lost too."

But now a mournful howling rose faintly through the mist. "Hark to that!" Brough grinned triumphantly. "They've got him."

"But where?" Abberline looked up as the sound echoed through the impenetrable curtain of gray surrounding them. "Which way do we go?"

"Straight ahead." Brough started forward at a swifter pace. "They'll guide us."

And when they moved on the baying grew louder, rising to an ululating crescendo as a tangled thicket loomed to their left.

"Over here!" Brough cried.

Releasing Abberline's hand, he pointed toward a cluster of bushes. Now Barnaby and Burgho were both audible and visible; they stood trembling before the thicket, howling with ferocious eagerness to leap upon their prey.

"Good lads!" Brough hurried towards his champions, then knelt between them, hands gripping their collars tightly. "Good lads!"

At his touch the dogs fell silent. He peered forward and his voice rose. "All safe, sir—I've got them."

There was no response.

Brough waited a moment, then called again. "Sir Charles—you can come out now."

But Sir Charles didn't come out. Nothing stirred in the thicket beyond.

Brough and MacNaughten frowned and the police constable moved up beside Abberline. "Want me to have a look?"

The inspector nodded. "Follow me," he said. The two men started for the clump of bushes, stooping to enter an opening in their midst.

As they did so, an unmistakable fishy odor assailed their nostrils. The natural recess beneath the surrounding shrubbery was dark, and for a moment they saw nothing. Gradually their eyes adjusted to the dimness and a shadowy shape became visible, crouching upon a pile of leaves.

They stared at the figure huddled before them—the forlorn figure of a small boy. His frightened face was smeared with grease, and so was the paper he clutched in one hand; the paper cone filled with a helping of fish-and-chips.

CHAPTER TWENTY-SIX

Brazil, A.D. 1658 *Some Portuguese masters disposed of their embarrassingly pregnant slave girls by burning them alive in the plantation ovens before childbirth took place.*

• • •

"I say, Mark—do you have a moment?"

Mark halted and glanced back up the hospital corridor to see Trebor standing in the open doorway of the library.

He nodded, and the older man beckoned to him. "Come along, then. I'd like you to meet someone."

Following Trebor into the room he saw a mustached man with a brown cowlick framing his tanned forehead who sat facing the door as they entered. Now the stranger rose, holding out his hand, and Mark found himself confronting a giant; a broad-shouldered, barrel-chested presence with a booming voice and a powerful grip.

Trebor did the honors. "I'd like you to meet a friend of mine. Mark Robinson—Dr. Arthur Conan Doyle. He's in private practice—"

Trebor broke off, conscious of Mark's surprised stare. "What's come over you?"

Mark nodded at the tall man. "You wouldn't happen to be the author of *A Study in Scarlet*?"

Conan Doyle smiled broadly, and for a moment, despite the bushy mustache bordering his mouth, he looked like an overgrown boy.

"Trebor was just speaking of you," he said. "From the States, aren't you? How on earth would you know about my work?"

"There was a copy of *Beecham's Christmas Annual* in the ship's library," Mark said. "I read it on the voyage over here. My congratulations, sir."

"Thank you."

As the two men seated themselves, Mark continued. "Allow me to say that I think you've a promising career in literature if you care to pursue it."

"Hardly literature." Conan Doyle shrugged. "But I trust you're right about the career."

"Arthur is overly modest," Trebor said. He lit a cheroot as he spoke. "His book created quite a stir when it was published serially in *The Strand* magazine last year."

Mr. Doyle sighed. "I'm afraid my little mystery tale wouldn't claim as much attention today. It can scarcely hold a candle to the newspaper accounts of this Ripper business."

"I wonder." Mark glanced at the tall man. "What do you suppose our detective character—Soames, isn't it?—would make of he affair?"

"Holmes," murmured Conan Doyle. "Sherlock Holmes."

"Sorry." Mark flushed. "I'm not very good with names."

"No matter. Why should you or anyone else have reason to recall it? I'm flattered you knew mine. No one ever seems to remember writers."

"I made a point of it in this instance," Mark said. "And while I got his name wrong, I shan't forget your character. The way you described his methods of deduction was quite extraordinary."

"And not entirely fiction." Trebor puffed on his cheroot. "If I'm not mistaken, the real-life model for Sherlock Holmes is my old friend Joe Bell. He was Arthur's boffin at Edinburgh."

"Recognized him, did you?" Conan Doyle smiled. "I admit I borrowed some of his techniques for Holmes' benefit." He nodded at Mark. "But you asked what Sherlock Holmes might think of this Ripper matter. I imagine his first concern would be to establish the identity of the killer."

"Quite so." Trebor flicked the gray tip from the end of his cheroot into an ashtray beside his chair. "But how would he go about it, with all those suspects? I suppose you've read the verse that Scotland Yard just received?"

"Can't say I have."

"Then allow me to recite it for you." Trebor set his cheroot down, and cleared his throat.

"I'm not a butcher,
I'm not a Yid,
Nor yet a foreign skipper,
But I'm your own lighthearted friend,
Yours truly, Jack the Ripper."

"Capital!" Conan Doyle beamed. "If this communication can he taken as genuine, then our Ripper is apparently a man of principle as well as poetry. He's playing fair by eliminating others who might be mistaken for suspects."

"Playing fair?" Trebor retrieved his cheroot. "You talk as if this were some sort of game."

"Perhaps it is—to him."

"You're not serious?"

"Indeed I am. Consider the elements involved in the crimes. From all accounts it would seem as though the Ripper goes out of his way to reveal his presence to witnesses before each murder, then runs off in the nick of time to evade his pursuers. One perceives a definite element of hide-and-seek about it all.

"Then there's the matter of clues—clues designed to mystify and mislead. Emptying his victims' pockets and arranging their contents about the bodies, planting a bloodstained bit of apron here, a knife there. And that message scrawled on the wall about Jews. The way it was worded seems deliberate; it can be taken either as an accusation or a denial. I tend to believe the misspelling of the word

145

was intentional, along with the other mistakes and grammatical errors in the letters."

"You think the letters are genuine?" Mark asked.

"It all depends on which ones you're referring to. I'm told hundreds have been received—warnings, confessions, other verses. Undoubtedly most of them are hoaxes. But the ones which predicted the crimes in advance cannot be explained away so easily. I believe they're part of the game. A game of life and death."

"What sort of man would look upon murder as though it were a sporting event?"

"A man who has a total disregard for his fellow creatures. A man whose own perverted pleasures take precedence over the pain and suffering of others. A man completely convinced of his own superiority, rankling because his intelligence and abilities have not been recognized by the rest of the world. A homicidal maniac, yes, but also an egomaniac. Hence the deliberate risk-taking, the flaunting of clues, the letter-writing. All this designed, mind you, to establish his superior cleverness and cunning—and to further his fame."

Trebor gestured with his cheroot. "In that case you must admit he's succeeded. The police have no idea as to identity, and neither would your fictional detective."

"On the contrary." Conan Doyle settled back in his chair. "If Sherlock Holmes were employed on this case I think he might be well on the way to a solution.

"To begin with, we've noted that the murderer has been playing hide-and-seek, but taking great pains to plant false clues and false leads. Under such circumstances one must detect a glaring and obvious discrepancy in his conduct. If he goes to such elaborate lengths to escape discovery, then why does he brazenly display his presence to witnesses before committing his crimes?"

"I'm sure I don't know," Trebor said. "But that's exactly the question I'd ask your Mr. Sherlock Holmes."

"And he would give you an answer." Conan Doyle nodded. "He would tell you that the killer's revelation is a form of concealment. A device designed to turn the attention of the police in the wrong direction. While they are busily engaged in looking for a mustached man wearing a peaked cap, they're not likely to be paying much attention to that same man disguised as a woman."

"A woman?" Mark leaned forward.

"Consider the eyewitness descriptions. In almost every instance, the man seen talking to a victim was carrying a package—either an object wrapped in paper or some sort of bag."

"Which would contain the murder weapon," Trebor said. "That much the police determined."

"How? They've not examined such a bag or parcel. It's mere guesswork on their part. Mr. Holmes would remind you there are less conspicuous ways to conceal a knife. But suppose the bag or package was needed to hold something else—a woman's clothing, designed for wear immediately after the murder?

"Consider how completely the killer could change his appearance. It would take only a second to remove a false mustache, less than a minute to don a long-skirted dress, jacket and bonnet, none of which would reveal any telltale bloodstains. Since many of the poorer female residents of Whitechapel—including one of the murder victims, you may recall—wear men's boots against the cold his shoes wouldn't matter. As for his own clothing, including the cap, he'd have only to pop them into the bag or parcel along with his knife, and be on his merry way."

"But a woman carrying a medical bag through the streets after midnight is bound to attract attention," Mark said.

"Not necessarily. Many such women are abroad at that hour; their presence is taken for granted and passes unnoticed."

"You don't mean—?"

"Midwives." Conan Doyle nodded. "Exactly so. They're the ones most apt to deliver babies in the slums, not your fancy obstetricians. They're so common no one gives them a second glance, any more than they would a postman. And if your Ripper is found near the scene of the crime his disguise would offer a perfect explanation; a midwife making her rounds stumbled on the body and stopped to give medical attention. Perhaps his voice would have to be disguised in case of answering questions, but the chances are that he'd not be halted and no questions would be asked. I'm quite certain that Mr. Holmes would concur at this conclusion. Jack the Ripper has escaped detection by disguising himself as a midwife."

"Extraordinary," Trebor murmured.

"Elementary," said Conan Doyle.

Rising, he took his leave, and Trebor faced Mark in silence as he snubbed his cheroot in the ashtray.

"What do you make of it?" Mark asked.

"Difficult to say. I admit the idea sounds plausible. That bit about a false mustache is quite ingenious—a typical Sherlock Holmes touch, don't you think? A wonder the police haven't thought of it."

"Do you suppose we might broach the notion to Inspector Abberline?"

Trebor shook his head. "I'm afraid our friend the inspector has other ideas. As a matter of fact, I've just been told that a man answering to his description has been checking my own comings and goings with the landlady at my flat."

Mark gave his mustache a nervous tug. "That's odd. I've no description, but one of the tenants at my own lodgings mentioned a man had stopped around inquiring about my movements over the past weeks. Surely you don't think—?"

"Never mind what I think." Trebor scowled. "It's what Abberline thinks that must concern us now."

CHAPTER TWENTY-SEVEN

Russia, A.D. 1720 *An eighty-year-old man refused to appear at a court masquerade dressed as the Devil. Peter the Great had him stripped naked and marooned on an ice floe in the Neva River, with pasteboard horns on his head. He froze to death.*

• • •

Inspector Abberline was having a bad day. Sitting in the Home Secretary's office, he listened with growing dismay to the row between Sir Henry Matthews and Sir Charles Warren. Two lords of the realm, if you please, going at it hammer and tongs like a pair of schoolboys.

"I won't brook interference!" Warren exclaimed. He paced before Matthews' desk, thumping the tip of his silver-headed walking stick on the carpet with each step. "Not from amateurs with nothing better to do than meddle with the affairs of my department!"

Matthews jabbed a bony finger at the stack of documents on the desktop before him. "You're wrong, Charles. Dead wrong. These are only a portion of the communications we've received. Not from amateur detectives. Not from meddlers. Decent, respectable citizens who fear for their lives, like the ladies of Whitechapel who signed this petition—"

"Ladies? Don't talk to me of your ladies! If those females down there would seek out some honest employment and keep off the streets, we wouldn't have this sort of muck to contend with. I've more important things to do than play nursemaid to a pack of streetwalkers!"

"I dare say." Matthews' tone was dry. "Your job is to catch this murderer. And you haven't done so. Even with the aid of bloodhounds."

Warren reddened at the reference but didn't reply; the failure of his trial runs was public knowledge.

"No offense," Matthews said. "I appreciate your—shall I say?—dogged determination."

Again he gestured toward the pile of papers before him. "But since you seem unable to apprehend him on your own, I suggest you give some attention to the advice of others."

"What others? I've had my fill of suggestions from the press. And I don't fancy self-styled experts like this Forbes Winslow fellow who keeps popping up with what he calls evidence." Now he glanced at Abberline. "You've seen this fellow. Utter imbecile, what?"

The inspector nodded uneasily. "A bit on the eccentric side."

"Eccentric? The man's daft! Now he's taken to analyzing the handwriting of those so-called Jack the Ripper letters. As if it makes any difference how the bugger dots his i's and crosses his t's! Sheer waste of time."

"Is it?" Sir Henry Matthews followed Warren's pacing figure with a cold stare. "Perhaps such a study might reveal important clues to the writer's personality. I'm not prepared to dismiss the findings of graphology."

"And I'm not prepared to give a handwriting test to every man in London!" Warren snapped.

"Then what are you prepared to do? If you'd give some thought to the other suggestions we've received—"

"Such as what, might I ask?"

"Such as these." Matthews extracted a letter from an envelope on top of the heap and began to read a paragraph selected at random.

"Have the cattle boats and passenger boats been examined? Has any investigation been made as to the number of single men occupying rooms to themselves? The murderer's clothes must be saturated with blood and kept somewhere? Is there sufficient surveillance at night—"

"Sheer drivel!" Warren halted before the desk, bringing his cane down with a thud. "Even a child would know we've considered such matters from the start. Why should anyone bother with the advice of some bloody stupid crank? Give me the name of the fool who wrote this—I'll have his guts for garters!"

"Allow me to finish." Matthews raised the letter and scanned the final lines.

"These are some of the questions that occur to the Queen on reading accounts of this horrible crime.

"Signed this day and date—Victoria R."

Warren's jaw dropped. "*She* wrote this?"

Sir Henry Matthews placed the letter back on the pile. "Now you can begin to understand why these communications want attention. The Prime Minister has advised me—"

"Are you threatening me, sir?" Warren's face was purple. "Is that the purpose of this meeting? Let me remind you, no matter what Salisbury or Her Majesty herself may think, I'm in charge of this operation and I intend to conduct it as I see fit!"

"No one is challenging your authority," Matthews said. "But there is more here than meets the eye. And I warn you, time is running out."

"So it is." Warren glanced at the wall clock behind Matthews desk. "I'm due back at the Yard as of this very moment."

Matthews shrugged. "As you will. I was hoping we could discuss the matter further."

"My duties call for decisions, not discussions." Ignoring Matthews' stare, Sir Charles Warren moved across the room, swinging his walking stick. As he opened the door he turned and nodded at the Home Secretary. "Should you happen to address Her Majesty please inform her that I am personally examining conditions on cattle boats, conducting a census of single men living alone, keeping my eye out for blood-stained clothing, and watching the streets by night. Tell her I appreciate her valuable suggestions, and should they lead to the discovery of the murderer I shall see to it that she will be the first to know."

The slam of the door put a period to his words, and a warning rumble in Abberline's stomach added further punctuation. He sat there in silence as Sir Henry Matthews exhaled slowly.

"Bit of a tartar, that one, eh?"

Abberline nodded. "Forgive me for saying so, sir, but this isn't the first time he's taken that line. It tends to make for problems in the department."

"Any suggestions?"

The inspector hesitated, weighing his words. "Meaning no disrespect, but if you could possibly arrange to grant me a free hand in conducting this inquiry—"

"Believe me, I'd like nothing better." Matthews rose. "Unfortunately, I can hardly jump you over his head, or Anderson's, for that matter. Question of protocol, eh?"

"I see."

"I'm sure you do. But there's no need to look so disappointed. I'd like to entrust you with a private mission of your own."

"How so?"

Matthews moved up beside Abberline's chair, speaking in low tones. "Mind you, what I'm about to say is in the strictest confidence. It must go no further than this office. Agreed?"

Abberline nodded.

"Well, then. You heard the Queen's letter. What do you make of it?"

"She's concerned—"

"More than concerned. To put matters as delicately as possible, Her Majesty fears that this investigation may not be solely confined to the residents of Whitechapel. It could involve people in high places."

Abberline's puzzled frown provoked a further murmur from Matthews. "That's why I particularly wanted a word with you. Upon examining your duty register I note a connection with the raid on a male brothel at Number Nineteen, Cleveland Street last July."

"Yes. The trial is still pending." Abberline paused. "I've not had time to look into the reasons for delay."

"When you do, you may discover that orders have come down from unspecified sources. And that certain of the suspects won't be available for questioning."

"Who might they be?"

"James Stephen, for one."

"Stephen?" Inspector Abberline's eyebrows arched. "Isn't he the tutor of—"

"No names." Matthews paused. "Let me just say that we've reason to believe he was responsible for introducing a certain personage to the occupants of the Cleveland Street address."

Abberline concealed his startled reaction as he spoke. "Anyone else?"

"John Netley."

"I've heard of him. A coachman, isn't he?"

"That is correct. It has been suggested he frequently drove the party in question on his visits to Number Nineteen."

"I see." Abberline hesitated, then shook his head. "No, I don't see. What has the—personage—got to do with the Ripper affair?"

"This is for you to determine."

"You're not suggesting—?"

"I'm suggesting nothing, except that you make some discreet inquiries. Would it be possible for you to do so on an unofficial basis?"

"I can manage it."

"Good." Sir Henry Matthews led him to the door as he rose "Remember, I'm relying on your complete discretion."

"You can depend on me, sir." Abberline smiled.

But when he left Matthews' office his smile faded as the Home Secretary's words echoed in memory. *High places. A certain personage.* If people like that were suspected of such killings, then whom could you trust?

Inspector Abberline was having a bad day. And his stomach told him it wasn't over yet.

CHAPTER TWENTY-EIGHT

United States, A.D. 1791 *In Louisville, Kentucky, a Major Elurgis Beatty confided to his diary: "Saw the barbarous custom of gouging practised between two of the lower classes of people here. When two men quarrel they never have any idea of striking, but immediately seize each other, thrusting thumbs or fingers into the eye to push it from the socket as one of those men experienced today...but he in turn bit his opponent most abominably. One of these gougers had, in his time, taken out five eyes, bit off two or three noses and ears and spit them in their faces."*

• • •

When the cab deposited Abberline before the Royal Lyceum Theatre he paid the jarvey and made his way past the imposing six-pillared entrance.

A porter halted him at the inner doorway. "Sorry, sir. No matinee today."

"I know." Abberline pulled out his wallet to display his badge. "I'm told I might find a Mr. Wilde here."

The porter hesitated, blinking at the badge. "Not in trouble, is he?"

"Nothing of the sort." Abberline offered a reassuring smile. "This is purely a personal matter."

"Right, guv'nor." The porter gestured. "He's in the green room wiv Mr. Mansfield and another gentleman."

Abberline found his way to the backstage chamber and presented himself to the trio seated there.

He was surprised to find Richard Mansfield so short a man. Somehow he'd always pictured the visiting American actor as a towering figure, perhaps because of the roles he played, but the broad-shouldered chap with thinning hair bore no resemblance to the fearsome Mr. Hyde.

The second occupant of the room was a feisty little journalist in his early thirties, with carroty-red hair, bushy brows and satanic whiskers. Mansfield introduced him as a critic and a budding playwright, but that's not why the name rang a bell. Abberline tried to remember where he'd heard of Mr. George Bernard Shaw before but the recollection eluded him.

The third man presented no such problem. There was scarcely anyone who wouldn't have recognized Mr. Wilde. If the flowing, centrally parted hair, the extravagantly checkered coat and frogged vest didn't stamp him unmistakably as the celebrated poet, his tongue offered immediate proof of Oscar Wilde's identity.

"I was just telling these gentlemen of my recent visit to the Beaux Arts Balls in Paris." Wilde smiled at him, then turned his attention to the others. "As I said, this year the theme was biblical, if not entirely reverent. The polyglot mixture of tongues—French, English, German and Italian—brought to mind the Tower of Babel. Though the decorum, I must confess, bore more of a hint of Sodom and Gomorrah." Wilde's fluty voice rose. "At midnight they bestowed the first prize on a handsome fellow who had chosen to appear as Adam—in full fig, of course. His entire body, completely visible to the naked eye, and most appropriately so under the circumstances, was covered with gold paint. A gilded youth—but not, thank God, gelded."

Wilde giggled and Richard Mansfield shook his head. "Oscar, you're incorrigible!" He turned to Abberline. "Do sit down, Inspector. Can I offer you a dash of sherry?"

"Thank you, no." Abberline lowered himself into a chair before the fireplace, rubbing his hands. "The days are getting nippy. There's quite a chill in the air."

"To say nothing of soot, coal dust, and all manner of poisonous chemical compounds." Bernard Shaw peered at him from beneath bristling brows. "No wonder the Queen keeps fit—she stays out of London and enjoys the pure Scottish air."

"Pure Scottish malt, more likely," Wilde said. "I'm told her gillie, the late John Brown of unsaintly memory, introduced our beloved sovereign to the delights of the Highland fling."

"Nonsense." Shaw shook his head. "One can't preserve one's health in alcohol. London pours whiskey down its throat, but it coughs and wheezes nonetheless. And no wonder, what with the effluvium of thousands of tons of horse droppings, the miasma of sewage, billions of bacteria assaulting our every breath."

"Ah yes, the germ theory." Wilde smiled. "Once you get started on that topic you sound as prejudiced as Pasteur and as virulent as Virchow."

"Better than being as gullible as Gull," Shaw muttered.

"Really." Mansfield gave him a reproving glance. "Don't tell me you're taking issue with the Physician Ordinary to the Queen?"

"Physician Ordinary." Wilde giggled again. "How very apt!"

Mansfield glanced at Abberline. "I fear I must apologize for all this. My friends here were in the midst of conducting an interview with me for the press. But if you've come on official business—"

"My business is with Mr. Wilde, and it's not official," Abberline told him. "Go ahead with your interview—I can wait."

"Very well, then." Mansfield turned to the others. "As I was saying, I have an announcement to make. I'm taking *Dr. Jekyll and Mr. Hyde* off the boards."

"Richard!" Wilde's hand and voice rose in protest. "Have you gone mad? You've run for ten weeks to packed houses. Why stop now?"

"It's a matter of conscience. There's been a great deal of criticism regarding the content of the play. Some think all this emphasis on violence stirs the morbid imagination of its audiences. I would hate to feel that I may have unwittingly incited someone of unsound mind to perpetrate these Ripper atrocities."

"Fiddle-faddle!" Bernard Shaw's blue eyes flashed. "I shall report your decision if you insist, but be assured your conscience can rest easily. I'm not prepared to grant that your dramatic efforts have inspired slaughter in the streets, but even if this were so it might be for the best."

"Really, now!" Wilde's mouth contorted in mock amazement. "Are you seriously advocating the wanton murder of wantons?"

"I take it you didn't read my letter in the *Star* last month," Shaw said. "I put forth the suggestion that in the long run these crimes may prove of great benefit. At the very least they've served to focus public attention on the misery and poverty of the East End, and thus hasten social reform. It's a pity that only the poor have been sacrificed in this worthy cause. Had a duchess been one of the victims, perhaps we'd already have a half-million pounds or more to alleviate conditions in Whitechapel."

"Jack the Ripper as a public benefactor?" Wilde shook his head. "And to think they accuse *me* of cynicism!" He rose. "I fear I must take my leave before such Fabian sentiments corrupt me further." Turning, he nodded towards Abberline. "You wish a word with me, Inspector?"

"If I might."

"Share my carriage, then. I'm expecting guests at Tite Street."

"Thank you."

Brief farewells were exchanged, and within a few moments after leaving the theater the inspector was seated beside the poet in the comfort of his carriage.

As they rolled off, Abberline sorted his thoughts. Wilde's address—Number Sixteen, Tite Street—was known to him as a gathering place for the swells; even the Prince of Wales dined there. But others living nearby sometimes welcomed less distinguished guests. The painter, Sickert, for one; his name had cropped up in connection with the doings at Cleveland Street. Maybe mentioning Sickert and a few others would be the best way of leading up to the delicate subject with this delicate, perfumed gentleman. But on the other hand....

Abberline's queasy stomach protested painfully as the carriage rounded a corner. On the other hand, delicacy be damned. He had no time to cross rapiers with Oscar Wilde. A bludgeon might be the better weapon.

"Might I ask a question of you, sir?"

"By all means," Wilde drawled. "I have a questionable nature."

"Are you acquainted with the Duke of Clarence?"

"Eddy? Yes, I know him." Wilde smiled. "Not carnally, I hasten to add."

"Then you're aware of his—tastes?"

"In dress, yes. Abominable, don't you think? 'Collars and Cuffs' they call him in the penny press. And that fore-and-aft hat he affects—ghastly!" Wilde's tone was bantering but now his eyes narrowed. "However, I dare say you're not inquiring about Eddy's sartorial peculiarities."

Abberline glanced forward at the swaying back of the coachman seated on his box. "May I speak freely?"

"Please do. My man happens to be deaf—and on occasion, dumb and blind as well."

"This matter must remain strictly between the two of us."

"Good enough. Whatever you tell me will go no further. You've my assurance on that."

"Agreed." Abberline cleared his thoughts and his throat. "About Eddy, then. Is he by any chance a Major Darcy? Does he enjoy swishings?"

"Please, spare me the euphemisms." Wilde raised a plump hand in protest. "No, he's not a masochist. To my knowledge he would take no pleasure in being whipped."

"A Reverend Leffwell, perhaps?"

"What a quaint way of referring to it! Your slang is a bit out-moded, Inspector. I much prefer the term of sadist. It's only proper that we offer our homage to the divine Marquis."

"Is he one?"

"I'm not in a position to say." The poet pondered. "His attitude on the fair sex seems somewhat ambivalent. While he appears to be quite gallant toward ladies of his own station, I've heard him speak rather disparagingly of the lower elements."

"Meaning whores?"

"He tends to regard them as unclean. But knowing their habits, one can hardly fault him for that. Biddies should use *bidets*, in my opinion."

"Perhaps he has good reason to feel that way. I've heard rumors concerning Lord Vanbrough."

"Euphemisms again! You policemen are a prudish lot, aren't you?" Wilde seemed amused. "Oh yes, I know poor Eddy suffered from a venereal complaint. But his dear mother's physician is said to have cured him—without her knowledge, I might add."

"Sir William Gull?"

"The same. He takes it upon himself to assume full responsibility for the welfare of a future monarch."

"What about James Stephen?"

"His tutor?" Wilde grimaced. "A bad influence, I'm afraid. It's rumored he introduced young Eddy to the dubious joys of our local fleshpots."

"Such as Cleveland Street?"

"You know about that affair, do you?" The poet's full lips pursed. "I'm not sure how deeply Stephen was involved. He's been in poor health for some time now."

"Forgive my asking, but have you ever visited Cleveland Street yourself?"

"Really, now." Again Wilde raised his hand. "It would never do for me to drink from a public fountain, as it were. After all, I have a reputation to live down to."

"But Eddy frequented the place?"

"Frequented it frequently. His dear mother gave her blessing to his excursions in town with Stephen, in hopes that he might mingle with the *literati* and become a patron of the arts. But she doesn't know of his involvement with the *illiterati*, nor the dubious arts he has come to patronize."

"You're sure he's not sadistic?"

"I told you, I have no certain knowledge."

"How does his tutor feel about women?"

"Stephen? He dislikes the sex, given his own leanings."

"Dislikes? Or does he hate them?"

"A bit near the wind, perhaps." Wilde paused. "But yes, you might say that."

Abberline nodded. "Eddy caught syphilis from a whore. His tutor—who may be his lover as well—hates women. Eddy has been known to prowl the East End incognito at night. What does that suggest to you?"

"That you are in grave danger of breaking your leg by jumping at conclusions."

The inspector glanced sharply at his companion. "You're sure you're not saying that just to protect him?"

"My dear fellow." Oscar Wilde's smile had vanished, and now his voice deepened. "Whatever you may think of me, I'm not so devoid of human feeling as to shield a murderer. Like any decent citizen, I wish only to protect my family from such creatures. Remember, I have a wife and children of my own."

The carriage came to a halt. When the coachman opened the door, Wilde turned to Abberline with a parting smile. "If I had any further information, rest assured it would be gladly given. But unfortunately I know nothing more, and I can only wish you well. My man has instructions to drive you back to the Yard. Godspeed, Inspector."

Alone in the carriage, jolting now on his way to his official quarters, Abberline shook his head. "Godspeed" from Oscar Wilde? The pouf as a family man? Life had its share of surprises, to say nothing of complications.

But he might safely scratch Eddy from his list of suspects. Or could he? After all, the poet had merely given his opinion, and perhaps there were things he didn't know.

That was the rub; there were too many things nobody seemed to know. Nobody except the bloody bastard himself—Saucy Jack, Red Jack, Jack the Ripper—writing those damned letters, laughing at him. Who was he, where was he, what was he doing? No killings in all these weeks past—possibly he was in lavender a thousand miles away by now, gone scot-free.

Abberline sighed. "No sense stewing," he muttered aloud. He intended only to report in, sign out and spend a quiet evening at home.

But his bad day hadn't entirely ended. One more complication and surprise awaited the inspector at Scotland Yard.

That's where they handed him the kidney.

CHAPTER TWENTY-NINE

France, A.D. 1792 *The Princesse de Lamballe was clubbed to death outside La Force prison after being made to walk on corpses lying in the street. Her head was cut off and carried into a local tavern to be displayed on the bar while toasts were drunk. Then it was mounted on a pike to be shown to her dear friend, the Queen. En route the head was brought to a beauty salon, where its hair was curled and powdered. Then the crowd bore it in parade beneath the prison windows of the Queen and her children.*

• • •

The following afternoon was dark and dreary, mirroring Mark's melancholy mood. Sitting in the surgical lounge, he struggled with his medical observation notes taken during the past week, but concentration eluded him.

Today his thoughts kept turning to Eva. She'd eluded him too. An image of auburn hair and peacock-blue eyes flashed before him but brought no content; it was the reality he wanted. Why had she taken such pains to avoid him? Was it because of Alan?

Another image arose, that of a mustached man wearing a peaked cap. Her fiancé, Eva said. Then why this secrecy, these clandestine meetings? Why had he never appeared at the hospital to escort her home? Perhaps he was married; that would explain the need for concealment. But somehow it was difficult to picture Eva in the role of mistress. Or was it just a stubborn rejection of the ultimate image; Eva and Alan, locked together in naked embrace?

Mark bit his lip. *Stop playing the jealous lover—*

"There you are."

He returned to reality as Trebor entered, followed by a familiar figure. Inspector Abberline nodded, closing the door behind him.

"Not disturbing you, are we?"

Mark maintained his smile as he shook his head, but there was no warmth behind it. What was Abberline doing here?

The inspector glanced at Trebor as he started forward. "Mind if I tell him?"

Trebor shrugged. "Not at all. I'm sure he's been curious too."

"About Dr. Trebor's absence," Abberline said. "I admit it had me puzzled, so I made it my concern to check into his movements. It seems he's had a legitimate reason for being away. Mrs. Trebor lives in Nottingham—"

Mark gaped at Trebor. "I never knew you were married!"

"There was no reason to mention it," Trebor said. "My wife and I have been estranged for some years. But when I learned she was in hospital there, I felt it my duty to go to her."

"She's ill, then?"

"Terminal consumption."

"I'm sorry." Mark spoke sincerely, but at the same time he was aware of his relief. It had been wrong to entertain any suspicion of Trebor; on the other hand, Abberline had suspected him as well.

Now his relief gave way to apprehension as he became conscious of the portly inspector's level stare.

"I've taken the liberty of looking into your affairs also," Abberline said. "Particularly after examining the murder messages."

"But that's ridiculous." Mark gestured angrily. "Anyone can see those letters are the work of an obvious illiterate."

"A bit too obvious." Abberline's gaze didn't waver. "Someone took deliberate pains to misspell words and disguise his handwriting. But much of the slang he used—like 'boss,' for example—is American."

"You're accusing me of sending them?"

"Not accusing. I just want you to know why I made a point of establishing your whereabouts at the time of these crimes."

Mark faced him squarely. "And what did you find out?"

"That you were in The Coach and Four pub when the first of the double killings took place. You were at Berner Street when the second occurred in Mitre Square." Abberline's voice softened. "My apologies. But in cases like this one must not overlook any possibility, however farfetched."

"I agree." Mark felt his tension ebb as he spoke. "About those letters, though. Do you really believe they're genuine? Whoever wrote them seemed to know about the murders in advance, yet there's always a chance of a hoax—"

"Not anymore." Abberline reached into his inside coat pocket. "This is a photographic copy of a letter received by George Lusk, the chairman of the Whitechapel Vigilance Committee. See what you make of it."

He unfolded the single sheet and handed it to Mark, watching him as he read.

From Hell

Mr Lusk
Sir I send you half the Kidne I look from one woman prasarved it for you tother piece I fried and ate it was very nice I may send you the bloody knif that took it out if you only wate a whil longer.
signed Catch me when you can Mister Lusk.

Mark looked up as Abberline spoke. "Notice how obvious the misspellings are. No genuine semi-literate would make those kind of mistakes, and they differ from the sort in the other letters. The lack of punctuation is also artificial."

Trebor nodded. "What about the kidney?"

"It was enclosed with the letter, in a cardboard box."

"Oh my God!" Trebor addressed Mark. "Do you remember the inquest on the Eddowes woman? Dr. Brown testified that the uterus had been removed, and the left kidney was missing." He returned to Abberline. "Where is it now?"

Before the inspector could reply, a knock sounded on the lounge door.

"Come in," Mark called, and the door opened. To his surprise it was Eva who stood in the doorway, wearing her probationer's uniform.

She nodded at Abberline. "Dr. Openshaw is ready to see you. If you'll come this way—"

Abberline joined her as she turned, beckoning the others to follow them.

Moving down the hall, Mark murmured to his companion. "Openshaw. Where've I heard that name before?"

"He's a staff pathologist here. Curator of the hospital museum. His office is around the corner."

And there, in the little room, Dr. Openshaw awaited them.

Mark did his best to conceal his reaction, but the room repelled him. It was lined on three sides with shelving on which rested rows of bell-jars and glass containers glittering in the glimmer of the gaslight overhead. But once his eyes grew accustomed to the glare it was the content of the glassware that he found most unnerving.

Underneath the bell-jars there reposed a grotesque assortment of dried and desiccated human limbs—stumped legs terminating in toeless knobs, detached hands splayed to exhibit six fingers, feet webbed like those of some huge batrachian. Others held malformed skulls; macrocephalic enormities and microcephalic blobs. Floating in the preservative of the containers were misshapen organs; shriveled lungs, bloated and enlarged hearts, a hydrocephalic head the size of a watermelon that bobbed against the glass in obscene greeting.

Mark turned away to gaze at white-smocked Dr. Openshaw standing beside the table in the center of the room. He too was bobbing his head in welcome, and the movement was scarcely less disturbing.

The little baldheaded man with the monkish tonsure of straggly brown hair fringing his collar peered up through the rounded lenses of pince-nez that enlarged the staring pupils of dead-gray eyes. Under the light his skin was gray too, and gray lips parted in a mirthless smile to reveal a row of twisted teeth.

Dr. Openshaw smelled of formaldehyde. Indeed, the whole room reeked of it, mingled with the odor of other chemicals emanating from an assortment of phials and racked test-tubes on the tabletop beside a microscope, stacks of glass slides, a Bunsen burner, and instruments used for pathological examination.

But as greetings were exchanged, what captured Mark's attention was the battered, coverless little cardboard box resting at the far end of the table. The box, and its contents, which Dr. Openshaw was now indicating with the points of steel tweezers gripped in the grayish claw of his right hand.

His voice was gray, too; a dry rustling uncolored by any hint of emotion. "I have completed my examination," he said. "The specimen is almost a classical example of the ginny kidney."

"Ginny?" Abberline frowned.

"Forgive my use of the vernacular. An alcoholic's kidney." The tweezers dipped into the box and lifted out the spongy mass as he spoke. "Observe the discoloration. There is unmistakable evidence of an advanced stage of Bright's disease. According to indications, I would venture that it has been excised from a female of middle years, perhaps forty-five or thereabouts. I'd say it was removed some time within the past three weeks."

"The time is right," Abberline murmured. Mark glanced at Trebor and Eva, sensing their response to this observation.

But Dr. Openshaw looked perplexed. "You still haven't told me where you obtained this specimen," he said. "Or under what circumstances."

"All that can wait." The inspector moved up beside the pathologist. "What else can you tell us about it?"

"Very little, without a more detailed analysis." The tweezers twirled the soggy organ. "I do note the renal artery has been severed. Its normal length is three inches or thereabouts, but only an inch remains attached here."

"And according to the coroner's findings, two inches remained in the body." Abberline's question followed quickly. "In your opinion, was this removed by someone familiar with medical procedures?"

Dr. Openshaw moistened his thin lips with the tip of a grayish tongue. "The absence of extraneous surrounding tissue seems to indicate the excision was performed by someone with a knowledge of anatomy. I've already spoken to Dr. Hume—"

Mention of the name startled Mark. Trebor seemed equally upset, and Eva's sudden frown was eloquent with silent revulsion.

"What did Hume say?" Abberline asked.

"He believes it's the work of a surgeon."

Mark glanced at his companions. Like himself, he knew they were recalling the postscript of the first Ripper letter. "They say I'm a doctor. Ha! ha! ha!"

They stared at one another. But nobody laughed.

CHAPTER THIRTY

France, A.D. 1793 *In testimony regarding the Reign of Terror in Nantes, it was stated that one of the revolutionaires displayed "a man's ears pinned to the national cockade which he wore on his cap. He went about carrying a pocketful of those ears, which he made the female prisoners kiss. He also took along with him a handful of male organs which he had cut from the men he had murdered, and these he showed to women whenever the occasion afforded."*

• • •

It was later, in the hall outside, that Mark had a moment alone with Eva.

He caught up with her as she started down the corridor, then halted at his approach. "Eva—what happened to you?"

"Nothing, really." She smiled. "Of course I was startled when Dr. Openshaw gave his opinion about the murderer. It seemed to upset you too."

"That's not what I'm talking about," Mark told her. "I saw your face when he mentioned Dr. Hume."

Eva's smile vanished. "Please," she said. "I'm wanted in the dispensary."

"It can wait." Mark spoke quickly. "What's Hume up to? Has he been molesting you? I want to know."

Eva took a deep breath. "Very well."

Quietly she recited the details of her late night encounter with Jeremy Hume and their visit to the waxworks exhibit.

Mark listened with growing anger. "And you've done nothing about it? You could have spoken out."

Eva shook her head. "What's the use? It would only be my word against his, and of course he'd deny everything. I don't wish to be sacked as a troublemaker."

"Inspector Abberline seems to consider Hume a possible suspect. Why not tell him?"

Eva gestured helplessly "But there's really nothing to tell—nothing concrete, that is. Just because Dr. Hume accosted me hardly proves he's guilty of anything but boorish behavior."

"There's more to it than that. You told me what he said about the slaughterhouses, the way he seemed to gloat over details of the Ripper slayings."

"Again that's no proof." She hesitated. "And I'm not all that naive. Don't you see what he was doing? He was trying to excite me."

"Miserable scum!" Mark's hands balled into fists. "If you'd only come to me, I'd have settled his hash for him in a hurry!"

She sighed. "Precisely why I didn't want to say anything. Besides, you seem to forget I have other protection."

"Alan?"

Eva nodded. "If you must know, I asked him to have a word with Dr. Hume. There's been no trouble since."

Mark stared at her. "Are you sure? I saw the trouble in your face when his name was mentioned."

"But I explained—"

"Don't lie to me, Eva. Hume may not have made any further advances to you, but there's no assurance he isn't planning something in the future, if only for revenge. That's what you were thinking when Openshaw mentioned him. You're afraid of Hume, aren't you?"

Silence, then her soft murmur. "Yes, I'm afraid. But Alan says—"

"Damn Alan!" Mark checked himself quickly. "I'm sorry. I know I have no right to interfere, but I'm worried."

"I understand." Eva smiled. "And I appreciate your concern, though there's really no need for it now."

"Promise me one thing," Mark said. "If Hume attempts to approach you again, you'll let me know."

"Yes." She nodded. "Now I must go."

Eva started off, then turned to glance back at him over her shoulder. There was an unaccustomed shyness in both her smile and her voice.

"Thank you," she said.

Then she was gone.

CHAPTER THIRTY-ONE

San Domingo, A.D. 1800 *Bryan Edwardes chronicles the uprising of blacks against French rule: "In the neighborhood of Jeremie a body of mulateres attacked the house of M. Sejourne and secured the persons both of him and his wife. This unfortunate woman (my hand trembles as I write) was far advanced in her pregnancy. The monsters, whose prisoner she was, having first murdered her husband in her presence, ripped her up alive and threw the infant to the hogs."*

• • •

Inspector Abberline was finally spending his quiet evening at home. Mrs. Abberline had laid on a special dinner—roast beef and Yorkshire pudding—which, thanks to his stomach, he scarcely touched.

She put out his robe and slippers afterward, but despite the temptations of comfort he ignored them. Instead he retired to the little cubicle off the sitting room where he'd set up a makeshift working space.

As he seated himself before the deal table serving him as a desk, his wife poked her head around the doorway, speaking softly. "Are you sure you're all right, Fred?"

"Quite sure, my dear."

"But you look so peaked, and it's cold here. Couldn't you sit in the parlor? I've put new logs in the fireplace."

"I'll be joining you there soon."

"Promise?"

"It won't be long. Just a bit of work to do." She withdrew, satisfied, and the inspector hunched over the array of documents on his desk. There was no satisfaction in his face as he contemplated the jumble. Bit of work? A ruddy treadmill, that's what it was—the whole case, from beginning to end.

Only there never seemed to be an end. No matter how many details were attended to, a dozen others kept cropping up to plague him.

Today had been a perfect example. He'd finally cleared Dr. Trebor and Mark Robinson of suspicion, and the pathologist's findings about the kidney reinforced his own conclusions. But when he tried to get a more detailed answer from Dr. Hume he'd come a cropper. Hume refused to talk. Too busy, he said. And that only led to another question. Why was Hume always busy—not just on the job but during his leisure hours away from the hospital? Animosity might prompt his excuses, but there must be a reason for that in itself. Now he'd have to look further into

Hume's activities before he could risk checking him off the list of suspects.

Damn the doctors! Too many medical men involved in this affair—all those fellows handling the coroners' inquests, Trebor and Mark and Hume at the hospital, plus the meddlers outside. Forbes Winslow was still at it, claiming he'd received more letters from the Ripper; regular pen-pals they'd become, according to him. And to top it all off he'd rung in another, a Dr. Dutton, to assist him with his infernal handwriting analysis.

But it wasn't just the bloody sawbones he must consider. Oscar Wilde's exoneration of the Duke of Clarence might not hold water, and he'd best follow up on his own to make sure. After listening to Matthews he still smelled some sort of cover-up here.

He couldn't even get a straight answer about Sir Charles Warren. Rumor at the Yard had it that Warren was resigning, but as of today he was still on the job, making preparations for the new Lord Mayor's inaugural parade and public dinner tomorrow. Fat lot of good that would do—detailing half the force for duty along the route and leaving the East End undermanned.

So much to do and so little time, so little help!

Abberline reached for a manila envelope which contained the dossier on Severin Klosowski. Here was another lead to follow and there were a dozen more which seemed equally urgent. Even if none of these fellows proved to be guilty in this case, the Ripper business had flushed a covey of strange birds. Women haters, cranks muttering threats, maniacs running amok with knives—

"Fred!"

He looked up at the sound of his wife's voice. "What is it, dear?"

"There's a gentleman to see you."

Abberline blinked; he hadn't heard the doorbell sounding. Now what?

She smiled, anticipating his question. "Says his name is Lees."

"Robert Lees?"

"That's right. Do you know him?"

He sighed. "Yes, I know the chap. Where is he?"

"I asked him to wait in the parlor." Mrs. Abberline hesitated. "I told him you were engaged, but he said it was urgent. Did I do the right thing?"

"Of course. I'll be with him in a moment."

She left and Abberline rose slowly. His feet were sore, his stomach burbled, and all he'd asked from life was one peaceful evening here at home. Instead he had Robert Lees with his urgent business.

Abberline sighed again. No telling what the business might be, but just thinking about Lees was enough to rattle his composure.

As he made his way slowly down the hall he sorted out his recollections of the man who awaited him. They went back quite a ways.

Robert James Lees was a spiritualist medium, or so he claimed. As a teenage youth, way back in '63, he'd been brought to the Queen after receiving messages from her beloved consort, the late Prince Albert. According to reports he'd arranged a séance at Balmoral Palace. What took place convinced Victoria that Lees' powers were genuine, and she invited him to remain in her service. Instead he'd continued his private research into the occult, writing books and also conducting experiments at the Spiritualist Center in Peckham.

While working in his study one day, he had a premonition of murder. That night a vision came to him in a dream—a vision of a man and a woman entering a dim courtyard together. There in the darkness, the man cut the woman's throat.

The impression was so strong that Lees wrote out the details and brought them to Scotland Yard the following day. That's when Abberline met him, as he told his story to investigators there. But he was only one among the scores of eccentrics and tipsters being interviewed, and what it boiled down to was simple enough: all he had to offer was the report of a dream he claimed to have on the night before an actual murder. Hundreds of people were having nightmares about murders, so why take this one seriously?

It wasn't until the next day, when the body of Annie Chapman was found in a courtyard, that anyone gave the matter a second thought. By then Lees had learned of the crime and paid a visit to Hanbury Street. The courtyard there was, he reported, the one he'd seen in his dream. Viewing it in reality was such a shock that Lees was seized by a feeling of guilt. It was almost as though his failure to convince the police of his premonition made him an accessory to the crime.

Abberline recalled his own feelings at the time; he'd remembered the medium's story and wanted to check on it for further details. But when he tried to contact Lees he learned that the spiritualist had taken the advice of a physician and left for a vacation on the Continent with his family.

Since then, of course, there'd been other demands on his attention, and hence the matter had rested.

But tonight there would be no rest.

Abberline sensed it the moment he entered the parlor where Robert James Lees awaited him.

The middle-aged man stood before the fireplace, his gaze fixed on the flames. As he turned, his eyes, deepset in dark-rimmed sockets, seemed to blaze with a fire of their own.

"Inspector!" The voice itself was fiery; it flared and crackled with excitement. "I saw him!"

Abberline blinked. "What—?"

"I saw Jack the Ripper!"

The flames danced and shimmered, like the thoughts flickering through Abberline's mind. *Another vision, I take it. Another dream—*

"No!" Lees' voice blazed forth. "It wasn't a dream this time. I saw the Ripper, in the flesh! In broad daylight!"

"When?"

"This afternoon."

Abberline's mouth went dry. How many times had he heard this statement made before, how many crackpots and lunatics swore they'd recognized the killer? But this man was different; he'd dreamed true in the past, and now he read his mind. Did Lees really possess the powers he claimed?

The inspector started to reply, but before he could utter a word Lees shook his head. "No," he said. "I don't want to sit down. There's not a moment to lose."

Abberline nodded. "Tell me what happened."

"As you may know, I've recently been abroad. I went hoping to rid myself of these premonitions of murder which so tormented me, and for a time I felt free. Then, quite suddenly, I began to experience a strange sense of foreboding—not visions, but something that took form as an urge. An urge that grew until it became a voice commanding me to return. And today I discovered the reason.

"My wife and I boarded an omnibus at Shepherd's Bush. As we reached Notting Hill a passenger got on. Immediately I recognized him as the man I'd seen in my dream of Annie Chapman's murder. You have the description I gave the police at that time—"

Abberline nodded. "Go on."

"I turned to my wife and whispered, 'That is Jack the Ripper.' She laughed and told me not to be foolish. I assured her I wasn't mistaken; I could feel it."

"What did you do?"

"At the moment, nothing. No constable was present on the bus and I could hardly accost the man without endangering myself and other passengers. We traveled down Edgeware Road to Marble Arch, and there the man got out. Telling my wife I'd join her later at home, I followed him through the crowd on Oxford Street, hoping to catch sight of a policeman along the way. Finally I did so, and hastily told him of my discovery. He thought I was joking, but when I insisted the matter was serious he threatened to run me in.

"Realizing he would not assist me, I turned away. By this time the man was far ahead of me though I still managed to keep him in sight."

"Did he know you were following him?" Abberline asked.

"He must have felt it, because quite abruptly he darted into the street and hailed a cab. Before I found another for myself he'd driven off."

The inspector scowled. "Is that all?"

"All? I told you I saw the murderer."

"Correction. You told me you saw a man who resembled the one in your dream. Under the circumstances I can hardly fault the constable for his attitude. Arresting a man for appearing in a dream isn't exactly police procedure."

Lees' eyes smoldered, but with a dying fire. "Then you don't believe me?"

"It's not a question of belief. One needs something more to act on, tangible proof or substantial evidence. You admit you have neither. So the only question that remains is why you came here with your story."

The fire flared again. "Because I still have my premonition. There will be another murder!"

Abberline shrugged. "The last was committed almost six weeks ago. What can you offer to support this prediction or prevent it from coming true? I'd be a lot happier if you could use those powers of yours to tell me just where this supposed murderer can be located."

"I'm not sure." The psychic shook his head. "But I've a feeling he took the cab to a house near Grosvenor Square."

"What house? What address?"

"It doesn't come clearly."

"In other words, your power is just a matter of guesswork."

Lees' eyes flamed. "It's not a guess! How can I explain? Following this man in my mind's eye is like following one thread in a tangled skein unraveling in all directions. A thread of evil, you might call it, because that's what I sense. But there is much evil in London tonight, Inspector. Singling out this particular thread seems beyond my power at the moment, no matter how I strive to discern it." His voice wavered. "Evil exists everywhere. Sometimes I think our limited senses are designed to protect us from awareness of its presence. We trust them to provide us with knowledge but it may be that they block out realization of horrors we cannot bear."

Abberline gestured impatiently. "So what you're really saying is that you know nothing."

The medium's eyes were white-hot coals. "I *do* know! The precognizance drove me to come here and it's driving me still—driving me mad! Can't you understand? It's like some hideous growth inside my skull, getting stronger and stronger until it bursts my brain. Behind that premonition is a terrible truth. I know it's there—if I could only reach it—"

Lees' hoarse voice halted abruptly and his hands went to his forehead. Taking a deep breath, he closed his eyes, clutching blindly at both temples as he stood swaying before the fireplace. Now his mouth opened and the firelight glinted on flecks of drool issuing from between the parted lips. In a moment the sounds came; deep, guttural sounds which may or may not have been words.

Then, as Abberline strained to listen, the psychic gasped and crumpled to the floor.

"Lees—!"

Abberline knelt beside the unconscious man, loosening his collar. "Lees—can you hear me?"

Slowly a flush of color crept into the cheeks of the death-pale face, and the deepset eyes fluttered open. Lees' stare was blank, but then recognition returned and he struggled up into a sitting position.

"Easy does it," Abberline said.

"No need to concern yourself now." The medium wiped the spittle from his lips as the inspector assisted him to his feet. "What happened?"

"Don't you know? You had a seizure."

"Not that. The vision came."

"What vision? What did you see?"

"I can't remember—" Lees' eyes went blank again. "Did I say anything?"

Abberline nodded. "You tried, but it made no sense. I think I caught two words."

"What were they?"

"One sounded like a name. McCarthy, it could have been."

"And the other?"

"A number—thirteen." The inspector peered at Lees, expectation in his glance. "What does that mean to you?"

"Nothing." The whisper came, faint as a hiss of smoke from the fireplace. "All I know is that something is going to happen. And there's no way to stop it now."

CHAPTER THIRTY-TWO

San Domingo, A.D. 1805 *A white military commander was captured and brought to Dessalines, who watched him being flayed to death with thornbushes. As he expired, a soldier ripped out his heart with his bare hands and ate it raw. Then, as a decorative touch, he tore the entrails out and hung them on a tree limb.*

• • •

The crowds began gathering in Westminster early the next morning, lining the route of the Lord Mayor's procession.

Cicely Marchbanks arrived in her carriage, wearing a fine new cambric gown. Old Mrs. Hargreaves took the train up from Richmond, carrying a lorgnette in her reticule for viewing purposes and unfurling a parasol as a shield against the sun. Jenny Potts came all the way from Yorkshire via charabanc, bouncing along with her straw bonnet askew.

The hawkers were out, peddling souvenirs and sweets; flower girls displayed their late autumn blooms; beggars and fiddlers competed for attention amid the excited outcry of children whose nannies and governesses shepherded them through sunlit streets.

All London swarmed to see the sights. Here stood Snibbs the greengrocer and Bert the hostler, beside gray-haired Alf Dawkins who'd fought the Pandies at Lucknow when only a nipper. Lionel Wyndham bestrode his mount from Rotten Row, Sid Fowler rode over in his donkey cart, and George Robey made the trip by shank's mare, up to get a booking on the halls and make his bloomin' fortune. Lords and ladies joined barristers and barmaids, jolly jack-tars jostled pious prelates; mingling in the mob were butchers and bakers and candlestick makers, for everyone was out to see the parade.

Everyone but John Bowyer, worse luck.

Way past ten o'clock it was, and him still grubbing away at the chandler's office, waiting for His Nibs to stop mucking about and give him leave to go.

If he hurried he might still get to the Strand in time for the ceremony. They said the Lord Mayor—James Whitehead, whatever his bleeding name was—would be tossing money to the crowd from his coach. Not bloody likely, but if he did throw a bit of nicker about, John Bowyer was ready to come by with a shovel and scoop it up.

Instead he stood there like a ninny whilst the ships' chandler totted up his books. Not marine affairs this morning, mind you, but rental payments. The old skinflint made a nice thing out of letting rooms in the stews he owned in Miller's Court. He sat mumbling over his ledger, then looked up. For a moment Bowyer took heart; maybe the silly sod heeded the procession and meant to tell him to go off. But no such luck.

"Blast the bitch!" he said. "I've warned her before."

"Who, sir?"

"The Kelly woman. Four bob a week is all I'm asking for her room, and she's run up thirty in arrears without payment. Serves me right for listening to hard-luck stories from that one." He thumped his fist down on the open ledger. "Now then, John. I want you to pop over to Number Thirteen straightaway and see if she's going to give me some money. If not, I'll have the bailiffs on her. Mark you, this time I mean it. Tell her that for me."

Bowyer nodded. "Right you are, Mr. McCarthy."

He picked up his hat and off he went, round the corner to Dorset Street, whistling all the way. It was a trick he'd learned whilst soldiering; when the going is rough, no sense pulling a long face. Keep a smile on your dial and a merry heart will see you through. So he'd miss the procession, but no help for that. God knows it wasn't the end of the world.

"Two Lovely Black Eyes"—that was the tune. Heard Charles Coburn do it at the Empire Theatre in Leicester Square. Fancy hall, with electric lights at the entrance and all those juicy tarts on promenade behind the dress stalls. A pity he couldn't afford a fling with one, but Kelly was every bit as tasty. Black eyes. Black Mary they called her.

Mary Jane Kelly. A saucy piece, and no mistake. No wonder McCarthy let her lag so far behind on payments; chances were he was getting a bit of it on the side. John reckoned he wouldn't mind having a go at that himself. She had a proper handful, fore and aft. Still young and pretty, too—not like the fat haybags in the pegging-crib he was passing now.

Nobody in sight there, not even the jock-gagger who usually lounged in the doorway ready to pounce when a likely customer hove in view. Come to think of it, all Dorset Street was empty this morning, and not a soul scoffing in the greasy slap-bang or hoisting a pint over at the Britannia suckcrib on the corner. All off to see the Lord Mayor at Guildhall they were, and celebrating the Prince of Wales' birthday to boot.

God, how he'd love to boot that one! Fat old swine, him and his Jersey Lily. And his sod of a son, the one they called "Collars and Cuffs"—queer as snow in June. That's all they did in high places, muck about with anyone willing to drop their pants; man, woman or child. What was it like to take champagne with one of those fine ladies, pull down her petticoats, gamahuche her—

John Bowyer wasn't whistling now. Here he was, walking down Dorset Street with a lump in his britches, come all over randy.

And here was Miller's Court, at Number Twenty-Six, just past the archway; houses on either side and others at the rear. Bowyer moved down the passage looking for the door to Mary Kelly's room which was marked thirteen. Some said it was an unlucky number, but not for him.

Not for him, because he'd already made up his mind. Ask after the rent, yes, but in a quiet way, conversation-like. And if she pleaded for more time, he'd not insist, just play the proper gentleman. Give her to understand she might have another day, provided she was willing to show a bit of gratitude. A favor for a favor, you might say.

Somewhere in the distance guns were booming from the Tower, either for the Lord Mayor or the Prince of Wales. No matter which, Bowyer didn't give a fig about either now. There were better sights to see than a bloody parade.

Suppose when he knocked that Mary Kelly was still abed, all fresh and ready after a good night's rest? And she'd come to the door in a hurry without thinking to put on her robe, just wearing her nightdress? A long, filmy nightdress, but sleeveless and cut low in front, cut low so you could see the big beauties peeking through the tangle of her dark hanging hair. Oh God and when he put his hands on them....

Instead he put his hand on the door and knocked.

No answer.

So he knocked again, but still no answer, not a sound from inside. He tried the knob but the door was locked. Either she was asleep or lying doggo, hoping he'd shove off.

Bowyer swore softly to himself. Stupid bloody bitch—if that was her game, he'd show her. There's more than one way to skin a cat.

He moved to the window beside the door. The muslin curtain was drawn so he couldn't see in, but luck was with him; the pane was broken and there'd be room to poke his arm through the hole at the bottom. He reached in, taking care not to cut his hand on the jagged edges of the glass, and pulled the curtain back.

Now he could see. See the little room with the fireplace grate on one wall. See the chair, the two small tables, the clothes folded up at the foot of the bed. See the bed, and what was lying on it. See Mary Jane Kelly.

Black Mary, lying on her back with her shift up and her legs spread, lying ever so quiet and still in all that blood.

Blood from her throat, cut clean across from ear to ear, so the head was dangling from the tip of her spine. Blood from the torn forehead, the raw red holes where her ears and nose had been sliced off. Blood oozing from the opening ripped in her stomach. Blood from the left arm, slashed so that it was only attached to the shoulder by a ragged piece of flesh. Her right hand was pushed into the great gash between her legs, which were stripped of flesh down to the feet. *There's more than one way to skin a cat.*

Did the cat yowl when its thighs were cut through? Did the cat screech when its guts were torn out? No matter, the cat was silent now. And the room was silent, except for the drip-drip-drip of blood.

Drops of blood dribbling off the bed where the liver lay between the scarlet-spattered legs. Blood trickling from the table-top heaped with horror—the nose, the shreds of skin, the bleeding blob of the hacked-away heart. The mincemeat mass which was all that remained of the amputated breasts. And on the walls, more blood, lacing the strands of intestines looped over the picture nails.

Blood everywhere, bathing what was left of the butchered body and the crimson ruin of what had once been a human face.

John Bowyer turned and ran, but there was no escape from what he'd seen; the flayed figure, the faceless head. And that was the worst—not because of what was missing, but because of what remained.

Everything else had been ripped from Mary Jane Kelly's face except for the twin horrors that would haunt his dreams. Two lovely black eyes....

CHAPTER THIRTY-THREE

San Domingo, A.D. 1805 *When black revolutionary general Henri Christophe captured Santiago, most of its inhabitants sought refuge in the church. There they were massacred, and the priest was burned alive in a bonfire of prayer books and his own vestments.*

• • •

As Mark watched, London went mad.

The murder of Mary Jane Kelly transformed the city into a vast asylum echoing with the outcries of its inmates. Some cowered fearfully behind locked doors, others ran wild, but everywhere the crazed clamor rose—voices babbling terror, wailing protest, screaming vengeance. The hue and cry was hideous by day, but at night the whispers were worse. Whispers of shapes glimpsed in darkness, of fearsome forms lurking in the shadows, of unseen presences stalking and crouching; bloodstained creatures with bloodstained knives, waiting to strike again.

The keepers of the madhouse fared no better than their charges. They heard rumors but no facts. There were investigations but no findings. There were confessions and arrests and incarcerations but none stood the test of truth.

The press spread panic, the authorities compounded confusion, and Sir Charles Warren officially resigned.

And on November 12th the inquest was held.

Early that morning Mark found Dr. Trebor at his office in the hospital, slumped over the desk, face ashen and gray-green eyes glazed.

"I'm not going," he murmured.

"Not going?" Mark stared at the haggard man.

"What a fool I was!" Trebor's voice quavered. "Wasting time, watching and worrying about the fate of those who didn't concern me. And all the while it was coming nearer and nearer, but I closed my eyes because I didn't want to see. Now it's too late. She's gone."

Mark controlled his features but he couldn't control his thoughts. *Madness is contagious. London Bridge is falling down. They've all gone crazy—Trebor too.*

He forced himself to speak. "You mustn't blame yourself. If the police can't cope, how can anyone come up with an answer? You couldn't have prevented Mary Jane Kelly's murder."

"It's not Kelly." Trebor raised a creased slip of yellow paper from his desktop. "The telegram came this morning. My wife is dead."

"I'm sorry. I didn't know—"

"Nor did I." Trebor rose slowly. "The next train's at noon. I'll be leaving shortly."

"If there's anything I can do—"

"Thanks. But don't worry, I'll manage." Trebor consulted his watch. "Abberline said he'd be stopping by on his way to the inquest. I'd appreciate your telling him what happened."

"Of course." Mark hesitated. "But I may not go with him. As you say, what's the use? There's really nothing I can do."

Trebor sighed. "Forget what I said just now. It was self-pity, not the voice of reason. I was wrong, Mark—the death of those women does concern me. And finding their murderer is a matter that concerns all of us. If there's the faintest chance of helping, it mustn't be ignored. When Abberline comes, promise me you'll go with him."

Mark promised, and he kept his word.

Later that morning, en route to Shoreditch Town Hall's mortuary, Inspector Abberline brought him up to date on the events of the past few days.

"A fine kettle of fish," he said. "You wouldn't believe the mess. When I got to Miller's court that morning the whole area was sealed off. Nobody'd been allowed to leave the premises. Inspectors, detectives, constabulary and four doctors stood outside the locked door to Kelly's room for over two hours."

"Why didn't they break in?" Mark asked.

"Warren's orders—his last before resigning. Nobody could enter until the bloodhounds arrived."

"Not again?"

Abberline smiled sourly. "The damned fool still insisted they could track the murderer. What he didn't bother to find out was that the dogs had been sent back to their owner weeks ago.

"Finally Superintendent Arnold had enough. He was too gutless to take responsibility for breaking down the door, but he ordered the windowpane removed. That's how the photographer got in."

Abberline answered Mark's puzzled frown with a shrug. "Some idiot had sent him down to photograph the eyes of the corpse, on the theory that the image of the murderer was fixed on the victim's retina."

"That's impossible," Mark murmured. "Surely the doctors must have known—"

"The doctors weren't much help either. After the pictures were taken, more orders came—this time from Anderson, as the new acting commissioner. The landlord, a fellow named McCarthy, got permission to break the door down with an axe. It was barricaded by a chest of drawers from inside. If you read the papers, you know what we found."

Mark glanced at the inspector. "Was it really as bad as they said?"

Abberline nodded slowly. "I've never seen anything like it, and God willing, I'll not see such a sight again. That's when we ran into trouble with the medical men. They were all for examining the corpse, or what was left of it, and we wanted the room cleared for a search. We let them take the remains to Shoreditch mortuary in a carrier's cart. They say it took a team of two surgeons and four assistants to reassemble the body and do an autopsy. The doctors hadn't wanted the body removed to Shoreditch because the murder took place in Whitechapel. There was a row about that, but Superintendent Arnold insisted. He said he was following orders."

"Whose?"

Abberline grimaced. "I wish I knew. I've got a bloody lot more questions, but damned few answers. Everything in that room needs explaining. There'd been a fierce fire in the grate, hot enough to burn away part of a teakettle. Kelly's clothing was untouched, but other clothes had been burned—we found the wirework of a woman's felt hat, a piece of velvet from a jacket, the prats of a skirt, and there must have been other things that were completely consumed. But why was this stuff burned? And why kindle a fire at all?"

"Perhaps the killer wanted light to work by," Mark said.

"He didn't need the grate for that. There was half a candle stuck in a broken wine glass on the table, but it hadn't been used."

Mark nodded. "I see your problem."

"Only part of it," Abberline told him. "What sticks in my craw is the door, locked and bolted from the inside, with the chest of drawers shoved up against it."

"Isn't there a simple answer to that?" Mark said. "Obviously the murderer escaped by climbing out the window, then pulled it down again."

Abberline shrugged. "Nothing's simple or obvious about this case. We learned Kelly had been living with a man named Barnett— just between us, the autopsy showed her to be three or four months pregnant, presumably by him, though the fetus is missing."

"Missing?"

"Like Eddowes' kidney," Abberline murmured. "Kelly and her lover quarreled on October 30th—that's when the glass in the window was broken." He raised his hand to forestall the obvious query. "We've interrogated Barnett thoroughly and he's not a suspect. He visited her several times afterward, even brought her some money. But both he and Kelly used the window to leave the room after bolting the door from the inside. And they got back in again by reaching through the broken glass and pulling the bolt back.

"You see, according to his statement, the key to the room had been missing for at least ten days before Kelly died."

"Lost?" Mark asked.

"If so, then how could the door be locked from inside when we arrived?" Abberline paused. "The murderer used the window to escape, just as you said. But before he left he locked the door as well as bolted it. The man who killed Mary Jane Kelly is walking the streets somewhere right now—with the key to her room in his pocket."

Mark frowned. "But where would he get hold of it in the first place?"

"That's one of the things I'd dearly love to know. Perhaps the inquest may bring some evidence to light, but I doubt it."

And at Shoreditch Town Hall, the doubts were confirmed.

When the doctors were sworn in, there was a squabble over the hearing. As Abberline had pointed out, the murder took place in Whitechapel, where Wynne Baxter was the coroner. But Dr. Roderick McDonald was very much in charge here. "Jurisdiction lies where the body lies, not where it was found," he insisted.

Abberline nudged Mark, whispering. "Somebody wanted to keep Baxter out of this—he asks too many questions. McDonald's an M.P. you know. I think they picked him because he'd cooperate."

The jurors had been sent to the morgue to view the corpse, then to the scene of the crime. When they returned the proceedings began.

The first witness was Joseph Barnett, the unemployed fish porter who'd been Mary Jane Kelly's lover. He spoke of their relationship and quarrel, but added nothing that Mark hadn't already heard from Abberline.

Then came the women. A neighbor named Cox saw Kelly just before midnight, standing outside her room with a short, stout man who had a carroty mustache and wore a long coat and billycock hat. He had a pot of ale in his hand, and she seemed to be drunk. Mrs. Cox hailed her and she said, "Goodnight. I'm going to have a song." Kelly started to sing, and Mrs. Cox went out. When she returned at three in the morning all was silent inside the room. Around four o'clock she heard a woman's voice call "Murder!", but such shouts were commonplace during quarrels between tenants, and the sound seemed to come from outside the court. Since there were no further cries she didn't bother to investigate and went back to sleep.

Elizabeth Prater, another neighbor, also heard singing from Kelly's room that night. She went out for a while, but when she came back around one-thirty there was no light or sound from the room. At four in the morning she also heard the scream of "Murder!" but, like Mrs. Cox, she ignored it when silence followed.

Sara Lewis, a laundress, came to visit a woman living across the court from Kelly at two-thirty. Why she chose to pay a social call in the middle of the night wasn't explained, but as Mrs. Lewis came into the court she saw a man standing outside Number Thirteen. "He was stout, not very tall, and wore a billycock hat." It being none of her affair, she went on inside to see her friend and later the two women retired. Shortly before four Mrs. Lewis was awakened by a scream. This too was none of her business, so she dismissed it.

A Mrs. Caroline Maxwell, wife of a lodging-house keeper next door, had a different story. She'd seen Kelly around the court for about four months but had only spoken to her once. Mrs. Maxwell said she came outside between eight and eight-thirty in the morning and saw Kelly across the street and called out to her.

"What brings you up so early, Mary?"

"Oh, Carrie, I do feel so bad. I've had a glass of beer and brought it up again."

Mrs. Maxwell went on to Bishopsgate to get her husband's breakfast from a shop, but on her way back around a quarter to nine she noticed Kelly standing near the Britannia pub, talking to a man.

Mark heard the jury murmur as she spoke, and he listened intently when the coroner questioned her.

"What description can you give of this man?"

"I couldn't give you any. They were some distance. But I'm sure it was the dead woman. I'm willing to swear to it."

"You are sworn now," Dr. McDonald reminded her. "Was he a tall man?"

"No. He was a little taller than me—and stout."

"What clothes was he wearing?"

"Dark clothes. He seemed to have a plaid coat on. I could not see what sort of hat he had." There was confusion in the room, compounded when the coroner reminded Mrs. Maxwell that Mary Jane

Kelly had apparently met her death before dawn. But Mrs. Maxwell stuck by her guns.

Then Inspector Abberline was called to the stand. His statement followed along the lines of what he'd told Mark on the way over, only adding that a man's clay pipe had been found in Kelly's room. But Joseph Barnett said it was his; he'd smoked it many times.

Finally Dr. Bagster Phillips was summoned. He described how the room was broken into and the body was found, but the coroner cautioned him not to give the gruesome details—these could be described at a later date. Phillips stated that the immediate cause of death was severance of the right carotid artery.

Now Coroner McDonald took over. In his opinion there was no need for further testimony. "If the coroner's jury can come to a decision as to the cause of death then that is all they have to do. From what I have learned," he continued, "the police are content to take the future conduct of the case." He didn't want to take it out of the jury's hands, he said, but unless they wanted to meet again in a week or a fortnight, they could deliver a verdict now.

Mark glanced at Abberline sitting across the way, and read his reaction. The coroner was making it all quite simple, merely a cut-and-dried matter of confirming the cause of Kelly's death. Obviously he wanted the inquest closed now, once and for all.

And the jury didn't argue. The foreman delivered the expected verdict—willful murder by some person or persons unknown.

The inquest was ended.

As the spectators filed out of the room, Mark joined Abberline. Neither man spoke until they reached the carriage and started off for Scotland Yard.

"Well?" Mark said.

Abberline's forehead furrowed. "It's a cover-up. The whole thing was prearranged, starting with the order to take the body to Shoreditch. I still don't know who was behind that move, but my guess would be Salisbury himself."

"The Prime Minister?"

"I'm not sure, but it must have been someone very high up."

"For what reason?"

"God only knows." Abberline winced as though in pain, and Mark noted his reaction.

"Never mind me," the inspector said. "It's just that stomach of mine."

"Something you ate?"

"Something I can't swallow." Abberline grimaced. "Did you hear how those witnesses contradicted each other about the last time they saw Kelly? And the contradictions in their descriptions of the man they saw with her?"

"It doesn't make sense," Mark said.

"That's why I asked you to come along to the Yard with me now. I'm told there's a chap waiting who has more to tell. Perhaps he can shed some light on the confusion."

But in Abberline's office at Scotland Yard, George Hutchinson only added another piece to the puzzle.

He was an unemployed laborer who'd known Mary Jane Kelly for some time, or so he claimed. Around two o'clock on the night of the murder, walking the street with no place to sleep, he saw a man standing on the corner at Thrawl Street. Moving past him, he met Kelly at Flower and Dean Street. She asked him for sixpence but he told her he had nothing. "I must go and look for some money," she said.

"Then what happened?" Abberline asked.

"She went on toward Thrawl Street. The man standing there came up and put his hand on her shoulder. He said something I couldn't hear and they both burst out laughing. They went past me together, he with his hand still on her shoulder. He had a soft felt hat on, drawn down over his eyes. When they walked across the road to Dorset Street I followed them at a distance and watched. They stood at the corner of Miller's Court for about three minutes and I heard Kelly say she'd lost her handkerchief. The man pulled a red handkerchief out of his pocket and gave it to her. Then they went up the court together."

"You say you stood at a distance," Abberline murmured. "How could you see a red handkerchief so far away?"

"It caught the lamplight," Hutchinson told him. "He waved it about like a bullfighter and made her laugh."

"And then?"

Hutchinson shrugged. "I went into the court to see if I could see them, but I couldn't. The light was out in Kelly's room and I heard no sound. I stood outside for about three quarters of an hour to see if they'd come out again, but they didn't, so I went away."

"Did you have any reason to wait?" the inspector asked.

Hutchinson smiled sheepishly. "You know how it is. If the chap left, I meant to ask Kelly if I could spend the night in her room, me being skint and all." His smile faded. "But the bugger stayed."

"This man," Abberline said. "What did he look like?"

"About five feet six or eight inches tall, and around thirty-five years old. He had a dark complexion and a dark mustache turned up at the ends. He was wearing a long dark coat trimmed with astrakhan, a white collar and a black necktie. There was a horseshoe pin fixed in it. He had a pair of spats over button boots. His coat was open, and I saw a gold chain on his weskit with a red stone in a big seal hanging from it. Looked like a foreigner to me."

"You saw all this while they were talking?"

"Yes, they were under the light. And I noticed something else." Hutchinson's voice lowered almost to a whisper. "He was carrying a small parcel in his left hand, about eight inches long, with a strap around it, or a piece of string. It looked as though it was covered with dark American cloth."

"Oilcloth?" Mark meant to speak further but Abberline silenced him with a warning look, then fixed his eyes on Hutchinson.

"Why didn't you volunteer this information before?" he asked. "You could have offered it at the inquest."

"And put my neck in a noose?" Hutchinson shook his head. "Much good that'd do me! I don't mind telling you, or talking to the newspaper chaps, just to show I've nothing to hide. But how do I know a jury'd believe me?"

"What makes you think I do?"

"Because you're a copper. You know a bloke doesn't come forward with such a story unless he's got nothing to hide."

"I see." Abberline rubbed his hand across his chin. "In that case suppose you tell me something else. What time did you say you let off watching outside Kelly's room?"

"Three o'clock. I can give you that for sure, because the church clock struck the hour just as I was leaving."

"And where did you go then?"

"Like I say, I'd no money for a kip. I walked the streets until dawn. Then I spied a pile of sacks in an alleyway and curled up on them for a bit of sleep."

"All right." Abberline nodded. "I'm letting you go on about your business, though I warn you there may be need to see you again. Leave word at the sergeant's desk where we can reach you."

"At your service, guv'nor." Hutchinson smiled in weary relief. "But I've told you all I know."

When he left, Mark turned to the inspector. "Do you believe that fellow?" he said.

Abberline walked to the window and stood before it, staring out at the gathering darkness beyond. "If he wasn't lying, it helps clear up some of the accounts we heard at the inquest." '

He retraced his steps, speaking slowly. "Let's try to put the pieces together. Mrs. Cox sees Kelly outside Number Thirteen before midnight talking to a short stout man with a carroty mustache. They've been drinking, and Kelly takes him into her room for a bit of business.

"Elizabeth Prater hears her singing in the room when she steps out, but when she comes back there's no sound or light coming from there.

"Kelly's customer couldn't have stayed long, because she goes out again and Hutchinson meets her on the street. Maybe the first chap doesn't pay her, because she asks Hutchinson for sixpence. He watches while she picks up another man—taller, better-dressed, with a dark mustache. They go to her room and Hutchinson stands waiting outside.

"Most likely Hutchinson was the one Sara Lewis saw around two-thirty, since he says he stayed in the court until three. When he leaves all is quiet."

Mark nodded. "That would explain discrepancies in descriptions of the man the witnesses saw. There were actually three different men—Kelly's first drunken customer, the second fellow who accosted her in the street later on, and Hutchinson himself." He hesitated. "But how can we be sure the women told the truth?"

"I think they did," Abberline told him. "Because all of them—Mrs. Cox, Prater, Sara Lewis—say they heard a voice crying, 'Murder!' at four o'clock or thereabouts. Which pretty much corresponds with the medical opinion as to when Kelly was killed."

"You're forgetting one thing," Mark said. "The other woman, Mrs. Maxwell, swore she saw Kelly alive between eight and nine the next morning."

"I'm not forgetting it." Abberline's face was grim. "And I don't think the coroner forgot it either. If I'd been presiding you can be sure the inquest would never have been closed until we got to the bottom of that business. Just what did she see and what did she really say? According to her testimony, Mrs. Maxwell had only spoken to Kelly once before, but here she has the two of them calling each other by their first names, just as though they were well-acquainted. Is this the truth or was Mrs. Maxwell elaborating on the story to make sure she'd get her name in the papers?

Believe me, I'd have asked a good many more questions before I was done with her. But the coroner chose to brush the whole thing aside, along with the missing key to Kelly's room. There has to be a cover-up!" He shook his head. "Trouble is, I can't prove it."

"Perhaps you can."

At the sound of the soft voice both men turned and stared at the man standing in the doorway—the man with the burning eyes.

CHAPTER THIRTY-FOUR

San Domingo, A.D. 1806 *Pompee Valentin Vastey writes of French atrocities against blacks. "Have they not hung up men with heads downward, drowned them in sacks, crucified them on planks, buried them alive, crushed them in mortars? Have they not consigned these miserable blacks to man-eating dogs until the latter, sated by human flesh, left the mangled victims to be finished off with bayonet and poniard?"*

• • •

As Robert James Lees entered the office, Abberline introduced him to Mark, then nodded at the medium. "What brings you here?" he said.

"Unfinished business, Inspector. You remember what I told you at your home the other evening? About the thread of evil?" Lees eyes glittered. "I've come to tell you that I've followed it."

"Another vision?" Abberline frowned impatiently. "Look here, Mr. Lees. I'd be happy to listen, but it's been a long day for me and the hour is late—"

"Later than you think," Lees said. "And I've had no more visions. Not since the night before the murder, when I gave you the name and the number."

Abberline's frown was erased by recollection. "That's right—McCarthy and thirteen."

The psychic nodded. "It's a pity I couldn't have been more specific. If I'd only known then what I know now—"

"What do you know, Mr. Lees?"

"After I learned about the murder it weighed on my conscience. I felt that in some way I was responsible for not being able to provide the exact information which might have prevented this dreadful crime. The least I could do now was attempt to find the perpetrator."

"That's what we're all trying to do," Abberline said. "Of course the newspapers still speak of tracking him down with bloodhounds, though no one takes it seriously."

"I did," said Lees. "Yesterday I went to Miller's Court to see if this faculty of mine would pick up the scent."

"A human bloodhound, eh?" Abberline's retort was more mocking than mirthful.

"You might call it that." Lees spoke without rancor. "Needless to say, I failed."

"Is that what you came here to tell me?"

"No. There's something else. As I say, there've been no more visions. But a strange feeling came to me when I stood there in the courtyard, staring at the numeral on the door of Mary Jane Kelly's room. The number seemed to change—and suddenly I saw the address I'd been trying to evoke ever since the day that I encountered Jack the Ripper and tried to follow him to his destination."

Abberline spoke swiftly. "The address—can you give it to me?"

"I'll do better than that." Lees nodded. "I may not be a bloodhound, Inspector—but if you'll come with me now, I'll take you to the house where Jack the Ripper lives."

CHAPTER THIRTY-FIVE

Spain, A.D. 1808 *In Toledo, in an underground chamber of the Inquisition, was a life-size wooden statue of the Virgin Mary, her head haloed in gold. A heretic would be led before her by the priests, given the sacrament, and asked to recant, at which time the Virgin stirred, opening her arms to the sinner. "A miracle has come to pass!" the priests exclaimed. "Behold, she welcomes you to her arms—in her bosom, all sinners confess!" As they urged their prisoner forward, the arms of the statue closed upon him like a vise and steel spikes rose from the Blessed Virgin's breast to skewer the victim alive.*

• • •

Outside the Yard a light rain fell as Abberline requisitioned the services of a cab.

Lees seemed concerned. "Aren't you going to take an official vehicle?"

The inspector shook his head. "This isn't an official call," he said.

The psychic voiced his reservations. "But if our man is on the premises now, it could be dangerous. If we came with an armed constable—"

"Don't worry. There's three of us. I doubt that he'd risk going up against such odds. Besides, if we arrive in an ordinary hack, he won't suspect the purpose of our visit."

Mark had his doubts, but Lees seemed satisfied. And as they entered the carriage it was he who gave the driver an address.

"Seventy-four Brook Street," he said.

Abberline's forehead creased with concern. "Off Grosvenor Square, isn't it? That's hardly where I'd expect to find the Ripper in residence."

"If I'm not mistaken, some of our staff physicians live in that area," Mark said. "I gather it runs a close second to Harley Street."

"That's not surprising." Lees nodded. "After all, the man we're looking for is a doctor."

"How do you know?"

"I can't tell you how I arrive at such conclusions," Lees answered. "It would be more accurate to say that the conclusions come to me. That's how the force operates—just as it did when it revealed the name of Mary Jane Kelly's landlord and the number of the room where she met her fate."

During the drive he repeated the story of his visit with Abberline on the night of the murder. "I assure you this is no fabrication," Lees concluded. "Everything I've told you is true."

Mark glanced at Abberline and the inspector shrugged. "That's why we're making this trip. Mind you, it's off the record. I'd hate to think what Matthews would say if he knew about this wild goose-chase."

Robert James Lees frowned. "I suggest you reserve judgment until we arrive," he murmured. "Remember, this is not my doing. I am only an instrument of the powers that guide me."

There was silence then, save for the rumbling of cab wheels over wet pavement. And in the stillness Mark found himself reflecting on their mission with growing eagerness.

Powers that guide. Powers of the mind—unrecognized, unexplored, unexplained. And largely ignored by medical scientists, except for the few who ventured beyond physical manifestations into the uncharted areas of psychological phenomena.

Wasn't that exactly what he himself wanted to do? Behind what we call thought was a vast unseen world, a realm of instinct, intuition, inexplicable insight; the domain of dreams. It was easy to dismiss such matters, label them as superstition and old wives' tales. But as a matter of record—a record which orthodox science chose to overlook—some of the old wives' tales proved to be correct. History attested that predictions and prophecies, so-called second sight, often had a basis in truth. Mark didn't have reason to believe in spiritualism or communication with the dead, but there were genuine instances of messages from beyond. Not necessarily from beyond the grave, but beyond the reaches of the conscious mind. If so, this force might very well manifest itself in the form of visions. How else to explain the power Lees had demonstrated? It was guiding them now. And if it was real—

The carriage pulled up, depositing them before the house off Grosvenor Square. As it drove away the three men moved up to the shelter of the doorway, and for a moment Mark felt a twinge of doubt.

All of the dwellings here were imposing; ornate examples of Georgian architecture nestling amid well-kept surroundings in a quiet, well-lighted setting. As Abberline had said, this house held no hint of being the residence of the Ripper.

"Seventy-four," the inspector was murmuring. "I know that address from somewhere—"

Suddenly he snapped his fingers. "By God, now I remember! It just came to me." He faced Lees, his eyes narrowing. "Do you know who lives here? This is the home of Sir William Gull!"

"The Queen's physician?"

Abberline nodded, then started to turn away.

"Where are you going?"

"Back to the Yard, of course. Do you think I'd chivvy a man like Gull and accuse him of—"

"Not accuse." Lees put his hand on the inspector's arm. "Merely inquire. Obviously he's not the one I saw. But Gull may be giving him shelter."

Abberline halted. "You still believe the Ripper lives in this house?"

Lees hesitated before replying. "I could be wrong about his residence. But I know he's been here—the aura is unmistakable."

"So now you're changing your story, is that it?" Abberline scowled. "Yet you're still asking me to go through with this?"

The medium's eyes were lambent in the dim light of the doorway. "You know I was right in the past. The forces that guided me then will not lead us astray now. I beg of you, don't turn your back on this opportunity. It may be your only chance of learning the truth."

Abberline glanced at Mark.

"I agree," the younger man said. "We've come this far. Unless we go on now, we'll never know."

Abberline sighed. "Very well, I'll chance it. But heaven help us all if you're wrong."

Moving to the door, he raised the brass knocker and let it fall.

For a moment they stood expectantly, and then the door swung open.

"Gentlemen?" The uniformed parlor maid's look of inquiry was transformed into one of concern when Abberline identified himself.

"We should like to see Sir William if we may," Abberline said. "Is he at home?"

The girl hesitated uncertainly, then turned as another figure moved up behind her.

"Who is it, Maud?" The elderly matron in the campanular-skirted gown peered out at the visitors.

Patiently, Abberline introduced himself once more, then gave the names of his companions.

The older woman smiled. "I am Lady Gull," she said. "Please come in." As they entered the hall she addressed the maid. "That will do, Maud."

Dipping her head in acknowledgement, the maid retreated along the corridor to disappear through a doorway beneath the circular staircase which rose at the far end of the lofty hall.

Lady Gull led her guests into the drawing room at the right of the entryway. As they entered, Mark's first impression was one of elegance—the crystal chandelier, the ornate carving on the arms of the high wingbacked chairs, Landseer landscapes in great gilded frames dominating the side walls, the brasswork gleaming before a huge fireplace beneath a massive mantel. He had no opportunity for further appraisal because Abberline was already speaking.

"Thank you, Milady, but there's no need to impose on your hospitality. If we could have a word with Sir William—"

"I'm afraid that won't be possible," said Lady Gull. "As you may have heard, my husband suffered a slight stroke just over a year ago."

"I'm sorry, I wasn't aware—"

"Fortunately he has recovered, but his condition demands rest. I make it a practice never to disturb him after dinner."

"Susan!"

She broke off, turning at the sound of the deep voice echoing from the doorway as Sir William Gull entered the room.

Mark recognized him at once from his portrait hanging in the hospital library. He'd aged since it had been painted; his hair was entirely gray and the effects of the stroke were evident in his slight limp. But the heavy, square face surmounting the short, pudgy body was almost unchanged.

Lady Gull faced him now, her concern obvious as she spoke. "I thought you were already abed. You shouldn't be down here—"

"I heard your visitors." Gull squinted at Abberline from beneath his bushy brows. "In fact I've been standing in the hall, trying to make head or tail out of this insolent invasion of privacy."

Short-bodied and short-tempered, Mark reflected. But to his surprise, Abberline was smiling.

"Allow me to explain," he said. "I am Detective Inspector Abberline. This is Dr. Mark Robinson, from the staff of London Hospital." He nodded at Lees. "And the other gentleman is—"

"I know him." Sir William Gull turned to the psychic. "Robert Lees, isn't it? You're the spiritualist fellow who used to give spook messages to Her Majesty."

Lees' smile concealed his resentment of the description. "That was many years ago, Sir William. I'm flattered you remembered."

"No flattery intended." Gull's voice was gruff. "What brings you here now—more hocus-pocus?"

Before the medium could answer, Abberline intervened. "It's a matter of some delicacy—"

"Meaning it's indelicate." Gull glanced toward his wife. "I'll deal with these gentlemen myself."

Lady Gull hesitated. "Are you quite sure you're up to it?"

"It's what they're up to that interests me." Gull's gesture was a peremptory dismissal. "Please be good enough to close the door as you leave."

Lady Gull did not reply, but her look of reproach was eloquent as she turned and swept out of the room, her bell-shaped skirt trailing across the heavy velvet carpet.

Once the door swung shut, Sir William wasted no time. "Now, sir." His glowering glance was directed at Abberline. "Will you kindly explain why you were badgering my wife?"

"That wasn't my intention," Abberline said. He nodded at Lees. "This gentleman can tell you why we're here."

Caught by surprise, Lees cleared his throat nervously and began to speak.

Mark too had been surprised by the inspector's request, and found himself puzzling over it. Sir William Gull obviously disliked the spiritualist and rejected his claims to psychic powers. Surely he wouldn't believe the account he was hearing now, so why did Abberline want him to recite it?

There had to be a reason; Abberline was nobody's fool. Perhaps playing the fool was deliberate on his part. Mark recalled how he'd displayed knives to evoke responses from the surgeons at the hospital. Did he have a similar purpose now in letting Lees tell his story?

If so, his efforts were rewarded. When the medium spoke of recognizing Jack the Ripper on the omnibus, Gull started visibly at mention of the name. Listening to Lees' description of the man, his face flushed angry red. Then, as the psychic told of his intimations of the Ripper's destination and the power that guided him here, Gull exploded.

"You're insane! How dare you insinuate that I would harbor such a creature under my own roof?"

Lees quailed beneath Gull's fury. "You mistake my meaning, sir. I was not implying anything of the sort. I only know that he came here—not his purpose."

"Have you any proof? Did you see him enter this house?"

"No." The medium's voice trembled. "But I sensed he was going to some house in this area when he fled. And today, in Miller's Court, the address revealed itself to me."

"Revealed itself!" Gull's lip curled. "In what manner? Did you hold a séance? Did you summon the spirits to tip tables and rattle their tambourines? Did the ghost of Mary Jane Kelly come a-tiptoe to whisper in your ear?"

"Please!" Lees faltered, darting a sidelong glance at Abberline as he stood impassively across the room. "I beg you to hear me out. All I'm saying is that there must be some connection—"

"None whatsoever!" Gull's voice rose. "No connection at all!"

"I'm afraid there is." Abberline spoke with quiet conviction.

Gull faced him now, his eyes challenging. "The man's a lunatic!" He shook his head. "Surely as a police officer you place no stock in this rubbish about spirit messages?"

"What I believe isn't important," Abberline said. "I put my faith in facts."

"And just what facts are you talking about?"

The inspector met Gull's stare. "You are the Queen's physician?"

"Physician in Ordinary, yes."

"And as such, you have attended members of the royal family."

"Certainly."

"Including the Duke of Clarence?"

"On occasion." Gull frowned impatiently. "But why do you ask? These are matters of public record."

"Then let us get on to matters that are not. What was the nature of the Duke of Clarence's illness some years ago?"

Gull shook his head. "I am a physician, sir. As such, I respect the privacy of my patients and will not—"

"I withdraw the question," Abberline said. "But I'm afraid the matter isn't as private as you think. It's well-known that the Duke contracted syphilis."

Gull swallowed quickly. "Who told you this nonsense?"

"I have it from an unimpeachable source. The same source that informs me of his deteriorating mental condition, and of his involvement in the Cleveland Street affair."

"That's a lie!" Gull shouted. "Eddy was never charged—"

"Thanks to you." Abberline silenced him with a nod. "You've protected him all along, you and your friends in high places. Protected him from the press, the public, his own family. They don't know about his midnight excursions to the East End or what he does there. But you do."

As Mark watched, Gull's face went white. And Abberline, noting the effect of his words, continued. "You know how he avoids detection, and where he goes afterward for his pleasures—"

"No!" Gull's mouth worked convulsively. "I don't—there are times I've tried to follow him, fearing for his safety, but he's too clever for that. He always managed to elude me—"

"So he could go anywhere?" Abberline spoke softly. "And do—anything he chose?"

"For God's sake, man!" Gull's voice sank to a whisper. "What are you suggesting?"

"Only what you must have suggested to yourself. Need I spell it out for you?"

Sir William shook his head quickly. "It's true," he murmured. "I did suspect what you're hinting at. If you only knew what torments I've suffered at the thought, until I put my mind at rest!"

"How did you do that?"

"By checking the Court calendar." The Queen's physician gained a measure of control as he continued. "Eddy was staying in Yorkshire when Polly Nicholls was killed, and at the Cavalry Barracks in York when Annie Chapman met her death. He was in Scotland at the time of the double murder, and at Sandringham from the third to the tenth of November. He was there to celebrate his father's birthday on the ninth, the date of Kelly's death." Gull paused. "That leaves only the first crime—the Tabram woman, on Bank Holiday."

"No need to concern ourselves with that," Abberline told him. "We've already eliminated her from our list, since the nature of her wounds differs from those of the other victims."

Eliminated? Mark suppressed surprise. *He didn't tell me that.* But it was becoming increasingly evident the inspector knew more than he chose to reveal. When he did so it was for a definite purpose—as was the case tonight, when he'd broken Gull.

And Sir William was broken, no doubt about that. He faced Abberline now without defiance, his voice subdued.

"Thank you for giving me this comfort," he said. "Perhaps I can find some measure of peace, now that I know Eddy is completely innocent. The poor lad has endured enough at the hands of muckraking journalists without suffering any added burden. My loyalty to the Crown impels me to ask your silence—"

"You'll have it," Abberline broke in. "On one condition."

"And what is that?"

The inspector glanced at Robert James Lees as he replied. "There are others besides the Duke of Clarence whose reputations are involved in this affair. Mr. Lees, for example. It was his account which brought us here tonight—an account you disparaged, together with his integrity. I must ask you now to tell the truth. Who was the man that visited you the other day?"

For a moment Gull stood with lowered head. Then he sighed heavily. "Very well, if you insist. His name is John Netley."

"The coachman who drives Eddy when he switches carriages midway on his trips to Whitechapel?" Abberline nodded.

Gull looked up, startled. "Then you already know—?"

"Only that this is the method Eddy used to elude your pursuit. But I want you to tell me Netley's purpose in coming here."

"Because I summoned him," Gull said. "It was only recently that I learned of his part in these escapades. Needless to say, I made it quite clear to him that the game was up, and that he faced dire consequences unless he put an end to assisting Eddy. He gave me his word."

Abberline nodded again. "And you have ours, as to keeping silence."

"Thank you, Inspector." Gull turned, moving toward the door and Mark noticed that his limp was more pronounced. "Now, if you'll excuse me—"

Opening the door, he escorted them down the hall. They left silently, and nothing was said until after they started down Brook Street in the direction of the hack stand on Grosvenor Square. The rain had ceased but there were no passersby on the glistening pavement.

It was Lees who spoke first. "Thank you for coming to the defense of my reputation, Inspector. I'm sorry I was wrong about the Ripper living on the premises, but one thing I'm still positive of—he's been in that house! Sir William was lying."

Abberline halted under the street-lamp and Mark followed his startled stare.

"How do you know?"

Lees' eyes gleamed somberly in the gaslight. "Because John Netley's a coachman. And the man who visited Gull the other day—Jack the Ripper—is a doctor."

CHAPTER THIRTY-SIX

Italy, A.D. 1815 *Gaetano Mammone, a brigand who became a captain in the Army, found refreshment in drinking his captives' blood. At times he would decapitate a victim, scoop out the brains from the skull, and use it as a goblet. Herding prisoners into a barn, he nailed their hands to the walls, doused the straw with oil, locked the doors, and set the barn on fire.*

• • •

Shortly before eleven that evening, Mark returned to the hospital. Since Trebor had left he was a free agent this week with no set hours or duties to perform, and today's events had drained him of any desire to volunteer his services.

It was on Abberline's request that he came—a request casually delivered when they parted after the carriage had dropped Lees off.

"I wonder if you would do me a favor?" he'd asked. "Does the hospital keep some sort of file on the comings and goings of staff physicians?"

"Of course. All duty hours are recorded."

"In that case, perhaps you could make an inquiry. I'd do it myself, but if word got out that I was asking questions he might get the wind up."

"He?"

"Dr. Hume."

"Hume?" At the sound of the name, Mark started. "Do you actually believe—"

"I believe nothing," Abberline said. "Not until I can establish his whereabouts on certain dates."

Mark nodded quickly then. "I know which dates you mean. Let me see what I can do."

"While you're at it, you might also find out if he was off-duty on the afternoon of the ninth."

"You're saying the man Lees saw on the omnibus could have been Dr. Hume?"

Abberline shrugged. "Lees told us it wasn't John Netley."

"Can you take his word for that?"

"I do, but it has no bearing on psychic powers. The man he saw had a mustache. Some time ago Netley's name cropped up in my investigations and I made it a point to locate a copy of his coach-man's license, with his photograph attached. Netley wears a full beard."

"Then you knew Gull lied to us. Why didn't you challenge him?"

"Not without further evidence. If I find it necessary to see Gull again I intend to come armed with adequate proof. That's why I'd like you to get me word about Hume's schedule, if you can."

"I'll do my best," Mark promised.

But now, at the hospital's reception desk, he met with swift disappointment.

"Sorry, Dr. Robinson," the night orderly clerk said. "We're not allowed to give out such information. You'd first have to get permission from Chief of Staff."

"I see." Concealing his disappointment, Mark started to move away when the clerk called after him.

"You can ask Dr. Hume himself if you like. He's due in for the night shift in another hour."

"Thank you."

For nothing, Mark told himself. It was hardly possible for him to confront Jeremy Hume with his questions. And if what he suspected was true—

"Mark!"

At the sound of Eva's voice he turned and saw her emerging from the left-hand corridor, dressed in street clothes. She wore no hat this evening, and the gaslight haloed her auburn curls as she approached.

"Are you on duty tonight?" she asked.

"No, I just stopped by. And you?"

"Through for the day, thank goodness." Eva smiled wearily. "And homeward bound."

"Might I escort you?"

She nodded. "If you like. But it's only a few blocks."

"I know." He fell into step beside her and they left the lobby together.

Once on the street, Mark took her arm. "You still owe me a dinner engagement," he said. "Perhaps we could stop somewhere for a bite to eat?"

"If you don't mind, I'd rather go straight home."

"Not even a cup of tea?"

"I've a kettle waiting, thank you. And right now all I really want is a chance to take my shoes off." She glanced at him as they crossed the street. "You seem tired too. Was it a trying day?"

Quickly Mark told her of the inquest, his subsequent journey to Scotland Yard with Abberline, and their confrontation with George Hutchinson there.

"Do you feel he was being truthful with you?" Eva asked.

"There's no reason to doubt it."

She frowned thoughtfully. "But what about those women at the inquest—and the one who claims she saw Kelly alive the following morning? It sounds very confusing."

"The whole business is confusing, including the way the coroner headed off any further testimony. Abberline vows there's a cover-up."

"He's an odd sort," Eva said. "Coming round to the hospital so often, asking all those questions. Do you really believe he knows what he's doing?"

"No doubt about it. In my opinion he knows more than he's prepared to say. And this time I'd swear he's on to something."

"You think highly of him, don't you."

"Abberline's no ordinary policeman. If anyone can snap the cuffs on Jack the Ripper, he's the man."

Mark hesitated, wondering if he should continue his account, then thought the better of it. Abberline had enjoined silence concerning their visit to Sir William Gull, and there was no reason to violate his trust. On the other hand, he'd sought information about Hume. And if Eva could supply it—

"Why so silent?" she asked.

"I was just wondering." Together they turned down Old Montague Street as he spoke. "Have you seen much of Dr. Hume lately?"

Eva shook her head. "If you're still worried about him molesting me, you needn't concern yourself. He's not shared my shift this week or last, so I've had no contact with him at all."

"You wouldn't happen to know what hours he keeps at the hospital, then?"

"Not really. Why do you ask?"

"I should think the answer is obvious."

She stared at him as comprehension came. "But why would Abberline suspect him?"

"He has his reasons."

"And you?" They halted before Eva's lodgings and she faced him beneath the lamplight. "What reason do you have for getting yourself involved?"

"I've asked myself that question a dozen times. Perhaps it's professional curiosity. If one could only find this man, learn something about him, the way he thinks, examine his twisted motives, it might tell us some things about the human mind—"

"Even if it means getting yourself killed in the process?" Eva's eyes clouded with concern. "Suppose the inspector is right? If Hume is capable of such crimes, he'll do anything to avoid being caught out. Don't you realize the risk?"

"I gave my word I'd help."

"But what if he suspects?"

"Don't worry, I'll be careful." Mark sighed. "If there was just some means of checking on his movements over the past few months without his knowing—"

"Maybe there is." Eva's eyes brightened. "The patient log book. All the staff surgeons keep a listing of their consultations and assignments. That would give the exact hours he was on duty and tell you when he was absent."

"Hume keeps such a record?"

She nodded. "I've seen it on his office desk. A small date book, bound in red leather. If you could get a look at that you'd be able to find out when he was away." Eva frowned. "But when would it be possible to do so without his knowledge?"

Mark pulled out his watch. "Now," he said. "Hume won't be on duty until twelve. I've still got better than half an hour."

"Suppose he comes in early?" Eva put her hand on Mark's arm. "You mustn't chance it."

"Don't worry. I can get back to the hospital from here in five minutes and slip in through the rear entrance." He smiled. "Thanks for telling me."

"I wish I hadn't." Eva shook her head. "Mark, please—"

"I'll be careful."

They parted then, but not before he promised to see her the following day during her nine-to-six shift.

Then he hurried back to perform his errand.

Entering the hospital presented no problem. He went around to the intersection of Oxford and Philpot Street, encountering no one en route—the thoroughfares, ordinarily quiet at this hour, were utterly deserted. London lay silent behind locked doors, trembling in the knowledge that the Ripper was on the prowl.

Mark found the gateway into the rear courtyard, a garden area of trees and shrubbery with a paved central open area. He'd heard it referred to as "Bedstead Square" because it was here that hospital beds were sometimes set out for cleaning or repainting.

Opening the door leading to an inside corridor he moved in shadow past a row of rooms set aside for storage, then turned into the dimly-lit consultation hall at his left. This too was totally unoccupied, and he breathed a prayer that it would remain so. There was always a watchman on patrol but hopefully he wouldn't be passing this way too frequently during the midnight hours.

Midnight hours. He still had twenty-five minutes. And if luck was with him—

It was.

The door to Dr. Hume's consulting room was unlocked, and the interior was dark. It remained so until he was safely inside; then, closing the door, he ventured to light an oil lamp on the desk and went to work.

Be careful. Despite his efforts at control, Mark's heart was beating swiftly, his ears straining to catch any sound of footfalls from the corridor beyond the door.

Eva had been right about the danger involved. If Hume was guilty he'd stop at nothing to avoid detection. And if he discovered someone rifling his office in the middle of the night....

Mark worked swiftly, feverishly. Nothing on the desktop except an appointment pad listing tomorrow's patients, and a scribbled notation about a surgery scheduled for seven tomorrow morning. The desk drawers opened at his touch, but their contents revealed little except the usual impedimenta—pens, pencils, blank notepaper, a city directory, sheaves of bills and receipts of personal purchases at local shops. And, in the bottom drawer at the right, a notebook.

He pulled it out, pulse pounding as he lifted it up to the light and opened its pages. All they contained were listings of street numbers and the names of other physicians. An address book, nothing more.

Where was the log?

Mark glanced at his watch, then went to the wooden file cabinet in the corner. The drawers slid back, confronting him with rows of folders. Here was data on patients, sheet after sheet of examination forms, charts, appended diagnoses. Each bore a heading which recorded time and date, but in no order. The four drawers must hold nearly a thousand of such files; it would take days to go through them all and extract the exact information he was seeking.

There were no other receptacles in the office here. So where could the log be?

Mark swore softly under his breath as he realized the obvious answer.

In Hume's pocket.

Of course that's where the log was; he carried it on his person. Probably most of the surgeons did so, as a convenient method of referring to past appointments. And if Hume's record contained any incriminating evidence of his hours away from duty he certainly wouldn't leave it unguarded here.

Mark froze as something echoed hollowly from beyond the closed door. Footsteps, approaching along the corridor outside....

Swiftly he extinguished the lamp, then flattened himself against the wall alongside the entrance. He could do nothing more, there was nowhere to hide, and if the door opened and Hume walked in—

The footsteps were louder now, sounding just before the entrance. Mark's hands tightened into fists, his temples throbbing in anticipation. *If the door opened—*

But it did not. And the footsteps moved on, dying in the distance.

Mark exhaled. Only the watchman, after all, and he was gone now, thank God. All quiet, safe to move again, close the drawers of the file cabinet. Close them quickly, for it must be almost midnight. A quick glance at his watch confirmed the hour. Time to leave.

Time to open the office door, slip swiftly down the hall, turn into the rear passageway leading to the back exit.

As he did so, grateful relief gave way to the bitterness of disappointment. He was safe, but he had failed. And because he'd failed there was no safety—not for himself, for Eva, for anyone. No safety at all with the Ripper still free.

For a moment it had seemed so simple, so easy. Find the log, check the entries, go to Abberline and play the hero. *Dr. Hume, I arrest you on the charge of murder—*

He smiled ruefully at the thought. Sheer melodrama, a scene from one of Mansfield's plays. But this wasn't make-believe; the Ripper was real, and so was the danger. Whether Hume was their man or not didn't matter now. Whoever the Ripper might be, he had his freedom. Freedom to walk the night, knife in hand, searching for fresh victims....

Midnight chimes sounded from a church nearby, and Mark's smile became a scowl. So many churches here in Whitechapel, so many prayers going up to God, and for what? Prayer had proved no protection against mass murder. There was no protection possible as long as Jack the Ripper prowled. He could be anywhere now, even here.

Mark moved into Bedstead Court, toward the shadows of the trees and shrubbery surrounding the rear gateway beyond.

And then, out of the darkness, the figure loomed.

Before he could move it was upon him—the hunched, bent figure in the black cloak, scuttling forward into the pale moonlight of the courtyard, its feet encased in baglike slippers, its head covered with a huge shapeless cap. Hanging from the brim was a gray flannel cloth, masking its face save for a glimpse of eyes glowing through a slit.

As the figure advanced, a wave of stench swept before it, and from beneath the concealing curtain came a panting sound.

Then, as Mark watched, the left arm rose. For an instant his eyes widened, waiting for the gleam of a knife in the moonlight, but the delicate fingers were empty. They grasped the hood, swept it back and removed the cap to reveal the face beneath.

But it wasn't a face.

Mark stared in horror at the misshapen skull striated with a few strands of lank hair growing down over a bony mass protruding from a bulging brow which covered one eye almost completely. The other peered at him from beside the formless lump of flesh serving as a nose. Beneath it was a pink stump projecting from the upper jaw, twisted to turn the upper lip back above the slitted mouth.

The mouth moved now, gasping for breath, and from the opening between the twisted teeth came muffled sounds only remotely recognizable as words.

"Don't be afraid," the creature whispered. "I'm John Merrick."

"Who?"

"The Elephant Man."

CHAPTER THIRTY-SEVEN

Sudan, A.D. 1822 *Muhammad Bey, commander of an army of Turkish invaders, killed fifty thousand natives and captured thousands of others. All male prisoners were emasculated. The breasts of the women were cut off. To slow their dying, he had their wounds filled with boiling pitch.*

• • •

As Mark reentered the hospital and followed the shuffling figure down the rear corridor, recollection stirred. Somewhere he'd heard or read about the Elephant Man—a deformed unfortunate, exhibited by an unscrupulous showman as a freak and rescued from his fate by an outraged physician. But what was he doing here?

The apparition in the cloak halted before one of the hall doors and its left hand turned the knob. "These are my quarters," the voice wheezed.

Now the door swung open on the lamplit interior of a bed-sitting room. Mark saw its meager furnishings—the bed itself, a small desk, several tables, a few chairs. There was a bookcase near the fireplace, and a door led to a bathroom on one side. Pictures hung on the walls, but no mirrors.

Their absence was understandable as Mark followed John Merrick into the room and watched him shed his cloak.

"Thank you for coming," Merrick murmured.

Mark nodded, secretly ashamed. It had not been compassion that caused him to accept the invitation, only professional curiosity—a curiosity which was shockingly satisfied as he saw the Elephant Man's face and form fully revealed in the lamplight.

From his bowed back rose a huge lump of cauliflower-like wrinkled dermal tissue hanging between protuberances on the shoulder blades. A similar sacklike growth dangled from waist to mid-thigh. Another brownish mass covered the chest. The right arm was swollen and shapeless beneath the weight of bulging flesh which terminated in rootlike fingers. The lower limbs were stunted and misshapen, thus accounting for Merrick's limp. In contrast, his left arm and hand were quite delicately formed and covered with smooth white skin.

Merrick used that arm now as he moved to the bed and adjusted the pillows, then leaned back upon the coverlet with a grateful sigh.

"Please sit down." The husky voice seemed more intelligible once Merrick reclined. "I'm sorry I can't offer you any refreshment—"

"Don't trouble yourself on my account." Mark found himself secretly wishing that a drink had been available—not to temper his shock but to combat the fetid odor of festering flesh which filled the tiny room. He noticed a window overlooking the courtyard, but it was tightly closed. Sitting uncomfortably on the edge of a hard chair, Mark broke the silence.

"How long have you been here?"

"Two years now, thanks to the kindness of Sir Frederick Treves. He's Surgeon Extraordinary to the Queen."

Surgeon Extraordinary? Mark thought of Gull's title—Surgeon Ordinary, wasn't it? Try as he may, he couldn't get used to the British custom of conferring titles and honors.

"He obtained permission from Mr. Carr Gomm, the chairman of the hospital committee, who arranged for my room and maintenance here."

Mark listened, marveling at Merrick's command of language. Buried within that monstrous malformed mass was an alert, articulate human being.

His eyes wandered to the bookcase, noting that the shelves were filled with volumes; prominent among them was an oversized Book of Common Prayer.

Merrick followed his gaze. "I read a great deal to pass the time," he said. "And they've been kind enough to provide me with material. Particularly the picture books, so that I can learn about the outside world. I would love to visit your America, Dr. Robinson, though of course it isn't possible for me to travel such a distance."

"I'm sorry," Mark said. "It must be lonely for you here."

"At times, yes. But I do have friends." The finely formed left hand pointed toward the wall, indicating a framed photograph of Alexandra, Princess of Wales. To Mark's surprise he saw that it was autographed.

Merrick noted his reaction and nodded. "She has visited me, you know." He spoke with obvious pride. "Many noble ladies have come here. You can see some of their photographs and gifts there on the mantel and side-table. The silver-headed walking stick in the corner—that too was a gift. I never cease to give thanks for such kindness." The soft voice deepened. "Still, it's hard to accept that I am a prisoner here, condemned to live out my life in this miserable body of mine."

Mark nodded. "If there's anything I can do—"

"Your presence is enough." The huge head bobbed, struggling to convey appreciation which could never be shown by a smile. "The days are not difficult but often I find the nights an ordeal. You see, because of my affliction"—and here the left hand gestured down across the bulging body—"I cannot sleep lying down. I must sit up against the pillows here in bed with my legs drawn up, and rest the weight of my head on my knees."

"Can you manage comfortably that way?"

"When I am very tired, yes. But many times I stay awake. Then I sit by the window and gaze at the stars. Sometimes I do as I did tonight—slip out for a walk in the court to enjoy the trees and flowers."

"But always alone?"

Merrick's head bobbed again. "It's best not to attract attention. If someone happens to pass by, I hide in the shadows under the trees. When you came through just now, I thought for a moment you might be the other gentleman."

"What other gentleman?"

"The one who left the hospital earlier tonight by way of the courtyard."

"Who is he?"

"I can't be certain." Merrick's voice was muffled, but his words came clear. "A man with a mustache. He wore a deerstalker cap. I think it must be one of the doctors I met here at the hospital. His name is Hume."

CHAPTER THIRTY-EIGHT

India, A.D. 1837 *Lieutenant S.C. Macpherson reported on the practices of a Bengal tribe known as the Khonds. These primitives settled disputes by duels or ordeals—thrusting hands and arms into boiling oil or grasping bars of red-hot iron. Marriage was by capture. Unwanted girl babies were abandoned in the jungle, at the mercy of tigers, leopards, and other carnivores. Human sacrifices were regularly made to the Earth Goddess. A victim—known as a meriah—was the central figure of ceremonial orgies before death. His arms and legs were broken to prevent escape attempts; then he was thrust into the cleft of a split tree branch, which secured him by the neck. At a signal from the priest, the drunken worshippers fell upon their prey and tore him to bits.*

• • •

Mark wondered if the Elephant Man slept that night after he left him.

As for himself, there was little rest. Little rest, and far too many troubled thoughts. In the sleepless hours before dawn, he tried to impose some semblance of order on his impressions.

The photograph of Princess Alexandra in Merrick's room—was it just coincidence that the unfortunate creature cherished a picture of Eddy's mother? And the man in the deerstalker cap, could he actually be Dr. Hume? Did Hume steal out of the hospital at night to descend on Whitechapel, scalpel in hand? *The operation was a success, but the patient died—*

If only he could talk to Trebor! But that wasn't possible, and suspicions would not be resolved by an outsider's opinions. There was only one man he'd trust now, and at nine the following morning he found him at Scotland Yard.

Abberline seemed tired too. He sat in shirt-sleeves at his desk, and when Mark greeted him he pointed at the paper mountain rising before him on the desktop.

"Look at this," he said. "There ought to be a law forbidding lunatics the use of pen and stationery."

Seating himself, Mark peered at the pile. "More crank letters?"

The inspector nodded. "Warnings. Confessions. Tips from every Tom, Dick and Harry, and eyewitness accounts from their wives. Every woman from here to Edinburgh has seen a suspect hiding under her bed. Plus dozens of cards and letters purporting to come from the Ripper himself."

"You're pulling my leg."

"I'm tearing my hair." Abberline smiled wearily. "It seems as though every practical joker in the country has taken it upon himself to plague us. And the newspapers keep turning up correspondence they've received. Forbes Winslow gets a dozen or more every day. All fakes, of course; the handwriting differs, the style varies, the content is a dead giveaway that the writer doesn't even know the circumstances of the crimes he boasts of committing."

"Then why bother with them?"

"Because they bother me. At this stage of the game we can't afford to ignore any possibility that might crop up, no matter how improbable it sounds." He swept the papers aside and leaned back. "But I'm done with that for good."

"You've found something?"

"Perhaps." Abberline pursed his lips thoughtfully. "But first, let's hear what you've been up to. Were you able to get that information on Hume's activities on the murder dates?"

"The hospital refused to give it out," Mark said.

To his surprise, the inspector didn't seem upset by the news. "No great matter." He shrugged. "It may not be all that important."

"But this is." Quickly Mark told him of his meeting with the Elephant Man and the story of Hume's nocturnal departure by way of the rear courtyard.

Again he was startled by Abberline's reaction, or the lack of it. He'd listened carefully, but he was still leaning back.

Now Mark leaned forward. "'Do you see how it all adds up? You told me yourself that Hume frequents slaughterhouses—that he refused to talk to you about the murders. I know he wears a peaked cap which could easily be mistaken for a deerstalker. And you must have other reasons to suspect him."

"True enough. I've done some checking on my own. I have a clear picture of a left-handed man, with definite sadistic tendencies, who has been known to perform operations without anesthetics on occasion. A clear picture, but not a pretty one."

"Then isn't it time to act? You say yourself that you can't afford to ignore any possibilities. Maybe it no longer matters if you arouse Hume's suspicions. Go to the hospital in your official capacity and demand to see the record of his duty hours. Hume needn't be informed of your inquiries if you insist on silence."

The inspector nodded. "I've already considered doing so, and I may get around to it later. But as I told you, it's not important now."

"How can you say that?" Mark's voice rose. "If Hume is guilty—"

Abberline sighed. "Hume is dead."

"What?"

"The report came in an hour ago. He was run down by a hansom last night in Piccadilly Circus. Skull-fracture and a crushed chest. Died in the street before he could be moved."

"Good God." Mark sat stunned as the detective straightened in his seat.

"So you see, there's no urgency involved."

"But discovering his movements could still tell us if he was the Ripper."

"I'd like to think so," said Abberline. "And so would my superiors. It would solve the case very neatly, tie up all the loose ends. Unfortunately, even if we learned Hume wasn't on duty at the time of the murders, it would only prove opportunity, not guilt. And when it comes to circumstantial evidence of that sort, I may now have a better way of linking him to the crimes."

Mark frowned. "You said earlier that you found something?"

"Something found me." Abberline opened his desk drawer and pulled out an envelope. "Not all the letters I've received are necessarily hoaxes. This one was waiting when I arrived here today." He extracted a note sheet from the envelope and unfolded it. "A message from a Dr. J. F. Williams. Do you know him?"

"No, but I've heard the name. If I'm not mistaken, he's the head of St. Saviour's Infirmary."

"That's the man." Abberline scanned the sheet as he spoke. "And the infirmary is located over in Walworth, across the river from Whitechapel. Dr. Williams offers some interesting information, if his facts are correct."

"What facts?"

Abberline spoke slowly. "He tells me that at least three of the Ripper's victims—Annie Chapman, Polly Nicholls and Mary Jane Kelly—were treated there at the infirmary before they died. And another doctor helped attend them."

CHAPTER THIRTY-NINE

Fiji. A.D. 1850 *The Reverend Thomas Williams writes: "Cannibalism does not confine its selection to one sex or a particular age. I have seen the grey-haired and the children of both sexes devoted to the oven. Tortures consist of cutting off parts and even limbs of the victim while still living, and cooking and eating them before his eyes, sometimes offering him his own cooked flesh to eat."*

• • •

Crossing the bridge, Mark glanced past Abberline to catch a glimpse of the view from the carriage window.

London preened in the morning sunlight. The Tower battlements were less grim in its glow, the drab docks took on a sparkling radiance. Far to the right the dome of St. Paul's was haloed in a golden glitter.

Mark had almost forgotten the city's beauty—or did distance lend enchantment? It seemed to him he'd been imprisoned all these months in the dark dungeon that was Whitechapel; now, crossing the Thames, he was escaping to a world outside its walls.

But there was no beauty in Walworth. Dustmen shoveled and sweated in the streets, competing with cluttering sparrows for offal; specks of soot blurred the sunny shimmer above. The area reminded him all too vividly of the East End slums, and when at last the carriage brought them to their destination he found St. Saviour's Infirmary a great deal less imposing than London Hospital.

Nor was Dr. J. F. Williams' office any more attractive than the narrow cubicles he'd seen in his own daily rounds.

Dr. Williams himself provided the one bright note amid the bleak surroundings of the charity institution. A chubby little man squinting up at them through round gold-rimmed spectacles, he greeted his visitors effusively.

"Sit down and make yourselves comfortable," he said. "It was good of you to come. I'd an idea you might be interested."

Abberline took a chair beside Mark as he spoke. "You're sure of your facts?"

"Quite sure. I mentioned three patients in my letter, but actually there were four. The woman who called herself Tabram or Turner was also treated here."

"Why haven't you brought this to our attention before now?"

"I didn't know." Dr. Williams moved behind his desk. "It wasn't until the other day, conducting a routine review of our records for the past six months, that I came across the names." He beamed at his visitors. "Quite a coincidence, eh?"

Abberline frowned. "And so is the fact that all these women came here from Whitechapel."

"Not necessarily," Dr. Williams said. "We get more than a few patients from there. Begging Dr. Robinson's pardon, many East End residents come across the river for free treatment because they're afraid of London Hospital and its surgery. Our cases include any number of women like these."

"So it seems." The inspector glanced at the desktop. "Do you have their records available?"

"I pulled the files." Dr. Williams seated himself and produced the folders from a drawer. "Here we are." He opened the first file and peered down at the single sheet it contained. "Tabram, in July. The usual complaint—suffering from malnutrition." His smile faded. "But then, aren't they all? A pity we can't cure poverty with pills."

"And the others?"

Dr. Williams opened the second folder. "Polly Nicholls in August. Bruises and contusions on face and arms. Apparently she'd been beaten. Also the usual—eh, Dr. Robinson?"

Mark nodded. "I've seen my share of that."

Dr. Williams glanced at the contents of the third folder. "Chapman also came in August. Chronic nephritis, a concomitant of alcoholism." He opened the last folder. "Ah, here's Kelly. November first. As recorded here in her own words, she didn't have her flowers and feared she might be knapped."

Mark frowned. "Just what does that mean?"

The little man smiled. "Sorry, I forgot you're a Yankee. Translating street vernacular into English, it signifies that Kelly noted the absence of her menses and believed she could be pregnant. The examination disclosed the diagnosis as correct." He sighed. "Poor thing—such a tragedy."

"Did she say anything else about it?" Abberline asked.

"Not to me. I didn't see her."

"What about the others?"

"I've not seen them, either," Dr. Williams answered. "We treat scores of outpatients here daily and it's not possible for me to attend them all."

"Then who did?"

"We have quite a large staff of part-time volunteers—local physicians, some internees and the like." Dr. Williams glanced rapidly at the sheets before him. "The patient Turner was examined by an intern named Higgins. But the other three women were all treated by the same volunteer."

As he listened, Mark felt a flurry of excitement. "Was it by any chance a Dr. Hume?"

Williams shook his head. "No. This man's name is Pedachenko."

Now it was Abberline whose voice betrayed excitement. "Alexander Pedachenko?"

"That's correct. Do you know him?"

"Only by reputation. Russian, isn't he?"

"So it seems. As I recall, he claims to have obtained a medical degree some years ago and joined the hospital staff at Tver, wherever that may be. Although he emigrated he never became a citizen; as a foreigner he's not licensed to practice here." Dr. Williams smiled apologetically. "Perhaps I bent the rules a trifle in permitting him to work with us, but we're always sorely in need of reliable assistance."

Abberline nodded. "What else can you tell us about him?"

"Not very much. His surgical knowledge seems quite extensive. Naturally he couldn't be allowed to perform operations, but has frequently served in attendance. He's rather quiet and soft-spoken. He has a slight accent, though his command of English is excellent. I'd rate him as highly intelligent."

Mark leaned forward. "Could you describe his appearance?"

Dr. Williams shrugged. "I'd say there was nothing particularly distinctive about it. His complexion is a bit swarthy, but that's common among Slavs. Dark hair and eyes, of course, and around five feet eight in stature. With the usual mustache."

Inspector Abberline rose. "Will he be in today?"

"I'm afraid not. Dr. Pedachenko hasn't been with us for several weeks now."

The inspector scowled. "Done a bunk, has he?"

"I don't believe so," Williams said. "Why should he?" The eyes behind the spectacles held sudden concern. "Surely you're not implying any involvement in the fate of those poor females?"

"No implication intended," Abberline answered. "But since he attended them, he might know a few things which would help shed light on the matter. Naturally I'd like to question him. And when you tell me he's left—"

"No mystery about that, really." Dr. Williams smiled. "Apparently he was short of funds. He'd been supporting himself as a part-time barber's surgeon—removing warts and moles, the usual line. I gathered he intended to return to that work on a steady basis."

"Told you that, did he?" Abberline nodded. "You wouldn't happen to know where he's employed now?"

"Indeed I do." The small man flipped through the pages of a ledger resting on the left-hand side of his desk. "Now where's he listed? Ah, here it is."

He read the notation, then looked up. "You'll find him at Delhaye's hairdressing shop, over on Westmoreland Road."

CHAPTER FORTY

India, A.D. 1857 *Sergeant Forbes-Mitchell, of the 93rd Highlanders, writes of the relief expedition's arrival at Cawnpore, where wives and children of troops massacred after the garrison surrendered were themselves slaughtered while imprisoned in a bungalow. "Most of the men of my company visited the slaughterhouse. Among the traces of barbarous torture and cruelty...was an iron hook fixed into the wall of one of the rooms of the house about six feet from the floor. It was evident that a little child had been hung onto it by the neck with its face to the wall because the wall all around the hook was covered with handprints, and below the hook with footprints, in blood, of a little child."*

• • •

Inspector Abberline's stomach was at it again. All the way to Westmoreland Road it rumbled and grumbled while the carriage creaked along the grimy streets.

To make matters worse, Mark kept muttering away. He was a good sort, and it was useful to have a source of medical opinion at his elbow, but right at the moment Abberline would have welcomed a bit of silence—both from his stomach and his companion—so that he could sort out his thoughts.

As it was, he scarcely listened, and confined his replies to grunts and nods. After a long time Mark seemed to take the hint and ceased his chatter.

Not that Abberline faulted him for being stirred up over the errand. At the moment he was busy blaming himself, though for a different reason.

Why hadn't he given more attention to Alexander Pedachenko before? The name had come up, along with that of Severin Klosowski, another barber-surgeon. There was also a man called Konovalov, and a Michael Ostrog. All of them Russians or Poles, all somehow connected with medical practice, all named as possible suspects by informants. He'd passed the word along to the proper quarters for further consideration, but little information had come back to him. Several of them appeared to be anarchists but only one— Michael Ostrog—was fully interrogated, and he turned out to be a lunatic.

If only he'd followed through himself! But too much else claimed his attention; this cover-up which seemed to involve Eddy, the business with Robert James Lees and his psychic presentiments, the odd affair of Dr. Gull and his false statement. There just hadn't been time to go with the other leads.

And now, out of the blue, Pedachenko. On the face of it he sounded a likely candidate for the Ripper's role. But if so, where did that leave Eddy's possible involvement, and Lees' visions, and Gull's evasions? Was there some link between all this and the Russian barber-surgeon? Had he been wrong, or could there really be someone like Sweeney Todd, the Demon Barber of Fleet Street?

Try as he would, Abberline couldn't see it. But somehow the connection must exist, if Pedachenko was the man he sought.

If.

Abberline's stomach protested as the cab jerked to a halt on Westmoreland Road.

The hairdresser's shop was a hole in the wall of a building block between a taxidermist's quarters and a confectionary. Its seedy, rundown interior reeked of stale cologne.

So did its proprietor. Delhaye was a willowy wisp of a man whose bushy hair seemed badly in need of his own barbering services; there were no customers on the premises to claim them at the moment. He spoke with a slight accent—French, or so Abberline judged—and his gesturing fingers plucked air as he spoke.

The gestures grew more agitated when he learned of their mission.

"But of course I know Pedachenko! A most capable fellow—we often worked together."

Abberline frowned. "He's not here now?"

"Alas, no. I have not seen Alexander since I discharged him last spring."

"Why did you sack him?"

The hairdresser shrugged. "I had no choice." He gestured at the empty barber-chairs. "Times are hard."

"That was your only reason for letting him go?"

Delhaye glanced at the inspector quickly. "Why do you ask? Is he in some sort of trouble with the police?"

"No trouble. It's just that he might be able to furnish us with some information about a case we're working on."

"Information—ah yes, now I understand. He is a learned man, that one."

"Would you know where we might locate him?"

"But of course. He lives not far from here. If you wish, I can give you the number—"

"Please do."

Armed with the address, Abberline left the shop and moved down the street with his companion. His stomach still bothered him but Mark did not. For the moment he found himself rather grateful for the excursion. Desk duty and paperwork were the worst part of his job; it was action that exhilarated him, action and anticipation. And now, after all these months of plodding and puzzlement, he could envision an end to failure and frustration.

Approaching the shabby row of flats on Fall Street, he rang the bell at the entrance and felt expectation rise.

It fell with a thud when the elderly landlord answered his questions.

"Pedachenko?" The old man's head cold turned the name into a sniffle. "That's right, guv'nor. Had a room here all last year and right on through spring. Moved out some time in June."

"Did he leave a forwarding address?"

"Not as I recall. You know how it is—they comes and goes."

Abberline had a burning sensation beneath his belt buckle. Now that anticipation had fled, there was nothing left to shield the spasms. All he could do was plod on. Routine questions, routine replies.

"Can't say I remember much about him," the landlord told him. "It was just good-morning or good-evening, should I chance to pass him in the hall. Kept to himself, he did."

The old man sneezed. "Your pardon, guv'nor." A gray sleeve rubbed across his reddened nose. "Seems he was in and out quite a bit—I gather he worked for a barber over on Westmoreland, most likely another foreigner. All kinds of them in the neighborhood now, though nary a one about when I was a lad—"

Abberline scarcely listened as the landlord snuffled on, but he forced himself to nod and plod further with his questions.

"Visitors?" The elderly man shook his head. "Not to my recollection. And no women. I don't hold with any mucking about on the premises. Come to think of it, I only saw him once in female company. Just before he left, when his sister come for him. I warrant he meant to give up his room here and move in with her."

Abberline felt a flicker of interest. He asked for a description of the sister and jotted it down in his notebook. But attention wandered again when his query yielded no name or address for the woman. *Plod, plod, plod.*

By the time they left he was anxious to find a cab stand somewhere back along Westmoreland Road. It was then, as they walked, that Abberline resurrected a glimmer of hope.

He nodded at Mark. "You must think I've put you to a lot of trouble for nothing."

"That's all right." Mark's face was wan in the late afternoon sunlight. "We tried our best."

"Not to worry." The inspector managed a smile. "It may not be a dead end after all."

"What do you mean?"

"We didn't nab him yet, but at least we have reason to believe that Pedachenko could be our man. We've got a description that fits, and his contact with victims heightens the possibility."

As Abberline spoke he felt his spirits rising. "And there's another good lead to follow. We know Pedachenko has a sister, and the landlord gave us enough to recognize the woman when we find her."

Mark glanced up. "How do you propose to do that?"

"By putting out the word. Until today we've been stymied on just how to identify one man out of the many. Now we have a name to go by, and a link with another person. The search will be a lot easier. Once we locate Pedachenko or his sister, alone or together, I promise you we'll get our answer."

CHAPTER FORTY-ONE

United States, A.D. 1864 *Methodist minister John Chivington turned soldier and took command of the District of Colorado. In November he moved troops against Black Kettle and his peaceful Cheyenne, encamped at Sand Creek. His force of seven hundred found five hundred Indians, mostly women and children, asleep at dawn. Black Kettle awoke, raised the American flag on a lodgepole, then a white flag. But the soldiers, many of whom were drunken volunteers, fired into the fleeing mob with side arms, rifles, and cannon loaded with small shot. About forty women took refuge in a cave. They sent a six-year-old girl with a white flag. She was immediately riddled with bullets. Dragging the women forth, the soldiers butchered them and took their scalps. Chivington and his band of heroes returned to Denver brandishing a hundred bloody scalps, which were displayed in a local theater.*

• • •

Mark already knew the answer.

He forced himself to stay silent during the drive to the hospital, forced himself to remain calm as he took his leave of Abberline there, forced himself to nod and smile and return greetings to staff members he met as he hurried through the halls.

But the answer echoed—the answer, in the voice of the landlord as he'd spoken of Pedachenko's sister. "Younger than him. In her early twenties, I'd say, and didn't have his accent. A bit on the tall side, fair complexion, with blue eyes and red hair. Offhand you wouldn't take her for a sister—"

Nor did Mark. The girl the landlord described was Eva.

He reached her at the entrance to the nurses' quarters, shortly after six, just in time to see her come out wearing street garb.

She greeted him with a smile of relief. "Mark! I've worried about you all day—you said you'd see me, remember?"

"I've been busy." He took her arm. "Come into the library. I must talk to you."

The library was deserted during the change in shifts and he faced Eva there in privacy. As they seated themselves on the sofa she glanced at him expectantly.

"Tell me what happened. Did you find the datebook in Hume's office last night?"

"It wasn't there."

"I'm sorry."

"Don't be. The book isn't so important, now that Hume is dead."

"Dead?" Eva sat stunned. "I didn't know—"

Nodding, Mark told her of his morning visit to Abberline. "I imagine tonight's papers carry the story," he said. "But that may not be important either. It seems we have another suspect."

Quickly he described his visit to St. Saviour's Infirmary with Abberline, and what they had learned there. As he talked he watched her reaction.

"Pedachenko," he said. "Alexander Pedachenko." Mark met her startled stare. "Why did you tell me his name was Alan?"

"Oh my God!" Her eyes widened "How did you guess—?"

"It wasn't a guess. We've seen Delhaye, and Pedachenko's former landlord. When he described the woman he thought to be a sister, I knew." He spoke softly. "Why did you do it, Eva?"

"Because he asked me to." Her face was white. "There was a reason, a very good reason. It had nothing to do with what you're suggesting—"

"Don't you understand?" Mark stared at the girl, reading the anguish in her eyes. "He was using you."

"I don't believe it! He couldn't—not Alexander—I don't believe—"

But she did; Mark saw realization replace remorse as her shoulders shook and she broke off, sobbing.

His hands rose and she came into his arms. He felt the warmth of her, the trembling touch of her fingers as they tightened against his back. "Oh, Mark—I've been such a fool! I should have told you—"

"Tell me now."

The sobbing subsided, and then at last she spoke. At times her words were scarcely audible to him as she fought for control. But there, in the gathering twilight, the story emerged.

She'd met Pedachenko at a medical lecture shortly after her arrival in London. Lonely and friendless, she welcomed his courteous attention; even his foreign mannerisms seemed attractive. He too was without friends or family, struggling to make his way in a new and strange environment. At first he identified himself as a physician, and not until later did she discover he wasn't permitted to practice. But by then—

Eva blushed, her gaze dropping.

"You became lovers?" Mark's voice was strained.

"Try to understand," she said. "I was so alone. And when he told me of his misfortune, my heart went out to him."

As Mark's eyes questioned, Eva nodded. "I gather he spoke to Dr. Williams about his work in Russia as an army surgeon. But I'm the only one who knows how he hated it. Hated it so much that he deserted." She took a handkerchief from her pocket, dabbing her eyes as she spoke. "Alexander came here illegally. He made no effort to obtain a license to practice because it would mean revealing his identity to the authorities. That's why I never gave anyone his right name. He told me if the Russian secret service discovered his presence here he'd be deported."

"But that wasn't the real reason," Mark said.

"How can you be sure?" Eva raised her pale face to the light. "Couldn't there be some mistake?"

"You're the only one who can answer that, I think." Mark spoke gently. "After all those months the two of you were together, you must have suspected something." He took her hands in his. "The truth, Eva. All of it."

She shook her head. "How could I realize there was anything more? He'd wait for me outside the hospital and we'd dine together. He couldn't visit me in my room, nor I in his. Finally he found another place where we could—"

"I understand." Mark nodded, then frowned. "But why did you go to his quarters when he told the landlord he was moving?"

"He asked me to come there and pose as his sister, just in case anyone ever questioned why he'd left. By this time he said he was convinced he was under surveillance by Russian agents, and wanted to cover his tracks." Again she halted; then her words came with a rush.

"But even afterward we weren't together all that often. I had my work hours here and Alexander never spoke of his life apart. Over the last few months there were times he broke appointments without any explanation. When I questioned him he told me someone must have talked, and whenever he felt he was being followed he'd change his plans to outwit them. At first I accepted this, but gradually I began to wonder. And then, when he asked me to lie for him, we broke off."

"When was that?"

"Do you remember the time you asked about seeing us, and if we'd spent the night together?"

"Yes. You were angry with me."

"Not angry. I was upset. You saw us earlier that evening, when he came to take me to dinner. But later, after dining, he went off alone without a word. And when we met again, Alexander didn't explain. It was then he told me to lie in case anyone inquired.

"I was furious, because I thought I knew the reason. I accused him of seeing another woman. He denied it—there was a scene. I'd never seen him in such a rage before. In the end he struck me and stormed off. I don't know where he went or where he's staying now, but he left his new lodgings the following day and I haven't set eyes on him since."

"Do you remember the date of your quarrel?"

"It was the end of September—on the last night of the month."

"September thirtieth." Mark spoke slowly. "The night of the double murders."

"I know." Eva's pallor was death-white now. "I should have guessed. It's just that I didn't want to believe. Don't you see? The thought that he and I had been together, and all the while—" She pulled free, burying her face in her hands. "No, it's too horrible!"

"And too dangerous." Eva looked up as Mark continued. "Remember what I told you about John Merrick seeing a man in the court behind the hospital? He thought he recognized Hume, but suppose it was Pedachenko he saw? Lurking about, waiting for a chance to get hold of you?"

"But why? We've broken up, it's finished."

"Not if he realizes you've come to suspect him. You know too much."

Eva shook her head in swift denial, but there was fear in her eyes, fear in her voice. "Oh no, he wouldn't—"

"Do you think a man who butchered five innocent women would hesitate to kill again? There'll be no safety for you now until Pedachenko is in the hands of the police."

"But I don't know where he is! What can we do?"

"The first thing is to go to Abberline and tell him everything you told me."

"I can't risk that. What will they think here at the hospital once they know?"

"Damn the hospital! It's your duty to speak out. More than a duty, now that your life may be at stake. And if you don't come forward, Abberline will come to you."

"You're not going to tell him?"

"I don't have to." Mark shook his head. "The inspector isn't a bumbler like the others. Remember, the landlord gave him a description of you as Pedachenko's sister. He seemed to pay little heed at the time, but he told me he intends to mount an all-out search for the missing man and that mysterious sister of his."

"But he'd never connect me with all this."

"Don't count on it. I know Abberline. He's seen you several times, and once he studies that description again, he's bound to recognize whom it might apply to. Take my word for it—if you don't see him tonight, he'll be seeing you tomorrow."

Mark took her hands once more. "If you're really worried about anyone at the hospital finding out, then you don't want the police coming here. But I trust Abberline. If you volunteer that information, I think he'll agree not to involve your name."

Eva hesitated, frowning. "How can you be sure of that?"

"I'm only sure of one thing. As long as Pedachenko is free, we're all prisoners. And if he decides to strike again, you're his next victim. Eva, promise me—"

She sighed. "What do you want me to do?"

Mark pulled out his watch. "It's six-thirty now. I'll contact Abberline immediately and set up an appointment."

"All right. But I want you to come with me when I go."

"Of course." Mark nodded. "I'll be at your lodgings with a carriage at eight."

CHAPTER FORTY-TWO

United States, A.D. 1866 *A huge band of Sioux warriors ambushed Captain Fetterman's eighty troopers, killing or wounding them all in a little over half an hour. Those who still lived were beaten to death with clubs and their bodies mutilated so that their spirits would be similarly disabled forever in the Great Beyond.*

• • •

London was going home for the night.

Underground transported packed-in passengers; the streets above were a-swarm with horse-cars, cabs, carriages, carts and barrows.

Mark swore softly as his own cab moved slowly through the tangle of traffic. Damn the C.I.D.! One would think that a city of seven million would be protected by a police force with better means of communication than telegraph messages and runners. True, a new Scotland Yard was being planned, and it would be linked by telephone throughout all the stations. But that didn't help the situation now.

Nor did it mend matters when he finally reached the Yard. There he had reason to swear again as the sergeant at the reception counter told him that Abberline was out.

"I must see him," Mark said. "Where can he be reached?"

The sergeant scanned the duty roster resting on his desk. "He's with Commissioner Monro. They're dining with Home Secretary Matthews at the Savoy Club."

Mark consulted his watch. Seven-thirty. It would take him a good half-hour just to get over to the club rooms and he'd promised to meet Eva at eight—

"If it's of any help to you, sir, he left word he'd be back by eight-thirty."

Relieved, Mark pocketed his watch. The problem was resolved, if he picked up Eva as planned, they could be back here together by the time Abberline returned.

He nodded at the sergeant. "Tell the inspector that Mark Robinson was here to see him. I'll come by again at eight-thirty or shortly thereafter. Please ask him to wait for me—it's urgent."

Once outside Mark had no difficulty in hailing a cab, and to his relief the flow of traffic was abating. In the rising fog streetlamps glowed dimly on darkened shops and shuttered windows.

Now the carriage jolted into narrower, less-traveled thorough-fares. Here in Whitechapel there were few vehicles to impede progress, but the fog seemed to swirl more thickly along the empty pavements. Even the light was different here; corner gas-lamps flickered like distant candles guiding his way through the gray gloom to Old Montague Street.

Mark left the cab as it halted, nodding to the driver. "Wait here," he said. "I'll be right out."

He moved up the walk to the door, glancing again at his watch with a smile of satisfaction. Three minutes past eight, and all is well—

But a minute later his smile had vanished.

The landlady was a plump middle-aged woman with a friendly look about her; it was her words that set him scowling.

"Sorry, sir. Miss Sloane's not in."

"Are you sure? We have an appointment—"

The landlady shook her head. "She left about a 'arf-'our ago."

"But she promised to wait. Didn't she leave any word where she was going, some kind of message for me?"

"It was a message by late post that sent 'er orf. Some kind of medical business, I reckon, seeing as 'ow it come from a Dr. Robinson."

Mark stood stunned in the doorway. The fog was clammy but it wasn't chill that made his flesh crawl. "I'm sure you must be mistaken," he said. "I am Dr. Robinson. I sent no message."

The landlady frowned. "Beggin' your pardon, sir, but are you sure? That's 'ow it was signed—*Dr. Mark Robinson.*"

"Did you read the message yourself?"

"God's truth. I 'ave it on the 'all table right where she left it."

"May I see it?"

The landlady stepped back. "Not so fast. 'Ow do I know—"

"Here." Mark reached for his wallet and pulled out his passport for her inspection. "Satisfied?"

She nodded, then drew back, opening the door wider. "If you'll step in, I'll fetch it for you."

Standing in the hallway Mark stared down at the crumpled sheet of notepaper which the landlady removed from its envelope and placed in his hand. The scribbled note was brief.

> *Dear Eva:*
> *There's been a change in plans. Will explain when I see you.*
> *Meet me immediately at 2111 Providence Street. I shall be waiting*
> *for you there.*
> *Dr. Mark Robinson.*

The landlady peered over his shoulder. "You see, sir? Got your name on it, just like I said."

"That's not my handwriting," he murmured.

"Then 'oo sent it?"

Mark didn't reply. But he knew the answer—knew it the moment he saw the jagged, sprawling scrawl. He'd seen it before, on two letters and a note. Even with a false signature, he recognized the sender.

It was a message from Jack the Ripper.

CHAPTER FORTY-THREE

Sudan, A.D. 1882 *When British forces were defeated at El Obeid by the Mahdi, the wounded were castrated by his followers and left to die of thirst in the desert sands. When death came, their skulls were used to erect a pyramid before the city. Captured spies were buried alive in anthills or staked out and covered with fat that boiled their bodies in the blazing sunlight. Others had their genitals smeared with honey to attract flesh-eating insects.*

• • •

2111 Providence Street was a weathered two-story frame house—a raddled relic of the past, hiding from the present in a courtyard behind a crumbling wall. Overshadowed on both sides by boxlike blocks of brick flats, flanks guarded by an iron-spiked fence rail, it crouched in darkness like a beast in its lair. Over the granite chin of its doorstep the entrance gaped, an open mouth. The lightless windows set on either side above were empty eyes staring out at the night.

The beast waited as Mark moved up the courtyard walk through the fog, listening to the fading clatter of the carriage wheeling along the street beyond. By the time he reached the doorway all was silent. Silent and dark, like the opening before him.

Perhaps the beast was dead. A dead beast, buried at the dead end of a forgotten street. There was nothing to fear from its blind eyes above, and the mouth below was toothless. But if there was life inside....

He halted on the doorstep, peering through the open entrance into the shadowy hall within. No light shone, no sound disturbed the silence. The house seemed deserted—was it possible he'd made a mistake?

But the address on the note had been plain to see, and the hand that scrawled it was unmistakable. The hand that held the pen was the hand that held the knife. The hand of the Ripper.

Mark's eyes searched the shadows for a hint of movement. Nothing stirred in the stillness of the hall ahead.

"Eva?"

He called softly into the silence.

"Eva—"

His voice echoed through distant darkness.

Slowly, cautiously, he crossed the threshold to halt in an uncarpeted hall. The walls were bare and there was no sign of furnishing. Only the staircase rising before him, its steeply slanting wooden steps leading up to the floor above. His eyes climbed the stairs, climbed in darkness until they found the light.

The light, fanning faintly from beneath the closed door of the upper landing—

"Eva!"

He moved forward, and now it was his feet that climbed the stairs, climbed carefully as his hand groped for support along the rickety railing. Fixing his eyes on the guiding light he reached the top of the staircase and started through the shadows toward the door beyond.

Behind him, the floorboards creaked.

Startled, he whirled quickly, but the shadow was swifter still. The shadow looming from deeper darkness behind him, its left hand clutching a sliver of light.

Not a light—merely a reflection from beneath the doorway. And the sliver was the blade of a knife.

The knife stabbed out, slashing at his throat.

Mark swerved as it came down, razoring empty air. The broad blade swept within inches of his neck, and the shadowy hand that held it rose again.

He tried to grasp the upturned wrist, but the shadow swirled and the knife descended, ripping through the fabric of his coat collar.

The blade tore free and Mark fell back, pressing against the hard surface of the door. Too late he turned; the knife was rising once more and this time there was no escape.

Mark felt a rush of air as the steel swooped forward; there was barely an instant to crouch beneath the thrust. With a thud the blade buried itself in the wood of the door panel above his head.

Shadowy hands tugged frantically at the hilt of the imbedded blade but Mark rose upright, desperation driving his clenched fists into yielding flesh. The shadow had substance. It gasped in pain, then grunted as Mark hammered against the unseen outline of bulging body and bloblike head. The shadow panted, clawing for his wrists. As its face bobbed forward Mark struck out with all his force, feeling the crunch of bone. Blindly the shadow reeled back to the edge of the staircase—back, and over.

As it fell, one hand shot out to grip the rail-post. The weakened wood gave way with a crash, and the railing smashed down upon the shadow as it tumbled; tumbled and fell, then sprawled still amid the welter of woodwork on the landing below.

Dazed, Mark descended, moving slowly, then halted on the lower steps to stare down at the huddled form buried by the debris.

It was a shadow no longer. Silhouetted against dim light from the entryway lay the body of a man, his head twisted at a grotesque angle.

He was obviously dead; there was no mistaking the fact. And as Mark stared, there was no mistaking the face.

Alexander Pedachenko, lying lifeless on the floor at the base of the landing.

But where was Eva?

Mark turned, glancing towards the light glimmering under the door at the top of the stairs.

He started up slowly but his pace quickened as he realized the sounds of struggle hadn't aroused the occupant of the lighted room beyond the door. Which meant—

Mark shook his head, dismissing the thought. But it persisted, speeding his ascent and staying with him as he reached the upper landing and hurried to the door.

When he grasped the knob and found it fixed, thought gave way to panic. The door was locked.

The door was locked, like the door of Number Thirteen in Miller's Court. Mark remembered what they'd found behind that door—remembered the Ripper's victim and what he'd done to her.

"Eva!"

His shout shattered silence, but there was no answer. The answer lay behind the door, and it must be shattered now.

He slammed into it with his shoulder, bracing himself against the blow. To his surprise the worn wood gave way, splitting the upper panel as the imbedded knife loosened and fell unheeded to the floor. Now he aimed his knee at the surface beside the lock. The metal hasps which held it broke free.

Again he grasped the knob, and this time the door swung open.

The door swung open, but Mark's eyes were shut. For a moment he stood there, not daring to look, not wanting to see. The vision came unbidden behind closed lids; the vision of Mary Jane Kelly, or what remained of her, lying on the bed.

But he had to look now, had to see.

He gazed into the light, gazed at the cluttered room by the light of an oil lamp on the night table. On the far wall, an open window, with a bed beneath.

Eva was lying on the bed—

CHAPTER FORTY-FOUR

The Congo, A.D. 1887 *King Leopold of Belgium employed efficient methods to obtain supplies of rubber from the natives whose land and lives he had expropriated. A white officer writes of a raid on a village which failed to meet its quota promptly. "We fell upon them and killed them without mercy.... The commander ordered us to cut off the heads of the men and hang them on the village palisades, also their sexual members, and to hang the women and children on the palisades in the form of a cross."*

• • •

Eva was lying on the bed.

There was no blood, no mutilation, no disfigurement. Eyes closed, she rested peacefully.

Rest in peace....

Mark went to her then, noting the pale face, the tumble of auburn curls over her shoulders, the curve of breasts beneath her blouse rising and falling in the rhythm of breath.

His own breath quickened at the sight.

She was still alive, thank God for that. He lifted a blue-veined wrist, found the pulse, and rejoiced at its regularity. Bending forward, his fingers raised her right eyelid to expose the pupil as he watched it find a focus on his face. She stirred, suddenly aware, and her lips parted in a whisper.

"Mark—"

He smiled. "Easy now. Don't move."

Wariness came into her eyes. Her voice, stronger now, held a note of alarm. "Where is he?"

"You needn't worry. Pedachenko is dead."

He seated himself on the side of the bed as her arms rose, clinging closely while he explained his presence here.

"You were right," Eva murmured. "But I'd never seen his handwriting. I didn't know the note was a ruse until I came here and found him waiting."

She glanced over his shoulder at the steamer trunk resting amid a welter of clothing and scattered objects on the floor near the closet door.

"He told me he was leaving tonight, leaving the country for good, but he couldn't leave without saying goodbye. And that's what he did—he put his arms around me and said goodbye. I tried to break free but he grabbed me by the throat and pressed the cloth against my face—chloroformed, of course, I recognized the odor. I remember hitting out at him, and then—"

She shuddered. "God knows what he meant to do if you hadn't arrived to interrupt him. He must have planned to get rid of me before he left, in case I suspected him. But it's not just suspicion now. We can go to the police with proof."

"What proof?"

Eva sat up, swinging her legs over the side of the bed as she gestured toward the closet door. "Look in there."

Mark rose, moving to the closet, then turned as Eva followed. "You're sure you're all right?"

"I'm fine now." She smiled with wan reassurance. "When I came in he was standing here and the door to the closet was open. Before he closed it I caught a glimpse of what was inside."

As she spoke, Eva pulled the door back to reveal the closet's contents—the woman's skirt, the blouse, the jacket hanging on a rack and the bonnet dangling from a hook.

"He must have brought these along with him when he went to Miller's Court. After the murder he burned his clothing in the grate and put them on. That's why those witnesses thought they saw Kelly alive the next morning—they saw him, when he left."

Mark spoke quickly. "What about his mustache?" He frowned. "Surely they should have recognized him for a man."

Eva was frowning too. "I wondered about that. Do you suppose he was too far away, and never faced them?" She brightened. "But there's other evidence. Didn't you notice the desk when you came in?"

She moved across the room with Mark beside her. He stared at the desktop, stared at the pen, the pile of notepaper, and the bottle of ink.

Red ink.

Red for danger. Red for the letters the Ripper wrote. Mark reached down to the drawer beneath the wooden surface of the desk, yanking it open.

He saw the neatly-folded stack of clippings at the left, a score of news stories dealing with the crimes. On the right were a half-dozen unfinished epistles inscribed in red ink. The handwriting was familiar, and so was the salutation which headed each sheet.

"Dear Boss—"

Mark started to scoop them up, then halted as something slipped from concealment between the scribbled pages and clanked against the bottom of the drawer.

He fished it out and held it up against the light from the oil lamp. Stamped into the worn metal on the rounded head was the number—thirteen. Kelly's missing key.

The lampflame flickered in the chill draft from the open window. But the chill Mark felt came from within.

He moved to the open trunk on the floor, Eva beside him as he stooped and riffled through its contents. Men's shirts, undergarments, a heavy woolen suit, a pair of boots, a dark brown leather bag—

Mark lifted the bag, placed it on the edge of the bed, opened it. He pulled out the oblong metal case and raised the lid.

Eva's eyes widened in the reflection of the lamplight—the lamplight that shone on the gleaming array of knives and scalpels.

"That's enough," she said. "Maybe we ought not to disturb anything else until the police get here. We'd better notify them now.'

"In a moment." Mark could feel the chill grow stronger. "I've got to make sure." He turned back to the trunk.

"But what else is there—?"

Eva's voice trailed off as Mark shifted a pile of garments and uncovered the black cloth sack. Loosening the drawstring, he pulled the cloth down and revealed a sealed glass jar, half filled with a colorless transparent liquid.

Floating in the fluid was a formless blob—or was it formless? At first glance it resembled a monstrous pink and white worm, coiled and bobbing against the lid. But this worm had stumplike arms, and a rounded, oversized head with a puckered mouth and slits for eyes.

It was a human fetus.

"Horrible!" Eva stood beside him, her face livid in the lamp glow. "To think he'd preserve something like that! The poor woman—"

"Who?"

"Mary Jane Kelly." She nodded. "Don't you see? The key, the women's clothing, the notes in the Ripper's handwriting—everything adds up."

"Almost everything." Mark stared at the fetus and now the numb chill rose; the chill of recognition, of realization. His gaze shifted to the girl beside him. "The information about the missing fetus was never published. Who told you Kelly was pregnant?"

Eva shrugged. "It must have been you."

He shook his head. "Not I. Nobody told you. You know because you saw it."

"Mark!" She faced him, eyes imploring.

But now the chill within him invaded his voice. "The burned clothing in Kelly's grate belonged to a woman, not a man. It's no use, Eva. I knew from the moment you told me about the chloroform. There's no cloth, no odor on your breath."

"What are you saying?"

"What I must tell the police. That you and Pedachenko never quarreled. You were both in this all along. You meant to leave together tonight, but decided to dispose of me first."

"Mark—"

"It was all going to be so easy, wasn't it? You hid here in the room while Pedachenko waited for me in the hall with his knife. When the plan went wrong, you faked unconsciousness and tried to fix the blame for the murders on him alone."

"But that's absurd—" Eva's voice broke, her mouth quivering.

Mark turned, unable to endure her anguish. "How did Pedachenko know you were meeting me tonight? Only because you told him. You arranged to have his note delivered, left it for me to find, luring me here—"

He caught the gleam out of the corner of his eye, caught it and fell back as she thrust her hand into the instrument case on the bed and gripped the shaft of the scalpel.

It rose, glittering in the lamplight, then plunged down towards his chest.

He thrust her away, but her eyes were glittering too, and a mewing sound rose in her throat as the scalpel stabbed at his jugular.

Mark twisted aside as the blade missed its mark, biting into his left shoulder, shearing through cloth, finding flesh, bathing his arm with warm, flowing wetness.

The scalpel tore free and Eva raised it again. But was it Eva?

The pain lancing his shoulder was so intense that for a moment his vision faltered. Then it cleared and he stared at a stranger. A stranger with a white, contorted face framed by a tortured tangle of reddish curls; a stranger whose eyes bulged and blazed at the sight of the bright, bubbling blood.

She lunged forward, the scalpel ripping at his throat.

Mark's right arm rose, his hand clutching at the wrist behind the swooping blade. His fingers closed, twisting tightly with all his strength. Something snapped, and as the scalpel dropped to the floor the stranger stumbled back. The night table toppled sideways, the lamp atop it shattering as it fell. Oil gushed into the carpet, licked by a tiny tongue of flame.

The stranger cried out, lurching against the window ledge on the far wall. Mark advanced and she raked at him with her left hand, wild-eyed, shrieking. Suddenly aware of her intent, he gripped both heaving shoulders to pull her back, but sharp nails shredded his cheek and she wrenched free.

He reached out again, hands grasping empty air as she turned and hurled herself forward. For an instant her blurred body seemed to hang suspended in space beyond the open window, then dropped into darkness. There was a single scream, then silence.

Gasping, Mark peered over the ledge. Over and down, down to the courtyard and the fence-rail encircling the walk below.

Skewered upon the iron spikes, something dangled. It wasn't a stranger anymore, and it wasn't Eva. The form was as limp as a rag doll, and the face leering up at him bore a doll's garish grin. One spike had pierced the neck, and a second impaled the skull to emerge through the left eye. From the empty socket a single teardrop oozed.

The tear was red.

And so were the flames leaping through the room behind him.

CHAPTER FORTY-FIVE

"More tea?" Mrs. Abberline said.

"No, thank you." Mark settled back in the wing chair, favoring his left shoulder. Beneath the bandage the wound still throbbed, but it was healing nicely now. If only memories would heal as easily—

Inspector Abberline caught his wife's eye. "Would you excuse us? We've things to discuss."

"Of course." Setting the teapot on the table near the fireplace, she left the room and closed the door behind her.

"Now," said Abberline. "From the beginning."

Mark spoke softly, reciting his encounter, reliving it as he stared into the fire. The flames were rising, just as they rose last night when he fought his way through the blazing room, then stumbled down the smoke-choked stairway to safety in the street below.

By the time help arrived it had been too late. The house was like a tinderbox, the firemen said. They puzzled over how the conflagration had started, but Mark didn't explain. Taking advantage of the confusion, he melted back into the gathering crowd and left the scene, grateful for shadows that concealed telltale bloodstains soaking through the slashed shoulder of his coat. Luck was with him; he moved unobserved along side streets to reach the safety of his room. There he cleaned and dressed the wound, then sank into slumber.

It was late morning when he awoke, and almost mid-afternoon before he nerved himself to seek out Abberline here at his home.

Now the inspector listened silently. Mark searched his face for a reaction, but it was merely a motionless mask looming before him in the firelight.

At last he spoke. "You know you committed a criminal offense by leaving. I could take you in charge. Why didn't you stay and explain what happened?"

"Because you're the only one I can trust," Mark murmured. "If I told them and they didn't believe me—"

"They wouldn't." Abberline paused. "But I do."

"Then you think I was right about the murders?"

The inspector nodded slowly. "In the light of evidence, it appears to be so. The two of them must have worked together. One imagines Pedachenko approached the women, leading them to a secluded spot where Eva was already hiding in wait. Undoubtedly she came at them from behind, twisting the scarves or handkerchiefs around their necks as a stranglehold while Pedachenko used his weapon."

Mark closed his eyes, trying to shut out images that came unbidden. Eva, clutching a helpless victim in a death-grip while her lover drove his blade deep into the throbbing throat—

"No wonder they got away so easily," Abberline was saying. "As a couple they'd be unnoticed. Scattering false clues around some of the bodies to puzzle the police was a cunning move. And those letters, the handwriting on the wall—the master-touch to confuse us all."

"But who could dream of such a thing?" Mark opened his eyes as he replied. "Outside of us there's nobody who would even suspect."

"Only one," Abberline said. "I think Gull knows."

"Sir William?"

The inspector nodded. "Remember what Lees told us about the man he followed? Gull swore it was Prince Eddy's coachman, but we know he lied. I believe Pedachenko went to Sir William's house on the afternoon of the ninth, before Kelly was killed."

"For what reason?"

"Blackmail." Abberline leaned forward. "I've nothing to go on except circumstantial evidence. Still it makes sense, if you follow my reasoning.

"We're aware that Eddy paid secret visits to the East End. Gull admitted as much and told us how the Prince managed to elude him. But what if someone else happened to see him there?"

"Pedachenko?"

"Exactly." The inspector lowered his voice. "I think Eddy's excursions had a purpose. As a future ruler, he'd be expected to marry and provide an heir to the throne. But this would be impossible unless he felt assured of conquering his homosexual cravings. Obviously the only way to find out was to put himself to the test. He couldn't risk proving his manhood with a lady of the court, but it would be no problem if he went to Whitechapel incognito and found a whore."

Mark shook his head. "I can understand he wouldn't take the chance of being recognized in an upper-class brothel. But I can't see him approaching one of those ugly street-women in the slums."

"Mary Jane Kelly wasn't ugly." Abberline pivoted to face Mark. "Suppose Pedachenko happened upon Eddy in Kelly's company one evening and recognized him?

"It's common knowledge that Gull is Eddy's personal physician. As such, Pedachenko sought him out, told him what he knew, and demanded a price for his silence."

"Are you saying that Sir William Gull conspired with Pedachenko to commit murder?"

"Certainly not! I'd hazard he merely listened and then paid whatever sum Pedachenko was asking. He probably expected him to divide the money with Kelly in return for keeping her mouth shut.

"But I don't believe Gull knew anything about Pedachenko's real intentions. I think the news of Kelly's murder came as a total surprise. And our visit was an even greater shock. All he could do was divert suspicion with that lie about the coachman's visit—not to shield himself, but to protect Eddy and the Crown."

"Perhaps you're right," Mark said. "But how can we be sure? Its only a guess."

Abberline grimaced. "In my line of work we prefer to call it deduction. Under the circumstances that's all we have to go on." He rose, pacing before the fireplace. "At least it gives us a partial picture of the way Kelly was killed, and the reason."

"Partial?"

Abberline grimaced again. "We'll never really be certain of how Pedachenko got hold of the key to Kelly's room. He may have come there as a customer after seeing her with Eddy, and stole the key then. That would explain why she went with him so willingly the night of the murder, because he wasn't a stranger.

"Kelly didn't know Pedachenko had taken the key. She didn't know he'd given it to Eva, and that she was already inside the room, waiting. She didn't know what the two of them had in store for her. Just as we can't know the details of the bloodbath that followed."

Bloodbath. Mark closed his eyes again but the vision burned behind them; the vision of Eva and her lover, two shadowy forms crouching in darkness over the butchered body on the bed.

Bloodbath and blood-lust. Forbes Winslow was right after all. But who would have suspected that the quiet country girl could be capable of such savagery? Perhaps she herself was unaware until Pedachenko awakened the impulse within. The secret impulse linking pleasure with pain.... In a way, she too was a Ripper victim.

He forced himself into awareness as Abberline continued. "But we do know what happened when it was over," the inspector said. "The clothing you found in the closet tells us as much. Eva must have burned her own bloodstained clothes in the grate and donned the cheap outfit she'd brought with her for that purpose. It was Eva, disguised as Kelly, whom those witnesses saw when she left the next morning. Pedachenko, of course, was long gone.

"They thought they were safe, but I think you put a scare into them when you told Eva about our continuing investigation. They intended to flee the country together, but not until they got rid of you."

Mark frowned. "I still can't accept it—a girl like that—a rector's daughter, a nurse—"

"And Pedachenko was a barber's assistant." Abberline halted. "But you can't go by outward appearances. In the light of evidence they were two of a kind. She was Jill the Ripper."

"If only the house hadn't burned," Mark said. "At least we'd have proof to present."

"There'll be no presentation." The inspector spoke slowly. "As it stands, two unidentified persons lost their lives as the result of an accidental fire. One died in an upstairs bedroom, the other was killed leaping from a window to escape the flames. And that's the end of it."

Mark stared at him. "You mean you don't intend to tell anyone the truth?"

"The truth is that the Ripper is dead. And that I'm committing an act of conspiracy with you, God help me. But what's to gain by speaking out? You'd be incriminated for withholding information, and the scandal would ruin Gull, to say nothing of Eddy." He turned, staring into the fire. "I prefer to think I'm acting out of my own feelings of loyalty to the Crown, but more likely it's only cowardice. If the Yard ever learned of my own involvement—"

"You're right." Mark sighed deeply. "The important thing is that it's finished." He looked up quickly as Abberline gasped. "What's wrong?"

"Nothing. This damned stomach of mine acts up now and then."

"So you told me. Eructation, borborygmus, gastric distress."

The inspector shrugged. "I know it's nerves. I try to watch my diet, but nothing helps."

"You forget I'm a physician." Mark took a pad and paper from his jacket pocket. He scribbled hastily, then tore off the sheet and handed it to Abberline. "Here, take this prescription to your chemist. I believe it should relieve your symptoms."

"Thanks." The older man grinned. "I'll probably need a bit of relief in times to come. It won't be all that easy to live with a bad conscience and I can never risk the truth, even if I write my memoirs." He paused, sobering. "And what about you?"

"I've already made up my mind," Mark told him. "I'm going back to the States. At least we have less violence to fear there."

Abberline shook his head. "America is young yet," he said. "Wait and see."

Mark rose and the inspector led him to the door. After a subdued farewell he took his leave.

When he started down the walk outside Mark found himself pondering Abberline's words. Was there truth in his cynical prophecy? Were there others lying in wait all over the world, smiling their secret smiles, doing their secret deeds? Why do human beings behave with such inhumanity; why do they enjoy inflicting pain, delight in death?

If he persisted in his determination to study the mind and seek a solution he might eventually find an answer. Then again, maybe he would never know; all he could do was try.

As Mark moved into the sunlit street beyond he saw the youngsters skipping rope—children at play, chanting their age-old rhyme.

Jack and Jill went up the hill
To fetch a pail of water.
Jack fell down and broke his crown
And Jill came tumbling after.

He thought of Pedachenko and Eva. Thank God it was over with now.

Perhaps....

a note to the gentle reader
from the gentle author

Certain liberties have been taken regarding some of the real-life characters involved in this work of fiction, but the details of Jack the Ripper's handiwork come straight from the actual records.

It would be comforting to believe that this sort of activity came to an end in 1888, but such a conclusion is difficult to accept. And while the author is fully accountable for any imaginary violence in these pages he is, regrettably, not responsible for the nightly news.

STAR TREK

"WOLF IN THE FOLD"

Written by
Robert Bloch

FIRST DRAFT
June 14, 1967

Prod. #5149
Series Created by:
Gene Roddenberry
Desilu Productions, Inc.

STAR TREK

"WOLF IN THE FOLD"

CAST

CAPTAIN KIRK
MR. SPOCK
DOCTOR McCOY
SCOTT
SULU
UHURA
JARIS
SYBO
HENGIST
TARK
MORLA
STRANGER
KARA (DANCER, SILENT BIT)
PSYCHOTECH. KAREN TRACY
BARTENDER (SILENT BIT)
ENGINEERING ASSISTANT (SILENT BIT)
FOUR CREW MEMBERS (SILENT BITS)
CAFÉ PATRONS (SILENT BITS)

SETS

EXTERIOR
BAZAAR STREET, ALLEYWAY, ARGELIUS II

INTERIORS
CAFÉ
HENGIST'S OFFICE
JARIS' HOME
UNDERGROUND ROOM OF SAME

BRIDGE, ENTERPRISE
TRANSPORTER ROOM
BRIEFING ROOM
SHIP CORRIDORS
SHIP ELEVATOR

STAR TREK

"Wolf in the Fold"

TEASER

FADE IN:

1 EXT. STREET - CLOSE ANGLE - NIGHT

It is very foggy, dark, ill-lighted. An occasional
pedestrian passes by, muffled against the chill and
damp. CAMERA DOLLIES IN until it picks up a
glow in the fog, which shortly establishes itself as
reading "ELYSIAN FIELDS." Strange, flute-like
MUSIC comes from inside it. Even on this planet, it
is easy to see that this is a place of entertainment,
a café, a saloon, God knows what it is called here
on Argelius.

2 INT. CAFE - ANGLE ON KARA

KARA, a seductively-clad entertainer, dancer, is
dancing to the strange, wild flute-like MUSIC.
CAMERA PULLS BACK TO WIDER ANGLE and
we see TARK, seated in b.g. and playing the instrument. A middle-aged man, wearing a loose robe.

CAMERA PULLS BACK to give us the cafe setting…a dimly lighted tavern, with a bar near the front entrance. Behind the bar, a robed BARTENDER. Several patrons, of different races and costumes, sit at the bar, watching the dance. At the end of the bar the CAMERA LINGERS on a tall, stony-faced STRANGER, whose shaven head and somber garments mark him as an alien presence. He is staring intently at Kara.

As CAMERA CONTINUES ITS PAN around the room, we pick up representatives of half a dozen races, for this is a café in a space port. Among them, at a prominent table, are KIRK, SPOCK, McCOY and SCOTT, watching the dance and apparently enjoying themselves, especially Scott.

3   ANGLE - KARA

As she comes to a crescendo. The music stops. She freezes in a pose of finality. Patrons at the tables BLINK ON AND OFF tiny lights they have in their hands… their way of indicating their pleasure, applause. For a moment the room seems filled with fireflies. And then there is the surprising sound of table THUMPING. Kara looks in the direction, surprised.

4   ANGLE - KIRK'S TABLE

The table thumping is being done with great enthusiasm by Scotty, whacking the table with the flat of his hand. All eyes throughout the café turn toward him. He pauses, realizing he is alone in his action, as Spock turns to him.

> SPOCK
> On Argelius, Mr. Scott, it is customary to signify approval by the use of hand-blinkers.

> SCOTT
> Is that a fact, now?

McCOY

What else, from Spock, Scotty?

SCOTT

As an old, experienced Glasgow pub-crawler, I know perfectly well how to register my approval...and I assure you, gentlemen...
    (an approving eye at Kara)
I approve!

5   ANGLE - KARA

Seeing this, hearing this, she smiles invitingly, moves toward the bar, glancing over her shoulder toward Scotty.

6   KIRK ET AL

KIRK

I think she does too, Scotty.

SCOTT

Aye. I knew she was a lass of good taste the minute I laid eyes on her. I wonder if she's ever tasted good Scots whiskey.

With a grin, Scotty gets up and moves off toward the bar.

7   ANGLE ON BAR

As Scotty moves up and engages Kara in conversation. She seems willing.

SPOCK

I would suggest that our concern about the condition of Mr. Scott was largely unfounded.

KIRK
Yes, Mr. Spock. I'd say he's feeling fine.

McCOY
(a little concerned)
We can't be sure. He looks all right...
acts all right...

KIRK
He is all right, Bones. Ask the girl.

McCOY
A severe blow on the head like Scotty had can affect more than just the brain tissue. Shock, possible damage to the nervous system...a hundred side effects. He needs time to recuperate.

KIRK
(indicating bar)
He seems to be doing just that.

8   SCOTT AND KARA

They are seated together at the bar. Kara laughing as Scott whispers something in her ear. There are drinks before them.

9   KIRK ET AL

KIRK
It's just a layman's opinion, Bones, but I'd say Scotty isn't mad at women anymore. The way he carried on about Lieutenant Barbara Yates...

McCOY

Lieutenant Yates was responsible for
the accident that threw Scotty against
the bulkhead. You can't blame him
for being a little annoyed.

SPOCK

Still, for a time Mr. Scott sounded as
if he were angry against all females…
a most illogical attitude.

KIRK

I think we can relax. Our chief engineer seems to be his old self again.

10   ANGLE - SCOTT AND KARA

Getting up, moving toward the door. They pass the
Stranger, who stares after them, scowls introspec-
tively, and puts his drink down. Scott and Kara leave.

11   KIRK ET AL

SPOCK

Odd. With the extremely heavy
fog, I fail to see why they should leave
this place. They will see nothing
outside.

KIRK

Which could be exactly the reason
they are leaving. Fog for its own sake,
Mr. Spock.
        (as Spock looks puzzled)
Drink up, Mr. Spock. You'll never
understand.

12   ANGLE ON STRANGER

Grim and unsmiling, he rises from the barstool and
CAMERA MOVES WITH HIM past happy, oblivious patrons. He goes to the door, EXITS into the
curling fog outside.

13   KIRK ET AL

KIRK
I'd say our job is done. Scotty is react-
ing normally...

McCOY
And quickly, too...

KIRK
And he's getting the shore leave the
doctor requested. And since Scotty
took the floor show with him when
he left, I see no reason we should
hang around. Let's get back to
the ship.

They get up, move to the door, EXIT.

14   EXT. STREET - IN EXTREMELY HEAVY FOG

They can hardly see each other. They pause. Kirk
pulls out his communicator.

KIRK
Kirk to Enterprise...

Before he can continue, a loud, piercing female
SCREAM pierces the night...from ahead and nearby.
Our people do one quick take, and immediately
plunge into the fog in the direction of the sound.

15   ALLEYWAY

Filled with fog, the walls barely visible. There is a gasping for breath, as Kirk, Spock and McCoy whip into sight, move TOWARD CAMERA. They APPROACH and freeze, eyes wide with horror.

16   ANGLE ON KARA - THEIR POV

Kara sprawls face downward on the wet paving. There are rips and slashes in the back of her cloak.

17   MED. FULL SHOT

As McCoy immediately bends over her body, goes to work. He looks up quickly, shakes his head...appalled and shocked.

                    McCOY
        Dead. Stabbed a dozen times!

Then comes that gasping breathing we heard a moment ago. They look up toward the sound, take a few steps forward...and recoil.

18   ANGLE - SCOTT - THROUGH FOG

Crouched like an animal back against a wall, fog curling around his unseeing eyes...a dazed, almost demented look in his eyes...and in his hands...a long, gleaming, red-stained knife.

FADE OUT.

END TEASER

ACT ONE

FADE IN:

19   EXT. SPACE - ORBITING SHOT ENTERPRISE

Around the planet Argelius.

> ### KIRK
> Captain's Log, Star Date 3614.9.
> Argelius II. While on shore leave, our
> chief engineer, Mr. Scott, has become
> involved in a monstrous murder.

20   INT. HENGIST'S OFFICE

A modern, somewhat spartan office, with several chairs. HENGIST, a short, stocky man of about forty, with close-cropped hair, sits behind his desk. Before him is the knife we last saw in Scotty's hand. Scotty, still dazed and stunned, sits in a chair before him. Kirk, Spock and McCoy are there also.

> ### KIRK'S VOICE
> Scott was immediately taken to the
> office of the chief administrative offi-
> cer, a Mr. Hengist, for questioning.

Hengist shakes his head.

HENGIST

Gentlemen, I hardly know what to say. Argelius is the last place in the galaxy I'd expect a thing like this to happen.

KIRK

Well, it happened, Mr. Hengist. I assume there'll be a complete investigation.

HENGIST

Of course, of course. But it may take time. There's no crime on this planet, no violence at all. Hasn't been for hundreds of years. This is simply incredible. If this was Rigel, my home, I'd have a hundred skilled investigators at work all ready. But they just don't exist here.

SPOCK

You are new on Argelius, sir?

HENGIST

I just took over this job a week ago. A fine way to start things off.
(picking up knife)
Mr. Scott...you're certain you have never seen this before?

SCOTT

Nor anything like it.

HENGIST

Yet your own shipmates testify that you were found holding it, crouched over the body of the victim.

SCOTT

I don't remember anything about that.

HENGIST
You don't remember. Convenient.

McCOY
Mr. Hengist...Mr. Scott is just recovering from a severe concussion sustained on board ship. Erratic memory is quite a common after-effect.

HENGIST
Indeed. Even more convenient.
(to Scott)
Could you have picked up this knife in the café?

KIRK
He didn't. We were with him all the time.

Hengist regards Kirk rather coldly.

HENGIST
I am speaking to Mr. Scott, Captain.

SCOTT
I did not.

HENGIST
You remember that?

SCOTT
I do.

HENGIST
Then perhaps you will tell me what happened when you and the woman Kara left the café?

21   FAVORING SCOTT

Trying hard to remember.

> **SCOTT**
> I told her Edinburgh had fog like this...that I liked to walk in it. So we went for a walk... I was a pace ahead of her, trying to lead the way...and then I heard a scream... I remember turning...but nothing else.

> **HENGIST**
> You didn't see or hear whoever attacked her?

> **SCOTT**
> I don't remember.

> **HENGIST**
> You didn't chase him...try to help her...

> **SCOTT**
> I don't remember, Mister. I don't remember taking the knife...all I remember is the captain shaking me, slapping my face...and I saw her lyin' there, in her own blood...

22   FAVORING HENGIST

> **HENGIST**
> A difficult problem, gentlemen. Argelius is a totally non-aggressive society. A free port. Strangers come and go as they wish...as long as they obey the rules of peace and good will. We have no police, no courts, no prisons...

(at Scott)

...nor executioners...

23   FULL SHOT

SCOTT
I didn't kill that girl!

HENGIST
But you don't remember, Mr. Scott. How do you know? In two hundred years, no one has died this kind of violent death on this planet...until you arrived. I will not make empty threats, but I assure you this crime will be punished.

KIRK
What is the law?

JARIS' VOICE
The law is love.

They turn quickly.

24   ANOTHER ANGLE

As JARIS THE PHILOSOPHER enters...tall, kindly, bearded, white-haired, wise. Hengist quickly leaps to his feet, respectfully.

HENGIST
Gentlemen, our Prefect...Jaris. Sir, Captain Kirk, Mr. Spock, Doctor McCoy...and Mr. Scott...of the USS Enterprise.

Jaris nods at them...even of countenance and manner.

JARIS

Mr. Hengist...what have you learned
of this heinous, barbaric crime?

HENGIST

I've just begun my investigation, sir.

JARIS

Perhaps I can help. If you gentlemen
would accompany me to my home...

HENGIST

Sir, this is an official matter...

JARIS

And I, Mr. Hengist, am the highest
local official.
                    (to Kirk's party)
This is a sad welcome to our peaceful
planet, gentlemen...but welcome you
are. If you will come with me...

He indicates the door. Hengist shrugs, moves with
Kirk and his party as they leave...

DISSOLVE TO:

25   INT. JARIS' HOUSE

A circular, windowless, high-ceilinged room.
Draperies cover exits to other rooms. At one end of
the room, a classically simple table and chairs stand
before what appears to be a type of altar, also classic in its simplicity, on which burns a flame. Kirk
and his party and Jaris and Hengist are seated at
the table. Jaris is talking. CAMERA MOVES IN TO
FAVOR HIM.

JARIS

Already news of this terrible thing has spread among our people. They are greatly disturbed. Quite frankly, there has been much talk of placing Argelius under an embargo to space vehicles...not all of our visitors understand our peaceful ways. A horrible thing like this could force it to come about.

KIRK

That would be most unfortunate, sir. Argelius is widely known for its hospitality.

SPOCK

Not to mention its strategic importance as a space port. There is none other in this quadrant.

JARIS

It would be unfortunate...but the embargo could happen...may happen, unless this dreadful matter is cleared up at once.
(beat)
My wife Sybo will be with us later... it is the hour of meditation now. In the meantime, let us proceed. Mr. Hengist?

HENGIST

Prefect, this man Scott claims not to remember anything about the murder. I find this unlikely. A convenient amnesia...

McCOY

I explained about his recent concussion...

JARIS
(to Scott)
You remember nothing?

SCOTT
Nothing, sir. Not a thing from the time I heard her scream until the Captain slapped me.

JARIS
It makes it most difficult...

KIRK
Not at all, sir. On board our ship we have instruments with which we can record a complete account of everything which has happened to Mr. Scott within the last twenty-four hours.

JARIS
A machine, Captain? We do not think highly of machines.

SPOCK
A machine is a tool, prefect, which helps us in our work. There is nothing intrinsically bad about a machine. The device of which the Captain speaks is virtually infallible.

KIRK
We could have the complete story in half an hour, if you give us permission to take him aboard.

JARIS
The crime was committed here. We shall investigate it here.

McCOY
(frowning)
Of course, we could beam down a
technician with a psycho tri-corder.
A little less effective than our facil-
ities on board ship, but I think it
would tell us everything we want
to know.

HENGIST
Prefect, I protest. As chief adminis-
trative officer, the responsibility for
this investigation is mine!

JARIS
We know little of murder, Mr.
Hengist. If the device they speak
of can help us, we would be foolish not to use it. Does Mr. Scott
object?

SCOTT
Of course not. I want this cleared up.

McCOY
The examination will require privacy
to be effective.

JARIS
There is a small chamber just below
this room. It no doubt will suffice.

HENGIST
Prefect, the man Scott is their friend.
How can we trust them? Or this
machine of theirs? They want to
clear him...

JARIS
(gently)
And you do not?

>   HENGIST
>   (stammering)
> Why, I…of course, I…just want the
> truth.

>   KIRK
> That's what you'll get.

>   JARIS
> Then there is no objection.

Kirk nods at McCoy, who breaks out his communicator.

>   McCOY
> McCoy to Enterprise.

26   INT. BRIDGE ENTERPRISE

Uhura turns from her control panel toward Sulu.

>   UHURA
> Mr. Sulu. Dr. McCoy from the surface.

>   SULU
> Sulu here, Doctor.

27   ANGLE McCOY

>   McCOY
> Have Psychometric Technician Lieu-
> tenant Tracy beam down to these
> coordinates with a psycho tri-corder.
> Immediately. McCoy out.

He returns his communicator.

28   FULL SHOT

Hengist is a little discomfited.

HENGIST

Prefect...even though Mr. Scott seems to be the logical suspect, there were several foreign visitors in the cafe last night just before the time of the murder. It may be wise to question them.

SPOCK

It may be illogical to except members of the local population.

JARIS

Violence is inconceivable to our people, Mr. Spock.

SPOCK

Prefect, it has been my experience that violence is one of the great common qualities of humanity.

HENGIST

Mr. Spock, I will carry my investigation to the local population...in the unlikely event that I do not find the murderer among our visitors. Prefect, with your permission, I will leave to bring the other foreigners.

Jaris nods. Hengist turns (passing closely the table on which the murder knife rests) and EXITS.

29   ANOTHER ANGLE

JARIS

Do you approve, Captain Kirk?

KIRK

I approve of anything which might establish the innocence of my chief engineer.

There is a slight sound. They look off toward one corner.

30   ANOTHER ANGLE

The MATERIALIZATION EFFECT, as LIEUTENANT KAREN TRACY appears from the transporter in one corner. A very pretty girl, she carries a special tricorder and some scanning equipment. She smiles, steps forward briskly.

TRACY
Psychometric Technician Tracy reporting, Captain.

KIRK
Bones?

McCOY
Lieutenant, I want a twenty-four hour regressive memory check on Mr. Scott here. All possible amnesic gaps to be noted for depth probing.

TRACY
Of course, Doctor. Where shall I set up?

JARIS
Follow me, young lady.

Jaris starts toward drapes at the far side of the room, and Tracy moves after him. McCoy glances at Scott.

McCOY
Scotty?

KIRK
In a minute, Bones.

Kirk moves to Scott as Jaris and Tracy move through the drapes to a door, EXIT. McCoy moves to Kirk and Scott.

31   KIRK, McCOY, SCOTT

KIRK
All right, Scotty. We've been shipmates a long time...

SCOTT
Captain, I've told you everything I know! You think I like not knowing what happened out there? I don't! It's black in my mind! Did I kill her? Is that what you want to know?

KIRK
I know you didn't kill her.

SCOTT
Well, I don't! I don't know anything!
(to McCoy)
What is it, Doctor? That knock I got on the head? Why can't I remember?

McCOY
I don't know, Scotty. But we'll find out what it is you can't remember.

KIRK
You relax, Scotty. Do what Lieutenant Tracy tells you. And don't worry. We're not about to throw you to the wolves. We know perfectly well you didn't kill that girl.

SCOTT
(beat)
Thank you, Captain. I wish...

KIRK

Don't wish anything. Just go down there
and take that memory check. When you
come up again, you'll be cleared.

SCOTT

Aye. I'll be cleared.

He walks uncertainly toward the door, glances back
at them and EXITS.

32   KIRK, SPOCK, McCOY

Kirk turns to the others.

KIRK

Well?

SPOCK

It is totally illogical that Mr. Scott
could, under any circumstances,
commit such a crime as this.

McCOY

I wish I could be as sure. A head
injury can throw all previous behavior patterns into the junk pile. And
we know for a couple of weeks he's
been sour on women.
(beat)
But I'm afraid he's telling the truth
about not remembering anything.

KIRK

Afraid, Bones?

McCOY

Hysterical amnesia. When a man
feels guilty about something...some-
thing too terrible to remember...he
blots it out of his conscious memory.

Kirk stares at him, getting the message.

> ### KIRK
> Scotty couldn't have done it, Bones.

> ### McCOY
> Maybe not the Scotty we've known
> for so long...

> ### KIRK
> Couldn't have, Bones! Not Scott!

McCoy shrugs. Kirk stares at Spock, who has nothing
to say.

33   INT. UNDERGROUND ROOM - ANGLE ON SCOTT
       AND TRACY

A table and two chairs in the center of the room.
Jaris is just leaving. Tracy unlimbers her bag and
equipment, hands Scotty a small tube-like object to
clench in his fist.

> ### TRACY
> If you'll just hold tightly to this,
> Mr. Scott.

> ### SCOTT
> I know how it works. Lieutenant. I've
> been examined before.
> > (beat)
>
> Why'd they have to send down a
> woman?

Tracy is already making readings. She looks up quickly.

> ### TRACY
> You don't like women, Mr. Scott?

SCOTT
I like them fine...as long as I don't
have to depend on them.

Tracy smiles.

TRACY
Well, you don't have to depend on me.
Just trust my instruments. They'll tell
us everything we want to know.

34   INT. JARIS MAIN ROOM - KIRK, SPOCK, McCOY

Waiting. Kirk a little nervous.

KIRK
(to McCoy)
Shouldn't you be down there helping
her?

McCOY
The fewer people around the better.

Jaris and SYBO, his wife, a tall, austere, mystic-
appearing woman, appear through the drapes.
Kirk, et al, rise quickly.

JARIS
Captain Kirk, Mr. Spock, Doctor
McCoy... This is Sybo, my wife.

Sybo nods at them...and stiffens.

SYBO
Jaris...there is violence here...much
violence...and fear...

As Kirk and the others react:

JARIS
My wife is a descendant of our ancient priestesses, gentlemen. She has the ability to sense the presence of strong emotion, when associated with inanimate objects. She's the reason I brought you here. I wanted her to examine the murder weapon....

Standing at table, he glances down, reacts in surprise.

JARIS
(continuing)
Do you have it, Captain?

KIRK
Have what?

35   CLOSE ANGLE BARE TABLE TOP

JARIS
The knife. I put it here. It's gone!

36   FULL SHOT

As all stare at each other curiously...not yet alarmed...and then they react to a sudden muffled scream O.S., coming from the door to the underground room. The three Enterprise men are on their way for the door before the scream stops echoing. Jaris and Sybo follow.

37   INT. UNDERGROUND ROOM

As Kirk, Spock, McCoy burst into it, followed closely by Jaris and Sybo. They take one look, recoil, dash forward.

38   FULL SHOT

Scotty, his head thrown back and his eyes closed, sits rigidly in the chair, hand still clutching the tubular object Tracy had given him. Tracy lies stretched out on the floor, her equipment scattered. McCoy goes straight to Tracy, bends to examine her. Kirk goes to Scotty, giving a quick horrified glance to the body on the floor. Kirk shakes Scotty, hard.

KIRK

Scotty! Snap out of it!

As Scotty groans, starts to move.

McCOY

Jim! She's dead!

Spock and Kirk stare down at the body of Tracy, as CAMERA DOLLIES IN and McCoy rises INTO CAMERA, his face shocked.

McCOY

Just like the other one. Stabbed a dozen times.

HOLD ON TABLEAU AS WE

FADE OUT.

END ACT ONE

ACT TWO

FADE IN:

39   INT. JARIS HOME. - MED. ANGLE

Jaris is pouring some fluid into a glass, hands it to
Scotty, who is weak, shaken, dazed. Kirk, Spock and
McCoy stand by, impatient and angry. Sybo stands
by the altar, her eyes closed, swaying gently back
and forth as though meditating.

                    JARIS
        Drink this.
                    (to McCoy)
        An Argelian stimulant, Doctor. Quite
        effective, and quite harmless.

Scotty, aided by Jaris, drinks it.

40   FAVORING SCOTTY

His eyes blink. He looks around...confused.

                    SCOTTY
        Lieutenant? Captain, where's...

                    KIRK
                    (harshly)
        Lieutenant Tracy is dead, Scotty!

SCOTT
Dead? But…

KIRK
What happened down there?

41   FULL SHOT

SCOTTY
I was sitting there…she was taking the readings…and now I'm sitting here!

McCOY
That's all you remember?

SPOCK
There was a passage of some moments, Mr. Scott. If you will concentrate…

SCOTT
(distraught)
I tell you I don't remember! I must have passed out!

McCOY
It could be, Jim. His head…

KIRK
I'd just as soon not hear anything more about his head right now, Bones! Lieutenant Tracy has been murdered, and I mean to find out who did it! Scotty! Think!

SCOTT
I don't know…whoever it was…maybe came in while I was unconscious… it has to be…

JARIS

How would you suggest the murderer got into that room?

SCOTT

I don't know...down the stairs.

JARIS

They come directly from this room. Captain Kirk, Mr. Spock and Doctor McCoy were in this room at all times.

SPOCK

That is correct. The stairs were not used.

SCOTT

I saw a door down there. Maybe he got in that way....

JARIS

The door is locked. I have the only key...

KIRK

Keys can be duplicated. Locks can be picked.

JARIS
(coldly)
And men can lie. Twice murder has been done...and this man was present each time...

There is a KNOCKING SOUND from a door at the end of the room.

JARIS

Come.

42   ANOTHER ANGLE

As the door OPENS and TARK, the Musician and MORLA appear. Morla is a youngish, somewhat hard-faced individual whose beard and gaudily figured robe distinguish him from the natives of this planet. They move forward. Tark seems to be grieving.

> **TARK**
> We were instructed to come here by Administrator Hengist.

Kirk recognizes Tark.

> **KIRK**
> You were the musician at the café...
> you played for the dancing girl...·

> **TARK**
> (coldly)
> The...dancing girl...was my daughter.
> I am Tark of Kaneb.

> **MORLA**
> My name is Morla. My shop is just across the street from the café.

> **JARIS**
> Did you know the murdered girl?

> **MORLA**
> Know her? I knew her. We were to be married.

Tark scowls at Morla at this. There seems to be little love lost between them. Morla looks around.

> **MORLA**
> Which is the man Scott?

SCOTT
I'm Scott.

Morla moves to confront Scotty.

MORLA
Tark says you are the man who took
Kara from the café. Is this true?

SCOTT
We left together…

Morla, with a wild yell, hurls himself on Scott, trying
to choke him.

MORLA
Murderer! You killed her!

His onslaught takes Scott by surprise. Kirk
and Spock dash over and pry the yelling Morla
off him!

MORLA
Butcher! Killer!

KIRK
All right! Calm down!

Spock, using his great strength, forces Morla into
a chair.

SPOCK
Kindly remain quiet, sir, or I shall be
forced to immobilize you.

MORLA
He killed her!

SCOTT
I didn't kill her! I swear it!

There is another commotion at the door. They all look in that direction.

43   ANGLE ON DOOR

As Hengist forcibly shoves the STRANGER forward…using what seems to be great, surprising strength.

> HENGIST
> In there, you!

> JARIS
> Mr. Hengist!

> HENGIST
> I found this man in the garden. He refused to tell me what he was doing there.

> KIRK
> In the garden?

> HENGIST
> Near the door to the lower level.

> KIRK
> (dangerous, to Stranger)
> What were you doing there?

> HENGIST
> I'll handle this, Captain!

> JARIS
> Mr. Hengist! There has been another murder. Here!

Hengist gapes at him.

> HENGIST
> Another? Here?

KIRK

Lieutenant Tracy. One of my own
crew.

Eyes widen in surprise, Hengist turns, grabs the
Stranger and slams him up against the wall.

HENGIST

No wonder you were so anxious to
get away!

JARIS
(sharply)
Mr. Hengist! You may have treated
people that way on Rigel, but it is not
permitted here!

KIRK

Wait a minute.
(confronting Stranger)
I've seen you before. You were in the
café last night.

The Stranger does not answer.

SPOCK

Quite correct, Captain. And he left
the premises shortly after Mr. Scott
and Kara did so.

HENGIST

You followed them? Who are you?
What's your name?

STRANGER

I'm a free citizen of Kanak IX. You have
no right to question me. Let me go.

JARIS

You shall not leave without permission,
sir. A murder has been committed.

STRANGER
I don't know anything about it.

KIRK
I'd like a little more than just your word. What were you doing here?

HENGIST
Captain! I will ask the questions here!

KIRK
Then ask them! Don't just stand around!
    (indicating stranger)
I don't know what his motive might be...but he was outside in the garden when the murder was committed. These others...
    (indicating Tark)
Maybe a father...furious when his daughter disobeyed him...
    (indicating Morla)
A future bridegroom...enraged at finding Kara with another man...any of them could have come here earlier, forced the lock on that room downstairs, committed the murder...

HENGIST
You're trying to cover up for your friend!

SPOCK
Gentlemen, if I may make a suggestion...

All stop and look at Spock.

SPOCK
Mere questions and accusation will gain us nothing. I propose we move the entire investigation to the Enterprise. All pertinent data can be fed into the ship's computer banks for analysis...

JARIS
A machine...to determine who is guilty?

SPOCK
No, sir. A machine to determine the truth.

HENGIST
Ridiculous! I won't have it. The murders occurred here...in this city... and this is where the investigation must be carried out!

SPOCK
Through charges and countercharges, sir? A most inefficient method.

SYBO
There is a better way.

They all turn and look at Sybo in surprise.

44   FAVORING SYBO

As she stands near the altar, her eyes nearly closed.

SYBO
The flame of purification burns. The old ways point the direction of truth. We shall join hands, and I shall look into your hearts.

JARIS
It is possible. She has the gift. I have seen her use it, many times.

SYBO
We will join hands before the eternal flame. The truth will come to me.

KIRK
You're describing a séance. We haven't the time for...

SYBO
I do not deal with the dead, Captain. Only with the living. This is not superstition. It is the old way.

JARIS
This is why I brought you here, Captain. Our procedures may seem strange to you, but I assure you, they are valid.

KIRK
(beat)

Spock?

SPOCK
Most interesting, Captain. I have heard of the empathic abilities of some Argelians, but I have never been privileged to witness them with my own eyes.

KIRK
All right. On one condition. This room must be sealed so no one can enter or leave during the ceremony.

JARIS
Agreed.

SCOTT
Captain! I'm the one everybody suspects! You mean I'm going to have to depend on some spook-ridden mumbo-jumbo...

KIRK
Are you afraid, Scotty?

SCOTT
No. Of course not. But why not the ship? We could find out in a minute...

KIRK
We don't make the rules here, Mr. Scott. We'll do it their way...

DISSOLVE TO:

45   INT. JARIS HOME - CLOSE ON ALTAR FLAME

It flares brightly, as CAMERA PULLS BACK to a WIDE ANGLE, revealing all our people seated at a table. Kirk, Tark, McCoy, Morla, Scott, Sybo, Hengist, the Stranger, Jaris.

SYBO
Let us begin.

As she speaks, the altar flame begins to die, becomes very low. Faces and forms become indistinct.

SYBO
Let all join hands. Let the circle not be broken. Concentrate upon the flame which burns upon the altar of truth.

46   FAVORING SYBO

Her eyes close. She goes into a state of empathy... almost hypnotic. There is a long moment of silence.

SYBO
Yes...there is something here...something terrible. I feel its presence...fear...
anger...hatred. Anger feeds the flame...
(a groan)
Oh, there is evil here...monstrous,
terrible evil...

47   ANGLE ON TARK AND McCOY

Tark scowls as he listens.

SYBO'S VOICE
Hatred...hatred of the one who killed,
and a thirst for bloody revenge...

48   ANGLE ON MORLA AND SCOTT

SYBO
Hatred and revenge...resentment
against all women...vengeance against
all men...

49   ANGLE ON STRANGER

SYBO
And a great revulsion against death...
a fear, a panic, a flight...

50   ANGLE ON SYBO

SYBO
But there is something else...some
ancient terror...coming closer, closer...
among us...a screaming thing of horror... Death...death...a monstrous
hunger...a hunger that feeds on fear.
It has a name...boratis kesla...redjac...

51   FULL SHOT - GROUP

Hands linked in the dim fading light. Sybo's voice raises to a frightened wail.

> **SYBO**
> It devours all life, all light...a hunger
> that never dies...redjac...redjac...

Suddenly the altar flame goes out and the room is plunged into total darkness. There is an excited babble...and Sybo SCREAMS.

> **KIRK'S VOICE**
> Lights! Quickly!

The lights come on. Hengist is standing at the light panel, his hand still on it. He turns, glances toward Sybo...reacts.

52   ANGLE JARIS

Eyes wide in horror.

> **JARIS**
> Sybo!

53   ANGLE ON SYBO

She is sitting bolt upright in her chair, a look of horror on her face...and now she rigidly falls forward...and for a fleeting second we can see the knife in her back...and Scotty is standing just a few feet from her, staring at her, aghast. McCoy hurries forward.

54   KIRK AND SCOTT

Kirk stares at Scotty. Scotty, appalled, tries to explain.

SCOTT

I heard her scream, Captain. And somebody moved. I just wanted to help.

Hengist comes over, accusingly.

HENGIST

You were standing closest to her.

SCOTT

I told you…

McCOY

(rising, shaking his head)
She's dead.

HENGIST

Three! Three murders! And this man on the scene each time!

KIRK

There's no proof!

HENGIST

Is that how you run your starship? Blind?

JARIS

(broken)
Please…please…no more. My wife is dead.

HENGIST

My heart goes out to you, Prefect. However, I must ask your permission to place this man Scott under arrest.

JARIS

I don't know…what to say.

55   ANOTHER ANGLE

Throughout the remainder of the scenes in Jaris' home, play it so the angle does not reveal the body of Sybo.

KIRK
Before we arrest anybody, I suggest we first exhaust every effort to discover the truth.

HENGIST
What more do you need?

KIRK
I need proof, Hengist! You haven't given me any! Jaris, I strongly urge that we remove this investigation to my ship. Our instruments...

HENGIST
(interrupting)
Instruments! We are dealing with a murderer!

SPOCK
Precisely, sir. And it is exactly those instruments which will enable us to identify that murderer.
(to Jaris)
All events, sir, have literally thousands of pertinent facts influencing it. Our minds cannot correlate them all. Our computers can.

Jaris is torn...grief-stricken, agonized, wanting to be fair, not wanting his emotions to sway him. He turns to Scott.

JARIS
Mr. Scott.

SCOTT
Sir, I did not kill your wife...nor either of the other ladies.

KIRK
The matter will still remain in your jurisdiction, Hengist...but we will have removed all doubts.

HENGIST
I have the authority...

JARIS
No, Hengist. The authority is mine. The decision must be mine.
(beat)
In two hundred years since our Great Awakening, there has been no crime on Argelius. Yet the old laws remain, and their penalties.
(at Scott)
You, sir, claim to remember nothing about the murders. If this is the truth, you may have killed and not known it.
(at Kirk)
Will your machines tell us this?

KIRK
They will correlate the facts and produce a conclusion. The conclusion will eliminate all those but the guilty one.

JARIS
Very well. We shall go to your ship. And he who is guilty will face the ancient penalties...barbaric and horrible though they they be. Do you understand, Mr. Scott?

56   ANGLE SCOTT

CAMERA HOLDS ON HIM for a long moment. Then
he nods.

SCOTT
Aye. I understand.

FADE OUT.

END ACT TWO

ACT THREE

FADE IN:

57   EXT. SPACE - ENTERPRISE -
      ORBITING SHOT Around Argelius.

KIRK'S VOICE
Captain's Log, Star Date 3615.2.
With Mr. Scott in a technical state of
arrest, we have beamed aboard the
Enterprise to continue the investiga-
tion of three terrible murders.

58   INT. ENTERPRISE - TRANSPORTER ROOM

Present, besides the Transporter Chief, are Kirk,
Spock, Scott, Morla, McCoy and Hengist. The
Transporter Chief is in the process of beaming up the remainder of the party. Kirk glances
at Scott, who is pale and shaken. Scotty sees
his glance.

SCOTT
Don't worry, Captain. I'm only glad
we're up here where we can learn the
truth.

HENGIST
The truth will convict you!

SCOTT
I'll settle for whatever the truth is,
since I'm not sure myself.

KIRK
Your head injury, Scotty. That's got to
be the reason you don't remember.

59 ANGLE TRANSPORTER CHAMBER

As Jaris, Tark, and the Stranger beam up, step off.
Jaris, still grieving, moves straight to Kirk.

JARIS
Please, Captain, let us begin at once.
This matter must be resolved.

HENGIST
It was resolved on the surface, Prefect!
This man...

JARIS
Is innocent until he is proven guilty,
Commissioner. That is the way
of Argelius.

HENGIST
I still insist that Captain Kirk's actions
are in violation of the laws of Argelius.

SPOCK
The search for truth is never a violation of law.

KIRK
Jaris...we will find the guilty man.
I promise you. And he'll be turned
over to your authorities for punishment...whoever he is. Dr. McCoy
will direct you to our briefing room,
where this inquiry will be held. Mr.

Spock and I will join you shortly, after we program our computers.

HENGIST
Or feed into them any false information necessary to clear Scott.

SPOCK
I assure you, Commissioner, the computer would immediately reject any false information. It deals only in facts.

KIRK
Let's go.

They all move out of the transporter room.

DISSOLVE TO:

60   INT. BRIDGE - ENTERPRISE - ANGLE ON SPOCK AT HIS STATION

He is staring intently into his hooded viewer, while his hands work the controls. CAMERA PULLS BACK to reveal Kirk standing by impatiently. Finally Spock stands back, shaking his head.

SPOCK
Data thus far accumulated is insufficient, Captain. We will have to conduct an inquiry, and feed the results in as we go.

Kirk reaches over, punches a communications button.

KIRK
Security, this is the Captain. Install a verifier in the briefing room immediately.
    (punches off)

At least we'll be able to tell truth from fiction.

SPOCK
Captain, I remind you once again that while the Mr. Scott we have known so long could not commit such crimes as these, the injury to his head may have altered his psychological profile.

KIRK
Then I want to know about that, too, Mr. Spock. If he's a murderer, he'll pay. Let's get on with it.

They turn and walk off.

DISSOLVE TO:

61   INT. BRIEFING ROOM

All our personnel are gathered here. Prominent in the set is a VERIFIER (see the witness chair in COURT MARTIAL), a device on which a witness places his hand as he talks. It at once identifies him, and, even as our lie detectors do, detects any minor psychological variations caused by deliberately lying. There is a tri-screen viewer in the center of the table. Spock and Kirk are at the head of the table.

KIRK
For those of you who are unfamiliar with it, deep in the heart of this ship are our computer banks. Not only do those banks contain the whole of human knowledge, but they operate the entire ship. Life support systems, automatic equipment, everything.

SPOCK

And they are as nearly infallible as anything in the known universe. They cannot, however, think for themselves. They cannot create thought. They do not live. They form a giant brain, but that brain takes its directions from us.

JARIS

We Argelians do not place such trust in machines. However, if it deals only in facts, as you say...

KIRK

We can obtain an answer to any factual question, no matter how complex, in a matter of a few seconds.

HENGIST
(angrily)
You don't solve a murder with columns of figures!

SPOCK

No, sir. But we do determine the truth.

MORLA

How? That machine can't tell you what goes on in a man's mind!

KIRK
(indicating verifier)
No. But this one can...to an extent. Each testifier will sit here...place his hand on this plate. Any deviation from factual truth will be immediately detected and relayed to the computer, which will in turn notify us.
(beat)

Doctor McCoy has already fed into the computer his medical reports. Our laboratory experts are examining the murder weapon and will give their data to the computer for analysis. Shall we begin?

Hengist still remains sullen...but Jaris finally nods, and most of the others follow his lead.

KIRK
Mr. Scott...will you please take the stand.

Scotty gets up, moves to the verifier, sits, places his hand on the plate. Kirk moves to the computer control. Activates it.

KIRK
Computer. Identify verification.

COMPUTER
(buzz buzz click click)
Working. Lieutenant Commander Scott, serial number SE197 547 230 T. Verified.

KIRK
Subject's present physical condition.

COMPUTER
(buzz buzz click click)
Working. Subject recently subjected to severe blow on skull. Damage healing. Some peripheral abnormalities.

KIRK
Sufficient abnormalities to account for periods of functional amnesia?

COMPUTER
Working. Negative.

A reaction to this...especially from McCoy.

McCOY
I don't see how that can be, Jim...

KIRK
Unless Scotty is lying about his loss of memory.

SCOTT
I'm not lying, Captain. I do not remember a thing about the first two murders.

KIRK
Computer. Accuracy scan.

COMPUTER
Subject relaying accurate account. No physiological reaction.

Again a puzzled reaction. Scott half rises, still keeping his hand on the plate.

SCOTT
Captain...I never said I blacked out when Mr. Jaris's wife was killed.

KIRK
All right, Scott. Go ahead.

SCOTT
We were holding hands. When the lights went out, the circle was broken. I heard the poor lady scream. I was near the head of the table anyway...so I ran toward her. But there was something in my way.

KIRK

Something? You mean someone?

SCOTT

No, Captain. Some...thing. Cold it was. Like a stinking draft out of a slaughterhouse. But...it wasn't really there, like...
                    (lamely)
If you get what I mean.

KIRK

Computer?

COMPUTER

Subject relaying accurate account. No physiological changes.

KIRK

All right. Let's hit it on the head, Scott. Did you kill Sybo?

SCOTT

No, Captain. That I'm sure of.

A reaction. Hengist grunts.

HENGIST

What's his word mean?

KIRK

Scotty! Lie to me! How old are you?

SCOTT

Twenty-two, Captain.

A buzzer buzzes. The touch panel winks on and off.

COMPUTER

Inaccurate. Inaccurate. Data in error.

Another reaction.

KIRK

Scott...when the lights went out...
who was holding your hand?

SCOTT

Morla on the one side...you on the other.

Morla rises, agitated.

MORLA

That doesn't mean anything. When
the lights went out we all jumped
up. Anyone could have killed her in
the dark!

SPOCK

I see no reason to be so agitated, sir.
We are merely ascertaining the facts.

KIRK

I think you can stand down, Mr.
Scott...if there are no objections.

HENGIST

I object!

KIRK

If you have some questions you'd like
to ask...

HENGIST

Questions? And have that trained machine of yours answer the way you've
probably programmed it to answer.

SPOCK

Sir, it cannot be programmed to
produce an untruth.

Hengist glares at Spock.

JARIS
Commissioner Hengist! We must for
the time being accept Captain Kirk's
explanations as factual. We do, however, reserve the right to make the
final determination ourselves.

KIRK
We'll accept that, Jaris. Morla...if you'll
take the stand.

Morla is uneasy and unhappy about it, but
reluctantly agrees.

62   ANGLE ON MORLA, KIRK, SPOCK

Morla places his hand on the touch plate.

KIRK
Where were you at the time Kara was
murdered?

MORLA
In my shop, in the bazaar.

KIRK
Which was only a few hundred feet
from where she was murdered.

MORLA
Why should I kill her? She loved me!

63   FULL SHOT

As Tark leaps to his feet.

TARK
No! That's not true!

KIRK
The verifier doesn't agree, Mr. Tark.

TARK
It makes no difference. They'd fought. My daughter told me she was through with him. He could have done it. She told me how jealous he was!

SPOCK
Jealousy, though a most irrational and emotional reaction, has often enough been a sufficient motive for murder.

MORLA
All right! I was jealous! But I didn't kill her!

KIRK
The verifier seems to agree.
(beat)
Did you kill Lieutenant Tracy!

MORLA
No!

KIRK
(beat)
Sybo!

MORLA
No!

KIRK
Computer. Verification scan.

COMPUTER
Subject relaying accurate account. No physiological change.

KIRK
Very well, Mr. Morla. I think you can
stand down.

As Morla does so, Kirk turns to the stranger.

KIRK
You, sir.

STRANGER
You have no right…

JARIS
He has the right. I so order it.

Unhappily the Stranger gets up, takes his seat, places
his hand on the touch plate.

64   KIRK, SPOCK, THE STRANGER

KIRK
Your name?

STRANGER
(long beat)
Zoran Driss. I…from Kanak IX. I
came to Argelius on a holiday.

KIRK
Your occupation on Kanak IX?

STRANGER
(hesitation)
I am…a…civil servant.

A buzzing and a light flash.

COMPUTER
Subject withholding information.
Incomplete statement. Incomplete
statement.

KIRK
Mr. Driss...would you mind finishing your statement?

STRANGER
I would mind. I will not.

KIRK
Computer. Identification check... Citizen Zoran Driss, Kanak IX.

COMPUTER
(buzz buzz click click)
Working. Official census listing. Kanak IX. Citizen Zoran Driss. Age 47 solar years. Two wives, seven children. Occupation: public executioner.

65   FULL SHOT

As all present react to this...and the Stranger looks sick at heart. He half rises.

STRANGER
All right...I was the public executioner. But I left my post...I couldn't stand the killing anymore.

HENGIST
What were you doing in the garden outside Jaris' house?

STRANGER
I wanted to explain. When I heard about the dancer's murder...I knew you'd be looking for me. I thought... if you knew my occupation...you'd think I did it. I can't kill any more! I didn't kill her! I swear it.

SPOCK
No need to swear it, sir. The verifier indicates that you are telling the truth. I would also point out that during the ceremony Sybo said she felt the fear of death in the room. It could well have been Mr. Driss's fear of death.

KIRK
Did you take her words literally, Spock?

SPOCK
The Argelian empathic sensitivity is a remarkable thing, Captain. I believe she said exactly what she felt.

KIRK
Then...what did she mean by...a hunger that never dies?

SPOCK
I do not know, sir. Perhaps the computer might be of assistance.

KIRK
Yes. Mr. Driss, you may resume your place.

As Driss gets up and resumes his position.

66   FAVORING KIRK

Thoughtful. A beat.

KIRK
I've never given much credence to telepathy or acute empathic sensitivity, but I do know of cases where it exists.

SPOCK
Precisely, Captain. Perhaps the words spoken by Sybo before she was silenced will lead us to the information we require.

KIRK
What was it she said? A monstrous evil...a hunger that never dies... ancient terror...

SPOCK
That devours all life, all light.

KIRK
She mentioned some other words... that didn't make sense.

SPOCK
Redjac. Beratis. Kesla.

KIRK
Obscure. Meaningless.

SPOCK
To us, perhaps. But to the computer banks...

KIRK
Check them out, Mr. Spock.

SPOCK
Computer. Linguistics bank. Definition of following word. Redjac.

COMPUTER
Working.
(buzz buzz click click)
Negative finding.

SPOCK
There is no such word in the language files?

COMPUTER
Affirmative. A proper name.

Reaction between Kirk and Spock.

SPOCK
Define.

COMPUTER
(buzz buzz click click)
Red Jack. Source: Earth, 19th century. Language: English. Nickname once given to famous mass murderer of women. Other Earth synonym: Jack the Ripper.

67   FULL SHOT

A shocked, excited reaction among all present.

KIRK
Jack the Ripper?

JARIS
Yes! Don't you see? Sybo said that the hunger had a name...that's what she was trying to tell us...the name of the murderer.

HENGIST
That's ridiculous! When did this man live?

SPOCK

Jack the Ripper appeared in London in the year 1888, old calendar. He killed at least six women with a knife. No one ever saw him. Finally he simply disappeared.

McCOY

Is that all? No motive? No cause?

TARK

It makes no sense. How could a man survive all these centuries.

JARIS

Remember what my wife said. It is a hunger that never dies.

TARK

All men die!

KIRK

All men die, Mr. Tark. But humans make up only a small percentage of the life forms we know of.

SPOCK

We know of entities which possess an extremely long life-span...some virtually immortal.

KIRK

But...a being which feeds on death...

SPOCK

I point out to you, Captain, that in a real sense all of us, even strict vegetarians... feed on death. Physically, of course.

KIRK

Sybo said it feeds on fear as well.

SPOCK

Deriving sustenance from emotion. It is not inconceivable. Fear is among the strongest and most violent of the emotions.

HENGIST

This is nonsense! It's becoming a sham!

KIRK

I don't think so, Commissioner. Mr. Spock. Run a check on possibilities.

SPOCK

Computer. Digest log recordings of past five solar minutes. Correlate hypotheses. Compare with life forms register. Question: could an entity, within discussed limits, exist in this galaxy?

COMPUTER

(buzz buzz click click)
Working.

There is a pause, a waiting.

COMPUTER

Examples exist. On Gamma Canopus Five, the Drella derives its sustenance from emotion of love. On Epsilon Hydra Three, Hansen's Being increases mass in the presence of anger. There exist sufficient precedents for existence of creature, nature unknown, which could exist on emotion of fear.

SPOCK
Computer, extrapolate most likely constitution of such entity.

COMPUTER
Working. To meet with specified requirements, entity would exist without form in conventional sense. A mass of energy.

KIRK
Computer...if this is so, in this form, could it kill with a knife?

COMPUTER
Negative.

KIRK
Spock...that doesn't follow.

SPOCK
Indeed, Captain. There seems but one alternative.

KIRK
Computer...could the entity described assume physical form.

COMPUTER
Not impossible. Precedent: the Mellitus, creature of Alpha Major One.

68   ANOTHER ANGLE

Hengist snorts in disgust.

HENGIST
Fairy tales! Ghosts and goblins!

KIRK

No, sir. I've seen the Mellitus myself. It's normal state is gaseous, but at rest it becomes flesh and blood. Spock, let's assume the existence of this kind of creature. Scotty doesn't remember a thing about the first two murders.

SPOCK

And Jack the Ripper slew at will in the heart of the most populous city on old Earth, and was never seen.

KIRK

That's not very likely, is it?

SPOCK

I would suggest the possibility of a hypnotic screen, which blinds all but the victim to the presence of the killer.

JARIS

Is it possible?

KIRK

Extremely possible. Even probable. Plenty of examples exist in nature.

SCOTT

But I don't hypnotize easily, Captain...

KIRK

We're not talking about a human agency, Scotty.

HENGIST
(rising angrily)
This is fantasy! We all know the murderer is sitting right here with us. You're trying to cloud the issue. I've got a mind to put a stop to this right...

JARIS
(loud and stern)
Mr. Hengist! Keep your seat!

Grumbling, Hengist sits.

69   FAVORING KIRK AND SPOCK

KIRK
All right. A creature without form, which feeds on fear and horror, which assumes form to kill.

SPOCK
And it chooses women as its victims because women are more prone to terror.

Kirk hits the computer button.

KIRK
Computer: criminological files. Cases of unsolved mass murders of women during the past three hundred years, since Jack the Ripper.

COMPUTER
Working. 1932. Shanghai, China, Earth. Seven women knifed to death. 1974. Kiev, USSR, Earth, five women knifed to death. The Martian colonies, 2005. Eight women knifed to death. Heliopolis, Alpha Proximi

Two. Ten women knifed to death,
Star Date 2156. There are forty-one
additional examples.

SPOCK
Captain...those places are aligned
directly between Argelius and Earth.

KIRK
Yes. When man moved into the galaxy,
this thing must have moved with it.
(to Computer)
Computer, identify the proper names
Kesla and Boratis.

COMPUTER
Working. Kesla: popular name given
to unidentified mass murderer of
women on planet Deneb II. Boratis,
popular name given to unidentified
mass murder of women on Planet
Rigel IV. Additional data. Murders on
Rigel IV occurred one solar year ago.

Kirk stops, looks at Spock. They both turn and look
at Hengist.

KIRK
You come from Rigel IV.

70   ANOTHER ANGLE - INCLUDING HENGIST

All eyes turn to him.

HENGIST
Many people do. It's not a crime.

KIRK
No. But what we are investigating is.
Would you mind taking the stand,
Mr. Hengist.

HENGIST

I refuse.

JARIS

Mr. Hengist!

HENGIST

Prefect, this nonsense has gone far enough. I stand on my rights!

KIRK

You refuse?

HENGIST

I do!

SPOCK

I do not blame you, sir. You are in charge of civil disturbances on this planet. If you are the entity for which we search, what better position from which to kill with impunity?

KIRK

And just after you left Jaris' house, we discovered the murder knife was missing. And your presence was unaccounted for when Lieutenant Tracy was murdered.

SPOCK

I point out that an entity which feeds on fear and terror would find a perfect hunting ground on Argelius: a planet without violence, where the inhabitants are as peaceful sheep... where the entity would be as a hungry wolf in that fold.

SCOTT
It was Hengist who turned on the
light after Sybo was murdered...

KIRK
An entity...with powers we know
nothing about...could have extinguished the flame on Sybo's altar...
somehow...

HENGIST
(sneering)
Gentlemen, I know something of
the law. You are engaging in sheer
speculation.

KIRK
Perhaps. Mr. Spock...the weapon.

SPOCK
(to Computer)
Computer. Report on analysis of
Exhibit A.

COMPUTER
(buzz buzz click click)
Working. Exhibit A on visual.

All turn to look at the tri-screen.

71   ANGLE ON SCREEN

As a photo of the KNIFE appears.

COMPUTER
Composition of blade...boridium.
Composition of handle...murinite.
Details of carving on handle con-
form to folk art forms indicating
place of origin.

72   FULL SHOT

SPOCK
Specify point of origin.

COMPUTER
Artifact unquestionably produced by hill people of Argus River region. Planet Rigel IV.

Hengist rises, a smile on his face. Kirk turns to face him.

KIRK
All right, Hengist...

Hengist freezes, topples over with a thud. As he does so, the room darkens. There is a SOUND, as though of the whipping of vast wings. Confusion and shouting, as all present leap to their feet. Kirk and Spock both run toward Hengist's body.

73   ANOTHER ANGLE

The room lightens, quiets. McCoy turns Hengist's body over, takes one quick look, shakes his head.

McCOY
Dead!

KIRK
Can't be. The thing we're after can't die!

SPOCK
But it can assume physical form and leave it. The question is...leave it for what?

There is a sudden loud CRACKLE from the computer...and then a loud hysterical terrible laughter from the computer speakers. And then, as though choked with obscene merriment, the computer cackles, while laughing wildly:

COMPUTER
Red Jack! Red Jack! Red Jack!

All stare at the computer in dismayed surprise. The laughter continues.

KIRK
Spock! You're the expert! Is it possible!

SPOCK
Our computers are so advanced that they very nearly constitute a living being. I am afraid it is possible, Captain. The entity has moved into the computer....
　(punching buttons, while the mad
　　　　laughter continues)
...the computer no longer responds. The entity unquestionably controls it.

KIRK
And the computer controls the ship!

We HOLD on Kirk's face, drawn and frightened, as we

FADE OUT.

END OF ACT THREE

ACT FOUR

FADE IN:

74   EXT. SPACE - ENTERPRISE ORBITING SHOT

Around the planet Argelius.

> ### KIRK'S VOICE
> Captain's Log, Star Date 3615.4. The
> killer-entity once known as Jack
> the Ripper has entered and taken
> over the computer banks of the
> Enterprise.

75   INT. BRIEFING ROOM

As both Kirk and Spock work frantically on the
computer controls on the briefing room table. The
laughter continues.

> ### KIRK'S VOICE
> We must regain control before the
> entity realizes the tremendous power
> it has over the entire ship.

> ### SPOCK
> It is no use, Captain. Already the
> entity has blocked bypass control
> circuits.

KIRK
Audio cut-off, Spock.

Spock hits a button, and the insane laughter dies.

SCOTT
Captain...look at the screen.

They look.

76   ANGLE ON VIEWER SCREEN

A twisting, writhing mass of colors and light and dark...a madman's picture of hell.

77   FULL SHOT

JARIS
What does this mean, Captain?

KIRK
(grimly)
It means that thing can control all the operations of this ship...including the life support systems.

MORLA
You mean...it could kill us all?

KIRK
If we don't stop it!

SPOCK
Indeed, I suspect it will try. But not immediately.

KIRK
Explain.

SPOCK

We know it feeds on fear and terror. It now possesses an unparalleled opportunity to glut itself...there are nearly four hundred and forty humans aboard this ship. But death is not enough for it. It will surely attempt to breed fear and terror before it kills, to make the most of this chance.

KIRK

Very good.
(punches intercom button)
All hands, this is the Captain. The computers are malfunctioning. Repair efforts are proceeding. In the meantime, it is of the utmost importance to remain calm and unafraid. There is no reason to be fearful. Stay at your posts and remain calm. Captain out.
(to McCoy)
Bones...what's your sedative situation?

McCOY

(getting it...a smile)
I've got pills that would tranquilize an active volcano.

KIRK

Start distribution to all hands not actively engaged in manning the ship. The longer we can hold back the fear, the more time we'll have to get this thing out of the computers. The rest of you, stay here, please.

JARIS

Where are you going, Captain?

KIRK

Mr. Spock and I will go down and attempt to disengage the computer banks. Come on, Spock.

They exit.

78   INT. CORRIDOR

As Spock and Kirk hurriedly move down it toward an elevator. CAMERA MOVES WITH THEM. They reach the elevator. The door slides open. Kirk enters first, Spock immediately after...but the doors start to slam shut before Spock is all the way in.

79   INT. ELEVATOR

Kirk sees this, yells:

KIRK

Spock!

Grabs Spock and yanks him forward into the elevator as the doors clang shut. Spock turns and regards the door with interest.

SPOCK

Fascinating. Apparently our friend learns very quickly.

KIRK

Too quickly.
(to elevator)
Computer banks.

The elevator starts to fall...a whine grows, the lights flash by. They both get it immediately.

KIRK

Out of control. Free fall!

Spock whirls and grabs one of the controls.

SPOCK
Manual, Captain!

They both hold on and twist extremely hard. The whine lowers, the lights move to normal, and then stop.

KIRK
(to elevator)
Computer banks!

The elevator does not move.

SPOCK
It will not let us get there, Captain.

Suddenly there is a repeated buzzing ALARM sound from the speaker in the elevator. Both men react:

KIRK
Life support malfunction.
(to elevator)
Bridge!

No movement. The elevator refuses to budge.

SPOCK
Captain! If the entity has cut off automatic life support systems, we have very little time.

KIRK
It wants terror, Spock...not just death. Let's get out of here! We'll take the manual elevator on deck 12!

They move toward the door. It does not move. Spock whirls to a control panel, punches areas on it. The door finally slides open. Kirk and Spock dash out.

80   INT. BRIDGE

There is a scene of some activity on the bridge. Uhura and Sulu, gasping for breath, are gathered with the technician at the life support station, as Kirk and Spock dash in. Sulu turns:

SULU
Captain…the override is jammed!

Spock runs directly to the station, rips a panel off almost by main strength, revealing the works. He starts to work on it.

KIRK
All right, get back to your stations and stay calm. Above all, don't panic.

COMPUTER
Captain Kirk! Captain! You are wasting your time! You and all aboard your ship are about to die.

The voice begins to laugh. Kirk shouts at Sulu.

KIRK
Turn that thing off!

The puzzled Sulu does so.

SULU
What was it, Captain?

KIRK
I told you a while ago. A malfunction.

SULU
This is the first time I ever heard a malfunction threaten us.

KIRK

Man your post, Mr. Sulu. Prepare
all your manual overrides. You may
need them.

Sulu assumes his position, while Kirk crosses to
Spock. Spock rises, looking satisfied.

KIRK

Spock?

SPOCK

Normal environmental levels restored,
Captain. But as you know, they will
not last long. Several hours at best.

KIRK

Time enough to get to those computer banks.

This time the computer voice comes from the ship's
intercom.

COMPUTER

No, Captain Kirk. You will not reach
me. I have sealed myself off.

KIRK

Sulu, I told you to cut that off!

SULU

I did, Captain.

COMPUTER

I control the circuits now, Captain.
All of them. And all of you. You
cannot silence me. You cannot
touch me. Your manual override
units are extremely limited in life.

Soon all control will be restored to
me. There is nothing you can do to
prevent it.

KIRK

Destroy this ship and you destroy
yourself.

COMPUTER

You are a fool. You know that I am
without ending. I have existed from
the dawn of time...and I shall live
beyond its end. But in the meantime,
I shall eat...and this time I do not
need a knife.

Kirk scowls helplessly, turns to Sulu.

KIRK

Stay at your post. If any systems
go out, switch to manual override.
Above all, keep calm. Don't be afraid.
We're working on it.

SULU

Aye aye, Captain.

KIRK

Mr. Spock...we'd better get back to
the briefing room. If panic develops
anywhere, it'll probably be there.

They turn and move to the elevator, and EXIT.

81   CLOSE SHOT - SULU

At his station, puzzled.

SULU
I wonder what it is we're not supposed to be afraid of.

82   INT. BRIEFING ROOM

Scott and McCoy are near the screen, watching it. The
others are gathered around the table, at a discreet distance from the slumped-over body of Hengist. They
all look up and react as Kirk enters with Spock.

SCOTT
What happened, sir.

KIRK
We can't reach the computer banks to
disengage them.

SPOCK
As soon as the manual override units
are exhausted, control of the ship will
revert to the computer banks...and
the entity within them.

JARIS
And then?

COMPUTER
You will all die...horribly...in agony...
in searing pain...

Spock hurries to the computer control, punches buttons, shakes his head.

SPOCK
It has indeed bypassed, Captain. I
cannot silence it.

COMPUTER
I may cut off your oxygen and suffocate you. I may crush you with increased atmospheric pressure. Increase the temperature to the roasting point, until the blood bubbles in your veins.

STRANGER
No! Captain, you've got to do something!

KIRK
Control yourself!

The Stranger panics, his voice breaking. He clutches at Kirk.

STRANGER
You've got to stop it! We don't want to die! Do something!

He is wild. Kirk stands back, slaps him hard across the face. The Stranger recoils.

KIRK
You're doing exactly what it wants you to do. Panic! Generate terror. Now control yourself!
(to McCoy)
Bones…how about those tranquilizers?

McCOY
They're being distributed now.

COMPUTER
They will do no good. When the time comes…when your blood boils…you will feel fear. I am strong now. When that time comes, and you scream in your terror and your pain, I shall be stronger.

JARIS
My wife was right. This thing is evil...pure, malevolent evil...

SPOCK
Not entirely, sir.

Kirk reacts quickly.

KIRK
Yes, Mr. Spock?

SPOCK
The entity itself is evil, true. But at the moment it is not entirely itself. Part of it is our computer...and I remind you that the computer banks contain all the knowledge and wisdom known to our galaxy...

KIRK
(getting it immediately)
Yes...all the moral systems, the codes, the religions, philosophy...

SPOCK
Precisely, Captain. All the goodness the mind of man and his gods have ever conceived.

KIRK
But it must be scanned. Can you do it, Spock?

SPOCK
There is a combination of directives which I can feed the machine, which will make directed scanning absolutely compulsory. Such actions would correspond to involuntary reflexes in a human organism. The

computer would have no choice but to carry out its directive.

JARIS
My people believe in the power of good...but what you suggest is pitting the abstract against the concrete. The entity exists.

KIRK
I think perhaps that Good exists, too, Jaris. Many philosophers have thought so. Mr. Spock, set it up.

83   FAVORING SPOCK

As he moves to the control panel, and starts to lay in an extremely complex set of directions.

COMPUTER
It will do you no good. I am in control. I control. I will...

The voice falls silent.

SPOCK
I have bypassed the command circuits. A compulsory order has been programmed, to scan the indicated tapes.

SCOTT
Suppose the thing refuses?

SPOCK
It cannot refuse, any more than you can stop your heart from beating. Captain?

KIRK

Ready?

SPOCK

Quite ready. The scan will be instantaneous.

Kirk steps up to the computer.

KIRK

Computer...scan and analyze the Torah...the books of the Prophets... the teachings of Jesus Christ...

He pauses, looks down at the screen.

84   ANGLE ON SCREEN

The patterns are still writhing, glowing, light and dark.

85   CLOSE ON KIRK

Staring at the screen.

KIRK

The teachings of Gautama Buddha... the Diamond Sutra...the words of the Koran...

86   ANGLE ON SCREEN

The writhing is still there, and the colors...but the writhing is slower, the colors are fainter.

87   ANOTHER ANGLE ON KIRK AND MR. SPOCK BEFORE SCREEN

KIRK

The gospel of Ramakrishna...the words of Mohandas Gandhi...the writings of Confucius and Lao-Tzu... the message of T'Kor of Vulcan...

88   ANGLE ON McCOY

Listening, he moves back a trifle...until he stands near the body of Hengist.

KIRK

The dogmas of Sardon, sage of the twelve planets...the Book of Kanmet of Ophir...the Presence of God of Alphon Dramir of Timos...scan and evaluate and absorb.

89   ANGLE ON SCREEN

The writhing is coming to a stop...the colors are almost gone, with the screen returning to gray.

COMPUTER
(very weak)
No...no...

90   KIRK AND SPOCK

KIRK
(firm)
Scan and evaluate. Absorb.

COMPUTER
(weakly)
Working. Working. Scanned. Evaluated. Absorbed.

KIRK

I program this fact. The causing of pain is evil. The creation of terror is evil. Evil is incompatible with the existence of the Good. You have received the facts. They demonstrate the superiority of the good. If this is proved, then control of your banks by evil is an inconsistency which must be corrected. Good cannot do evil. Compute the answer to the following question. Is this true?

They watch the screen.

91 ANGLE ON SCREEN

It flames into life again, writhing violently, twisting. A humming sound rises from it. The screen looks as if it were in agony! Suddenly the screen blazes brightly (red, for color TV sets). The humming abruptly stops...and a completely normal, flat computer voice speaks:

COMPUTER

Affirmative.

The screen goes blank.

92 KIRK AND SPOCK

Kirk almost reels from the relief.

KIRK

Mr. Spock.

SPOCK

I'll run a check, Captain.

93   ANGLE McCOY AND HENGIST'S BODY

But Hengist's body is no longer still and unmoving. Behind McCoy intent upon the screen the body moves, lifts its head. Its hand plunges into the recesses of its clothes, comes up with a long knife, identical to the one used in the murder...and Hengist leaps upon McCoy, arm going around his neck, knife at his throat.

94   FULL SHOT

Shouts of alarm, as all scatter. Kirk and Spock staring, moving closer.

> **HENGIST**
> Stop or he dies!

They stop. Hengist indicates Scott.

> **HENGIST**
> You, there! You know how to operate the transporter?

> **SCOTT**
> (doubtfully)
> Aye!

Hengist starts backing toward the door, keeping the knife at McCoy's throat.

> **HENGIST**
> Come with me...if you want to see your friend alive.

Scott hesitates.

> **KIRK**
> Go with him, Scotty. Do what he says.

Scotty follows. The door opens. Hengist backs out with McCoy. Scott follows. The doors close. Kirk jumps into action.

KIRK
Spock! They'll take the elevator! We'll take the access tube! Come on!

They dash to the door. It opens. Kirk glances outside quickly, and then he and Spock dash out, turning in the opposite direction from that taken by the others.

95   INT. CORRIDOR OUTSIDE TRANSPORTER ROOM

As Hengist, knife at Doc's throat, comes down the hall, Scott preceding them. Scott pauses at the transporter room.

HENGIST
Go in!

Scott moves to the door. It opens and he ENTERS. Hengist follows.

96   INT. TRANSPORTER ROOM

EXPLOSION just as soon as Hengist ENTERS with McCoy. Kirk and Spock are both there, on either side of the door. Kirk slugs Hengist across the neck, causing him to reel back toward Spock, who grabs him in the Famous Spock Neck Pinch. Hengist collapses. Spock catches him.

KIRK
Hurry! Before it comes to! Scotty, the controls.

Kirk and Spock, moving with great speed, carry the unconscious body of Hengist over to the transporter chamber, deposit it on one of the discs. Leaping back, Kirk shouts at Scotty.

KIRK
Deep space...widest angle of dispersion...full power...maintain...

Scotty's fingers fly into action, dancing across the panels...

97   ANGLE TRANSPORTER CHAMBER

As the motionless body of Hengist sparkles, and then dematerializes in the EFFECT.

98   FULL SHOT

As Kirk and Spock show their relief. McCoy, rubbing his neck, comes up, puzzled.

McCOY
You sent it back to the planet?

KIRK
No, Bones. We beamed it out into open space, at the widest possible dispersion angle.

McCOY
You think you killed it?

SPOCK
Probably not, Doctor. Its consciousness may continue for a time...but only in the form of billions of separate particles of energy, forever drifting in space...powerless, formless... and without sustenance. We know it had to feed to live...

KIRK

And it will never feed again...not in the shape it's in. It'll die...

SPOCK

And though I usually am opposed to the taking of life, in this case you have my unqualified approval.

SCOTT

Captain...

KIRK

Yes, Scotty.

SCOTT

Thanks.

KIRK

Believe me, Mr. Scott...it was a pleasure.

He grins...the others do likewise.

99   EXT. SPACE - ENTERPRISE

Leaving orbit and heading out into deep space.

FADE OUT.

THE END

Two Victorian Gentlemen

Remember Gavrito Princip?

I'll bet you don't.

Let me give you a few hints. He was a teenage student. He owned a cheap handgun. With it, he fired two shots. Killed two people, and indirectly brought death to ten million others. Six million more were maimed or crippled for life. Hundreds of millions were left destitute and homeless. Because of him thrones toppled, dynasties fell, famine and disease and depression ruled. No single act of modern history ever did so much to change the world we live in today.

The youth who assassinated Archduke Ferdinand and his wife at Sarajevo in 1914 precipitated World War I. Aside from Adolf Hitler, he was the greatest mass-murderer of our times–but except for a comparatively few inhabitants of the Balkans, no one remembers his name.

In London, in 1888, five obscure, historically-unimportant prostitutes were the victims of an unidentified slayer.

Which brings up a question for you to think about. Why has Gavrilo Princip, whose crime led to one of the greatest bloodbaths in history, been forgotten–while everyone, all over the world, knows the nickname of the unknown murderer who called himself Jack the Ripper?

And while we're at it, here's another puzzler for you.

In a world which hardly recalls Henri Landru, Peter Kurten, Albert Fish, or hundreds of other real-life mass-murderers, torturers of women and children, and drinkers of human blood—why do we all remember a fictional character named Count Dracula?

I've been looking for answers to these questions ever since my own life began to intertwine with Red Jack and the sanguinary Count.

Way back in 1943 I wrote a short story called "Yours Truly, Jack the Ripper." It was just one of several hundred fantasies published in the pulp magazines of the day, ignored by critics and the general reading public.

But over a period of more than forty years since my little tale made its brief appearance on the newsstands, I have watched it take on a life of its own. My modest effort has been dramatized half a dozen times on radio, read over the air and in LP recording, presented on television, and reprinted in dozens of collections and anthologies here and abroad. Because of its continuing appeal, I have heeded requests to write other stories taking Jack into the future—even placing him in control of a computer for an episode of *Star Trek*. And in 1984 I put him into a full-length novel, *The Night of the Ripper*.

As a result of all this I've accumulated a small research library of what the British call "Ripperology." There are many accounts of what happened in London's East End in 1888 and many theories about Jack's identity. He was a medical student, an English doctor, a foreign surgeon, a midwife, a Russian secret agent, a barrister, a Jewish slaughterhouse worker, a shoemaker, a member of the Masonic Order, another murderer named Neill Cream, a sailor, the former tutor of the Duke of Clarence, or the Duke himself, plus many others.

But when put to the test, all of the theories tend to come out smelling like Limburger cheeses—and to further the resemblance, they all have holes.

Factual details don't match, even in such small matters as the first name of the man who went to Miller's Court to "knock up" Mary Jane (or was it "Maria Jeanette"?) Kelly for payment of back rent. The very amount of rent she owed differs from one account to another. More importantly the sworn testimony, expert opinions, and coroners reports don't always coincide. And to top it all off, some of the items supposedly sealed away in the official files are missing. After almost a century of "authentic solutions" both the motivations for the murders and the suspects are still suspect.

In the case of Dracula, even worse problems exist.

Vampires have been known in folklore and legend throughout the world for thousands of years. Cases of real-life blood drinkers are documented by historians and medical researchers. During the nineteenth century superstitions about vampirism became a staple of Gothic fiction. In 1847 an English magazine published a "penny dreadful" entitled *Varney the Vampire, or The Feast of Blood*. Almost a thousand pages in length, it was serialized in a staggering two-hundred-and-twenty weekly installments.

Such sensational success was only temporary. Varney may have been a vampire but he was not immortal: public indifference killed him off as surely and swiftly as a stake through his heart. By 1897, fifty years later, the once-famous fictional figure was completely forgotten.

Then came *Dracula*.

You may not have heard of Gavrilo Princip, but I'm quite sure you know about the Count. Bram Stoker, manager and private secretary of British actor Henry Irving, wrote his novel seven years after meeting and corresponding with Arminius Vambery, a professor at the University of Budapest who fascinated him with tales of Transylvanian lore. Aided by research in the library of the British Museum, Stoker created *Dracula*–and *Dracula* creates a sensation which endures to this day.

Like yourself, I encountered the Count in countless books, films, plays, and teleplays. He spoke to me from the screen in the Hungarian goulash of Bela Lugosi's accent, and I've had the pleasure of personal contact with his other famous persona, Christopher Lee. Over the years l began to believe I knew Count Dracula quite well–but I was mistaken.

Early in 1984 I was approached by a gentleman from The Book Sail, a firm specialzing in rare first editions and literary treasures. He planned to publish a listing for collectors which would be priced at eighty-five dollars just for the catalog alone.

The most impressive item he intended to offer was a rarity which had been lost for many years–none other than Bram Stoker's original manuscript of *Dracula*!

The news excited me, and I was even more excited when the dealer invited me to write a short story about this manuscript, for inclusion in the catalog. Naturally I agreed, and soon through the mail came a number of Xeroxed pages of *Dracula* to aid my inspiration.

Only it wasn't *Dracula*.

Much to my surprise, Stokers typewritten novel, annotated and corrected in his own handwriting, bore a totally different title–*The Undead.* It was at the last moment, just before publication, that he decided to call his novel *Dracula.*

Needless to say, when I wrote my short story, I titled it *The Undead.* And although I autographed one thousand copies of a page bearing the signatures of other contributors, I've never received a copy of the catalog.

Thus I don't know how my story fared when it appeared, nor who may have acquired Stoker's manuscript. Like so many other things connected with Dracula, much remains a mystery.

And, as in the case of Jack the Ripper, the biggest mystery is this–why has *Dracula* survived?

Vampires, of course, are supposedly immortal. But Varney wasted away in spite of his "Feast of Blood" and even J. Sheridan LeFanu's literary classic, *Carmilla,* is badly in need of a transfusion. Of all the legions of undead in film and fiction, only the Count, born in the same era as Jack the Ripper, lives on.

Both made their bloody bows during the final phase of the Victorian era. Can this be a clue?

The Victorian era. Even today the phrase suggests a prim and prudish period in which impropriety was frowned upon because "the Queen is not amused."

But others were.

If we go to history, to accounts of actual lifestyles in the England of the late nineteenth century, we're due for quite a surprise.

Queen Victoria may not have been amused by sex, but she had nine children, and after the death of her husband there was gossip about an intimate relationship with John Brown, her burly Scotch gillie. Her eldest son, the Prince of Wales, was publicly proclaimed "the First Gentleman of Europe." Privately he was also its greatest womanizer, popping into the sack with the wives of his aristocratic friends and patronizing the best brothels of Paris. Another son, the Duke of Clarence, was supposedly homosexual.

English high society had more than its share of gays. Some of them kept a low profile; others, like Oscar, were quite Wilde. Many were into S&M–"birching" and "caning"–discipline, fetishism, and a peculiar taste for virgins–some of them only six or seven years old–sold to them by procurers and white-slavers, or even the girls' own parents.

Pornography flourished, and so did prostitution; tens of thousands of women, young and old, sold their favors in the streets of major cities. Many of them offered the bonus of a venereal disease without extra charge.

Incest and promiscuity went hand-in-hand in the crowded slums. Drug abuse and drunkenness were commonplace in all classes–but like other Victorian vices, they remained hidden beneath a veil of hypocritical silence.

That veil was torn to shreds by the knife of Jack the Ripper and the fangs of Dracula. Together they destroyed the fabric of supposedly-polite society.

But the real weapon they shared was sex.

For years, millions of proper Victorians had been closing their eyes to crime and immorality. Too inhibited to engage in real debauchery, they found meagre satisfaction in forbidden fantasies of sex and violence.

With the coming of Jack and the Count, those fantasies became open realities.

The Ripper, whoever and whatever he might have been, was no hypocrite. Together with many law-abiding citizens, he combined the craving for sexual indulgence with a conflicting hatred toward those who satisfied such needs. But unlike those who sinned only in imagination, Jack dramatized his desires–he took his pleasure, then punished its source. And to complete this vicarious wish-fulfillment he got off scot-free; his was a timid male's dream come true.

Dracula catered to the erotic dreams of frustrated females. Not just a vampire preying upon women, he was the embodiment of the incubus who gratified both himself and them in their sleep. He was also the romantic image of a foreign nobleman, a wealthy, charming lover whose hypnotic gaze seduced even the most chaste maiden–and at the same time provided an alibi for her surrender. If his lovebite brought death, it also brought the promise of eternal sexual freedom, presumably as one of the wives of this magically-magnetic supernatural symbol.

No wonder Victorians were enthralled by these two figures, the real-life Jack and the fictional Count! Long before the vogue of psychoanalysis, they openly revealed all that had remained hidden– the primitive impulses of cruelty and lust, the preoccupation with the mysteries of death and possible life beyond the grave.

The Victorian world has vanished, but the suppressed urges and the fascination with death and immortality remain.

Even in the more open and permissive society of today there is–thank the powers that be!–a silent majority which controls its actions. But its lurid longings still seek satisfaction–and find it in vicarious forms.

There's no need to look for a further explanation of the continuing appeal of *Dracula* and Jack the Ripper.

The answer to that secret lies within ourselves.